Also available from Silhouette by

Nora Roberts

Nora Roberts
Treasures

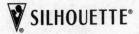 SILHOUETTE®

*Silhouette and Colophon are registered trademarks of
Harlequin Books S.A., used under licence.
Silhouette Books, Eton House, 18-24 Paradise Road,
Richmond, Surrey TW9 1SR*

TREASURES © Harlequin Books S.A. 2008

*The publisher acknowledges the copyright holder of the
individual works as follows:*

Secret Star © Nora Roberts 1998
Treasures Lost, Treasures Found © Nora Roberts 1986

ISBN: 978 0 263 86890 6

026-1108

*Printed and bound in Spain
by Litografia Rosés S.A., Barcelona*

CONTENTS

Secret Star

To generous hearts

Chapter 1

The woman in the portrait had a face created to steal a man's breath and haunt his dreams. It was, perhaps, as close to perfection as nature would allow. Eyes of laser blue whispered of sex and smiled knowingly from beneath thick black lashes. The brows were perfectly arched, with a flirty little mole dotting the downward point of the left one. The skin was porcelain-pure, with a hint of warm rose beneath—just warm enough that a man could fantasize that heat was kindling only for him. The nose was straight and finely sculpted.

The mouth—and, oh, the mouth was hard to ignore—was curved invitingly, appeared pillow-soft, yet strong in shape. A bold red temptation that beckoned as clearly as a siren's call.

Framing that staggering face was a rich, wild tumble of ebony hair that streamed over creamy bare shoulders.

Glossy, gorgeous, generous. The kind of hair even a strong man would lose himself in—fisting his hands in all that black silk, while his mouth sank deep, and deeper, into those soft, smiling lips.

Grace Fontaine, Seth thought, a study in the perfection of feminine beauty.

It was too damn bad she was dead.

He turned away from the portrait, annoyed that his gaze and his mind kept drifting back to it. He'd wanted some time alone at the crime scene, after the forensic team finished, after the M.E. took possession of the body. The outline remained, an ugly human-shaped silhouette marring the glossy chestnut floor.

It was simple enough to determine how she'd died. A nasty tumble from the floor above, right through the circling railing, now splintered and sharp-edged, and down, beautiful face first, into the lake-size glass table.

She'd lost her beauty in death, he thought, and that was a damn shame, too.

It was also simple to determine that she'd been given some help with that last dive.

It was, he mused, looking around, a terrific house. The high ceilings offered space and half a dozen generous sky-lights gave light, rosy, hopeful beams from the dying sun. Everything curved—the stairs, the doorways, the windows. Female again, he supposed. The wood was glossy, the glass sparkling, the furniture all obviously carefully selected antiques.

Someone was going to have a tough time getting the bloodstains out of the dove-gray upholstery of the sofa.

He tried to imagine how it had all looked before

whoever helped Grace Fontaine off the balcony stormed through the rooms.

There wouldn't have been broken statuary or ripped cushions. Flowers would have been meticulously arranged in vases, rather than crushed into the intricate pattern of the Oriental rugs.

There certainly wouldn't have been blood, broken glass, or layers of fingerprint dust.

She'd lived well, he thought. But then, she had been able to afford to live well. She'd become an heiress when she turned twenty-one, the privileged, pampered orphan and the wild child of the Fontaine empire. An excellent education, a country-club darling, and the headache, he imagined, of the conservative and staunch Fontaines, of Fontaine Department Stores fame.

Rarely had a week gone by that Grace Fontaine didn't warrant a mention in the society pages of the *Washington Post,* or a paparazzi shot in one of the glossies. And it usually hadn't been due to a good deed.

The press would be screaming with this latest, and last, adventure in the life and times of Grace Fontaine, Seth knew, the moment the news leaked. And they would be certain to mention all of her escapades. Posing nude at nineteen for a centerfold spread, the steamy and very public affair with a very married English lord, the dalliance with a hot heartthrob from Hollywood.

There'd been other notches in her designer belt, Seth remembered. A United States senator, a bestselling author, the artist who had painted her portrait, the rock star who, rumor had it, had attempted to take his own life when she dumped him.

She'd packed a lot of men into a short life.

Grace Fontaine was dead at twenty-six.

It was his job to find out not only the how, but the who. And the why.

He had a line on the why already. The Three Stars of Mithra—a fortune in blue diamonds, the impulsive and desperate act of a friend, and greed.

Seth frowned as he walked through the empty house, cataloging the events that had brought him to this place, to this point. Since he had a personal interest in mythology, had since childhood, he knew something about the Three Stars. They were the stuff of legends, and had once been grouped in a gold triangle that had been held in the hands of a statue of the god Mithra.

One stone for love, he remembered, skimming through details as he climbed the curved stairs to the second level. One for knowledge, and the last for generosity. Mythologically speaking, whoever possessed the Stars gained the god's power. And immortality.

Which was, logically, a crock, of course. Wasn't it odd, though, he mused, that he'd been dreaming lately of flashing blue stones, a dark castle shrouded in mist, a room of glinting gold? And there was a man with eyes as pale as death, he thought, trying to clear the hazy details. And a woman with the face of a goddess.

And his own violent death.

Seth shook off the uneasy sensation that accompanied his recalling the snippets of dreams. What he required now were facts, basic, logical facts. And the fact was that three blue diamonds weighing something over a hundred carats apiece were worth six kings' ransoms. And someone wanted them, and didn't mind killing to gain possession.

He had bodies piling up like cordwood, he thought, dragging a hand through his dark hair. In order of death, the first had been Thomas Salvini, part owner of Salvini, gem experts who had been contracted by the Smithsonian Institution to verify and assess the three stones. Evidence pointed to the fact that verifying and assessing hadn't been quite enough for Thomas Salvini, or his twin, Timothy.

Over a million in cash indicated that they'd had other plans—and a client who wanted the Stars for himself.

Added to that was the statement from one Bailey James, the Salvinis' stepsister, and eyewitness to fratricide. A gemologist with an impeccable reputation, she claimed to have discovered her stepbrothers' plans to copy the stones, sell the originals and leave the country with the profits.

She'd gone in to see her brothers alone, he thought with a shake of his head. Without contacting the police. And she'd decided to face them down after she shipped two of the stones to her two closest friends, separating them to protect them. He gave a short sigh at the mysterious minds of civilians.

Well, she'd paid for her impulse, he thought. Walking in on a vicious murder, barely escaping with her life—and with her memory of the incident and everything before it blocked for days.

He stepped into Grace's bedroom, his heavy-lidded gold-toned eyes cooly scanning the brutally searched room.

And had Bailey James gone to the police even then? No, she'd chosen a P.I., right out of the phone book. Seth's mouth thinned in annoyance. He had very little respect and no admiration for private investigators. Through blind luck, she'd stumbled across a fairly decent one, he acknowledged. Cade Parris wasn't as bad as most, and he'd managed—through more blind luck, Seth was certain—to sniff out a trail.

And nearly gotten himself killed in the process. Which brought Seth to death number two. Timothy Salvini was now as dead as his brother. He couldn't blame Parris overmuch for defending himself from a man with a knife, but taking the second Salvini out left a dead end.

And through the eventful Fourth of July weekend, Bailey James's other friend had been on the run with a bounty hunter. In a rare show of outward emotion, Seth rubbed his eyes and leaned against the door jamb.

M. J. O'Leary. He'd be interviewing her soon, personally. And he'd be the one telling her, and Bailey James, that their friend Grace was dead. Both tasks fell under his concept of duty.

O'Leary had the second Star and had been underground with the skip tracer, Jack Dakota, since Saturday afternoon. Though it was only Monday evening now, M.J. and her companion had managed to rack up a number of points—including three more bodies.

Seth reflected on the foolish and unsavory bail bondsman who'd not only set Dakata up with the false job of bringing in M.J., but also moonlighted with blackmail. The hired muscle who'd been after M.J. had likely been part of some scam of his and had killed him. Then they'd had some very bad luck on a rain-slicked road.

And that left him with yet another dead end.

Grace Fontaine was likely to be third. He wasn't certain what her empty house, her mangled possessions, would tell him. He would, however, go through it all, inch by inch and step by step. That was his style.

He would be thorough, he would be careful, and he would find the answers. He believed in order, he believed in laws. He believed, unstintingly, in justice.

Seth Buchanan was a third-generation cop, and had worked his way up the rank to lieutenant due to an inherent skill for police work, an almost terrifying patience, and a hard-edged objectivity. The men under him respected him—some secretly feared him. He was well aware he was often referred to as the Machine, and took no offense. Emotion, temperament, the grief and the guilt civilians could indulge in, had no place in the job.

If he was considered aloof, even cold and controlled, he saw it as a compliment.

He stood a moment longer in the doorway, the mahogany-framed mirror across the wide room reflecting him. He was a tall, well-built man, muscles toned to iron under a dark suit jacket. He'd loosened his tie because he was alone, and his nightwing hair was slightly disordered by the rake of his fingers. It was full and thick, with a slight wave. He pushed it back from an unsmiling face that boasted a square jaw and tawny skin.

His nose had been broken years before, when he was in uniform, and it edged his face toward the rugged. His mouth was hard, firm, and rare to smile. His eyes, the dark gold of an old painting, remained cool under straight black brows.

On one wide-palmed hand he wore the ring that had been his father's. On either side of the heavy gold were the words *Serve* and *Protect*.

He took both duties seriously.

Bending, he picked up a pool of red silk that had been tossed on the mountain of scattered clothing heaped on the Aubusson carpet. The callused tips of his fingers skimmed over it. The red silk gown matched the short robe the victim had been wearing, he thought.

He wanted to think of her only as the victim, not as the woman in the portrait, certainly not as the woman in those new and disturbing dreams that disrupted his sleep. And he was irritated that his mind kept swimming back to that stunning face—the woman behind it. That quality was—had been, he corrected—part of her power. That skill in drilling into a man's mind until he was obsessed with her.

She would have been irresistible, he mused, still holding the wisp of silk. Unforgettable. Dangerous.

Had she slipped into that little swirl of silk for a man? he wondered. Had she been expecting company—a private evening of passion?

And where was the third Star? Had her unexpected visitor found it, taken it? The safe in the library downstairs had been broken open, cleaned out. It seemed logical that she would have locked something that valuable away. Yet she'd taken the fall from up here.

Had she run? Had he chased her? Why had she let him in the house? The sturdy locks on the doors hadn't been tampered with. Had she been careless, reckless enough to open the door to a stranger while she wore nothing but a thin silk robe?

Or had she known him?

Perhaps she'd bragged about the diamond, even shown it off to him. Had greed taken the place of passion? An argument, then a fight. A struggle, a fall. Then the destruction of the house as cover.

It was an avenue, he decided. He had her thick address book downstairs, and would go through it name by name. Just as he, and the team he assigned, would go through the empty house in Potomac, Maryland, inch by inch.

But he had people to see now. Tragedy to spread and details to tie up. He would have to ask one of Grace Fontaine's friends, or a member of her family, to come in and officially identify the body.

He regretted, more than he wanted to, that anyone who had cared for her would have to look at that ruined face.

He let the silk gown drop, took one last look at the room, with its huge bed and trampled flowers, the scatter of lovely old antique bottles that gleamed like precious gems. He already knew that the scent here would haunt him, just as that perfect face painted beautifully in oils in the room downstairs would.

It was full dark when he returned. It wasn't unusual for him to put long, late hours into a case. Seth had no life to speak of outside of the job, had never sought to make one. The women he saw socially, or romantically, were carefully, even calculatingly, selected. Most tolerated the demands of his work poorly, and they rarely cemented a relationship. Because he knew how difficult and frustrating those demands of time, energy and heart were on those who waited, he expected complaints, sulking, even accusations, from the women who felt neglected.

So he never made promises. And he lived alone.

He knew there was little he could do here at the scene. He should have been at his desk—or at least, he thought, have gone home just to let his mind clear. But he'd been pulled back to this house. No, to this woman, he admitted.

It wasn't the two stories of wood and glass, however lovely, that dragged at him.

It was the face in the portrait.

He'd left his car at the top of the sweep of the drive, and walked to the house sheltered by grand old trees and well-trimmed shrubs green with summer. He'd let himself in, turned the switch that had the foyer chandelier blazing light.

His men had already started the tedious door-to-door of the neighborhood, hoping that someone, in another of the big, exquisite homes, would have heard something, seen anything.

The medical examiner was slow—understandably, Seth reminded himself. It was a holiday, and the staff was down to bare minimum. Official reports would take a bit longer.

But it wasn't the reports or lack of them that nagged at his mind as he wandered back, inevitably, to the portrait over the glazed-tile hearth.

Grace Fontaine had been loved. He'd underestimated the depth friendship could reach. But he'd seen that depth, and that shocked and racking grief in the faces of the two women he'd just left.

There had been a bond between Bailey James, M. J. O'Leary and Grace that was as strong as he'd ever seen. He regretted—and he rarely had regrets—that he'd had to tell them so bluntly.

I'm sorry for your loss.

Words cops said to euphemize the death they lived with—often violent, always unexpected. He had said the words, as he had too often in the past, and watched the fragile blonde and the cat-eyed redhead simply crumble. Clutching each other, they had simply crumbled.

He hadn't needed the two men who had ranged themselves as the women's champions to tell him to leave them alone with their grief. There would be no questions, no statements, no answers, that night. Nothing he could say or do would penetrate that thick curtain of grief.

Grace Fontaine had been loved, he thought again, looking into those spectacular blue eyes. Not simply desired by men, but loved by two women. What was behind those eyes, what was behind that face, that had deserved that kind of unquestioning emotion?

"Who the hell were you?" he murmured, and was answered by that bold, inviting smile. "Too beautiful to be real. Too aware of your own beauty to be soft." His deep voice, rough with fatigue, echoed in the empty house. He slipped his hands in his pockets, rocked back on his heels. "Too dead to care."

And though he turned from the portrait, he had the uneasy feeling that it was watching him. Measuring him.

He had yet to reach her next of kin, the aunt and uncle in Virginia who had raised her after the death of her parents. The aunt was summering in a villa in Italy and was, for tonight, out of touch.

Villas in Italy, he mused, blue diamonds, oil portraits over fireplaces of sapphire-blue tile. It was a world far removed from his firmly middle-class upbringing, and from the life he'd embraced through his career.

But he knew violence didn't play favorites.

He would eventually go home to his tiny little house on its postage-stamp lot, crowded together with dozens of other tiny little houses. It would be empty, as he'd never found a woman who moved him to want to share even that small private space. But his home would be there for him.

And this house, for all its gleaming wood and acres of gleaming glass, its sloping lawn, sparkling pool and trimmed bushes, hadn't protected its mistress.

He walked around the stark outline on the floor and started up the stairs again. His mood was edgy—he could admit that. And the best thing to smooth it out again was work.

He thought perhaps a woman with as eventful a life as Grace Fontaine would have noted those events—and her personal feelings about them—in a diary.

He worked in silence, going through her bedroom carefully, knowing very well that he was trapped in that sultry scent she'd left behind.

He'd taken his tie off, tucked it in his pocket. The weight from his weapon, snug in his shoulder harness, was so much a part of him it went unnoticed.

He went through her drawers without a qualm, though they were largely empty now, as their contents were strewn around the room. He searched beneath them, behind them and under the mattress.

He thought, irrelevantly, that she'd owned enough clothing to outfit a good-size modeling troupe, and that she'd leaned toward soft materials. Silks, cashmeres, satins, thin brushed wools. Bold colors. Jewel colors, with a bent toward blues.

With those eyes, he thought as they crept back into his mind, why not?

He caught himself wondering how her voice had sounded. Would it have fit that sultry face, been husky and low, another purr of temptation for a man? He imagined it that way, a voice as dark and sensual as the scent that hung on the air.

Her body had fit the face, fit the scent, he mused, stepping into her enormous walk-in closet. Of course, she'd helped nature along there. And he wondered why a woman would feel impelled to add silicone to her body to lure a man. And what kind of pea-brained man would prefer it to an honest shape.

He preferred honesty in women. Insisted on it. Which, he supposed, was one of the reasons he lived alone.

He scanned the clothes still hanging with a shake of his head. Even the killer had run out of patience here, it seemed. The hangers were swept back so that garments were crowded together, but he hadn't bothered to pull them all out.

Seth judged that the number of shoes totaled well over two hundred, and one wall of shelves had obviously been fashioned to hold handbags. These, in every imaginable shape and size and color, had been pulled out of their slots, ripped open and searched.

A cupboard had held more—sweaters, scarves. Costume jewelry. He imagined she'd had plenty of the real sparkles, as well. Some would have been in the now empty safe downstairs, he was sure. And she might have a lockbox at a bank.

That he would check on first thing in the morning.

She'd enjoyed music, he mused, scanning the wireless speakers. He'd seen speakers in every room of the house, and there had been CDs, tapes, even old albums, tossed around the living area downstairs. She'd had eclectic taste there. Everything from Bach to the B-52s.

Had she spent many evenings alone? he wondered. With music playing through the house? Had she ever curled up in front of that classy fireplace with one of the hundreds of books that lined the walls of her library?

Snuggled up on the couch, he thought, wearing that little red robe, with her million-dollar legs tucked up. A glass of brandy, the music on low, the starlight streaming through the roof windows.

He could see it too well. He could see her look up, skim that fall of hair back from that staggering face, curve those tempting lips as she caught him watching her. Set the book aside, reach out a hand in invitation, give that low, husky purr of a laugh as she drew him down beside her.

He could almost taste it.

Because he could, he swore under his breath, gave himself a moment to control the sudden upbeat of his heart rate.

Dead or alive, he decided, the woman was a witch. And the damn stones, preposterous or not, only seemed to add to her power.

And he was wasting his time. Completely wasting it, he told himself as he rose. He was covering ground best covered through rules and routine. He needed to go back, light a fire under the M.E., push for an estimated time of death. He needed to start calling the numbers in the victim's address book.

He needed to get out of this house that smelled of this woman. All but breathed of her. And stay out of it, he determined, until he was certain he could rein in his uncharacteristic imaginings.

Annoyed with himself, irked by his own deviation from strict routine, he walked back through the bedroom. He'd just started down the curve of the stairs when a movement caught his eye. His hand reached for his weapon. But it was already too late for that.

Very slowly, he dropped his hand, stood where he was

and stared down. It wasn't the automatic pointed at his heart that stunned him motionless. It was the fact that it was held, steady as a rock, in the hand of a dead woman.

"Well," the dead woman said, stepping forward into the halo of light from the foyer chandelier. "You're certainly a messy thief, and a stupid one." Those shockingly blue eyes stared up at him. "Why don't you give me one good reason why I shouldn't put a hole in your head before I call the police?"

For a ghost, she met his earlier fantasy perfectly. The voice was a purr, hot and husky and stunningly alive. And for the recently departed, she had a very warm flush of temper in her cheeks. It wasn't often that Seth's mind clicked off. But it had. He saw a woman, runway-fresh in white silk, the glint of jewels at her ears and a shiny silver gun in her hand.

He pulled himself back roughly, though none of the shock or the effort showed as he met her demand with an unsmiling response. "I *am* the police."

Her lips curved, a generous bow of sarcasm. "Of course you are, handsome. Who else would be creeping around a locked house when no one's at home but an overworked cop on his beat?"

"I haven't been a beat cop for quite some time. I'm Buchanan. Lieutenant Seth Buchanan. If you'd aim your weapon just a little to the left of my heart, I'll show you my badge."

"I'd just love to see it." Watching him, she slowly shifted the barrel of the gun. Her heart was thudding like a jackhammer with a combination of fear and anger, but she took another casual step forward as he reached two fingers into his pocket. The badge looked real enough, she mused. What she could see of the identification with the gold shield on the flap that he held up.

And she began to get a very bad feeling. A worse sinking in the stomach sensation than she'd experienced when she pulled up to the drive, saw the strange car and the lights blazing inside her empty house.

She flicked her eyes from the badge up to his again. Damned if he didn't look more like a cop than a crook, she decided. Very attractive, in a straight-edged, buttoned-down sort of fashion. The solid body, broad of shoulder and narrow of hip, appeared ruthlessly disciplined.

Eyes like that, cool and clear and golden brown, that seemed to see everything at once, belonged to either a cop or a criminal. Either way, she imagined, they belonged to a dangerous sort of man.

Dangerous men usually appealed to her. But at the moment, as she took in the oddity of the situation, her mood wasn't receptive.

"All right, Buchanan, Lieutenant Seth, why don't you tell me what you're doing in my house." She thought of what she carried in her purse—what Bailey had sent her only days before—and felt that unsettling sensation in her stomach deepen.

What kind of trouble are we in? she wondered. And just how do I slide out of it with a cop staring me down?

"Have you got a search warrant to go along with that badge?" she demanded.

"No, I don't." He'd have felt better, considerably better, if she'd put the gun down altogether. But she seemed content to hold it, aiming it lower now, no less steadily, but lower. Still, his composure had snapped back. Keeping his eyes on hers, he came down the rest of the stairs and stood in the lofty foyer, facing her. "You're Grace Fontaine."

She watched him tuck his badge back into his pocket, while those unreadable cop's eyes skimmed over her face. Memorizing features, she thought, irritated. Making mental note of any distinguishing marks. Just what the hell was going on?

"Yes, I'm Grace Fontaine. This is my property, my home. And as you're in it, without a proper warrant, you're trespassing. As calling a cop seems superfluous, maybe I'll just call my lawyer."

He angled his head, and unwillingly caught a whiff of that siren's scent of hers. Perhaps it was that, and feeling its instant and unwelcome effect on his system, that had him speaking without thought.

"Well, Ms. Fontaine, you look damn good for a dead woman."

Chapter 2

Her response was to narrow her eyes, arch a brow. "If that's some sort of cop humor, I'm afraid you'll have to translate."

It annoyed him that she'd jarred the remark out of him. It wasn't professional. Cautious, he brought a hand up slowly, tipped the barrel of the gun farther to the left. "Do you mind?" he said, then, quickly, before she could agree, he twisted it neatly out of her hand, pulled out the clip. It wasn't the time to ask if she had a license to carry, so he merely handed her back the empty gun and pocketed the clip.

"It's best to keep both hands on your weapon," he said easily, and with such sobriety that she suspected amusement lurked beneath. "And, if you want to keep it, not to get within reach."

"Thanks so much for the lesson in self-defense." Obviously irritated, she opened her bag and dumped the gun inside. "But you still haven't answered my initial question, Lieutenant. Why are you in my house?"

"You've had an incident, Ms. Fontaine."

"An incident? More copspeak?" She blew out a breath. "Was there a break-in?" she asked, and for the first time took her attention off the man and glanced past him into the foyer. "A robbery?" she added, then caught sight of an overturned chair and some smashed crockery through the archway in the living area.

Swearing, she started to push past him. He curled a hand over her arm to stop her. "Ms. Fontaine—"

"Get your hand off me," she snapped, interrupting him. "This is my home."

He kept his grip firm. "I'm aware of that. Exactly when was the last time you were in it?"

"I'll give you a damn statement after I've seen what's missing." She managed another two steps and saw from the disorder in the living area that it hadn't been a neat or organized robbery. "Well, they did quite a job, didn't they? My cleaning service is going to be very unhappy."

She glanced down to where Seth's fingers were still curled around her arm. "Are you testing my biceps, Lieutenant? I do like to think they're firm."

"Your muscle tone's fine." From what he could see of her in the filmy ivory slacks, it appeared more than fine. "I'd like you to answer my question, Ms. Fontaine. When were you home last?"

"Here?" She sighed, shrugged one elegant shoulder. Her mind was flitting around the annoying details that were the backwash of a robbery. Calling her insurance agent, filing a claim, giving statements. "Wednesday af-

ternoon. I went out of town for a few days." She was more
shaken than she cared to admit that her house had been
robbed and ransacked in her absence. Her things touched
and taken by strangers. But she slid him a smiling glance
from under her lashes. "Aren't you going to take notes?"

"As a matter of fact, I am. Shortly. Who was staying in
the house in your absence?"

"No one. I don't care to have people in my home when
I'm away. Now if you'll excuse me…" She gave her arm
a quick, hard jerk and strode through the foyer and under
the arch. "Good God." The anger came first, quick and
intense. She wanted to kick something, no matter that it
was broken and ruined already. "Did they have to break
what they didn't cart out?" she muttered. She glanced up,
saw the splintered railing and swore again. "And what the
devil did they do up there? A lot of good an alarm system
does if anyone can just…"

She stopped her forward motion, her voice trailing
off, as she saw the outline on the gleaming chestnut
wood of the floor. As she stared at it, unable to tear her
eyes away, the blood drained out of her face, leaving it
painfully cold and stiff.

Placing one hand on the back of the stained sofa for
balance, she stared down at the outline, the diamond glitter
of broken glass that had been her coffee table, and the
blood that had dried to a dark pool.

"Why don't we go into the dining room?" he said
quietly.

She jerked her shoulders back, though he hadn't touched
her. The pit of her stomach was cased in ice, and the flashes
of heat that lanced through her did nothing to melt it. "Who
was killed?" she demanded. "Who died here?"

"Up until a few minutes ago, it was assumed you did."

She closed her eyes, vaguely concerned that her vision was dimming at the edges. "Excuse me," she said, quite clearly, and walked across the room on numb legs. She picked up a bottle of brandy that lay on its side on the floor, fumbled open a display cabinet for a glass. And poured generously.

She took the first drink as medicine. He could see that in the way she tossed it back, shuddered twice, hard. It didn't bring the color back to her face, but he imagined it had shocked her system into functioning again.

"Ms. Fontaine, I think it would be better if we talked about this in another room."

"I'm all right." But her voice was raw. She drank again before turning to him. "Why did you think it was me?"

"The victim was in your house, dressed in a robe. She met your general description. Her face had been... damaged by the fall. She was your approximate height and weight, your age, your coloring."

Her coloring, Grace thought on a wave of staggering relief. Not Bailey or M.J., then. "I had no houseguest while I was gone." She took a deep breath, knowing the calm was there, if only she could reach it. "I have no idea who the woman was, unless it was one of the burglars. How did she—" Grace looked up again at the broken railing, the viciously sharp edges of wood. "She must have been pushed."

"That has yet to be determined."

"I'm sure it has. I can't help you as to who she was, Lieutenant. As I don't have a twin, I can only—" She broke off, her color draining a second time. Now her free hand fisted and pressed hard to her stomach. "Oh, no. Oh, God."

He understood, didn't hesitate. "Who was she?"

"I— It could have been... She's stayed here before while I was away. That's why I stopped leaving a spare key outside. She might have had it copied, though. She'd think nothing of that."

Turning her gaze away from the outline, she walked back through the debris, sat on the arm of the sofa. "A cousin." Grace sipped brandy again, slowly, letting it ease warmth back into her system. "Melissa Bennington— No, I think she took the Fontaine back a few months ago, after the divorce. I'm not sure." She pushed a hand through her hair. "I wasn't interested enough to be sure of a detail like that."

"She resembles you?"

She offered a weak, humorless smile. "It's Melissa's mission to *be* me. I went from finding it mildly flattering to mildly annoying. In the last few years I found it pathetic. There's a surface resemblance, I suppose. She's augmented it. She let her hair grow, dyed it my color. There was some difference in build, but she...augmented that, as well. She shops the same stores, uses the same salons. Chooses the same men. We grew up together, more or less. She always felt I got the better deal on all manner of levels."

She made herself look back, look down, and felt a wash of grief and pity. "Apparently I did, this time around."

"If someone didn't know you well, could they mistake you?"

"A passing glance, I suppose. Maybe a casual acquaintance. No one who—" She broke off again, got to her feet. "You think someone killed her believing her to be me? Mistaking her for me, as you did? That's absurd. It was a break-in, a burglary. A terrible accident."

"It's possible." He had indeed taken out his book to note down her cousin's name. Now he glanced up, met her eyes. "It's also more than possible that someone came here, mistook her for you, and assumed she had the third Star."

She was good, he decided. There was barely a flicker in her eyes before she lied. "I have no idea what you're talking about."

"Yes, you do. And if you haven't been home since Wednesday, you still have it." He glanced down at the bag she continued to hold.

"I don't generally carry stars in my purse." She sent him a smile that was shaky around the edges. "But it's a lovely, almost poetic, thought. Now, I'm very tired—"

"Ms. Fontaine." His voice was clipped and cool. "This victim is the sixth body I've dealt with today that traces back to those three blue diamonds."

Her hand shot out, gripped his arm. "M.J. and Bailey?"

"Your friends are fine." He felt her grip go limp. "They've had an eventful holiday weekend, all of which could have been avoided if they'd contacted and cooperated with the police. And it's cooperation I'll have from you now, one way or the other."

She tossed her hair back. "Where are they? What did you do, toss them in a cell? My lawyer will have them out and your butt in a sling before you can finish reciting the Miranda." She started toward the phone, saw it wasn't on the Queen Anne table.

"No, they're not in a cell." It goaded him, the way she snapped into gear, ready to buck the rules. "I imagine they're planning your funeral right about now."

"Planning my—" Her fabulous eyes went huge with

distress. "Oh, my God, you told them I was dead? They think I'm dead? Where are they? Where's the damn phone? I have to call them."

She crouched to push through the rubble, shoving at him when he took her arm again. "They're not home, either of them."

"You said they weren't in jail."

"And they're not." He could see he'd get nothing out of her until she'd satisfied herself. "I'll take you to them. Then we're going to sort this out, Ms. Fontaine—I promise you."

Grace didn't speak as he drove her toward the tidy suburbs edging D.C. He'd assured her that Bailey and M.J. were fine, and her instincts told her that Lieutenant Seth Buchanan was saying nothing but the truth. Facts were his business, after all, she thought. But she still gripped her hands together until her knuckles ached.

She had to see them, touch them.

Guilt was already weighing on her, guilt that they should be grieving for her, when she'd spent the past few days indulging her need to be alone, to be away. To be somewhere else.

What had happened to them over the long weekend? Had they tried to contact her while she was out of reach? It was painfully obvious that the three blue diamonds Bailey had been assessing for the museum were at the bottom of it all.

As the afterimage of that stark outline on the chestnut floor flashed into her head, Grace shuddered once again.

Melissa. Poor, pathetic Melissa. But she couldn't think of that now. She couldn't think of anything but her friends.

"They're not hurt?" she managed to ask.

"No." Seth left it at that, drove through the wash of streetlights and headlights. Her scent was sliding silkily through his car, teasing his senses. Deliberately he opened his window and let the light, damp breeze chase it away. "Where have you been the last few days, Ms. Fontaine?"

"Away." Weary she laid her head back, shut her eyes. "It's one of my favorite spots."

She jerked upright again when he turned down a tree-lined street, then swung into the drive of a brick house. She saw a shiny Jaguar, then an impossibly decrepit boat of a car. But no spiffy MG, no practical little compact.

"Their cars aren't here," she began, tossing him a look of distrust and accusation.

"But they are."

She climbed out and, ignoring him, hurried toward the front door. Her knock was brisk, businesslike, but her fist trembled. The door opened, and a man she'd never seen before stared down at her. His cool green eyes flickered with shock, then slowly warmed. His flash of a smile was blinding. Then he reached out, laid a hand gently on her cheek.

"You're Grace."

"Yes, I—"

"It's absolutely wonderful to see you." He gathered her into his arms, one of which was freshly bandaged, with such easy affection that she didn't have time to register surprise. "I'm Cade," he murmured, his gaze meeting Seth's over Grace's head. "Cade Parris. Come on in."

"Bailey. M.J."

"Just in here. They'll be fine as soon as they see you." He took her arm, felt the quick, hard tremors in it. But in the doorway of the living room, she stopped, laid a hand over his arm.

Inside, Bailey and M.J. stood, facing away, hands linked. Their voices were low, with tears wrenching through them. A man stood a short distance away, his hands thrust in his pockets and a look of helplessness on his bruised and battered face. When he saw her, his eyes, the gray of storm clouds, narrowed, flashed. Then smiled.

Grace took one shuddering breath, exhaled it slowly. "Well," she said in a clear, steady voice, "it's gratifying to know someone would weep copiously over me."

Both women whirled. For a moment, all three stared, three pair of eyes brimming over. To Seth's mind, they all moved as one, as a unit, so that their leaping rush across the room to each other held an uncanny and undeniably feminine grace. Then they were fused together, voices and tears mixing.

A triangle, he thought, frowning. With three points that made a whole. Like the golden triangle that held three priceless and powerful stones.

"I think they could use a little time," Cade said quietly, and gestured to the other man. "Lieutenant?" He motioned down the hall, lifting his brows when Seth hesitated. "I don't think they're going anywhere just now."

With a barely perceptible shrug, Seth stepped back. He could give them twenty minutes. "I need your phone."

"There's one in the kitchen. Want a beer, Jack?"

The third man grinned. "You're playing my song."

"Amnesia," Grace said a little time later. She and Bailey were huddled together on the sofa, with M.J. sitting on the floor at their feet. "Everything just blanked?"

"Everything." Bailey kept her hold on Grace's hand tight, afraid to break the link. "I woke up in this horrible little hotel room with no memory, over a million in cash, and the diamond. I picked Cade's name out of the phone book. Parris." She smiled a little. "Funny, isn't it?"

"I'm going to get you to France yet," Grace promised.

"He helped me through everything." The warmth in her tone had Grace sharing a quick look with M.J. This was something to be discussed in detail later. "I started to remember, piece by piece. You and M.J., just flashes. I could see your faces, even hear your voices, but nothing fit. He's the one who narrowed it down to Salvini, and when he took me there... He broke in."

"Shortly before we did," M.J. added. "Jack could tell the rear locks had been picked."

"We got inside," Bailey continued, and her tear-ravaged eyes went glassy. "And I remembered, I remembered it all then, how Thomas and Timothy were planning to steal the stones, copy them. How I'd shipped one off to each of you to keep it from happening. Stupid, so stupid."

"No, it wasn't." Grace slid an arm around Bailey's shoulders. "It makes perfect sense to me. You didn't have time for anything else."

"I should have called the police, but I was so sure I could turn things around. I was going into Thomas's office to have a showdown, tell them it was over. And I saw..." She trembled again. "The fight. Horrible. The lightning flashing through the windows, their faces. Then Timothy grabbed the letter opener, the knife. The power went out, but the lightning kept flashing, and I could see what he was doing...to Thomas. All the blood."

"Don't," M.J. murmured, rubbing a comforting hand on Bailey's knee. "Don't go back there."

"No." Bailey shook her head. "I have to. He saw me, Grace. He would have killed me. He came after me. I had grabbed the bag with their deposit money, and I ran through the dark. And I hid down under the stairs. In this little cave under the stairs. But I could see him hunting for me, blood all over his hands. I still don't remember how I got out, got to that room."

Grace couldn't bear to imagine it—her quiet, serious-minded friend, pursued by a murderer. "The important thing is that you did get away, and you're safe." Grace looked down at M.J. "We all are." She tried a bolstering grin. "And how did you spend your holiday?"

"On the run with a bounty hunter, handcuffed to a bed in a cheap motel, being shot at by a couple of creeps— with a little detour up to your place in the mountains."

Bounty hunter, Grace thought, trying to keep pace. The man named Jack, she supposed, with the bronze-tipped ponytail and the stormy gray eyes. And the killer grin. Handcuffs, cheap motels, and shootings. Pressing finger-tips to her eyes, she latched on to the least disturbing detail.

"You were at my place? When?"

"It's a long story." M.J. gave a quick version of a handful of days from her first encounter with Jack, when he'd tried to take her in, believing her to be a bail jumper, to the two of them escaping that setup and working their way back to the core of the puzzle.

"We know someone's pulling the strings," M.J. concluded. "But we haven't gotten very far on figuring that out yet. The bail bondsman-cum-blackmailer who gave

Jack the fake paperwork on me is dead, the two guys who came after us are dead, the Salvinis are dead."

"And Melissa," Grace murmured.

"It was Melissa?" Bailey turned to Grace. "In your house?"

"It must have been. When I got home, the cop was there. The place was torn up, and they'd assumed it was me." It took a moment, a carefully indrawn breath, a steady exhale, before she could finish. "She'd fallen off the balcony—or been pushed. I was miles away when it happened."

"Where did you go?" M.J. asked her. "When Jack and I got to your country place, it was locked up tight. I thought…I was sure you'd just been there. I could smell you."

"I left late yesterday morning. Got an itch to be near the water, so I drove down the Eastern Shore, found a little B-and-B. I did some antiquing, rubbed elbows with tourists, watched a fireworks display. I didn't leave until late today. I nearly stayed over another night. But I called both of you from the B-and-B and got your machines. I started feeling uncomfortable about being out of contact, so I headed home."

She shut her eyes a moment. "Bailey, I hadn't been really thinking. Just before I left for the country, we lost one of the children."

"Oh, Grace, I'm sorry."

"It happens all the time. They're born with AIDS or a crack addiction or a hole in the heart. Some of them die. But I can't get used to it, and it was on my mind. So I wasn't really thinking. When I started back, I started to think. And I started to worry. Then the cop was there in my house. He asked about the stone. I didn't know what you wanted me to tell him."

"We've told the police everything now." Bailey sighed. "Neither Cade nor Jack seem to like this Buchanan very much, but they respect his abilities. The two stones are safe now, as we are."

"I'm sorry for what you went through, both of you. I'm sorry I wasn't here."

"It wouldn't have made any difference," M.J. declared. "We were scattered all over—one stone apiece. Maybe we were meant to be."

"Now we're together." Grace took each of their hands in hers. "What happens next?"

"Ladies." Seth stepped into the room, skimmed his cool gaze over them, then focused on Grace. "Ms. Fontaine. The diamond?"

She rose, picked up the purse she'd tossed carelessly on the end of the couch. Opening it, she took out a velvet pouch, slid the stone out into her palm. "Magnificent, isn't it?" she murmured, studying the flash of bold blue light. "Diamonds are supposed to be cold to the touch, aren't they, Bailey? Yet this has…heat." She lifted her eyes to Seth's as she crossed to him. "Still, how many lives is it worth?"

She held her open palm out. When his fingers closed around the stone, she felt the jolt—his fingers on her skin, the shimmering blue diamond between their hands.

Something clicked, almost audibly.

She wondered if he'd felt it, heard it. Why else did those enigmatic eyes narrow, or his hand linger? The breath caught in her throat.

"Impressive, isn't it?" she managed, then felt the odd

wave of emotion and recognition ebb when he took the stone from her hand.

He didn't care for the shock that had run up his arm, and he spoke bitingly. "I imagine this one's out of even your price range, Ms. Fontaine."

She merely smiled. No, she told herself, he couldn't have felt anything—and neither had she. Just imagination and stress. "I prefer to decorate my body in something less...obvious."

Bailey rose. "The Stars are my responsibility, unless and until the Smithsonian indicates otherwise." She looked over at Cade, who remained in the doorway. "We'll put them in the safe. All of them. And I'll speak with Dr. Linstrum in the morning."

Seth turned the stone over in his hand. He imagined he could confiscate it, and its mates. They were, after all, evidence in several homicides. But he didn't relish driving back to the station with a large fortune in his car.

Parris was an irritant, he reflected. But he was an honest one. And, technically, the stones were in Bailey James's keeping until the Smithsonian relieved her of them. He wondered just what the powers at the museum would have to say about the recent travels of the Three Stars.

But that wasn't his problem.

"Lock it up," he said, passing the stone off to Cade. "And I'll be talking with Dr. Linstrum in the morning, as well, Ms. James."

Cade took one quick, threatening step forward. "Look, Buchanan—"

"No." Quietly, Bailey stepped between them, a cool breeze between two building storms. "Lieutenant Buchanan's right, Cade. It's his business now."

"That doesn't stop it from being mine." He gave Seth one last, warning look. "Watch your step," he said, then walked away with the stone.

"Thank you for bringing Grace by so quickly, Lieutenant."

Seth looked down at the extended, and obviously dismissing, hand Bailey offered him. Here's your hat, he thought, what's your hurry. "I'm sorry you were disturbed, Ms. James." His gaze flicked over to M.J. "Ms. O'Leary. You'll keep available."

"We're not going anywhere." M.J.'s chin angled, a cocky gesture as Jack crossed to her. "Drive carefully, Lieutenant."

He acknowledged the second dismissal with a slight nod. "Ms. Fontaine? I'll drive you back."

"She's not leaving." M.J. jumped in front of Grace like a tiger defending her cub. "She's not going back to that house tonight. She's staying here, with us."

"You may not care to go back home, Ms. Fontaine," Seth said coolly. "You may find it more comfortable to answer questions in my office."

"You can't be serious—"

He cut Bailey's protest off with a look. "I have a body in the morgue. I take it very seriously."

"You're a class act, Buchanan," Jack drawled, but the sound was low and threatening. "Why don't you and I go in the other room and…talk about our options?"

"It's all right." Grace stepped forward, working up a believable smile. "It's Jack, isn't it?"

"That's right." He took his attention from Buchanan long enough to smile at her. "Jack Dakota. Pleased to meet you…Miss April."

"Oh, my misspent youth survives." With a little laugh, she kissed his bruised cheek. "I appreciate the offer to beat up the lieutenant for me, Jack, but you look like you've already gone several rounds."

Grinning now, he stroked a thumb over his bruised jaw. "I've got a few more rounds in me."

"I don't doubt it. But, sad to say, the cop's right." She pushed her hair to her back and turned that smile, several degrees cooler now, on Seth. "Tactless, but right. He needs some answers. I need to go back."

"You're not going back to your house alone," Bailey insisted. "Not tonight, Grace."

"I'll be fine. But if it's all right with your Cade, I'll deal with this, pick up a few things and come back." She glanced over at Cade as he came back into the room. "Got a spare bed, darling?"

"You bet. Why don't I go with you, help you pick up your things and bring you back?"

"You stay here with Bailey." She kissed him, as well— a casual and already affectionate brush of lips. "I'm sure Lieutenant Buchanan and I will manage." She picked up her purse, turned and embraced both M.J. and Bailey again. "Don't worry about me. After all, I'm in the arms of the law."

She eased back, shot Seth one of those full candle-power smiles. "Isn't that right, Lieutenant?"

"In a manner of speaking." He stepped back and waited for her to walk to the door ahead of him.

She waited until they were in his car and pulling out of the drive. "I need to see the body." She didn't look at him, but lifted a hand to the four people crowded at the front door, watching them drive away. "You need— She'll have to be identified, won't she?"

It surprised him that she'd take the duty on. "Yes."

"Then let's get it over with. After—afterwards, I'll answer your questions. I'd prefer we handle that in your office," she added, using that smile again. "My house isn't ready for company."

"Fine."

She'd known it would be hard. She'd known it would be horrible. Grace had prepared herself for it—or she'd thought she had. Nothing, she realized as she stared down at what remained of the woman in the morgue, could have prepared her.

It was hardly surprising that they'd mistaken Melissa for her. The face Melissa had been so proud of was utterly ruined. Death had been cruel here, and, through her involvement with the hospital, Grace had reason to know it often was.

"It's Melissa." Her voice echoed flatly in the chilly white room. "My cousin, Melissa Fontaine."

"You're sure?"

"Yes. We shared the same health club, among other things. I know her body as well as I know mine. She has a sickle-shaped birthmark at the small of her back, just left of center. And there's a scar on the bottom of her left foot, small, crescent-shaped, in the ball of her foot, where she stepped on a broken shell in the Hamptons when we were twelve."

Seth shifted, found the scar, then nodded to the M.E.'s assistant. "I'm sorry for your loss."

"Yes, I'm sure you are." With muscles that felt like glass, she turned, her dimming vision passing over him. "Excuse me."

She made it nearly to the door before she swayed. Swearing under his breath, Seth caught her, pulled her out into the corridor and put her in a chair. With one hand, he shoved her head between her knees.

"I'm not going to faint." She squeezed her eyes tightly shut, battling fiercely against the twin foes of dizziness and nausea.

"Could have fooled me."

"I'm much too sophisticated for something as maudlin as a swoon." But her voice broke, her shoulders sagged, and for a moment she kept her head down. "Oh, God, she's dead. And all because she hated me."

"What?"

"Doesn't matter. She's dead." Bracing herself, she sat up again, let her head rest against the cold white wall. Her cheeks were just as colorless. "I have to call my aunt. Her mother. I have to tell her what happened."

He gauged this woman, studying the face that was no less staggeringly lovely for being bone-white. "Give me the name. I'll take care of it."

"It's Helen Wilson Fontaine. I'll do it."

He didn't realize until her hand moved that he'd placed his own over it. He pulled back on every level, and rose. "I haven't been able to reach Helen Fontaine or her husband. She's in Europe."

"I know where she is." Grace shook back her hair, but didn't try to stand. Not yet. "I can find her." The thought of making that call, saying what had to be said, squeezed her throat. "Could I have some water, Lieutenant?"

His heels echoed on tile as he strode off. Then there was silence—a full, damning silence that whispered of what kind of business was done in such places. There were

scents here that slid slyly under the potent odors of anti-
septics and industrial cleaning solutions.

She was pitifully grateful when she heard his footsteps
on the return journey.

She took the paper cup from him with both hands,
drinking slowly, concentrating on the simple act of swallowing liquid.

"Why did she hate you?"

"What?"

"Your cousin. You said she hated you. Why?"

"Family trait," she said briefly. She handed him back
the empty cup as she rose. "I'd like to go now."

He took her measure a second time. Her color had yet
to return, her pupils were dilated, the electric-blue irises
were glassy. He doubted she'd last another hour.

"I'll take you back to Parris's," he decided. "You can
get your things in the morning, come in to my office to
make your statement."

"I said I'd do it tonight."

"And I say you'll do it in the morning. You're no good
to me now."

She tried a weak laugh. "Why, Lieutenant, I believe
you're the first man who's ever said that to me. I'm
crushed."

"Don't waste the routine on me." He took her arm, led
her to the outside doors. "You haven't got the energy for
it."

He was exactly right. She pulled her arm free as they
stepped back into the thick night air. "I don't like you."

"You don't have to." He opened the car door, waited.
"Any more than I have to like you."

She stepped to the door, and with it between them met

his eyes. "But the difference is, if I had the energy—or the inclination—I could make you sit up and beg."

She got in, sliding those long, silky legs in.

Not likely, Seth told himself as he shut the door with a snap. But he wasn't entirely sure he believed it.

Chapter 3

She felt like a weakling, but she didn't go home. She'd needed friends, not that empty house, with the shadow of a body drawn on the floor.

Jack had gone over, fetched her bags out of her car and brought them to her. For a day, at least, she was content to make do with that.

Since she was driving in to meet with Seth, Grace had made do carefully. She'd dressed in a summer suit she'd just picked up on the Shore. The little short skirt and waist-length jacket in buttercup yellow weren't precisely professional—but she wasn't aiming for professional. She'd taken the time to catch her waterfall of hair back in a complicated French braid and made up her face with the concentration and determination of a general plotting a decisive battle.

Meeting with Seth again felt like a battle.

Her stomach was still raw from the call she'd made to her aunt, and the sickness that had overwhelmed her after it. She'd slept poorly, but she had slept, tucked into one of Cade's guest rooms, secure that those who meant most to her were close by.

She would deal with the relatives later, she thought, easing her convertible into the lot at the station house. It would be hard, but she would deal with them. For now, she had to deal with herself. And Seth Buchanan.

If anyone had been watching as she stepped from her car and started across the lot, he would have seen a transformation. Subtly, gradually, her eyes went from weary to sultry. Her gait loosened, eased into a lazy, hip-swinging walk designed to cross a man's eyes. Her mouth turned up slightly at the corners, into a secret, knowing female smile.

It wasn't really a mask, but another part of her. Innate and habitual, it was an image she could draw on at will. She willed it now, flashing a slow under-the-lashes smile at the uniform who stepped to the door as she did. He flushed, moved back and nearly bobbled the door in his hurry to open it for her.

"Why, thank you, Officer."

Heat rose up his neck, into his face, and made her smile widen. She was right on target. Seth Buchanan wouldn't see a pale, trembling woman this morning. He'd see Grace Fontaine, just hitting her stride.

She sauntered up to the sergeant on duty at the desk, skimmed a fingertip along the edge. "Excuse me?"

"Yes, ma'am." His Adam's apple bobbed three times as he swallowed.

"I wonder if you could help me? I'm looking for a

Lieutenant Buchanan. Are you in charge?" She skimmed her gaze over him. "You must be in charge, Commander."

"Ah, yes. No. It's sergeant." He fumbled for the sign-in book, the passes. "I— He's— You'll find the lieutenant upstairs, detective division. To the left of the stairs."

"Oh." She took the pen he offered and signed her name boldly. "Thank you, Commander. I mean, Sergeant."

She heard his little expulsion of breath as she turned, and felt his gaze on her legs as she climbed the stairs.

She found the detective division easily enough. One sweeping glance took in the front-to-front desks, some manned, some not. The cops were in shirtsleeves in an oppressive heat that was barely touched by what had to be a faulty air-conditioning unit. A lot of guns, she thought, a lot of half-eaten meals and empty cups of coffee. Phones shrilling.

She picked her mark—a man with a loosened tie, feet on the desk, a report of some kind in one hand and a Danish in the other. As she started through the crowded room, several conversations stopped. Someone whistled softly—it was like a sigh. The man at the desk swept his feet to the floor, swallowed the Danish.

"Ma'am."

About thirty, she judged, though his hairline was receding rapidly. He wiped his crumb-dusted fingers on his shirt, rolled his eyes slightly to the left, where one of his associates was grinning and pounding a fist to his heart.

"I hope you can help me." She kept her eyes on his, and only his, until a muscle began to twitch in his jaw. "Detective?"

"Yeah, ah, Carter, Detective Carter. What can I do for you?"

"I hope I'm in the right place." For effect, she turned her head, swept her gaze over the room and its occupants. Several stomachs were ruthlessly sucked in. "I'm looking for Lieutenant Buchanan. I think he's expecting me." Gracefully she brushed a loose flutter of hair away from her face. "I'm afraid I just don't know the proper procedure."

"He's in his office. Back in his office." Without taking his eyes from her he jerked a thumb. "Belinski, tell the lieutenant he has a visitor. A Miss…"

"It's Grace." She slid a hip onto the corner of the desk, letting her skirt hike up a dangerous inch. "Grace Fontaine. Is it all right if I wait here, Detective Carter? Am I interrupting your work?"

"Yes— No. Sure."

"It's so exciting." She brought the temperature of the overheated room up ten more degrees with a dazzling smile. "Detective work. You must have so many interesting stories."

By the time Seth had finished the phone call he was on when he was notified of Grace's arrival, shrugged back into the jacket he'd removed as a concession to the heat and made his way into the bull pen, Carter's desk was completely surrounded. He heard a low, throaty female laugh rise out of the center of the crowd.

And saw a half a dozen of his best men panting like puppies over a meaty bone.

The woman, he decided, was going to be an enormous headache.

"I see all cases have been closed this morning, and miraculously crime has come to a halt."

His voice had the desired effect. Several men jerked straight. Those less easily intimidated grinned as they skulked back to their desks. Deserted, Carter flushed from his neck to his receding sandy hairline. "Ah, Grace—that is, Miss Fontaine to see you, Lieutenant. Sir."

"So I see. You finish that report, Detective?"

"Working on it." Carter grabbed the papers he'd tossed aside and buried his nose in them.

"Ms. Fontaine." Seth arched a brow, gestured toward his office.

"It was nice meeting you, Michael." Grace trailed a finger over Carter's shoulder as she passed.

He'd feel the heat of that skimming touch for hours.

"You can cut the power back now," Seth said dryly as he opened the door to his office. "You won't need it."

"You never know, do you?" She sauntered in, moving past him, close enough for them to brush bodies. She thought she felt him stiffen, just a little, but his eyes remained level, cool, and apparently unimpressed. Miffed, she studied his office.

The institutional beige of the walls blended depressingly into the dingy beige of the aging linoleum floor. An overburdened department-issue desk, gray file cabinets, computer, phone and one small window didn't add any spark to the no-nonsense room.

"So this is where the mighty rule," she murmured. It disappointed her that she found no personal touches. No photos, no sports trophies. Nothing she could hold on to, no sign of the man behind the badge.

As she had in the bull pen, she eased a hip onto the

corner of his desk. To say she resembled a sunbeam would have been a cliché. And it would have been incorrect, Seth decided. Sunbeams were tame—warm, welcoming. She was an explosive bolt of heat lightning— Hot. Fatal.

A blind man would have noticed those satiny legs in the snug yellow skirt. Seth merely walked around, sat, looked at her face.

"You'd be more comfortable in a chair."

"I'm fine here." Idly she picked up a pen, twirled it. "I don't suppose this is where you interrogate suspects."

"No, we have a dungeon downstairs for that."

Under other circumstances, she would have appreciated his dust-dry tone. "Am I a suspect?"

"I'll let you know." He angled his head. "You recover quickly, Ms. Fontaine."

"Yes, I do. You had questions, Lieutenant?"

"Yes, I do. Sit down. In a chair."

Her lips moved in what was nearly a pout. A luscious come-on-and-kiss-me pout. He felt the quick, helpless pull of lust, and damned her for it. She moved, sliding off the desk, settling into a chair, taking her time crossing those killer legs.

"Better?"

"Where were you Saturday, between the hours of midnight and 3:00 a.m.?"

So that was when it had happened, she thought, and ignored the ache in her stomach. "Aren't you going to read me my rights?"

"You're not charged, you don't need a lawyer. It's a simple question."

"I was in the country. I have a house in western Maryland. I was alone. I don't have an alibi. Do I need a lawyer now?"

"Do you want to complicate this, Ms. Fontaine?"

"There's no way to simplify it, is there?" But she flicked a hand in dismissal. The thin diamond bracelet that circled her wrist shot fire. "All right, Lieutenant, as uncomplicated as possible. I don't want my lawyer—for the moment. Why don't I just give you a basic rundown? I left for the country on Wednesday. I wasn't expecting my cousin, or anyone, for that matter. I did have contact with a few people over the weekend. I bought a few supplies in the town nearby, shopped at the gardening stand. That would have been Friday afternoon. I picked up some mail on Saturday. It's a small town, the postmistress would remember. That was before noon, however, which would give me plenty of time to drive back. And, of course, there was the courier who delivered Bailey's package on Friday."

"And you didn't find that odd? Your friend sends you a blue diamond, and you just shrug it off and go shopping?"

"I called her. She wasn't in." She arched a brow. "But you probably know that. I did find it odd, but I had things on my mind."

"Such as?"

Her lips curved, but the smile wasn't reflected in her eyes. "I'm not required to tell you my thoughts. I did wonder about it and worried a little. I thought perhaps it was a copy, but I didn't really believe that. A copy couldn't have what that stone has. Bailey's instructions in the package were to keep it with me until she contacted me. So that's what I did."

"No questions?"

"I rarely question people I trust."

He tapped a pencil on the edge of the desk. "You stayed alone in the country until Monday, when you drove back to the city."

"No. I drove down to the Eastern Shore on Sunday. I had a whim." She smiled again. "I often do. I stayed at a bed-and-breakfast."

"You didn't like your cousin?"

"No, I didn't." She imagined that quick shift of topic was an interrogation technique. "She was difficult to like, and I rarely make the effort with difficult people. We were raised together after my parents were killed, but we weren't close. I intruded into her life, into her space. She compensated for it by being disagreeable. I was often disagreeable in return. As we got older, she had a less...successful talent with men than I. Apparently she thought by enhancing the similarities in our appearance, she'd have better success."

"And did she?"

"I suppose it depends on your point of view. Melissa enjoyed men." To combat the guilt coating her heart, Grace leaned back negligently in the chair. "She certainly enjoyed men—which is one of the reasons she was recently divorced. She preferred the species in quantity."

"And how did her husband feel about that?"

"Bobbie's a..." She trailed off, then relieved a great deal of her own tension with a quick, delighted and very appealing laugh. "If you're suggesting that Bobbie—her ex—tracked her down to my house, murdered her, trashed the place and walked off whistling, you couldn't be more wrong. He's a cream puff. And he is, I believe, in England, even as we speak. He enjoys tennis and never misses Wimbledon. You can check easily enough."

Which he would, Seth thought, noting it down. "Some people find murder distasteful on a personal level, but not at a distance. They just pay for a service."

This time she sighed. "We both know Melissa wasn't the target, Lieutenant. I was. She was in my house." Restless, she rose, a graceful and feline movement. Walking to the tiny window, she looked out on his dismal view. "She's made herself at home in my Potomac house twice before when I was away. The first time, I tolerated it. The second, she enjoyed the facilities a bit too enthusiastically for my taste. We had a spat about it. She left in a huff, and I removed the spare key. I should have thought to change the locks, but it never occurred to me she'd go to the trouble of having copies made."

"When was the last time you saw her or spoke with her?"

Grace sighed. Dates ran through her head, people, events, meaningless social forays. "About six weeks ago, maybe eight. At the health club. We ran into each other in the steam room, didn't have much conversation. We never had much to say to each other."

She was regretting that now, Seth realized. Going over in her head opportunities lost or wasted. And it would do no good. "Would she have opened the door to someone she didn't know?"

"If the someone was male and was marginally attractive, yes." Weary of the interview, she turned back. "Look, I don't know what else I can tell you, what help I can possibly be. She was a careless, often arrogant woman. She picked up strange men in bars when she felt the urge. She let someone in that night, and she died for it. Whatever she was, she didn't deserve to die for that."

She brushed at her hair absently, tried to clear her mind as Seth simply sat, waiting. "Maybe he demanded she give him the stone. She wouldn't have understood. She paid for her trespassing, for her carelessness and her ignorance. And the stone is back with Bailey, where it belongs. If you haven't spoken to Dr. Linstrum yet this morning, I can tell you that Bailey should be meeting with him right now. I don't know anything else to tell you."

He kicked back for a moment, his eyes cool and steady on her face. If he discounted the connection with the diamonds, it could play another way. Two women, at odds all their lives. One of them returns home unexpectedly to find the other in her home. An argument. Escalating into a fight. And one of them ends up taking a dive off a second-floor balcony into a pool of glass.

The first woman doesn't panic. She trashes her own home to cover herself, then drives away. Puts distance between herself and the scene.

Was she a skilled enough actress to fake that stark shock, the raw emotion he'd seen on her face the night before?

He thought she was.

But despite that, the scene just didn't click. There was the undeniable connection of the diamonds. And he was dead sure that if Grace Fontaine had caused her cousin's fall, she would have been just as capable of picking up the phone and coolly reporting an accident.

"All right, that's all for now."

"Well." Her breath was a huff of relief. "That wasn't so bad, all in all."

He stood up. "I'll have to ask you to stay available."

She switched on the charm again, a hot, rose-colored light. "I'm always available, handsome. Ask anyone." She picked up her purse, moved with him to the door. "How long before I can have my house dealt with? I'd like to put things back to order as quickly as possible."

"I'll let you know." He glanced at his watch. "When you're up to going through things and doing an inventory to see what's missing, I'd like you to contact me."

"I'm on my way over now to do just that."

His brow furrowed a moment as he juggled responsibilities. He could assign a man to go with her, but he preferred dealing with it himself. "I'll follow you over."

"Police protection?"

"If necessary."

"I'm touched. Why don't I give you a lift, handsome?"

"I'll follow you over," he repeated.

"Suit yourself," she began, and grazed a hand over his cheek. Her eyes widened slightly as his fingers clamped on her wrist. "Don't like to be petted?" She purred the words, surprised at how her heart had jumped and started to race. "Most animals do."

His face was very close to hers, their bodies were just touching, with the heat from the room and something even more sweltering between them. Something old, and almost familiar.

He drew her hand down slowly, kept his fingers on her wrist.

"Be careful what buttons you push."

Excitement, she realized with surprise. It was pure, primal excitement that zipped through her. "Wasted advice," she said silkily, daring him. "I enjoy pushing new ones. And apparently you have a few interesting buttons just begging for attention." She skimmed her gaze deliberately down to his mouth. "Just begging."

He could imagine himself shoving her back against the door, moving fast into that heat, feeling her go molten. Because he was certain she was aware of just how perfectly a man would imagine it, he stepped back, released her and opened the door to the din of the bull pen.

"Be sure to turn in your visitor's badge at the desk," he said.

He was a cool one, Grace thought as she drove. An attractive, successful, unmarried—she'd slipped that bit of data out of an unsuspecting Detective Carter—and self-contained man.

A challenge.

And, she decided as she passed through the quiet, well-designed neighborhood, toward her home, a challenge was exactly what she needed to get through the emotional upheaval.

She'd have to face her aunt in a few hours, and the rest of the relatives soon after. There would be questions, demands, and, she knew, blame. She would be the recipient of all of it. That was the way her family worked, and that was what she'd come to expect from them.

Ask Grace, take from Grace, point the finger at Grace. She wondered how much of that she deserved, and how much had simply been inherited along with the money her parents left her.

It hardly mattered, she thought, since both were hers, like it or not.

She swung into her drive, her gaze sweeping over and up. The house was something she'd wanted. The clever and unique design of wood and glass, the gables, the cornices, the decks and the ruthlessly groomed grounds. She'd wanted the space, the elegance that lent itself to entertaining, the convenience to the city. The proximity to Bailey and M.J.

But the little house in the mountains was something she'd needed. And that was hers, and hers alone. The relatives didn't know it existed. No one could find her there unless she wanted to be found.

But here, she thought as she set the brakes, was the neat, expensive home of one Grace Fontaine. Heiress, socialite and party girl. The former centerfold, the Radcliffe graduate, the Washington hostess.

Could she continue to live here, she wondered, with death haunting the rooms? Time would tell.

For now, she was going to concentrate on solving the puzzle of Seth Buchanan, and finding a way under that seemingly impenetrable armor of his.

Just for the fun of it.

She heard him pull in and, in a deliberately provocative move, turned, tipped down her shaded glasses and studied him over the tops.

Oh, yes, she thought. He was very, very attractive. The way he controlled that lean and muscled body. Very economical. No wasted movements. He wouldn't waste them in bed, either. And she wondered just how long it would be before she could lure him there. She had a hunch—and she rarely doubted her hunches where men were concerned—that there was a volcano bubbling under that calm and somewhat austere surface.

She was going to enjoy poking at it until it erupted.

As he crossed to her, she handed him her keys. "Oh, but you have your own now, don't you?" She tipped her glasses back into place. "Well, use mine…this time."

"Who else has a set?"

She skimmed the tip of her tongue over her top lip, darkly pleased when she saw his gaze jerk down. Just for an instant, but it was progress. "Bailey and M.J. I don't give my keys to men. I'd rather open the door for them myself. Or close it."

"Fine." He dumped the keys back in her hand, looking amused when her brows drew together. "Open the door."

One step forward, two steps back, she mused, then stepped up on the flagstone portico and unlocked her home.

She'd braced for it, but it was still difficult. The foyer was as it had been, largely undisturbed. But her gaze was drawn up now, helplessly, to the shattered railing.

"It's a long way to fall," she murmured. "I wonder if you have time to think, to understand, on the way down."

"She wouldn't have."

"No." And that was better, somehow. "I suppose not." She stepped into the living area, forced herself to look at the chalk outline. "Well, where to begin?"

"He got to your safe down here. Emptied it. You'll want to list what was taken out."

"The library safe." She moved through, under an arch and into a wide room filled with light and books. A great many of those books littered the floor now, and an art deco lamp in the shape of an elongated woman's body— a small thing she'd loved—was cracked in two. "He wasn't subtle, was he?"

"I say he was rushed. And pissed off."

"You'd know best." She walked to the safe, noting the open door and the empty interior. "I had some jewelry— quite a bit, actually. A few thousand in cash."

"Bonds, stock certificates?"

"No, they're in my safe-deposit box at the bank. One doesn't need to take out stock certificates and enjoy the way they sparkle. I bought a terrific pair of diamond earrings just last month." She sighed, shrugged. "Gone now. I have a complete list of my jewelry, and photographs of each piece, along with the insurance papers, in my safety box. Replacing them's just a matter of—"

She broke off, made a small, distressed sound and rushed from the room,

The woman could move when she wanted, Seth thought as he headed upstairs after her. And she didn't lose any of that feline grace with speed. He turned into her bedroom, then into her walk-in closet behind her.

"He wouldn't have found it. He couldn't have found it." She repeated the words like a prayer as she twisted a knob on the built-in cabinet. It swung out, revealing a safe in the wall behind.

Quickly, her fingers not quite steady, she spun the combination, wrenched open the door. Her breath expelled in a whoosh as she knelt and took out velvet boxes and bags.

More jewelry, he thought with a shake of his head. How many earrings could one woman wear? But she was opening each box carefully, examining the contents.

"These were my mother's," she murmured, with a catch of undiluted emotion in the words. "They matter. The sapphire pin my father gave her for their fifth anniversary, the necklace he gave her when I was born. The pearls. She wore these the day they married." She stroked the creamy white strand over her cheek as if it were a loved one's hand. "I had this built for them, didn't keep them with the others. Just in case."

She sat back on her heels, her lap filled with jewelry that meant so much more than gold and pretty stones. "Well," she managed as her throat closed. "Well, they're here. They're still here."

"Ms. Fontaine."

"Oh, call me Grace," she snapped. "You're as stuffy as my Uncle Niles." Then she pressed a hand to her forehead, trying to work away the beginnings of a tension headache. "I don't suppose you can make coffee."

"Yes, I can make coffee."

"Then why don't you go down and do that little thing, handsome, and give me a minute here?"

He surprised her, and himself, by crouching down first, laying a hand on her shoulder. "You could have lost the pearls, lost all of it. You still wouldn't have lost your memories."

Uneasy that he'd felt compelled to say it, he straightened and left her alone. He went directly to the kitchen, pushing through the mess to fill the coffeepot. He set it up to brew and switched the machine on. Stuck his hands in his pockets, then pulled them out.

What the hell was going on? he asked himself. He should be focused on the case, and the case alone. Instead, he felt himself being pulled, tugged at, by the woman upstairs—by the various faces of that woman. Bold, fragile, sexy, sensitive.

Just which was she? And why had he spent most of the night with her face lodged in his dreams?

He shouldn't even be here, he admitted. He had no official reason to be spending this time with her. It was true he felt the case warranted his personal attention. It was serious enough. But she was only one small part of the whole.

And he'd be lying to himself if he said he was here strictly on an investigation.

He found two undamaged cups. There were several broken ones lying around. Good Meissen china, he noted. His mother had a set she prized dearly. He was just pouring the coffee when he sensed her behind him.

"Black?"

"That's fine." She stepped in, and winced as she took a visual inventory of the kitchen. "He didn't miss much, did he? I suppose he thought I might stick a big blue diamond in my coffee canister or cookie jar."

"People put their valuables in a lot of odd places. I was involved in a burglary case once where the victim saved her in-house cash because she'd kept it in a sealed plastic bag in the bottom of the diaper pail. What self-respecting B-and-E man is going to paw through diapers?"

She chuckled, sipped her coffee. Whether or not it had been his purpose, his telling of the story had made her feel better. "It makes keeping things in a safe seem foolish. This one didn't take the silver, or any of the electronics. I suppose, as you said, he was in too much of a hurry, and just took what he could stuff in his pockets."

She walked to the kitchen window and looked out. "Melissa's clothes are upstairs. I didn't see her purse. He might have taken that, too, or it could just be buried under the mess."

"We'd have found it if it had been here."

She nodded. "I'd forgotten. You've already searched through my things." She turned back, leaned on the counter and eyed him over the rim of her cup. "Did you go through them personally, Lieutenant?"

He thought of the red silk gown. "Some of it. You have your own department store here."

"I'd come by that naturally, wouldn't I? I have a weakness for things. All manner of things. You make excellent coffee, Lieutenant. Isn't there anyone who brews it for you in the morning?"

"No. Not at the moment." He set his coffee aside. "That wasn't very subtle."

"It wasn't intended to be. It's not that I mind competition. I just like to know if I have any. I still don't think I like you, but that could change." She lifted a hand to finger the tail of her braid. "Why not be prepared?"

"I'm interested in closing a case, not in playing games with you...Grace."

It was such a cool delivery, so utterly dispassionate it kindled her spirit of competition. "I suppose you don't like aggressive women."

"Not particularly."

"Well, then." She smiled as she stepped closer to him. "You're just going to hate this."

In a slick and practiced move, she slid a hand up into his hair and brought his mouth to hers.

Chapter 4

The jolt, lightning wrapped in black velvet, stabbed through him in one powerful strike. His head spun with it, his blood churned, his belly ached. No part of his system was spared the rapid onslaught of that lush and knowing mouth.

Her taste, unexpected yet familiar, plunged into him like hot spiced wine that rushed immediately to his head, leaving him dazed and drunk and desperate.

His muscles bunched, as if poised to leap. And in leaping, he would possess what was somehow already his. It took a vicious twist of will to keep his arms locked at his sides, when they strained to reach out, take, relish. Her scent was as dark, as drugging, as her flavor. Even the low, persuasive hum that sounded in her throat as she moved that glorious fantasy of a body against his was a tantalizing hint of what could be.

For a slow count of five, he fisted his hands, then relaxed them and let the internal war rage while his lips remained passive, his body rigid in denial.

He wouldn't give her the satisfaction of response....

She knew it was a mistake. Even as she moved toward him, reached for him, she'd known it. She'd made mistakes before, and she tried never to regret what was done and couldn't be undone.

But she regretted this.

She deeply regretted that his taste was utterly unique and perfect for her palate. That the texture of his hair, the shape of his shoulders, the strong wall of his chest, all taunted her, when she'd only meant to taunt him, to show him what she could offer. If she chose.

Instead, swept into need, rushed into it by that mating of lips, she offered more than she'd intended. And he gave nothing back.

She caught his bottom lip between her teeth, one quick, sharp nip, then masked an outrageous rush of disappointment by stepping casually back and aiming an amused smile at him.

"My, my, you're a cool one, aren't you, Lieutenant?"

His blood burned with every heartbeat, but he merely inclined his head. "You're not used to being resistible, are you, Grace?"

"No." She rubbed a fingertip lightly over her lip in a movement that was both absent and provocative. The essence of him clung stubbornly there, insisting it belonged. "But then, most of the men I've kissed haven't had ice water in their veins. It's a shame." She took her finger from her own lip, tapped it on his. "Such a nice mouth. Such potential. Still, maybe you just don't care for...women."

The grin he flashed stunned her. His eyes glowed with it, in fascinating tones of gold. His mouth softened with a charm that had a wicked and unpredictable appeal. Suddenly he was approachable, nearly boyish, and it made her heart yearn.

"Maybe," he said, "you're just not my type."

She gave one short, humorless laugh. "Darling, I'm every man's type. Well, we'll just chalk it up to a failed experiment and move on." Telling herself it was foolish to be hurt, she stepped to him again, reached up to straighten the tie she'd loosened.

He didn't want her to touch him, not then, not when he was so precariously perched on the edge. "You've got a hell of an ego there."

"I suppose I do." With her hands still on his tie, she looked up, into his eyes. The hell with it, she thought, if they couldn't be lovers, maybe they could be cautious friends. The man who had looked at her and grinned would be a good, solid friend.

So she smiled at him with a sweetness that was without art or guile, lancing his heart with one clean blow. "But then, men are generally predictable. You're just the exception to the rule, Seth, the one that proves it."

She brushed her hands down, smoothing his jacket and said something more, but he didn't hear it over the roaring in his ears. His control broke; he felt the snap, like the twang of a sword violently broken over an armored knee. In a movement he was hardly aware of, he spun her around, pressed her back against the wall, and was ravaging her mouth.

Her heart kicked in her chest, drove the breath out of her body. She gripped his shoulders as much for balance as in response to the sudden, violent need that shot from him to her and fused them together.

She yielded, utterly, then locked her arms around his neck and poured herself back.

Here, was all her dazzled mind could think. Oh, here, at last.

His hands raced over her, molded and somehow recognized each curve. And the recognition seared through him, as hot and real as the surge of desire. He wanted that taste, had to have it inside him, to swallow it whole. He assaulted her mouth like a man feeding after a lifelong fast, filled himself with the flavors of her, all of them dark, ripe, succulent.

She was there for him, had always been there—impossibly there. And he knew that if he didn't pull back, he'd never be able to survive without her.

He slapped his hands on the wall on either side of her head to stop himself from touching, to stop himself from taking. Fighting to regain both his breath and his sanity, he eased out of the kiss, stepped away.

She continued to lean back against the wall, her eyes closed, her skin luminous with passion. By the time her lashes fluttered up and those slumberous blue eyes focused, he had his control snapped back ruthlessly in place.

"Unpredictable," she managed, barely resisting the urge to press both hands to her galloping heart. "Very."

"I warned you about pushing the wrong buttons." His voice was cool, edging toward cold, and had the effect of a backhand slap.

She flinched from it, might have reeled, if she hadn't been braced by the wall. His eyes narrowed fractionally at the reaction. Hurt? he wondered. No, that was ridiculous. She was a veteran game player and knew all the angles.

"Yes, you did." She straightened, pride stiffening her spine and forcing her lips to curve in a casual smile. "I'm just so resistant to warnings."

He thought she should be required by law to carry one—Danger! Woman!

"I've got work to do. I can give you another five minutes, if you want me to wait while you pack some things."

Oh, you bastard, she thought. How can you be so cool, so unaffected? "You toddle right along, handsome. I'll be fine."

"I'd prefer you weren't in the house alone for the moment. Go pack some things."

"It's my home."

"Right now, it's a crime scene. You're down to four and a half minutes."

Fury vibrated through her in hot, pulsing beats. "I don't need anything here." She turned, started out, whirling back when he took her arm. "What?"

"You need clothes," he said, patient now. "For a day or two."

"Do you really think I'd wear anything that bastard might have touched?"

"That's a foolish and a predictable reaction." His tone didn't soften in the least. "You're not a foolish or a predictable woman. Don't be a victim, Grace. Go pack your things."

He was right. She could have despised him for that alone. But the frustrated need still fisted inside her was a much better reason. She said nothing at all, simply turned again and walked away.

When he didn't hear the front door slam, he was satisfied that she'd gone upstairs to pack, as he'd told her to. Seth turned off the coffeemaker, rinsed the cups and set them in the sink, then went out to wait for her.

She was a fascinating woman, he thought. Full of temperament, energy and ego. And she was undoing him, knot by carefully tied knot. How she knew exactly what strings to pull to do so was just one more mystery.

He'd taken this case on, he reminded himself. Riding a desk and delegating were only part of the job. He needed to be involved, and he'd involved himself with this—and therefore with her. Grace's part of the whole was small, but he needed to treat her with the same objectivity that he treated every other piece of the case with.

He looked up, his gaze drawn to the portrait that smiled down so invitingly.

He'd have to be more machine than man to stay objective when it came to Grace Fontaine.

It was midafternoon before he could clear his desk enough to handle a follow-up interview. The diamonds were the key, and he wanted another look at them. He hadn't been surprised when his phone conversation with Dr. Linstrum at the Smithsonian resulted in a testimonial to Bailey James's integrity and skill. The diamonds she'd gone to such lengths to protect remained at Salvini, and in her care.

When Seth pulled into the parking lot of the elegant corner building just outside D.C. that housed Salvini, he nodded to the uniformed cop guarding the main door. And felt a faint tug of sympathy. The heat was brutal.

"Lieutenant." Despite a soggy uniform, the officer snapped to attention.

"Ms. James inside?"

"Yes, sir. The store's closed to the public for the next week." He indicated the darkened showroom through the thick glass doors with a jerk of the head. "We have a guard posted at every entrance, and Ms. James is on the lower level. It's easier access through the rear, Lieutenant."

"Fine. When's your relief, Officer?"

"I've got another hour." The cop didn't wipe his brow, but he wanted to. Seth Buchanan had a reputation for being a stickler. "Four-hour rotations, as per your orders, sir."

"Bring a bottle of water with you next time." Well aware that the uniform sagged the minute his back was turned, Seth rounded the building. After a brief conversation with the duty guard at the rear, he pressed the buzzer beside the reinforced steel door. "Lieutenant Buchanan," he said when Bailey answered through the intercom. "I'd like a few minutes."

It took her some time to get to the door. Seth visualized her coming out of the workroom on the lower level, winding down the short corridor, passing the stairs where she'd hidden from a killer only days before.

He'd been through the building himself twice, top to bottom. He knew that not everyone could have survived what she'd been through in there.

The locks clicked, the door opened. "Lieutenant." She smiled at the guard, silently apologizing for his miserable duty. "Please come in."

She looked neat and tidy, Seth thought, with her trim blouse and slacks, her blond hair scooped back. Only the faint shadows under her eyes spoke of the strain she'd been under.

"I spoke with Dr. Linstrum," Seth began.

"Yes, I expect you did. I'm very grateful for his understanding."

"The stones are back where they started."

She smiled a little. "Well, they're back where they were a few days ago. Who knows if they'll ever see Rome again. Can I get you something cold to drink?" She gestured toward a soft-drink machine standing brightly against a dark wall.

"I'll buy." He plugged in coins. "I'd like to see the diamonds, and have a few words with you."

"All right." She pressed the button for her choice, and retrieved the can that clunked down the shoot. "They're in the vault." She continued to speak as she led the way. "I've arranged to have the security and alarm system beefed up. We've had cameras in the showroom for a number of years, but I'll have them installed at the doors, as well, and for the upper and lower levels. All areas."

"That's wise." He concluded that there was a practical streak of common sense beneath the fragile exterior. "You'll run the business now?"

She opened a door, hesitated. "Yes. My stepfather left it to the three of us, with my stepbrothers sharing eighty percent between them. In the event any of us died without heirs, the shares go to the survivors." She drew in a breath. "I survived."

"That's something to be grateful for, Bailey, not guilty about."

"Yes, that's what Cade says. But you see, I once had the illusion, at least, that they were family. Have a seat, I'll get the Stars."

He moved into the work area, glanced at the equipment, the long worktable. Intrigued, he stepped closer, examining the glitter of colored stones, the twists of gold. It was going to be a necklace, he realized, running a fingertip over the silky length of a closely linked chain. Something bold, almost pagan.

"I needed to get back to work," she said from behind him. "To do something…different, my own, I suppose, before I faced dealing with these again."

She set down a padded box that held the trio of diamonds.

"Your design?" he asked, gesturing to the piece on the worktable.

"Yes. I see the piece in my head. I can't draw worth a lick, but I can visualize. I wanted to make something for M.J. and for Grace to…" She sighed, sat on the high stool. "Well, let's say to celebrate survival."

"And this is the one for Grace."

"Yes." She smiled, pleased that he'd sensed it. "I see something more streamlined for M.J. But this is Grace." Carefully she set the unfinished work in a tray, slid the padded box containing the Three Stars between them. "They never lose their impact. Each time I see them, it stuns."

"How long before you're finished with them?"

"I'd just begun when—when I had to stop." She cleared her throat. "I've verified their authenticity. They are blue diamonds. Still, both the museum and the insurance carrier prefer more in-depth verification. I'll be running a number of other tests beyond what I've already started or completed. A metallurgist is testing the triangle, but that will be given to me for further study in a day or two. It shouldn't take more than a week altogether before the museum can take possession."

He lifted a stone from the bed, knew as soon as it was in his hand that it was the one Grace had carried with her. He told himself that was impossible. His untrained eye couldn't tell one stone from either of its mates.

Yet he felt her on it. In it.

"Will it be hard to part with them?"

"I should say no, after the past few days. But yes, it will."

Grace's eyes were this color, Seth realized. Not sapphire, but the blue of the rare, powerful diamond.

"Worth killing for," he said quietly, looking at the stone in his hand. "Dying for." Then, annoyed with himself, he set the stone down again. "Your stepbrothers had a client."

"Yes, they spoke of a client, argued about him. Thomas wanted to take the money, the initial deposit, and run."

The money was being checked now, but there wasn't much hope of tracing its source.

"Timothy told Thomas he was a fool, that he'd never be able to run far or fast enough. That he—the client— would find him. He's not even human. Timothy said that, or something like it. They were both afraid, terribly afraid, and terribly desperate."

"Over their heads."

"Yes, I think very much over their heads."

"It would have to be a collector. No one could move these stones for resale." He glanced at the gems sparkling in their trays like pretty stars. "You acquire, buy and sell to collectors of gems."

"Yes—certainly not on a scale like the Three Stars, but yes." She skimmed her fingers absently through her hair. "A client might come to us with a stone, or a request for one. We'd also acquire certain gems on spec, with a particular client in mind."

"You have a client list, then? Names, preferences?"

"Yes, and we have records of what a client had purchased, or sold." She gripped her hands together. "Thomas would have kept it, in his office. Timothy would have copies in his. I'll find them for you."

He touched her shoulder lightly before she could slide from the stool. "I'll get them."

She let out a breath of relief. She had yet to be able to face going upstairs, into the room where she'd seen murder. "Thank you."

He took out his notebook. "If I asked you to name the top gem collectors, your top clients, what names come to mind? Off the top of your head?"

"Oh." Concentrating, she gnawed on her lip. "Peter Morrison in London, Sylvia Smythe-Simmons of New York, Henry and Laura Muller here in D.C., Matthew Wolinski in California. And I suppose Charles Van Horn here in D.C., too, though he's new to it. We sold him three lovely stones over the last two years. One was a spectacular opal I coveted. I'm still hoping he'll let me set it for him. I have this design in my head...."

She shook herself, trailed off when she realized why he was asking. "Lieutenant, I know these people. I've dealt with them personally. The Mullers were friends of my stepfather's. Mrs. Smythe-Simmons is over eighty. None of them are thieves."

He didn't bother to glance up, but continued to write. "Then we'll be able to check them off the list. Taking anything or anyone at face value is a mistake in an investigation, Ms. James. We've had enough mistakes already."

"With mine standing out." Accepting that fact, she nudged her untouched soft drink over the table. "I should have gone to the police right away. I should have turned the information—at the very least, my suspicions—over to the authorities. Several people would still be alive if I had."

"It's possible, but it's not a given." Now he did glance up, noted the haunted look in those soft brown eyes. Compassion stirred. "Did you know your stepbrother was being blackmailed by a second-rate bail bondsman?"

"No," she murmured.

"Did you know that someone was pulling the strings, pulling them hard enough to turn your stepbrother into a killer?"

She shook her head, bit down hard on her lip. "The things I didn't know were the problem, weren't they? I put the two people I love most in terrible danger, then I forgot about them."

"Amnesia isn't a choice, it's a condition. And your friends handled themselves. They still are—in fact, I saw Ms. Fontaine just this morning. She doesn't look any the worse for wear to me."

Bailey caught the disdainful note and turned to face him. "You don't understand her. I would have thought a man who does what you do for a living would be able to see more clearly than that."

He thought he caught a faint hint of pity in her voice, and resented it. "I've always thought of myself as clear-sighted."

"People are rarely clear-sighted when it comes to Grace. They only see what she lets them see—unless they care enough to look deeper. She has the most generous heart of any person I've ever known."

Bailey caught the quick flicker of amused disbelief in his eyes and felt her anger rising against it. Furious, she pushed off the stool. "You don't know anything about her, but you've already dismissed her. Can you conceive of what she's going through right now? Her cousin was murdered—and in her stead."

"She's hardly to blame for that."

"Easy to say. But she'll blame herself, and so will her family. It's easy to blame Grace."

"You don't."

"No, because I know her. And I know she's dealt with perceptions and opinions just like yours most of her life. And her way of dealing with it is to do as she chooses, because whatever she does, those perceptions and opinions rarely change. Right now, she's with her aunt, I imagine, and taking the usual emotional beating."

Her voice heated, became rushed, as emotions swarmed. "Tonight, there'll be a memorial service for Melissa, and the relatives will hammer at her, the way they always do."

"Why should they?"

"Because that's what they do best." Running out of steam she turned her head, looked down at the Three Stars. Love, knowledge, generosity, she thought. Why did it seem there was so little of it in the world? "Maybe you should take another look, Lieutenant Buchanan."

He'd already taken too many, he decided. And he was wasting time. "She certainly inspires loyalty in her friends," he commented. "I'm going to look for those lists."

"You know the way." Dismissing him, Bailey picked up the stones to carry them back to the vault.

* * *

Grace was dressed in black, and had never felt less like grieving. It was six in the evening, and a light rain was beginning to fall. It promised to turn the city into a massive steam room instead of cooling it off. The headache that had been slyly brewing for hours snarled at the aspirin she'd already taken and leaped into full, vicious life.

She had an hour before the wake, one she had arranged quickly and alone, because her aunt demanded it. Helen Fontaine was handling grief in her own way—as she did everything else. In this case, it was by meeting Grace with a cold, damning and dry eye. Cutting off any offer of support or sympathy. And demanding that services take place immediately, and at Grace's expense and instigation.

They would be coming from all points, Grace thought as she wandered the large, empty room, with its banks of flowers, thick red drapes, deep pile carpeting. Because such things were expected, such things were reported in the press. And the Fontaines would never give the public media a bone to pick.

Except, of course, for Grace herself.

It hadn't been difficult to arrange for the funeral home, the music, the flowers, the tasteful canapés. Only phone calls and the invocation of the Fontaine name were required. Helen had brought the photograph herself, the large color print in a shining silver frame that now decorated a polished mahogany table and was flanked with red roses in heavy silver vases that Melissa had favored.

There would be no body to view.

Grace had arranged for Melissa's body to be released from the morgue, had already written the check for the cremation and the urn her aunt had chosen.

There had been no thanks, no acknowledgment. None had been expected.

It had been the same from the moment Helen became her legal guardian. She'd been given the necessities of life—Fontaine-style. Gorgeous homes in several countries to live in, perfectly prepared food, tasteful clothing, an excellent education.

And she'd been told, endlessly, how to eat, how to dress, how to behave, who could be selected as a friend and who could not. Reminded, incessantly, of her good fortune—unearned—in having such a family behind her. Tormented, ruthlessly, by the cousin she was there tonight to mourn, for being orphaned, dependent.

For being Grace.

She'd rebelled against all of it, every aspect, every expectation and demand. She'd refused to be malleable, biddable, predictable. The ache for her parents had eventually dimmed, and with it the child's desperate need for love and acceptance.

She'd given the press plenty to report. Wild parties, unwise affairs, unrestricted spending.

When that didn't ease the hurt, she'd found something else. Something that made her feel decent and whole.

And she'd found Grace.

For tonight, she would be just what her family had come to expect. And she would get through the next endless hours without letting them touch her.

She sat heavily on a sofa with overstuffed velvet seats. Her head pounded, her stomach clutched. Closing her eyes, she willed herself to relax. She would spend this last hour alone, and prepare herself for the rest.

But she'd barely taken the second calming breath when

she heard footsteps muffled on the thick patterned carpet. Her shoulders turned to rock, her spine snapped straight. She opened her eyes. And saw Bailey and M.J.

She let her eyes close again, on a pathetic rush of gratitude. "I told you not to come."

"Yeah, like we were going to listen to that." M.J. sat beside her, took her hand.

"Cade and Jack are parking the car." Bailey flanked her other side, took her other hand. "How are you holding up?"

"Better." Tears stung her eyes as she squeezed the hands clasped in hers. "A lot better now."

On a sprawling estate not so many miles from where Grace sat with those who loved her, a man stared out at the hissing rain.

Everyone had failed, he thought. Many had paid for their failures. But retribution was a poor substitute for the Three Stars.

A delay only, he comforted himself. The Stars were his, they were meant to be his. He had dreamed of them, had held them in his hands in those dreams. Sometimes the hands were human, sometimes not, but they were always his hands.

He sipped wine, watched the rain, and considered his options.

His plans had been delayed by three women. That was humiliating, and they would have to be made to pay for that humiliation.

The Salvinis were dead—Bailey James.

The fools he'd hired to retrieve the second Star were dead—M. J. O'Leary.

The man he'd sent with instructions to acquire the third Star at any cost was dead—Grace Fontaine.

And he smiled. That had been indiscreet, as he'd disposed of the lying fool himself. Telling him there'd been an accident, that the woman had fought him, run from him, and fallen to her death. Telling him he'd searched every corner of the house without finding the stone.

That failure had been irritating enough, but then to discover that the wrong woman had died and that the fool had stolen money and jewels without reporting them. Well, such disloyalty in a business associate could hardly be tolerated.

Smiling dreamily, he took a sparkling diamond earring out of his pocket. Grace Fontaine had worn this on her delectable lobe, he mused. He kept it now as a good-luck charm while he considered what steps to take next.

There were only days left before the Stars would be in the museum. Extracting them from those hallowed halls would take months, if not years, of planning. He didn't intend to wait.

Perhaps he had failed because he had been overcautious, had kept his distance from events. Perhaps the gods required a more personal risk. A more intimate involvement.

It was time, he decided, to step out of the shadows, to meet the women who had kept his property from him, face-to-face. He smiled again, excited by the thought, delighted with the possibilities.

When the knock sounded on the door, he answered with great cheer and good humor. "Enter."

The butler, in stern formal black, ventured no farther than the threshold. His voice held no inflection. "I beg your pardon, Ambassador. Your guests are arriving."

"Very well." He sipped the last of his wine, set the empty crystal flute on a table. "I'll be right down."

When the door closed, he moved to the mirror, examined his flawless tuxedo, the wink of diamond studs, the gleam of the thin gold watch at his wrist. Then he examined his face—the smooth contours, the pampered, pale gold skin, the aristocratic nose, the firm, if somewhat thin, mouth. He brushed a hand over the perfectly groomed mane of silver-threaded black hair.

Then, slowly, smilingly, met his own eyes. Pale, almost translucent blue smiled back. His guests would see what he did, a perfectly groomed man of fifty-two, erudite and educated, well mannered and suave. They wouldn't know what plans and plots he held in his heart. They would see no blood on his hands, though it had been only twenty-four short hours since he used them to kill.

He felt only pleasure in the memory, only delight in the knowledge that he would soon dine with the elite and the influential. And he could kill any one of them with a twist of his hands, with perfect immunity.

He chuckled to himself—a low, seductive sound with shuddering undertones. Tucking the earring back in his pocket, he walked from the room.

The ambassador was mad.

Chapter 5

Seth's first thought when he walked into the funeral parlor was that it seemed more like a tedious cocktail party than like a memorial service. People stood or sat in little cliques and groups, many of them nibbling on canapés or sipping wine. Beneath the strains of a muted Chopin étude, voices murmured. There was an occasional roll or tinkle of laughter.

He heard no tears.

Lights were respectfully dimmed, and set off the glitter and gleam of gems and gold. The fragrance of flowers mixed and merged with the scents worn by both men and women. He saw faces, both elegant and bored.

He saw no grief.

But he did see Grace. She stood looking up into the face of a tall, slim man whose golden tan set off his golden hair and bright blue eyes. He held one of her hands in his and smiled winningly. He appeared to be speaking quickly, persuasively. She shook her head once, laid a hand on his chest, then allowed herself to be drawn into an anteroom.

Seth's lip curled in automatic disdain. A funeral was a hell of a place for a flirtation.

"Buchanan." Jack Dakota wandered over. He scanned the room, stuck his hands in the pockets of the suit coat he wished fervently was still in his closet, instead of on his back. "Some party."

Seth watched two women air kiss. "Apparently."

"Doesn't seem like one a sane man would want to crash."

"I have business," he said briefly. Which could have waited until morning, he reminded himself. He should have let it wait. It annoyed him that he'd made the detour, that he'd been thinking of Grace—more, that he'd been unable to lock her out of his head.

He pulled a copy of a mug shot out of his pocket, handed it to Jack. "Recognize him?"

Jack scanned the picture, considered. Slick-looking dude, he thought. Vaguely European in looks, with the sleek black hair, dark eyes and refined features. "Nope. Looks like a poster boy for some wussy cologne."

"You didn't see him during your amazing weekend adventures?"

Jack took one last, harder look, handed the shot back. "Nope. What's his connection?"

"His prints were all over the house in Potomac."

Jack's interest rose. "He the one who killed the cousin?"

Seth met Jack's eyes coolly. "That has yet to be determined."

"Don't give me the cop stand, Buchanan. What'd the guy say? He stopped by to sell vacuum cleaners?"

"He didn't say anything. He was too busy floating facedown in the river."

With an oath, Jack's gaze whipped around the room again. He relaxed fractionally when he spotted M.J. huddled with Cade. "The morgue must be getting crowded. You got a name?"

Seth started to dismiss the question. He didn't care for professions that stood a step back from the police. But there was no denying that the bounty hunter and the private investigator were involved. And there was no avoiding the connection, he told himself.

"Carlo Monturri."

"Doesn't ring a bell either."

Seth hadn't expected it would, but the police—on several continents—knew the name. "He's out of your league, Dakota. His type keeps a fancy lawyer on retainer and doesn't use the local bail bondsman to get sprung."

As he spoke, Seth's eyes moved around the room as a cop's did, sweeping corner to corner, taking in details, body language, atmosphere. "Before he took his last swim, he was expensive hired muscle. He worked alone because he didn't like to share the fun."

"Connections in the area?"

"We're working on it."

Seth saw Grace come out of the anteroom. The man who was with her had his arm draped over her shoulders, pulled her close in an intimate embrace, kissed her. The flare of fury kindled in Seth's gut and bolted up to his heart.

"Excuse me."

Grace saw him the moment he started across the room. She murmured something to the man beside her, dislodged him, then dismissed him. Straightening her spine, she fixed on an easy smile.

"Lieutenant, we didn't expect you."

"I apologize for intruding in your—" he flicked a glance toward the golden boy, who was helping himself to a glass a wine "—grief."

The sarcasm slapped, but she didn't flinch. "I assume you have a reason for coming by."

"I'd like a moment of your time—in private."

"Of course." She turned to lead him out and came face-to-face with her aunt. "Aunt Helen."

"If you could tear yourself away from entertaining your suitors," Helen said coldly, "I want to speak to you."

"Excuse me," Grace said to Seth, and stepped into the anteroom again.

Seth debated moving off, giving them privacy. But he stayed where he was, two paces from the doorway. He told himself murder investigations didn't allow for sensitivity. Though they kept their voices low, he heard both women clearly enough.

"I assume you have Melissa's things at your home," Helen began.

"I don't know. I haven't been able to go through the house thoroughly yet."

Helen said nothing for a moment, simply studied her niece through cold blue eyes. Her face was smooth and showed no ravages of grief in the carefully applied makeup. Her hair was sleek, lightened to a tasteful ash blond. Her hands were freshly manicured and glittered with the diamond wedding band she continued to wear, though she'd shared little but her husband's name in over a decade, and a square-cut sapphire given to her by her latest lover.

"I sincerely doubt Melissa came to your home without a bag. I want her things, Grace. All of her things. You'll have nothing of hers."

"I never wanted anything of hers, Aunt Helen."

"Didn't you?" There was a crackle in the voice—a whip flicking. "Did you think she wouldn't tell me of your affair with her husband?"

Grace merely sighed. It was new ground, but sickeningly familiar. Melissa's marriage had failed, publicly. Therefore, it had to be someone else's fault. It had to be Grace's fault.

"I didn't have an affair with Bobbie. Before, during or after their marriage."

"And whom do you think I would believe? You, or my own daughter?"

Grace tilted her head, twisted a smile on her face. "Why, your own daughter, of course. As always."

"You've always been a liar and a sneak. You've always been ungrateful, a burden I took on out of family duty who never once gave anything back. You were spoiled and willful when I opened my door to you, and you never changed."

Grace's stomach roiled viciously. In defense, she smiled, shrugged. Deliberately careless, she smoothed a hand over the hair sleeked into a coiled twist at the nape of her neck. "No, I suppose I didn't. I'll just have to remain a disappointment to you, Aunt Helen."

"My daughter would be alive if not for you."

Grace willed her heart to go numb. But it ached, and it burned. "Yes, you're right."

"I warned her about you, told her time and again what you were. But you continually lured her back, playing on her affection."

"Affection, Aunt Helen?" With a half laugh, Grace pressed her fingers to the throb in her left temple. "Surely even you don't believe she ever had an ounce of affection for me. She took her cue from you, after all. And she took it well."

"How dare you speak of her in that tone, after you've killed her!" In the pampered face, Helen's eyes burned with loathing. "All of your life you've envied her, used your wiles to influence her. Now your unconscionable life-style has killed her. You've brought scandal and disgrace down on the family name once again."

Grace went stiff. This wasn't grief, she thought. Perhaps grief was there, buried deep, but what was on the surface was venom. And she was weary of being struck by it. "That's the bottom line, isn't it, Aunt Helen? The Fontaine name, the Fontaine reputation. And, of course, the Fontaine stock. Your child is dead, but it's the scandal that infuriates you."

She absorbed the slap without a wince, though the blow printed heat on her cheek, brought blood stinging to the surface. She took one long, deep breath. "That should end things appropriately between the two of us," she said evenly. "I'll have Melissa's things sent to you as soon as possible."

"I want you out of here." Helen's voice shook for the first time—whether in grief or in fury, Grace couldn't have said. "You have no place here."

"You're right again. I don't. I never did."

Grace stepped out of the alcove. The color that had

drained out of her face rose slightly when she met Seth's eyes. She couldn't read them in that brief glance, and didn't want to. Without breaking stride, she continued past him and kept walking.

The drizzle that misted the air was a relief. She welcomed the heat after the overchilled, artificial air inside, and the heavy, stifling scent of funeral flowers. Her heels clicked on the wet pavement as she crossed the lot to her car. She was fumbling in her bag for her keys when Seth clamped a hand on her shoulder.

He said nothing at first, just turned her around, studied her face. It was white again—but for the red burn from the slap—the eyes a dark contrast and swimming with emotion. He could feel the tremors of that emotion under the palm of his hand.

"She was wrong."

Humiliation was one more blow to her overwrought system. She jerked her shoulder, but his hand remained in place. "Is that part of your investigative technique, Lieutenant? Eavesdropping on private conversations?"

Did she realize, he wondered, that her voice was raw, her eyes were devastated? He wanted badly to lift a hand to that mark on her face, cool it. Erase it. "She was wrong," he said again. "And she was cruel. You aren't responsible."

"Of course I am." She spun away, jabbing her key at the door lock. After three shaky attempts, she gave up, and they dropped with a jingling splash to the wet pavement as she turned into his arms. "Oh, God." Shuddering, she pressed her face into his chest. "Oh, God."

He didn't want to hold her, wanted to refuse the role of comforter. But his arms came around her before he could stop them, and one hand reached up to brush the smooth twist of her hair. "You didn't deserve that, Grace. You did nothing to deserve that."

"It doesn't matter."

"Yes, it does." He found himself weakening, drawing her closer, trying to will her trembling away. "It always does."

"I'm just tired." She burrowed into him while the rain misted her hair. There was strength here, was all she could think. A haven here. An answer here. "I'm just tired."

Her head lifted, their mouths met, before either of them realized the need was there. The quiet sound in her throat was of relief and gratitude. She opened her battered heart to the kiss, locking her arms around him, urging him to take it.

She had been waiting for him, and, too dazed to question why, she offered herself to him. Surely comfort and pleasure and this all-consuming need were reason enough. His mouth was firm—the one she'd always wanted on hers. His body was hard and solid—a perfect match for hers.

Here he is, she thought with a ragged sigh of joy.

She trembled still, and he could feel his own muscles quiver in response. He wanted to gather her up, carry her out of the rain to someplace quiet and dark where it was only the two of them. To spend years where it would only be the two of them.

His heart pounded in his head, masking the slick sound of traffic over the rain-wet street beyond the lot. Its fast, demanding beat muffled the warning struggling to sound in the corner of his brain, telling him to step back, to break away.

He'd never wanted anything more in his life than to bury himself in her and forget the consequences.

Swamped with emotions and needs, she held him close. "Take me home," she murmured against his mouth. "Seth, take me home, make love with me. I need you to touch me. I want to be with you." Her mouth met his again, in a desperate plea she hadn't known herself capable of.

Every cell in his body burned for her. Every need he'd ever had coalesced into one, and it was only for her. The almost vicious focus of it left him vulnerable and shaky. And furious.

He put his hands on her shoulders, drew her away. "Sex isn't the answer for everyone."

His voice wasn't as cool as he'd wanted, but it was rigid enough to stop her from reaching for him again. Sex? she thought as she struggled to clear her dazzled mind. Did he really believe she'd been speaking about something as simple as sex? Then she focused on his face, the hard set of his mouth, the faint annoyance in his eyes, and realized he did.

Her pride might have been tattered, but she managed to hold on to a few threads. "Well, apparently it's not for you." Reaching up, she smoothed her hair, brushed away rain. "Or if it is, you're the type who insists on being the initiator."

She made her lips curve, though they felt cold now and stiff. "It would have been just fine and dandy if you'd made the move. But when I do, it makes me—what would the term be? Loose?"

"I don't believe it's a term I used."

"No, you're much too controlled for insults." She bent down, scooped up her wet keys, then stood jingling them in her hand while she studied him. "But you wanted me right back, Seth. You're not quite controlled enough to have masked that little detail."

"I don't believe in taking everything I want."

"Why the hell not?" She gave a short, mirthless laugh. "We're alive, aren't we? And you, of all people, should know how distressingly short life can be."

"I don't have to explain to you how I live my life."

"No, you don't. But it's obvious you're perfectly willing to question how I live mine." Her gaze skimmed past him, back toward the lights glinting in the funeral home. "I'm quite used to that. I do exactly what I choose, without regard for the consequences. I'm selfish and self-involved and careless."

She lifted a shoulder as she turned and unlocked her door. "As for feelings, why should I be entitled to them?"

She slipped into her car, flipped him one last look. Her mouth might have curved with seductive ease, but the sultry smile didn't reach her eyes, or mask the misery in them. "Well, maybe some other time, handsome."

He watched her drive off into the rain. There would be another time, he admitted, if for no other reason than that he hadn't shown her the picture. Hadn't, he thought, had the heart to add to her unhappiness that night.

Feelings, he mused as he headed to his own car. She had them, had plenty of them. He only wished he understood them. He got into his car, wrenched his door shut. He wished to God he understood his own.

For the first time in his life, a woman had reached in and clamped a hand on his heart. And she was squeezing.

Seth told himself he wasn't postponing meeting with Grace again. The morning after the memorial service had been hellish with work. And when he did carve out time to leave his office, he'd headed toward M.J.'s. It was true he could have assigned this follow-up to one of his men. Despite the fact that the chief of police had ordered him to head the investigation, and give every detail his personal attention, Mick Marshall—the detective who had taken the initial call on the case—could have done this next pass with M. J. O'Leary.

Seth was forced to admit that he wanted to talk to her personally and hoped to slide a few details out of her on Grace Fontaine.

M.J.'s was a cozy, inviting neighborhood pub that ran to dark woods, gleaming brass and thickly padded stools and booths. Business was slow but steady in midafternoon. A couple of men who looked to be college age were sharing a booth, a duet of foamy mugs and an intense game of chess. An older man sat at the bar working a crossword from the morning paper, and a trio of women with department store shopping bags crowding the floor around them huddled over drinks and laughter.

The bartender glanced at Seth's badge and told him he'd find the boss upstairs in her office. He heard her before he saw her.

"Look, pal, if I'd wanted candy mints, I'd have ordered candy mints. I ordered beer nuts. I want them here by six. Yeah, yeah. I know my customers. Get me the damn nuts, pronto."

She sat behind a crowded desk with a battered top. Her short cap of red hair stood up in spikes. Seth watched her rake her fingers through it again as she hung up the phone and pushed a pile of invoices aside. If that was her idea of filing, he thought, it suited the rest of the room.

It was barely big enough to turn around in, crowded with boxes, files, papers, and one ratty chair, on which sat an enormous and overflowing purse.

"Ms. O'Leary?"

She looked up, her brow still creased in annoyance. It didn't clear when she recognized her visitor. "Just what I needed to make my day perfect. A cop. Listen, Buchanan, I'm behind here. As you know, I lost a few days recently."

"Then I'll try to be quick." He stepped inside, pulled the picture out of his pocket and tossed it onto the desk under her nose. "Look familiar?"

She pursed her lips, gave the slickly handsome face a slow, careful study. "Is this the guy Jack told me about? The one who killed Melissa?"

"The Melissa Fontaine case is still open. This man is a possible suspect. Do you recognize him?"

She rolled her eyes, pushed the photo back in Seth's direction. "No. Looks like a creep. Did Grace recognize him?"

He angled his head slightly, his only outward sign of interest. "Does she know many men who look like creeps?"

"Too many," M.J. muttered. "Jack said you came by the memorial service last night to show Grace this picture."

"She was…occupied."

"Yeah, it was a rough night for her." M.J. rubbed her eyes.

"Apparently, though she seemed to have been handling it well enough initially." He glanced down at the photo again, thought of the man he'd seen her kiss. "This looks like her type."

M.J.'s hand dropped, her eyes narrowed. "Meaning?"

"Just that." Seth tucked the photo away. "If one's going by type, this one doesn't appear, on the surface, too far a step from the one she was cozy with at the service."

"Cozy with?" The narrowed eyes went hot, angry green flares. "Grace wasn't cozy with anyone."

"About six-one, a hundred and seventy, blond hair, blue eyes, five-thousand-dollar Italian suit, lots of teeth."

It only took her a moment. At any other time, she would have laughed. But the cool disdain on Seth's face had her snarling. "You stupid son of a bitch, that was her cousin Julian, and he was hitting her up for money, just like he always does."

Seth frowned, backtracked, played the scene through his mind again. "Her cousin…and that would be the victim's…?"

"Stepbrother. Melissa's stepbrother—her father's son from a previous."

"And the deceased's stepbrother was asking Grace for money at his stepsister's memorial?"

This time she appreciated the coating of disgust over his words. "Yeah. He's slime—why should the ambience stop him from shaking her down? Most of them squeeze her for a few bucks now and then." She rose, geared up. "And you've got a hell of a nerve coming in here with your attitude and your superior morals, ace. She wrote that pansy-faced jerk a check for a few thousand to get him off her back, just like she used to pass bucks to Melissa, and some of the others."

"I was under the impression the Fontaines were wealthy."

"Wealth's relative—especially if you live the high life and your allowance from your trust fund is overdrawn, or if you've played too deep in Monte Carlo. And Grace has more of the green stuff than most of them, because her parents didn't blow the bucks. That just burns the relatives," she muttered. "Who do you think paid for that wake last night? It wasn't the dearly departed's mama or papa. Grace's witch of an aunt put the arm on her, then put the blame on her. And she took it, because she thinks it's easier to take it and go her own way. You don't know anything about her."

He thought he did, but the details he was collecting bit by bit weren't adding up very neatly. "I know that she's not to blame for what happened to her cousin."

"Yeah, try telling her that. I know that when we realized she'd left and we got back to Cade's, she was in her room crying, and there was nothing any of us could do to help her. And all because those bastards she has the misfortune to be related to go out of their way to make her feel rotten."

Not just her relatives, he thought with a quick twinge of guilt. He'd had a part in that.

"It seems she's more fortunate in her friends than in her family."

"That's because we're not interested in her money, or her name. Because we don't judge her. We just love her. Now, if that's all, I've got work to do."

"I need to speak with Ms. Fontaine." Seth's voice was as stiff as M.J.'s had been passionate. "Would you know where I might find her?"

Her lips curled. She hesitated a moment, knowing Grace wouldn't appreciate the information being passed along. But the urge to see the cop's preconceptions slapped down was just too tempting. "Sure. Try Saint Agnes's Hospital. Pediatrics or maternity." Her phone rang, so she snatched it up. "You'll find her," she said. "Yeah, O'Leary," she barked into the phone, and turned her back on Seth.

He assumed she was visiting the child of a friend, but when he asked at the nurses' station for Grace Fontaine, faces lit up.

"I think she's in the intensive care nursery." The nurse on duty checked her watch. "It's her usual time there. Do you know the way?"

Baffled, Seth shook his head. "No." He listened to the directions, while his mind turned over a dozen reasons why Grace Fontaine should have a usual time in a nursery. Since none of them slipped comfortably into a slot, he headed down corridors.

He could hear the high sound of babies crying behind a barrier of glass. And perhaps he stopped for just a moment outside the window of the regular nursery, and his eyes might have softened, just a little, as he scanned the infants in their clear-sided beds. Tiny faces, some slack in sleep, others screwed up into wrinkled balls of fury.

A couple stood beside him, the man with his arm over the woman's robed shoulders. "Ours is third from the left. Joshua Michael Delvecchio. Eight pounds, five ounces. He's one day old."

"He's a beaut," Seth said.

"Which one is yours?" the woman asked.

Seth shook his head, shot one more glance through the glass. "I'm just passing through. Congratulations on your son."

He continued on, resisting the urge to look back at the new parents lost in their own private miracle.

Two turns down the corridor away from the celebration was a smaller nursery. Here machines hummed, and nurses walked quietly. And behind the glass were six empty cribs.

Grace sat beside one, cuddling a tiny, crying baby. She brushed away tears from the pale little cheek, rested her own against the smooth head as she rocked.

It struck him to the core, the picture she made. Her hair was braided back from her face and she wore a shapeless green smock over her suit. Her face was soft as she soothed the restless infant. Her attention was totally focused on the eyes that stared tearfully into hers.

"Excuse me, sir." A nurse hurried up. "This is a restricted area."

Absently, his eyes still on Grace, Seth reached for his badge. "I'm here to speak with Ms. Fontaine."

"I see. I'll tell her you're here, Lieutenant."

"No, don't disturb her." He didn't want anything to spoil that picture. "I can wait. What's wrong with the baby she's holding?"

"Peter's an AIDS baby. Ms. Fontaine arranged for him to have care here."

"Ms. Fontaine?" He felt a fist lodge in his gut. "It's her child?"

"Biologically? No." The nurse's face softened slightly. "I think she considers them all hers. I honestly don't know what we'd do without her help. Not just the foundation, but her."

"The foundation?"

"The Falling Star Foundation. Ms. Fontaine set it up a few years ago to assist critically ill and terminal children and their families. But it's the hands-on that really matters." She gestured back toward the glass with a nod of her head. "No amount of financial generosity can buy a loving touch or sing a lullaby."

He watched the baby calm, drift slowly to sleep in Grace's arms. "She comes here often?"

"As often as she can. She's our angel. You'll have to excuse me, Lieutenant."

"Thank you." As she walked away, he stepped closer to the isolation glass. Grace started toward the crib. It was then that her eyes met his.

He saw the shock come into them first. Even she wasn't skilled enough to disguise the range of emotions that raced over her face. Surprise, embarrassment, annoyance. Then she smoothed the expressions out. Gently, she laid the baby back into the crib, brushed a hand over his cheek. She walked through a side door and disappeared.

It was several minutes before she came out into the corridor. The smock was gone. Now she was a confident woman in a flame-red suit, her mouth carefully tinted to match. "Well, Lieutenant, we meet in the oddest places."

Before she could complete the casual greeting she'd practiced while she tidied her makeup, he took her chin firmly in his hand. His eyes locked intently on hers, probed.

"You're a fake." He said it quietly, stepping closer. "You're a fraud. Who the hell are you?"

"Whatever I like." He unnerved her, that long, intense and all-too-personal study with those golden-brown eyes. "And I don't believe this is the place for an interrogation. I'd like you to let me go now," she said steadily. "I don't want any scenes here."

"I'm not going to cause a scene."

She lifted her brows. "I might." Deliberately she pushed his hand away and started down the corridor. "If you want to discuss the case with me, or have any questions regarding it, we'll do it outside. I won't have it brought in here."

"It was breaking your heart," he murmured. "Holding that baby was breaking your heart."

"It's my heart." Almost viciously, she punched a finger at the button for the elevator. "And it's a tough one, Seth. Ask anyone."

"Your lashes are still wet."

"This is none of your business." Her voice was low and vibrating with fury. "Absolutely none of your business."

She stepped into the crowded elevator, faced front. She wouldn't speak to him about this part of her life, she promised herself. Just the night before, she'd opened herself to him, only to be pushed away, refused. She wouldn't share her feelings again, and certainly not her feelings about something as vital to her as the children.

He was a cop, just a cop. Hadn't she spent several miserable hours the night before convincing herself that was all he was or could be to her? Whatever he stirred in her would have to be stopped—or, if not stopped, at least suppressed.

She would not share with him, she would not trust him, she would not give to him.

By the time she reached the lobby doors, she was steadier. Hoping to shake him quickly, she started toward the lot. Seth merely took her arm, steered her away.

"Over here," he said, and headed toward a grassy area with a pair of benches.

"I don't have time."

"Make time. You're too upset to drive, in any case."

"Don't tell me what I am."

"Apparently that's just what I've been doing. And apparently I've missed several steps. That's not usual for me, and I don't care for it. Sit down."

"I don't want—"

"Sit down, Grace," he repeated. "I apologize."

Annoyed, she sat on the bench, found her sunglasses in her bag and slipped them on. "For?"

He sat beside her, removed the shielding glasses and looked into her eyes. "For not letting myself look beneath the surface. For not wanting to look. And for blaming you because I don't seem able to stop wanting to do this."

He took her face in his hands and captured her mouth with his.

Chapter 6

She didn't move into him. Not this time. Her emotions were simply too raw to risk. Though her mouth yielded beneath his, she lifted a hand and laid it on his chest, as if to keep him at a safe distance.

And still her heart stumbled.

This time she was holding back. He sensed it, felt it in the press of her hand against him. Not refusing, but resisting. And with a knowledge that came from somewhere too deep to measure, he gentled the kiss, seeking not only to seduce, but also to soothe.

And still his heart staggered.

"Don't." It made her throat ache, her mind haze, her body yearn. And it was all too much. She pulled away from him and stood staring out across the little patch of grass until she thought she could breathe again.

"What is it with timing?" Seth wondered aloud. "That makes it so hard to get right?"

"I don't know." She turned then to look at him. He was an attractive man, she decided. The dark hair and hard face, the odd tint of gold in his eyes. But she'd known many attractive men. What was it about this one that changed everything and made her world tilt? "You bother me, Lieutenant Buchanan."

He gave her one of his rare smiles—slow and full and rich. "That's a mutual problem, Ms. Fontaine. You keep me up at night. Like a puzzle where the pieces are all there, but they change shape right before your eyes. And even when you put it all together—or think you have—it doesn't stay the same."

"I'm not a mystery, Seth."

"You are the most fascinating woman I've ever met." His lips curved again when she lifted her brows. "That isn't entirely a compliment. Along with fascination comes frustration." He stood, but didn't step toward her. "Why were you so upset that I found you here, saw you here?"

"It's private." Her tone was stiff again, dismissive. "I go to considerable trouble to keep it private."

"Why?"

"Because I prefer it that way."

"Your family doesn't know about your involvement here?"

The fury that seared through her eyes was burning-cold. "My family has *nothing* to do with this. Nothing. This isn't a Fontaine project, one of their charitable sops for good press and a tax deduction. It's mine."

"Yes, I can see that," he said calmly. Her family had hurt her even more than he'd guessed. And more, he thought, than she had acknowledged. "Why children, Grace?"

"Because they're the innocents." It was out before she realized she meant to say it. Then she closed her eyes and sighed. "Innocence is a precious and perishable commodity."

"Yes, it is. Falling Star? Your foundation. Is that how you see them, stars that burn out and fall too quickly?"

It was her heart he was touching simply by understanding, by seeing what was inside. "It has nothing to do with the case. Why are you pushing me on this?"

"Because I'm interested in you."

She sent him a smile—half inviting, half sarcastic. "Are you? You didn't seem to be when I asked you to bed. But you see me holding a sick baby and you change your tune." She walked toward him slowly, trailed a fingertip down his shirt. "Well, if it's the maternal type that turns you on, Lieutenant—"

"Don't do that to yourself." Again his voice was quiet, controlled. He took her hand, stopped her from backtracking the trail of her finger. "It's foolish. And it's irritating. You weren't playing games in there. You care."

"Yes, I do. I care enormously. And that doesn't make me a hero, and it doesn't make me any different than I was last night." She drew her hand away and stood her ground. "I want you. I want to go to bed with you. That irritates you, Seth. Not the sentiment, but the bluntness of the statement. Isn't it games you'd prefer? That I'd pretend reluctance and let you conquer?"

He only wished it was something just that ordinary. "Maybe I want to know who you are before we end up in bed. I spent a long time looking at your face—that portrait of you in your house. And, looking, I wondered about you. Now, I want you. But I also want all those pieces to fit."

"You might not like the finished product."

"No," he agreed. "I might not."

Then again, she thought… Considering, she angled her head. "I have a thing tonight. A cocktail party hosted by a major contributor to the hospital. I can't afford to skip it. Why don't you take me, then we'll see what happens next?"

He weighed the pros and cons, knew it was a step that would have ramifications he might not be able to handle smoothly. She wasn't simply a woman, and he wasn't simply a man. Whatever was between them had a long reach and a hard grip.

"Do you always think everything through so carefully?" she asked as she watched him.

"Yes." But in her case it didn't seem to matter, he realized. "I can't guarantee my evenings will be free until this case is closed." He shifted times and meetings and paperwork in his head. "But if I can manage it, I'll pick you up."

"Eight's soon enough. If you're not there by quarter after, I'll assume you were tied up."

No complaints, he thought, no demands. Most of the women he'd known shifted to automatic sulk mode when his work took priority. "I'll call if I can't make it."

"Whatever." She sat again, relaxed now. "I don't imagine you came by to see my secret life, or to make a tentative date for a cocktail party." She slipped her sunglasses back on, sat back. "Why are you here?"

He reached inside his jacket for the photo. Grace caught a brief glimpse of his shoulder holster, and the weapon snug inside it. And wondered if he'd ever had occasion to use it.

"I imagine your time is taken up mainly with administration duties." She took the picture from him, but continued to look at Seth's face. "You wouldn't participate in many, what—busts?"

She thought she caught a faint glint of humor in his eyes, but his mouth remained sober. "I like to keep my hand in."

"Yes," she murmured, easily able to imagine him whipping the weapon out. "I suppose you would."

She shifted her gaze, scanned the face in the photo. This time the humor was in her eyes. "Ah, Joe Cool. Or more likely Juan or Jean-Paul Cool."

"You know him?"

"Not personally, but certainly as a type. He likely speaks the right words in three languages, plays a steely game of baccarat, enjoys his brandy and wears black silk underwear. His Rolex, along with his monogrammed gold cufflinks and diamond pinkie ring, would have been gifts from admirers."

Intrigued, Seth sat beside her again. "And what are the right words?"

"You're the most beautiful woman in the room. I adore you. My heart sings when I look into your eyes. Your husband is a fool, and darling, you must stop buying me gifts."

"Been there?"

"With some variations. Only I've never been married and I don't buy trinkets for users. His eyes are cold," she added, "but a lot of women, lonely women, would only see the polish. That's all they want to see." She took a quick, short breath. "This is the man who killed Melissa, isn't it?"

He started to give her the standard response, but she looked up then, and he was close enough to read her eyes through the amber tint of her glasses. "I think it is. His prints were all over the house. Some of the surfaces were wiped, but he missed a lot, which leads me to think he panicked. Either because she fell or because he wasn't able to find what he'd come for."

"And you're leaning toward the second choice, because this isn't the type of man to panic because he'd killed a woman."

"No, he isn't."

"She couldn't have given him what he'd come for. She wouldn't have known what he was talking about."

"No. That doesn't make you responsible. If you indulge yourself by thinking it does, you'd have to blame Bailey, too."

Grace opened her mouth, closed it again, breathed deep. "That's clever logic, Lieutenant," she said after a moment. "So I shed my sackcloth and ashes and blame this man. Have you found him?"

"He's dead." He took the photo back, tucked it away. "And my clever logic leads me to believe that whoever hired him decided to fire him, permanently."

"I see." She felt nothing, no satisfaction, no relief. "So, we're nowhere."

"The Three Stars are under twenty-four-hour guard. You, M.J. and Bailey are safe, and the museum will have its property in a matter of days."

"And a lot of people have died. Sacrifices to the god?"

"From what I've read about Mithra, it isn't blood he wants."

"Love, knowledge and generosity," she said quietly. "Powerful elements. The diamond I held, it has vitality. Maybe that's the same as power. Does he want them because they're beautiful, priceless, ancient, or because he truly believes in the legend? Does he believe that if he has all of them in their triangle, he'll possess the power of the god, and immortality?"

"People believe what they choose to believe. Whatever reason he wants them, he's killed for them." Staring out across the grass, he stepped over one of his own rules and shared his thoughts with her. "Money isn't the driving force. He's laid out more than a million already. He wants to own them, to hold them in his hands, whatever the cost. It's more than coveting," he said quietly, as a murky scene swam into his mind.

A marble altar, a golden triangle with three brilliantly blue points. A dark man with pale eyes and a bloody sword.

"And you don't think he'll stop now. You think he'll try again."

Baffled and uneasy with the image, he shook it off, turned back to logic and instinct. "Oh, yeah." Seth's eyes narrowed, went flat. "He'll try again."

Seth made it to Cade's at 8:14. His final meeting of the day, with the chief of police, had gone past seven, and that had barely given him time to get home, change and drive out again. He'd told himself half a dozen times that he'd be better off staying at home, putting the reports and files away and having a quiet evening to relax his mind.

The press conference set for nine sharp the next morning would be a trial by fire, and he needed to be sharp. Yet here he was, sitting in his car feeling ridiculously nervous and unsettled.

He'd tracked a homicidal junkie through a condemned tenement without breaking a sweat, with a steady pulse he'd interrogated cold, vicious killers—but now, as the white ball of the sun dipped low in the sky, he was as jittery as a schoolboy.

He hated cocktail parties. The inane conversations, the silly food, the buffed faces, all feigning enthusiasm or ennui, depending on their style.

But it wasn't the prospect of a few hours socializing with strangers that unnerved him. It was spending time with Grace without the buffer of the job between them.

He'd never had a woman affect him as she did. And he couldn't deny—at least to himself—that he had been deeply, uniquely affected, from the moment he saw her portrait.

It didn't help to tell himself she was shallow, spoiled, a woman used to men falling at her feet. It hadn't helped before he discovered she was much more than that, and it was certainly no good now.

He couldn't claim to understand her, but he was beginning to uncover all those layers and contrasts that made her who and what she was.

And he knew they would be lovers before the night was over.

He saw her step out of the house, a charge of electric blue from the short strapless dress molded to her body, the long, luxurious fall of ebony hair, the endless and perfect legs.

Did she shock every man's system, Seth wondered, just the look of her? Or was he particularly, specifically vulnerable? He decided either answer would be hard to live with, and got out of his car.

Her head turned at the sound of his door, and that heart-stopping face bloomed with a smile. "I didn't think you were going to make it." She crossed to him, unhurried, and touched her mouth to his. "I'm glad you did."

"I'd said I'd call if I wouldn't be here."

"So you did." But she hadn't counted on it. She'd left the address of the party inside, just in case, but she'd resigned herself to spending the evening without him. She smiled again, smoothed a hand down the lapel of his suit. "I never wait by the phone. We're going to Georgetown. Shall we take my car, or yours?"

"I'll drive." Knowing she expected him to make some comment on her looks, he deliberately kept silent as he walked around the car to open her door.

She slipped in, her legs sliding silkily inside. He wanted his hands there, right there where the abbreviated hem of her dress kissed her thighs. Where the skin would be tender as a ripened peach and smooth as white satin.

He closed the door, walked back around the car and got behind the wheel. "Where in Georgetown?" was all he said.

It was a beautiful old house, with soaring ceilings, heavy antiques and deep, warm colors. The lights blazed down on important people, people of influence and wealth, who carried the scent of power under their perfumes and colognes.

She belonged, Seth thought. She'd melded with the whole from the moment she stepped through the door to exchange sophisticated cheek brushes with the hostess.

Yet she stood apart. In the midst of all the sleek black, the fussy pastels, she was a bright blue flame daring anyone to touch and be burned.

Like the diamonds, he thought. Unique, potent…irresistible.

"Lieutenant Buchanan, isn't it?"

Seth shifted his gaze from Grace and looked at the short, balding man who was built like a boxer and dressed in Savile Row. "Yes. Mr. Rossi, counsel for the defense. If the defense has deep enough pockets."

Unoffended, Rossi chuckled. "I thought I recognized you. I've crossed you on the stand a few times. You're a tough nut. I've always believed I'd have gotten Tremaine off, or at least hung the jury, if I'd have been able to shake your testimony."

"He was guilty."

"As sin," Rossi agreed readily, "but I'd have hung that jury."

As Rossi started to rehash the trial, Seth resigned himself to talking shop.

Across the room, Grace took a glass from a passing waiter and listened to her hostess's gossip with half an ear. She knew when to chuckle, when to lift a brow, purse her lips, make some interesting comment. It was all routine.

She wanted to leave immediately. She wanted to get Seth out of that dark suit. She wanted her hands on him, all over him. Lust was creeping along her skin like a hot rash. Sips of champagne did nothing to cool her throat, and only added to the bubbling in her blood.

"My dear Sarah."

"Gregor, how lovely to see you."

Grace shifted, sipped, smiled at the sleek, dark man

with the creamy voice who bent gallantly over their hostess's hand. Mediterranean, she judged, by the charm of the accent. Fiftyish, but fit.

"You're looking particularly wonderful tonight," he said, lingering over her hand. "And your hospitality, as always, is incomparable. And your guests." He turned smiling pale silvery-blue eyes on Grace. "Perfect."

"Gregor." Sarah simpered, fluttered, then turned to Grace. "I don't believe you've met Gregor, Grace. He's fatally charming, so be very careful. Ambassador DeVane, I'd like to present Grace Fontaine, a dear friend."

"I am honored." He lifted Grace's hand, and his lips were warm and soft. "And enchanted."

"Ambassador?" Grace slipped easily into the role. "I thought ambassadors were old and stodgy. All the ones I've met have been. That is, up until now."

"I'll just leave you with Grace, Gregor. I see we have some late arrivals."

"I'm sure I'm in delightful hands." With obvious reluctance, he released Grace's fingers. "Are you perhaps a connection of Niles Fontaine?"

"He's an uncle, yes."

"Ah. I had the pleasure of meeting your uncle and his charming wife in Capri a few years ago. We have a mutual hobby, coins."

"Yes, Uncle Niles has quite a collection. He's mad for coins." Grace brushed her hair back, lifted it off her bare shoulder. "And where are you from, Ambassador DeVane?"

"Gregor, please, in such friendly surroundings. Then I might be permitted to call you Grace."

"Of course." Her smile warmed to suit the new intimacy.

"I doubt you would have heard of my tiny country. We are only a small dot in the sea, known chiefly for our olive oil and wine."

"Terresa?"

"Now I am flattered again that such a beautiful woman would know my humble country."

"It's a beautiful island. I was there briefly, two years ago, and very much enjoyed it. Terresa is a small jewel in the sea, dramatic cliffs to the west, lush vineyards in the east, and sandy beaches as fine as sugar."

He smiled at her, took her hand again. The connection was as unexpected as the woman, and he found himself compelled to touch. And to keep. "You must promise to return, to allow me to show you the country as it should be seen. I have a small villa in the west, and the view would almost be worthy of you."

"I'd love to see it. How difficult it must be to spend the summer in muggy Washington, when you could be enjoying the sea breezes of Terresa."

"Not at all difficult. Now." He skimmed a thumb over her knuckles. "I find the treasures of your country more and more appealing. Perhaps you would consider joining me one evening. Do you enjoy the opera?"

"Very much."

"Then you must allow me to escort you. Perhaps—" He broke off, a flicker of annoyance marring his smooth features as Seth stepped up to them.

"Ambassador Gregor DeVane of Terresa, allow me to introduce Lieutenant Seth Buchanan."

"You are military," DeVane said, offering a hand.

"Cop," Seth said shortly. He didn't like the ambassador's looks. Not one bit. When he saw DeVane with

Grace, he'd had a fast, turbulent impulse to reach for his weapon. But, strangely, his instinctive movement hadn't been up, to his gun, but lower on the side. Where a man would carry a sword.

"Ah, the police." DeVane blinked in surprise, though he already had a full dossier on Seth Buchanan. "How fascinating. I hope you'll forgive me for saying it's my fondest wish never to require your services." Smoothly DeVane slipped a glass from a passing tray, handed it to Seth, then took one for himself. "But perhaps we should drink to crime. Without it, you'd be obsolete."

Seth eyed him levelly. There was recognition, inexplicable, and utterly adversarial, when their eyes locked, pale silver to dark gold. "I prefer drinking to justice."

"Of course. To the scales, shall we say, and their constant need for balancing?" Gregor drank, then inclined his head. "You'll excuse me, Lieutenant Buchanan, I've yet to greet my host. I was—" he turned to Grace and kissed her hand again "—beautifully distracted from my duty."

"It was a pleasure to meet you, Gregor."

"I hope to see you again." He looked deeply into her eyes, held the moment. "Very soon."

The moment he turned away, Grace shivered. There had been something almost possessive in that last, long stare. "What an odd and charming man," she murmured.

Energy was shooting through Seth, the need to do battle. His system sparked with it. "Do you usually let odd and charming men drool over you in public?"

It was small of her, Grace supposed, but she enjoyed a kick of satisfaction at the annoyance in Seth's tone. "Of course. Since I so dislike them drooling over me in private." She turned into him, so that their bodies brushed lightly. Then slanted a look up from under that thick curtain of lashes. "You don't plan to drool, do you?"

He could have damned her for shooting his system from slow burn up to sizzle. "Finish your drink," he said abruptly, "and say your goodbyes. We're going."

Grace gave an exaggerated sigh. "Oh, I do love being dominated by a strong man."

"We're about to put that to the test." He took her half-finished drink, set it aside. "Let's go."

DeVane watched them leave, studied the way Seth pressed a hand to the small of Grace's back to steer her through the crowd. He would have to punish the cop for touching her.

Grace was his property now, DeVane thought as he gritted his teeth painfully tight to suppress the rage. She was meant for him. He'd known it from the moment he took her hand and looked into her eyes. She was perfect, flawless. It wasn't just the Three Stars that were fated for him, but the woman who had held one, perhaps caressed it, as well.

She would understand their power. She would add to it.

Along with the Three Stars of Mithra, DeVane vowed, Grace Fontaine would be the treasure of his collection.

She would bring the Stars to him. And then she would belong to him. Forever.

As she stepped outside, Grace felt another shudder sprint down her spine. She hunched her shoulder blades against it, looked back. Through the tall windows filled with light she could see the guests mingling.

And she saw DeVane, quite clearly. For a moment, she would have sworn their eyes met—but this time there was no charm. An irrational sense of fear lodged in her stomach, had her turning quickly away again.

When Seth pulled open the car door, she got in without complaint or comment. She wanted to go, to get away from those brilliantly lit windows and the man who seemed to watch her from beyond them. Briskly she rubbed the chill from her arms.

"You wouldn't be cold if you'd worn clothes." Seth stuck the key in the ignition.

The single remark, issued with cold and savage control, made her chuckle and chased the chill away. "Why, Lieutenant, and here I was wondering how long you would let me keep on what I am wearing."

"Not a hell of a lot longer," he promised, and pulled out into the street.

"Good." Determined to see that he kept that promise, she squirmed over and began to nibble his ear. "Let's break some laws," she whispered.

"I could already charge myself with intent."

She laughed again, quick, breathless, and had him hard as iron.

He wasn't sure how he managed to handle the car, much less drive it through traffic out of D.C. and back into Maryland. She worked his tie off, undid half the buttons of his shirt. Her hands were everywhere, and her mouth teased his ear, his neck, his jaw, while she murmured husky promises, suggestions.

The fantasies she wove with unerring skill had the blood beating painfully in his loins.

He pulled to a jerky stop in his driveway, then dragged

her across the seat. She lost one shoe in the car and the other halfway up the walk as he half carried her. Her laughter, dark, wild, damning, roared in his head. He all but broke his own door down to get her inside. The instant they were, he pushed her back against the wall and savaged her mouth.

He wasn't thinking. Couldn't think. It was all primal, violent need. In the darkened hallway, he hiked up her skirt with impatient hands, found the thin, lacy barrier beneath and ripped it aside. He freed himself, then, gripping her hips, plunged into her where they stood.

She cried out, not in protest, not in shock at the almost brutal treatment. But in pure, overwhelming pleasure. She locked herself around him, let him drive her ruthlessly, crest after torrential crest. And met him thrust for greedy, desperate thrust.

It was mindless and hot and vicious. And it was all that mattered. Sheer animal need. Violent animal release.

Her body shattered, went limp, as she felt him pour into her.

He slapped his hand against the wall to keep his balance, struggled to slow his breathing, clear his fevered brain. They were no more than a step inside his door, he realized, and he'd mounted her like a rutting bull.

There was no point in apologies, he thought. They'd both wanted fast and urgent. No, *wanted* was too tame a word, he decided. They'd craved it, the way starving animals craved meat.

But he'd never treated a woman with less care, or so completely ignored the consequences.

"I meant to get you out of that dress," he managed, and was pleased when she laughed.

"We'll get around to it."

"There's something else I didn't get around to." He eased back, studied her face in the dim light. "Is that going to be a problem?"

She understood. "No." And though it was rash and foolish, she felt a twinge of regret that there would be no quickening of life inside her as a result of their carelessness. "I take care of myself."

"I didn't want this to happen." He took her chin in his hand. "I should have been able to keep my hands off you."

Her eyes glimmered in the dark—confident and amused. "I hope you don't expect me to be sorry you didn't. I want them on me again. I want mine on you."

"While they are." He lifted her chin a little higher. "No one else's are. I don't share."

Her lips curved slowly as she kept his gaze. "Neither do I."

He nodded, accepting. "Let's go upstairs," he said, and swept her into his arms.

Chapter 7

He switched on the light as he carried her into his room. This time he needed to see her, to know when her eyes clouded or darkened, to witness those flickers of pleasure or shock.

This time he would remember man's advantage over the animal, and that the mind and heart could play a part.

She got a sense of a room of average size, simple buff-colored curtains at the windows, clean-lined furniture without color, a large bed with a navy spread tucked in with precise, military tidiness.

There were paintings on the walls that she told herself she would study later, when her heart wasn't skipping. Scenes both urban and rural were depicted in misty, dreamy watercolors that made a personal contrast to the practical room.

But all thoughts of art and decor fled when he set her

on her feet beside the bed. She reached out, undid the final buttons of his shirt, while he shrugged out of his jacket. Her brows lifted when she noted he wore his shoulder holster.

"Even to a cocktail party?"

"Habit," he said simply, and took it off, hung it over a chair. He caught the look in her eye. "Is it a problem?"

"No. I was just thinking how it suits you. And wondering if you look as sexy putting it on as you do taking it off." Then she turned, scooped her hair over her shoulder. "I could use some help."

He let his gaze wander over her back. Instead of reaching for the zipper, he drew her against him and lowered his mouth to her bare shoulder. She sighed, tipped her head back.

"That's even better."

"Round one took the edge off," he murmured, then slid his hands around her waist, and up, until they cupped her breasts. "I want you whimpering, wanting, weak."

His thumbs brushed the curves just above the bold blue silk. Focused on the sensation, she reached back, linked her arms around his neck. Her body began to move, timed to his strokes, but when she tried to turn, he held her in place.

She moaned, shifted restlessly, when his fingers curved under her bodice, the backs teasing her nipples, making them heat and ache. "I want to touch you."

"Whimpering," he repeated, and ran his hands down her dress to the hem, then beneath. "Wanting." And cupped her. "Weak." Pierced her.

The orgasm flooded her, one long, slow wave that swamped the senses. The whimper he'd waited for shuddered through her lips.

He toed off his shoes, then lowered her zipper inch by inch. His fingers barely brushed her skin as he spread the parted material, eased it down her body until it pooled at her feet. He turned her, stepped back.

She wore only a garter, in the same hot blue as the dress, with stockings so sheer they appeared to be little more than mist. Her body was a fantasy of generous curves, and satin skin. Her hair fell like wild black rain over her shoulders.

"Too many men have told you you're beautiful for it to matter that I say it."

"Just tell me you want me. That matters."

"I want you, Grace." He stepped to her again, took her into his arms, but instead of the greedy kiss she'd expected, he gave her one to slowly drown in. Her arms clutched around him, then went limp, at this new assault to the senses.

"Kiss me again," she murmured when his lips wandered to her throat. "Just like that. Again."

So his mouth met hers, let her sink a second time. With a dreamy hum of pleasure, she slipped his shirt away, let her hands explore. It was lovely to be savored, to be given the gift of a slow kindling flame, to feel the control slip out of her hands into his. And to trust.

He let himself learn her body inch by generous inch. Pleasured them both by possessing those full firm breasts, first with hands, then with mouth. He lowered his hands, flicked the hooks of her stockings free one by one— hearing her quick catch of breath each time. Then slid his hands under the filmy fabric to flesh.

Warm, smooth. He lowered her to the bed, felt her body yield beneath his. Soft, willing. Her lips answered his. Eager, generous.

They watched each other in the light. Moved together.

First a sigh, then a groan. She found muscle, the rough skin of an old scar, and the taste of man. Shifting, she drew his slacks down, feasted on his chest as she undressed him. When he took her breasts again, pulled her closer to suckle, her arms quivered and her hair drifted forward to curtain them both.

She felt the heat rising, sliding through her blood like a fever, until her breath was short and shallow. She could hear herself saying his name, over and over, as he patiently built her toward the edge.

Her eyes went cobalt, fascinating him. Her pillowsoft lips trembled, her glorious body quaked. Even as the need for release clawed at him, he continued to savor. Until he finally shifted her to her back and, with his eyes locked on hers, buried himself inside her.

She arched upward, her hands fisting in the sheets, her body stunned with pleasure. "Seth." Her breath expelled in a rush, burned her lungs. "It's never… Not like this. Seth—"

Before she could speak again, he closed her mouth with his and took her.

When sleep came, Grace dreamed she was in her garden in the mountains, with the woods, thick and green and cool, surrounding her. The hollyhocks loomed taller than her head and bloomed in deep, rich reds and clear, shimmering whites. A hummingbird, shimmering sapphire and emerald, drank from a trumpet flower. Cosmos and coneflowers, dahlias and zinnias made a cheerful wave of mixed colors.

Pansies turned their exotic little faces toward the sun and smiled.

Here she was happy, at peace with herself. Alone, but never lonely. Here there was no sound but the song of the breeze through the leaves, the hum of bees, the faint music of the creek bubbling over rocks.

She watched deer walk quietly out of the woods to drink from the slow-moving creek, their hooves lost in the low-lying mist that hugged the ground. The dawn light shimmered like silver, sparkled off the soft dew, caught rainbows in the mist.

Content, she walked through her flowers, fingers brushing blooms, scents rising up to please her senses. She saw the glint among the blossoms, the bright, beckoning blue, and, stooping, plucked the stone from the ground.

Power shimmered in her hand. It was a clean, flowing sensation, pure as water, potent as wine. For a moment, she stood very still, her hand open. The stone resting in her palm danced with the morning light.

Hers to guard, she thought. To protect. And to give.

When she heard the rustle in the woods, she turned, smiling. It would be him, she was certain. She'd waited for him all her life, wanted so desperately to welcome him, to walk into his arms and know they would wrap around her.

She stepped forward, the stone warming her palm, the faint vibrations from it traveling like music up her arm and toward her heart. She would give it to him, she thought. She would give him everything she had, everything she was. For love had no boundaries.

All at once, the light changed, hazed over. The air went cold and whipped with the wind. By the creek, the deer lifted their heads, alert, alarmed, then turned as one and fled into the sheltering trees. The hum of bees died into a rumble of thunder, and lightning snaked over the dingy sky.

There in the darkened wood, close, too close to where her flowers bloomed, something moved stealthily. Her fingers clutched reflexively, closing fast over the stone. And through the leaves she saw eyes, bright, greedy. And watching.

The shadows parted and opened the path to her.

"No." Frantic, Grace pushed at the hands that held her. "I won't give it to you. It's not for you."

"Easy." Seth pulled her up, stroked her hair. "Just a nightmare. Shake it off now."

"Watching me…" She moaned it, pressed her face into his strong, bare shoulder, drew in his scent and was soothed. "He's watching me. In the woods, watching me."

"No, you're here with me." Her heart was pounding hard enough to bring real concern. Seth tightened his grip, as if to slow it and block the tremors that shook her. "It's a dream. There's no one here but me. I've got you."

"Don't let him touch me. I'll die if he touches me."

"I won't." He tipped her face back. "I've got you," he repeated, and warmed her trembling lips with his.

"Seth." Relief shuddered through her as she clutched at him. "I was waiting for you. In the garden, waiting for you."

"Okay. I'm here now." To protect, he thought. And then to cherish. Shaken by the depth of that, he eased her backward, brushed the tumbled hair away from her face. "Must have been a bad one. Do you have a lot of nightmares?"

"What?" Disoriented, trapped between the dream and the present, she only stared at him.

"Do you want the light?" He didn't wait for an answer, but reached around her to switch on the bedside lamp. Grace turned her face away from the glare, pressed her fisted hand against her heart. "Relax now. Come on." He took her hand, started to open her fingers.

"No." She jerked it back. "He wants it."

"Wants what?"

"The Star. He's coming for it, and for me. He's coming."

"Who?"

"I don't...I don't know." Baffled now, she looked down at her hand, slowly opened it. "I was holding the stone." She could still feel the heat, the weight. "I had it. I found it."

"It was a dream. The diamonds are locked in a vault. They're safe." He tipped a finger under her chin until her eyes met his. "You're safe."

"It was a dream." Saying it aloud brought both relief and embarrassment. "I'm sorry."

"It's all right." He studied her, saw that her face was white, her eyes were fragile. Something moved inside him, shifted, urged his hand to reach out, stroke that pale cheek. "You've had a rough few days, haven't you?"

It was just that, the quiet understanding in his voice, that had her eyes filling. She closed them to will back the tears and took careful breaths. The pressure in her chest was unbearable. "I'm going to get some water."

He simply reached out and drew her in. She'd hidden all that fear and grief and weariness inside her very well, he realized. Until now. "Why don't you let it go?"

Her breath hitched, tore. "I just need to—"

"Let it go," he repeated, and settled her head on his shoulder.

She shuddered once, then clung. Then wept.

He offered no words. He just held her.

At eight the next morning, Seth dropped her off at Cade's. She'd protested the hour at which he shook her out of sleep, tried to curl herself into the mattress. He'd dealt with that by simply picking her up, carrying her into the shower and turning it on. Cold.

He'd given her exactly thirty minutes to pull herself together, then packed her into the car.

"The gestapo could have taken lessons from you," she commented as he pulled up behind M.J.'s car. "My hair's still wet."

"I didn't have the hour to spare it must take to dry all that."

"I didn't even have time to put my makeup on."

"You don't need it."

"I suppose that's your idea of a compliment."

"No, it's just a fact."

She turned to him, looking arousing, rumpled and erotic in the strapless dress. "You, on the other hand, look all pressed and tidy."

"I didn't take twenty minutes in the shower." She'd sung in the shower, he remembered. Unbelievably off-key. Thinking of it made him smile. "Go away. I've got work to do."

She pouted, then reached for her purse. "Well, thanks for the lift, Lieutenant." Then laughed when he pushed her back against the seat and gave her the long, thorough kiss she'd been hoping for.

"That almost makes up for the one miserly cup of coffee you allowed me this morning." She caught his bottom lip between her teeth, and her eyes sparkled into his. "I want to see you tonight."

"I'll come by. If I can."

"I'll be here." She opened the door, shot him a look over her shoulder. "If I can."

Unable to resist, he watched her every sauntering step toward the house. The minute she closed the front door behind her, he shut his eyes.

My God, he thought, he was in love with her. And it was totally impossible.

Inside, Grace all but danced down the hall. She was in love. And it was glorious. It was new and fresh and the first. It was what she'd been waiting for her entire life. Her face glowed as she stepped into the kitchen and found Bailey and Cade at the table, sharing coffee.

"Good morning, troops." She all but sang it as she headed to the coffeepot.

"Good morning to you." Cade tucked his tongue in his cheek. "I like your pajamas."

Laughing, she carried her cup to the table, then leaned down and kissed him full on the mouth. "I just adore you. Bailey, I just adore this man. You'd better snap him up quick, before I get ideas."

Bailey smiled dreamily into her coffee, then looked up, eyes shining and damp. "We're getting married in two weeks."

"What?" Grace bobbled her mug, sloshed coffee dangerously close to the rim. "What?" she repeated, and sat heavily.

"He won't wait."

"Why should I?" Reaching over the table, Cade took Bailey's hand. "I love you."

"Married." Grace looked down at their joined hands. A perfect match, she thought, and let out a shaky sigh. "That's wonderful. That's incredibly wonderful." Laying a hand over theirs, she stared into Cade's eyes. And saw exactly what she needed to see. "You'll be good to her." It wasn't a question, it was acceptance.

After giving his hand a quick squeeze, she sat back. "Well, a wedding to plan, and a whole two weeks to do it. That ought to make us all insane."

"It's just going to be a small ceremony," Bailey began. "Here at the house."

"I'm going to say one word." Cade put a plea in his voice. *"Elopement."*

"No." With a shake of her head, Bailey drew back, picked up her mug. "I'm not going to start our life together by insulting your family."

"They're not human. You can't insult the inhuman. Muffy will bring the beasts with her."

"Don't call your niece and nephew beasts."

"Wait a minute." Grace held up a hand. Her brows knit. "Muffy? Is that Muffy Parris Westlake? She's your sister?"

"Guilty."

Grace managed to suppress most of the snort of laughter. "That would make Doro Parris Lawrence your other sister." She rolled her eyes, picturing the two annoying and self-important Washington hostesses. "Bailey, run for your life. Go to Vegas. You and Cade can get married by a nice Elvis-impersonator judge and have a delightful, quiet life in the desert. Change your names. Never come back."

"See?" Pleased, Cade slapped a hand on the table. "She knows them."

"Stop it, both of you." Bailey refused to laugh, though her voice trembled with it. "We'll have a small, dignified ceremony—with Cade's family." She smiled at Grace. "And mine."

"Keep working on her." Cade rose. "I've got a couple things to do before I go into the office."

Grace picked up her coffee again. "I don't know his family well," she told Bailey. "I've managed to avoid that little pleasure, but I can tell you from what I do know, you've got the cream of the crop."

"I love him so much, Grace. I know it's all happened quickly, but—"

"What does time have to do with it?" Because she knew they were both about to get teary, she leaned forward. "We have to discuss the important, the vital, aspects of this situation, Bailey." She took a deep breath. "When do we go shopping?"

M.J. staggered in to the sound of laughter, and scowled at both of them. "I hate cheerful people in the morning." She poured coffee, tried to inhale it, then turned to study Grace. "Well, well," she said dryly. "Apparently you and the cop got to know each other last night."

"Well enough that I know he's more than a badge and an attitude." Irritated, she pushed her mug aside. "What have you got against him?"

"Other than the fact he's cold and arrogant, superior and stiff, nothing at all. Jack says they call him the Machine. Small wonder."

"I always find it interesting," Grace said coolly, "when people only skim the surface, then judge another human being. All those traits you just listed describe a man you don't know."

"M.J., drink your coffee." Bailey rose to get the cream. "You know you're not fit to be around until you've had a half a gallon."

M.J. shook her head, fisted a hand on a hip covered with a tattered T-shirt and equally tattered shorts. "Just because you slept with him, doesn't mean you know him, either. You're usually a hell of a lot more careful than that, Grace. You might let other people assume you pop into bed with a new guy every other night, but we know better. What the hell were you thinking of?"

"I was thinking of *me*," she shot back. "I wanted him. I needed him. He's the first man who's ever really touched me. And I'm not going to let you stand there and make something beautiful into something cheap."

No one spoke for a moment. Bailey stood near the table, the creamer in one hand. M.J. slowly straightened from the counter, whistled out a breath. "You're falling for him." Staggered, she raked a hand through her hair. "You're really falling for him."

"I've already hit the ground with a splat. So what?"

"I'm sorry." M.J. struggled to adjust. She didn't have to like the man, she told herself. She just had to love Grace. "There must be something to him, if he got to you. Are you sure you're okay with it?"

"No, I'm not sure I'm okay with it." Temper drained, and doubt snuck in. "I don't know why it's happened or what to do about it. I just know it is. It wasn't just sex." She remembered how he had held her while she cried. How he'd left the light on for her without her having to ask. "I've been waiting for him all my life."

"I know what that means." Bailey set the creamer down, took Grace's hand. "Exactly."

"So do I." With a sigh, M.J. stepped forward. "What's happening to us? We're three sensible women, and suddenly we're guarding ancient mythical stones, running from bad guys and falling headlong into love with men we've just met. It's crazy."

"It's right," Bailey said quietly. "You know it feels right."

"Yeah." M.J. laid her hand over theirs. "I guess it does."

It wasn't easy for Grace to go back into her house. This time, though, she wasn't alone. M.J. and Jack flanked her like bookends.

"Man." Scanning the wreck of the living area, M.J. hissed out a breath. "I thought they did a number on my place. Of course, you've got a lot more toys to play with."

Then her gaze focused on the splintered railing. And the outline below. "You don't want to do this now, Grace."

"The police cleared the scene. I have to get started on it sometime."

M.J. shook her head. "Where?"

"I'll start in the bedroom." Grace managed a smile. "I'm about to make my dry cleaner a millionaire."

"I'll see what I can do with the railing," Jack told her. "Jury-rig something so it's safe until you have it rebuilt."

"I'd appreciate it."

"Go on up," M.J. suggested. "I'll get a broom. And a bulldozer." She waited until Grace was upstairs before she turned to Jack. "I'm going to do this down here. Get rid of…things." Her gaze wandered to the outline. "She shouldn't have to handle that."

He leaned down to kiss her forehead. "You're a stand-up pal, M.J."

"Yeah, that's me." She inhaled sharply. "Let's see if we can dig up the stereo or the TV out of this mess. I could use some racket in here."

It took most of the afternoon before Grace was satisfied that the house was cleared out enough to call in her cleaning service. She wanted every room scrubbed before she lived there again.

And she was determined to do just that. To live, to be at home, to face whatever ghosts remained. To prove to herself that she could, she separated from M.J. and Jack and went shopping for the first replacements. Then, because the entire day had left her feeling raw, she stopped by Salvini.

She needed to see Bailey.

And she needed to see the Stars.

Once she was buzzed in, she found Bailey up in her office on the phone. With a smile, Bailey gestured her in. "Yes, Dr. Linstrum, I'm faxing the report to you now, and I'll bring you the original personally before five. I can complete the final tests you've ordered tomorrow."

She listened a moment, ran a finger down the soapstone elephant on her desk. "No, I'm fine. I appreciate your concern, and your understanding. The Stars are my priority. I'll have full copies of all the reports for your insurance carrier by end of business day Friday. Yes, thank you. Goodbye."

"You're working very quickly," Grace commented.

"Despite all that happened, hardly any time was lost. And everyone will feel more comfortable when the stones are in the museum."

"I want to see them again, Bailey." She let out a little

laugh. "It's silly, but I really need to. I had this dream last night—nightmare, really."

"What kind of dream?"

Grace sat on the edge of the desk and told her. Though her voice was steady, her fingers tapped with nerves.

"I had dreams, too," Bailey murmured. "I'm still having them. So is M.J."

Uneasy, Grace shifted. "Like mine?"

"Similar enough to be more than coincidence." She rose, held out a hand for Grace's. "Let's go take a look."

"You're not breaking any laws, are you?"

As they walked downstairs together, Bailey sent her an amused look. "I think after what I've already done, this is a minor infraction." She tried to block it, but a shudder escaped as they descended the last flight of steps, under which she'd once hidden from a killer.

"Are you going to be all right here?" Instinctively Grace hooked an arm around Bailey's shoulder. "I hate thinking of what happened, and now thinking of you working here, remembering it."

"It's getting better. Grace, I've had my stepbrothers cremated. Or rather, Cade took care of the arrangements. He wouldn't let me handle any of it."

"Good for him. You don't owe them anything, Bailey. You never did. We're your family. We always will be."

"I know."

She passed into the vault room and approached the massive reinforced-steel doors. The security system was complex and intricate, and even with the ease of long practice, it took Bailey three full minutes to disengage.

"Maybe I ought to have one of these installed in my house," Grace said lightly. "That bastard popped my library safe like it was a gumball machine. He must have fenced the jewelry fast. I hate losing the pieces you made for me."

"I'll make you more. In fact—" Bailey picked up a square velvet box "—let's start now."

Curious, Grace opened the box to a pair of heavy gold earrings. The smooth crescent-shaped gold was studded with stones in deep, dark hues of emerald, ruby and sapphire.

"Bailey, they're beautiful."

"I'd just finished them before…well, before. As soon as I had, I knew they were yours."

"It's not my birthday."

"I thought you were dead." Bailey's voice shook, then strengthened when Grace looked up. "I thought I would never see you again. So let's consider these a celebration of the rest of our lives."

Grace removed the simple studs in her ears, began to replace them with Bailey's gift. "When I'm not wearing them, I'll keep them with my mother's jewelry. The things that matter most."

"They look perfect on you. I knew they would." Bailey turned, took the heavy padded box from its shelf in the vault. Holding it between them, she opened it.

Grace let out a long, uneven sigh. "I honestly thought one would be gone. I would drive up to the mountains and find it in my garden, sitting on the ground beneath the flowers. It was so real, Bailey."

Reaching out, Grace took a stone. Her stone. "I felt it in my hand, just as I do now. It pulsed in my hand like a heart." She laughed a little, but the sound was hollow. "My heart. That's what it seemed like. I didn't realize that until now. It was like holding my own heart."

"There's a link." A little pale, Bailey took another stone from the box. "I don't understand it, but I know it. This is the Star I had. If M.J. was here, she'd have picked hers."

"I never thought I believed in this sort of thing." Grace turned the stone in her hand. "I was wrong. It's incredibly easy to believe it. To know it. Are we protecting them, Bailey, or are they protecting us?"

"I like to think it's both. They brought me Cade." Gently, she replaced her stone, touched a fingertip to the second Star in its hollow. "Brought M.J. Jack." Her face softened. "I opened up the showroom for them a little while ago," she told Grace. "Jack dragged her in and bought her a ring."

"A ring?" Grace lifted a hand to her heart as it swelled. "An engagement ring?"

"An engagement ring. She argued the whole time, kept telling him not to be a jerk. She didn't need any ring. He just ignored her and pointed to this lovely green tourmaline—square-cut, with diamond baguettes. I designed it a few months ago, thinking that it would make a wonderful, nontraditional engagement ring for the right woman. He knew she was the right woman."

"He's perfect for her." Grace brushed a tear from her lashes and beamed. "I knew it as soon as I saw them together."

"I wish you'd seen them today. There she is, grumbling, rolling her eyes, insisting all this fuss is a waste of time and effort. Then he put that ring on her finger. She got this big, sloppy grin on her face. You know the one."

"Yeah." And she could see it, perfectly. "I'm so happy for her, for you. It's like all that love was there, waiting, and the stones…" She looked down at them again. "They opened the door for it."

"And you, Grace? Have they opened the door for you?"

"I don't know if I'm ready for that." Nerves suddenly sprang to her fingertips. She laid the stone back in its bed. "Seth certainly wouldn't be. I don't think he'd believe in magic of any sort. And as for love…even if that door is wide open and the opportunity is there, he's not a man to fall easily."

"Easy or not—" Bailey closed the lid, replaced the box "—when you're meant to fall, you fall. He's yours, Grace. I saw that in your eyes this morning."

"Well." Grace swallowed the nerves. "I think I may wait awhile to let him in on that."

Chapter 8

There were flowers waiting for her when Grace returned to Cade's. A gorgeous crystal vase was filled with long spears of paper-white long-stemmed roses. Her heart thudded foolishly into her throat as she snatched up the card, tore open the envelope.

Then it deflated and sank.

Not from Seth, she noted. Of course, it had been silly of her to think that he'd have indulged in such a romantic and extravagant gesture. The card read simply:

Until we meet again,

Gregor

The ambassador with the oddly compelling eyes, she mused, and leaned forward to sniff at the tender, just-opening blooms. It had been sweet of him, she told herself.

A bit over-the-top, as there were easily three dozen roses in the vase, but sweet.

And she was irritated to realize that if they had been from Seth, she would have mooned over them like a star-struck teenager, would likely have pressed one between the pages of a book, even shed a few tears. She berated herself for being six times a fool.

If these appalling highs and lows were side effects of being in love, Grace thought she could have waited quite a bit longer to experience the sensation. She was just about to toss the card on the table when the phone rang.

She hesitated, as both Cade's and Jack's cars were in the drive, but when the phone rang the third time, she picked it up. "Parris residence."

"Is Grace Fontaine available?" The crisp tones of a well-trained secretary sounded in her ear. "Ambassador DeVane calling."

"Yes, this is she."

"One moment, please, Ms. Fontaine."

Lips pursed thoughtfully, Grace flipped the edge of the card against her palm. The man certainly had had no trouble tracking her down, Grace mused. And just how was she going to handle him?

"Grace." His voice flowed through the phone. "How delightful to speak with you again."

"Gregor." She flipped her hair behind her shoulder, edged a hip onto the table. "How extravagant of you. I've just walked in to your roses." She tipped one down, sniffed again. "They're glorious."

"Merely a token. I was disappointed not to have more time with you last evening. You left so early."

She thought of the wild ride to Seth's, the wilder sex. "I had…a previous engagement."

"Perhaps we can make up for it tomorrow evening. I have a box at the theater. *Tosca*. It's such a beautiful tragedy. There's nothing I would enjoy more than sharing it with you, then a late supper, perhaps."

"It sounds lovely." She rolled her eyes toward the flowers. Oh, dear, she thought. This would never do. "I'm so terribly sorry, Gregor, but I'm not free." With no regret whatsoever, she set the card aside. "Actually, I'm involved with someone, quite seriously."

For me, in any case, she thought. Then she looked through the glass panels of the front door, and her face lit up with surprise and pleasure when she saw Seth's car pull in.

"I see." She was too busy trying to steady her abruptly dancing pulse to notice how his voice had chilled. "Your escort of last evening."

"Yes. I'm terribly flattered, Gregor, and if I were any less involved, I'd leap at the invitation. I hope you'll forgive me, and understand."

Struggling not to squirm with delight, she crooked her finger in invitation as Seth stepped up to the door.

"Of course. If your circumstances change, I hope you'll reconsider."

"I certainly will." With a sultry smile, she walked her fingers up Seth's chest. "And thank you again, Gregor, so much, for the flowers. They're divine."

"It was my pleasure," he said, and his hands balled into bone-white fists as he hung up the receiver.

Humiliated, he thought, snapping his teeth together, grinding them viciously. Rejected for a suitful of muscles and a badge.

She would pay, he promised himself, taking her photo from his file and gently tapping a well-manicured finger against it. She would pay dearly. And soon.

With the ambassador completely forgotten the moment the connection was broken, Grace tipped her face up to Seth's. "Hello, handsome."

He didn't kiss her, but looked at the flowers, then at the card she'd tossed carelessly beside them. "Another conquest?"

"Apparently." She heard the cold distance in his tone and wasn't certain whether to be flattered or annoyed. She opted for a different tack altogether, and purred. "The ambassador was interested in an evening at the opera and...whatever."

The spurt of jealousy infuriated him. It was a new experience, and one he detested. It left him helpless, made him want to drag her out to his car by the hair, cart her off, lock her up where only he could see and touch and taste.

But more, there was fear, for her. A bone-deep sense of danger.

"It seems the ambassador—and you—move quickly."

No, she realized, the temper was going to come. There was no stopping it. She eased off the table, her smile an icy dare. "I move however it suits me. You should know."

"Yes." He dipped his hands into his pockets to keep them off her. "I should. I do."

Crushed, she angled her chin, aimed those laser blue eyes. "Which am I now, Lieutenant? The whore or the goddess? The ivory princess atop the pedestal, or the tramp? I've been them all—it just depends on the man and how he chooses to look."

"I'm looking at you," he said calmly. "And I don't know what I see."

"Let me know when you make up your mind." She started to move around him, came up short when he took her arm. "Don't push me." She tossed her head so that her hair flew out, settled.

"I could say the same, Grace."

She drew in one hot, deep breath, shoved his hand aside. "If you're interested, I gave the ambassador my regrets and told him I was involved with someone." She flashed a frigid smile and swung toward the stairs. "That, apparently, was my mistake."

He scowled after her, considered striding up the stairs of a house that wasn't his own and finishing the confrontation—one way or the other. Appalled, he pinched the bridge of his nose between his thumb and forefinger and tried to squeeze off the bitter headache plaguing him.

His day had been grueling, and had ended ten long hours after it began, with him staring at the group of photos on his board. Photos of the dead who were waiting for him to find the connection.

And he was already furious with himself because he'd already begun to run a search for data on Gregor DeVane. He couldn't be sure if he had done so due to a basic cop's hunch, or a man's territorial instinct. Or the dreams. It was a question, and a conflict, he'd never had to face before.

But one answer was clear as glass. He'd been out of line with Grace. He was still standing by the foyer table, frowning at the steps and weighing his options, when Cade strolled in from the rear of the house.

"Buchanan." More than a little surprised to see the homicide lieutenant standing in his foyer scowling, Cade stopped, scratched his jaw. "Ah, I didn't know you were here."

He had no business being there, Seth reminded himself. "Sorry. Grace let me in."

"Oh." After one beat, Cade pinpointed the source of the heat still flashing in the air. "Oh," he said again, and wisely controlled a grin. "Fine. Something I can do for you?"

"No. I'm just leaving."

"Have a spat?"

Seth turned his head, met Cade's obviously amused eyes blandly. "Excuse me?"

"Just a wild stab in the dark. What did you do to tick her off?" Though Seth didn't answer, Cade noted that his gaze shifted briefly to the roses. "Oh, yeah. Guess you didn't send them, huh? If some guy sent Bailey three dozen white roses, I'd probably have to stuff them down his throat, one at a time."

It was the gleam of appreciation that flashed briefly in Seth's eyes that made Cade decide to revise his stance. Maybe he could like Lieutenant Seth Buchanan after all.

"Want a beer?"

The casual and friendly invitation threw Seth off balance. "I— No, I was leaving."

"Come on out back. Jack and I already popped a couple of tops. We're going to fire up the grill and show the women how real men cook." Cade's grin spread charmingly. "Besides, oiling yourself with a couple of brews will make it easier for you to crawl. You're going to crawl anyway, so you might as well be comfortable."

Seth hissed out a breath. "Why the hell not?"

Grace stayed stubbornly in her room for an hour. She could hear laughter, music, and the silly whack of mallets striking balls as people played an enthusiastic game of croquet. She knew Seth's car was still in the drive, and had promised herself she wouldn't go back down until it was gone.

But she was feeling deprived, and hungry.

Since she'd already changed into shorts and a thin cotton shirt, she paused at the mirror only long enough to freshen her lipstick, spritz on some perfume. Just to make him suffer, she told herself, then sauntered downstairs and out onto the patio.

Steaks were smoking on the grill with Cade at the helm wielding an enormous barbecue fork. Bailey and Jack were arguing over the croquet match, and M.J. was sulking at a picnic table while she nibbled on potato chips.

"Jack knocked me out of the game," she complained, and gestured with her beer. "I still say he cheated."

"Any time you lose," Grace pointed out as she picked up a chip, "it's because someone cheated." Then she slid her gaze to Seth.

He'd taken off his tie, she noted, and his jacket. He still wore his holster. She imagined that was because he didn't feel comfortable hanging his gun over a tree branch. He, too, had a beer in his hand, and was watching the game with apparent interest.

"You still here?"

"Yeah." He'd had two beers, but didn't think crawling was going to be any more comfortable with the lubricant. "I've been invited to dinner."

"Isn't that cozy?" Grace spied what she recognized as a pitcher of M.J.'s special margaritas and poured herself a glass. The taste was tart, icy, and perfect. In dismissal, she wandered over to the grill to kibitz.

"I know what I'm doing," Cade was saying, and

shifted to guard his territory as Seth joined them. "I marinated these vegetable kabobs personally. Go away and leave this to a man."

"I was merely asking if you preferred your mushrooms blackened."

Cade sent her a withering look. "Get her off my back, Seth. An artist can't work with critics breathing down his neck and picking on his mushrooms."

"Let's go over here." Seth took her elbow, and was braced for her jerk. He kept his grip firm and hauled her away into the rose garden.

"I don't want to talk to you," Grace said furiously.

"You don't have to talk. I'll talk." But it took him a minute. Apologies didn't come easily to a man who made it a habit not to make mistakes. "I'm sorry. I overreacted."

She said nothing, simply folded her arms and waited.

"You want more?" He nodded, didn't bother to sigh. "I was jealous, an atypical reaction for me, and I handled it poorly. I apologize."

Grace shook her head. "That's the weakest excuse for an apology I've ever heard. Not the words, Seth, the delivery. But fine, I'll accept it in the same spirit it was offered."

"What do you want from me?" he demanded, frustrated enough to raise his voice and grab her arms. "What the hell do you want?"

"That." She tossed back her head. "Just that. A little emotion, a little passion. You can take your cardboard-stiff apology and stuff it, just like you can stuff the cold, deliberate and dispassionate routine you gave me over the flowers. That icy control doesn't cut it with me. If you feel something—whatever the hell it is—then let me know."

She sucked in her breath, stunned, when he yanked her against him, savaged her mouth with heat and anger and need. She twisted once and was hauled roughly back. Then was left weak and singed and shaken by the time he drew away.

"Is that enough for you?" He hauled her to her toes, his fingers digging in. His eyes weren't dispassionate now, weren't cool, but turbulent. Human. "Enough emotion, enough passion? I don't like to lose control. You can't afford to lose control on the job."

Her breath was heaving. And her heart was flying. "This isn't the job."

"No, but it was supposed to be." He willed his grip to loosen. "You were supposed to be. I can't get you out of my head. Damn it, Grace. I can't get you out."

She laid a hand on his cheek, felt the muscle twitch. "It's the same for me. Maybe the only difference right now is that I want it to be that way."

For how long? he wondered, but he didn't say it. "Come home with me."

"I'd love to." She smiled, stroked her fingers back, into his hair. "But I think we'd better stay for dinner, at least. Otherwise, we'd break Cade's heart."

"After dinner, then." It wasn't difficult at all, he discovered, to bring her hands to his lips, linger over them, then look into her eyes. "I am sorry. But, Grace—?"

"Yes?"

"If DeVane calls you again, or sends flowers?"

Her lips twitched. "Yes?"

"I'll have to kill him."

With a delighted laugh, she threw her arms around Seth's neck. "Now we're talking."

* * *

"That was nice." With a satisfied sigh, Grace sank down in the seat of Seth's car and watched the moon shimmer in the sky. "I like seeing the four of them together. But it's funny. It's as if I blinked, and everyone took this huge, giant step forward."

"Red light, green light."

Confused, Grace turned her head to look at him. "What?"

"The game—the kid's game? You know, the person who's it has to say, 'Green light,' turn his back. Everybody can go forward, but then he says, 'Red light' and spins around. If he sees anybody move, they have to go back to the start."

When she gave a baffled laugh, it was his turn to look. "Didn't you ever play games like that when you were a kid?"

"No. I was given the proper lessons, lectured on etiquette and was instructed to take brisk daily walks for exercise. Sometimes I ran," she said softly, remembering. "Fast, and hard, until my heart was bumping in my chest. But I guess I always had to go back to the start."

Annoyed with herself, she shook her shoulders. "My, doesn't that sound pathetic? It wasn't, really. It was just structured." She scooped back her hair, smiled at him. "So what other games did young Seth Buchanan play?"

"The usual." Didn't she know how heartbreaking it was to hear that wistfulness in her voice, then see that quick, careless shrug as she pushed it all aside? "Didn't you have friends?"

"Of course." Then she looked away. "No. It doesn't matter. I have them now. The best of friends."

"Do you know any one of the three of you can start a sentence and either of the other two can finish it?"

"We don't do that."

"Yes, you do. A dozen times tonight, at least. You don't even realize it. And you have this code," he continued. "Little quirks and gestures. M.J.'s half smirk or eye roll, Bailey's downsweep of the lashes or hair-around-the-finger twist. And you lift your left brow, just a fraction, or catch your tongue between your teeth. When you do, you let each other know the joke's your little secret."

She hummed in her throat, not at all sure she liked being deciphered so easily. "Aren't you observant…."

"That's my job." He pulled into his driveway, turned to her. "It shouldn't bother you."

"I haven't decided if it does or not. Did you become a cop because you're observant, or are you observant because you're a cop?"

"Hard to say. I was never really anything else."

"Not even when you were young Seth Buchanan?"

"It was always part of my life. My grandfather was a cop. And my father. My father's brother. Our house was filled with them."

"So it was expected of you?"

"It was understood," he corrected. "If I'd wanted to be a plumber or a mechanic, that would have been fine. But it was what I wanted."

"Why?"

"There's right and there's wrong."

"Just that simple?"

"It should be." He looked at the ring on his finger. "My father was a good cop. Straight. Fair. Solid. You can't ask for more than that."

She laid a hand over his. "You lost him."

"Line of duty. A long time ago." The hurt had passed a long time before, as well, and left room for pride. "He was a good cop, a good father, a good man. He always said there was a choice between doing the right thing or the wrong thing. Either one had a price. But you could pay up on the first and still look yourself in the eye every morning."

Grace leaned over, kissed him lightly. "He did the right thing by you."

"Always. My mother was a cop's wife, steady as a rock. Now she's a cop's mother, and she's still steady. Still there. When I got my gold shield, it meant as much to her as it did to me."

There was a bond, she realized. Deep and true and un-questioned. "But she worries about you."

"Some. But she accepts it. Has to," he added, with the ghost of a smile. "I've got a younger brother and sister. We're all cops."

"It runs through the blood," she murmured. "Are you close?"

"We're family," he said simply, then thought of hers and remembered that such things weren't simple. They were precious. "Yes, we're close."

He was the oldest, she mused. He would have taken his generational placement seriously, and, when his father died, his responsibilities as man of the house with equal weight.

It was hardly a wonder, then, that authority, respon-sibility, duty, sat so naturally on him. She thought of the weapon he wore, touched a fingertip to the leather strap.

"Have you ever…" She lifted her gaze to his. "Have you ever had to?"

"Yes. But I can still look myself in the eye in the morning."

She accepted that without question. But the next subject was more difficult. "You have a scar, just here." Her memory of it was perfect as she touched her finger just under his right shoulder now. "You were shot?"

"Five years ago. One of those things." There was no point in relaying the details. The bust gone wrong, the shouts and the electric buzz of terror. The insult of the bullet and the bright, stupefying pain. "Most police work is routine—paperwork, tedium, repetition."

"But not all."

"No, not all." He wanted to see her smile again, wanted to prolong what had evolved into a sweet and intimate interlude in a darkened car. Just conversation, without the sizzle of sex. "You've got a tattoo on your incredibly perfect bottom."

She laughed then, and tossed her hair back. "I didn't think you'd noticed."

"I noticed. Why do you have a tattoo of a winged horse on your butt, Grace?"

"It was an impulse, one of those wild-girl things I dragged M.J. and Bailey into."

"They have winged horses on their—"

"No, and what they do have is their little secret. I wanted the winged horse because it was free. You couldn't catch it unless it wanted to be caught." She lifted a hand to his face, changed the mood subtly. "I never wanted to be caught. Before."

He nearly believed her. Lowering his head, he met her lips with his, let the kiss spin out. It was quiet, without urgency. The slow meeting of tongues, the lazy change of angles and depths. Easy sips. Testing nibbles.

Her body shifted fluidly, her hands sliding up his chest to link at the nape of his neck. A purr sounded in her throat. "It's been a long time since I necked in the front seat of a car."

He nudged her hair aside so that his mouth could find that sweet, sensitive curve between neck and shoulder. "Want to try the back seat?"

Her laugh was low and delighted. "Absolutely."

The need had snuck up on him, crept into his bloodstream to stagger his heart. "We'll go inside."

Her breath was a bit unsteady as she leaned back, grinned at him in the shimmer of moonlight. "Chicken."

His eyes narrowed fractionally, making her grin widen. "There's a perfectly good bed in the house."

She made a soft clucking noise, then, chuckling, rubbed her lips over his. "Let's pretend," she whispered, pressing her body to his, sliding it against his. "We're on a dark, deserted road and you've told me the car's broken down."

He said her name, an exasperated sound against her tempting lips. It was only another challenge to her.

"I pretend I believe you, because I want to stay, I want you to…persuade me. You'll say you just want to touch me, and I'll pretend I believe that, too." She took his hand, laid it on her breast and felt the quick thrill when his fingers flexed. "Even though I know that's not all you want. It's not all you want, is it, Seth?"

What he wanted was that dark, slippery slide into her. His hands moved under her shirt, found flesh. "We're not going to make it into the back seat," he warned her.

She only laughed.

He wasn't sure if he felt smug or stunned by his own behavior when he finally unlocked his front door. Had he been this randy as a teenager? he wondered. That ridiculously reckless. Or was it only Grace who made such things as making desperate love in his own driveway one more adventure?

She stepped inside, lifted the hair off her neck, then let it fall in a gesture that simply stopped his heart. "My place should be ready by tomorrow, the next day at the latest. We'll have to go there. We can skinny-dip in my pool. It's so hot out now."

"You're so beautiful."

She turned, surprised at the mix of resentment and desire in his voice. He stood just inside the door, as if he might turn at any moment and leave her.

"It's a dangerous weapon. Lethal."

She tried to smile. "Arrest me."

"You don't like to be told." He let out a half laugh. "You don't like to be told you're beautiful."

"I didn't do anything to earn how I look."

She said it, he realized, as if beauty were more of a curse than a gift. And in that moment he felt a new level of understanding. He stepped forward, took her face gently in his hands, looked deep and long.

"Well, maybe your eyes are a little too close together."

Her hitch of laughter was pure surprise. "They are not."

"And your mouth, I think it might be just a hair off center. Let me check." He measured it with his own, lingering over the kiss when her lips curved. "Yeah. Just a hair, but it does throw things off, now that I really look. And let's see…" He turned her head to each side, paused to consider. "Yep. The left profile's weak. Are you getting a double chin there?"

She slapped his hand away, torn between insult and laughter. "I certainly am not."

"I really should check that, too. I don't know if I want to take this whole thing any further if you're getting a double chin."

He grabbed her, tugging her head back gently by the hair so that he could nibble freely under her jaw. She giggled— a young, foolish sound—and squirmed. "Stop that, you idiot." She let out a shriek when he hauled her up into his arms.

"You're no lightweight, either, by the way."

Her eyes went to slits. "Okay, buster, that's all. I'm leaving."

It was a delight to watch him grin—that quick, boyish flash of humor. "I forgot to tell you," he said as he headed for the stairs. "My car's broken down. I'm out of gas. The cat ate my homework. I'm just going to touch you."

He'd made it up two steps when the phone rang. "Damn." He brushed his lips absently over her brow. "I have to get that."

"It's all right. I'll remember where you were." Though he set her down, she didn't think her feet hit the floor. Love was a cushy buffer.

But her smile faded as she saw his eyes change. Suddenly they were flat again, unreadable. She knew as she walked across the room toward him that he'd shifted seamlessly from man to cop.

"Where?" His voice was cool again, controlled. "Is the scene secured?" He swore lightly, barely a whisper under the breath. "Get it secured. I'm on my way." As he hung up, his eyes skimmed over her, focused. "I'm sorry, Grace, I have to go."

She moistened her lips. "Is it bad?"

"I have to go," was all he'd say. "I'll call for a black-and-white to take you back to Cade's."

"Can't I wait here for you?"

"I don't know how long I'll be."

"It doesn't matter." She offered a hand, but wasn't sure she could reach him. "I'd like to wait. I want to wait for you."

No woman ever had. That thought passed quickly through his mind, distracting him. "If you get tired of waiting, call the precinct. I'll leave word there for a uniform to drive you home if you call in."

"All right." But she wouldn't call in. She would wait. "Seth." She moved into him, brushed her lips against his. "I'll see you when you get back."

Chapter 9

Alone, Grace switched on the television, settled on the sofa. Five minutes later, she was up and wandering the house.

He didn't go in for knickknacks, she mused. Probably thought of them as dustcatchers. No plants, no pets. The living room furniture was simple, masculine, and good quality. The sofa was comfortable, of generous size and a deep hunter green. She would have spruced it up with pillows. Burgundy, navy, copper. The coffee table was a square of heavy oak, highly polished and dust-free.

She decided he had a weekly housekeeper. She just couldn't picture Seth wielding a polishing rag. There was a bookcase under the side window and, crouching, she scanned the titles. It pleased her that they had read many of the same books. There was even a gardening book she'd studied herself.

That she could see, she decided. Yes, she could see Seth working out in the yard, turning the earth, planting something that would last.

There was art in this room, as well. She moved closer, certain the watercolor portraits grouped on the wall were the work of the same artist who had done the cityscape and rural scene in his bedroom. She searched for the signature first, and found Marilyn Buchanan looped in the lower corner.

Sister, mother, cousin? she wondered. Someone he loved, and who loved him. She shifted her gaze and studied the first painting.

Seth's father, Grace realized with a jolt. It had to be. The resemblance was there, in the eyes, clear, intense, tawny. The jaw, squared off, almost chiseled. The artist had seen strength, a touch of sadness, and honor. A whisper of humor around the mouth and an innate pride in the set of the head. All were evident in the three-quarter profile view that had the subject staring off at something only he could see.

The next portrait was a woman, perhaps in her forties. It was a pretty face, but the artist hadn't hidden the faint and telltale lines of age, the touches of gray in the dark, curling hair. The hazel eyes looked straight ahead, with humor and with patience. And there was Seth's mouth, Grace thought, smiling easily.

His mother, she concluded. How much strength was contained inside those quiet gray eyes? Grace wondered. How much was required to stand and accept when everyone you loved faced danger daily?

Whatever the amount, this woman possessed it.

There was another man, young, twenty-something,

with a cocky grin and daredevil eyes shades darker than
Seth's. Attractive, sexy, with a dark shock of hair falling
carelessly over his brow. His brother, certainly.

The last was of a young woman with a shoulder-length
sweep of dark hair, the tawny eyes alert, the sculpted
mouth just curved in the beginnings of a smile. Lovely,
with more of Seth's seriousness about her than the young
man. His sister.

She wondered if she would ever meet them, or if she
would know them only through their portraits. Seth would
take the woman he loved to them, she thought, and let the
little slice of hurt pass through her. He would want to—
need to—bring her into his mother's home, watch how she
melded and mixed with his family.

It was a door he'd have to open on both sides in
welcome. Not just because it was traditional, she realized,
but because it would matter to him.

But a lover? No, she decided. It wasn't necessary to
share a lover with family. He'd never take a woman with
whom he shared only sex home to meet his mother.

Grace closed her eyes a moment. Stop feeling sorry for
yourself, she ordered briskly. You can't have everything
you want or need, so you make the best of what there is.

She opened her eyes again, once more scanned the portraits. Good faces, she thought. A good family.

But where, Grace wondered, was Seth's portrait? There
had to be one. What had the artist seen? Had she painted
him with that cool cop's stare, that surprisingly beautiful
smile, the all-too-rare flash of that grin?

Determined to find out, she left the television blaring and
went on the hunt. In the next twenty minutes, she discovered that Seth lived tidily, kept a phone and notepad in

every room, used the second bedroom as a combination guest room and office, had turned the tiny third bedroom into a minigym and liked deep colors and comfortable chairs.

She found more watercolors, but no portrait of the man.

She circled the guest room, curious that here, and only here, he'd indulged in some whimsy. Recessed shelves held a collection of figures, some carved in wood, others in stone. Dragons, griffins, sorcerers, unicorns, centaurs. And a single winged horse of alabaster caught soaring in midflight.

Here the paintings reflected the magical—a misty landscape where a turreted castle rose silver into a pale rose-colored sky, a shadow-dappled lake where a single white deer drank.

There were books on Arthur, on Irish legends, the gods of Olympus, and those who had ruled Rome. And there, on the small cherrywood desk, was a globe of blue crystal and a book on Mithra, the god of light.

It made her tremble, clutch her arms. Had he picked up the book because of the case? Or had it already been here? She touched a hand to the slim volume and was certain it was the latter.

One more link between them, she realized, forged before they'd even met. It was so easy for her to accept that, even to be grateful. But she wondered if he felt the same.

She went downstairs, oddly at home after her self-guided tour. It made her smile to see their coffee cups from that morning still in the sink, a little touch of intimacy. She found a bottle of wine in the refrigerator, poured herself a glass and took it with her into the living room.

She went back to the bookcase, thinking of curling up on the couch with the TV for company and a book to pass the time. Then a chill washed over her, so quick, so intense, the wine shook in her hand. She found herself staring out the window, her breath coming short, her other hand clutched on the edge of the bookcase.

Someone watching. It pounded in her brain, a frightened, whispering voice that might have been her own.

Someone watching.

But she saw nothing but the dark, the shimmer of moonlight, the quiet house across the street.

Stop it, she ordered herself. There's no one there. There's nothing there. But she straightened and quickly twitched the curtains closed. Her hands were shaking.

She sipped wine, tried to laugh at herself. The late-breaking bulletin on the television had her turning slowly. A family of four in nearby Bethesda. Murdered.

She knew where Seth had gone now. And could only imagine what he was dealing with.

She was alone. DeVane sat in his treasure room, stroking an ivory statue of the goddess Venus. He'd come to think of it as Grace. As his obsession festered and grew, he imagined Grace and himself together, immortal through time. She would be his most prized possession. His goddess. And the Three Stars would complete his collection of the priceless.

Of course, she would have to be punished first. He knew what had to be done, what would matter most to her. And the other two women were not blameless—they had complicated his plans, caused him to fail. They would have to die, of course.

After he had the Stars, after he had Grace, they would die. And their deaths would be her punishment.

Now she was alone. It would be so easy to take her now. To bring her here. She'd be afraid, at first. He wanted her to be afraid. It was part of her punishment. Eventually he would woo her, win her. Own her. They would have, after all, several lifetimes to be together.

In one of them he would take her back to Terresa. He would make her a queen. A god could settle for no less than a queen.

Take her tonight. The voice that spoke louder and louder in his head every day taunted him. He couldn't trust it. DeVane steadied his breathing, shut his eyes. He would not be rushed. Every detail had to be in place.

Grace would come to him when he was prepared. And she would bring him the Stars.

Seth downed one last cup of sludgy coffee and rubbed at the ache at the back of his neck. His stomach was still raw from what he'd seen in that neat suburban home. He knew civilians and rookie cops believed the vets became immune to the results of violent death—the sights, the smells, the meaningless waste.

It was a lie.

No one could become used to seeing what he'd seen. If they could, they shouldn't wear a badge. The law needed to retain its sense of disgust, of horror, for murder.

What drove a man to take the lives of his own children, of the woman he'd made them with, and then his own? There'd been no one left in that neat suburban home to answer that question. He knew it would haunt him.

Seth scrubbed his hands over his face, felt the knots of

tension and fatigue. He rolled his shoulders once, twice, then squared them before cutting through the bull pen, toward the locker room.

Mick Marshall was there, rubbing his sore feet. His wiry red hair stood up like a bush that needed trimming from a face lined with weariness. His eyes were shadowed, his mouth was grim.

"Lieutenant." He pulled his socks back on.

"You didn't have to come in on this, Detective."

"Hell, I heard the gunshots from my own living room." He picked up one of his shoes, but just rested his elbows on his knees. "Two blocks over. Jesus, my kids played with those kids. How the hell am I going to explain this?"

"How well did you know the father?"

"Didn't, really. It's just like they always say, Lieutenant. He was a quiet guy, polite, kept to himself." He gave a short, humorless laugh. "They always do."

"Mulrooney's taking the case. You can assist if you want. Now go home, get some sleep. Go in and kiss your kids."

"Yeah." Mick scraped his fingers through his hair. "Listen, Lieutenant, I got some data on that DeVane guy."

Seth's spine tingled. "Anything interesting?"

"Depends on what floats your boat. He's fifty-two, never married, inherited a big fat pile from his old man, including this big vineyard on that island, that Terresa. Grows olives, too, runs some cattle."

"The gentleman farmer?"

"Oh, he's got more going than that. Lots of interests, spread out all over hell and back. Shipping, communications, import-export. Lots of fingers in lots of pies generating lots of dough. He was made ambassador to the U.S. three years ago. Seems to like it here. He bought some nifty place on Foxhall Road, big mansion, likes to entertain. People don't like to talk about him, though. They get real nervous."

"Money and power make some people nervous."

"Yeah. I haven't gotten a lot of information yet. But there was a woman about five years ago. Opera singer. Pretty big deal, if you're into that sort of thing. Italian lady. Seems like they were pretty tight. Then she disappeared."

"Disappeared." Seth's waning interest snapped back. "How?"

"That's the thing. She just went poof. Italian police can't figure it. She had a place in Milan, left all her things—clothes, jewelry, the works. She was singing at that opera house there, in the middle of a run, you know? Didn't show for the evening performance. She went shopping on that afternoon, had a bunch of things sent back to her place. But she never went back."

"They figure kidnapping?"

"They did. But then there was no ransom call, no body, no sign of her in nearly five years. She was…" Mick screwed up his face in thought. "Thirty, supposed to be at the top of her form, and a hell of a looker. She left a big pile of lire in her accounts. It's still there."

"DeVane was questioned?"

"Yeah. Seems he was on his yacht in the Ionian Sea, soaking up rays and drinking ouzo, when it all went down. A half-dozen guests on board with him. The Italian cop I talked to—big opera fan, by the way—he didn't think DeVane seemed shocked enough, or upset enough. He smelled something, but couldn't make anything stick. Still, the guy offered a reward, five million lire, for her safe return. No one ever collected."

"I'd say that was fairly interesting. Keep digging." And, Seth thought, he'd start doing some digging himself.

"One more thing." Mick cracked his neck from side to side. "And I thought this was interesting too—the guy's a collector. He has a little of everything—coins, stamps, jewelry, art, antiques, statuary. He does it all. But he's also reputed to have a unique and extensive gem collection—rivals the Smithsonian's."

"DeVane likes rocks."

"Oh, yeah. And get this. Two years ago, more or less, he paid three mil for an emerald. Big rock, sure, but its price spiked because it was supposed to be a magic rock." The very idea made Mick's lips curl. "Merlin was supposed to have, you know, conjured it up for Arthur. Seems to me a guy who'd buy into that would be pretty interested in three big blue rocks and all that god and immortality stuff that goes with them."

"I just bet he would." And wasn't it odd, Seth mused, that DeVane's name hadn't been on Bailey's list? A collector whose U.S. residence was only miles from Salvini, yet he'd never done business with them?

No, the lack was too odd to believe.

"Get me what you've got when you go on shift, Mick. I'd like to talk to that Italian cop personally. I appreciate the extra time you put into this."

Mick blinked. Seth never failed to thank his men for good work, but it was generally mechanical. There had been genuine warmth this time, on a personal level. "Sure, no sweat. But you know, Lieutenant, even if you can tie this guy to the case, he'll bounce. Diplomatic immunity. We can't touch him."

"Let's tie him first, then we'll see." Seth glanced over,

distracted, when a locker slammed open nearby as a cop was coming on shift. "Get some sleep," he began, then broke off. There, taped to the back of the locker, was Grace, young, laughing and naked.

Her head was tossed back, and that teasing smile, that feminine confidence, that silky power, sparkled in her eyes. Her skin was like polished marble, her curves were generous, with only that rainfall of hair, artfully draped to drive a man insane, covering her.

Mick turned his head, saw the centerfold and winced. Cade had filled him in on the lieutenant's relationship with Grace, and all Mick could think was that someone— very likely the cop currently standing at his locker whistling moronically—was about to die.

"Ah, Lieutenant..." Mick began, with some brave thought of saving his associate's life.

Seth merely held up a hand, cut Mick off and walked to the locker. The cop changing his shirt glanced over. "Lieutenant."

"Bradley," Seth said, and continued to study the glossy photo.

"She's something else, isn't she? One of the guys on day shift said she'd been in and looked just as good in person."

"Did he?"

"You bet. I dug this out of a pile of magazines in my garage. None the worse for wear."

"Bradley." Mick whispered the name and buried his head in his hands. The guy was dead meat.

Seth took a long breath, resisted the urge to rip the photo down. "Female officers share this locker room, Bradley. This is inappropriate." Where was the tattoo?

Seth thought hazily. What had she been when she posed for this? Nineteen, twenty? "Find somewhere else to hang your art."

"Yes, sir."

Seth turned away, then shot one last look over his shoulder. "And she's better in person. Much better."

"Bradley," Mick said as Seth strode out, "you just dodged one major bullet."

Dawn was breaking when Seth let himself into the house. He'd gone by the book on the case in Bethesda. It would close when the forensic and autopsy reports confirmed what he already knew. A man of thirty-six who made a comfortable living as a computer programmer had gotten up from his sofa, where he was watching television, loaded his revolver and ended four lives in the approximate space of ten minutes.

For this crime, Seth could offer no justice.

He could have headed home two hours earlier. But he'd made use of the time difference in Europe to make calls, ask questions, gather data. He was slowly putting together a picture of Gregor DeVane.

A man of wealth he had never sweated for. One who enjoyed prestige and power, who traveled in exalted circles, and had no family.

There was no crime in any of that, Seth thought as he closed his front door behind him.

There was no crime in sending white roses to a beautiful woman.

Or in once being involved with one who'd disappeared. But wasn't it interesting that DeVane had been involved with another woman? A Frenchwoman, a prima ballerina of great beauty who'd been considered the finest dancer of the decade. And who had been found dead of a drug overdose in her Paris home.

The verdict had been suicide, though those closest to her insisted she had never used drugs. She had been fiercely disciplined about her body. DeVane had been questioned in that matter, as well, but only as a matter of form. He had been dining at the White House at the very hour the young dancer slipped into a coma, and then into death.

Still, Seth and the Italian detective agreed it was quite a fascinating coincidence.

A collector, Seth mused, switching off lights automatically. An acquirer of beautiful things, and beautiful women. A man who would pay double the value of an emerald to possess a legend, as well.

He would see how many more threads he could tie, and he would, he decided, have an official chat with the ambassador.

He stepped into the living room, started to hit the next switch, and saw Grace curled upon the couch.

He'd assumed she'd gone home. But there she was, curled into a tight, protective ball on his couch, sleeping. What the hell was she doing here? he wondered.

Waiting for you. Just as she said she would. As no woman had waited before. As he'd wanted no woman to wait.

Emotion thudded into his chest, flooded into his heart. It undid him, he realized, this irrational love. His heart wasn't safe here, wasn't even his own any longer. He wanted it back, wanted desperately to be able to turn away, leave her and go back to his life.

It terrified him that he wouldn't. Couldn't.

She was bound to get bored before too much longer, to lose interest in a relationship he imagined was fueled by impulse and sex on her part. Would she just drift away, he wondered, or end it cleanly? It would be clean, he decided. That would be her way. She wasn't, as he'd once wanted to believe, callous or cold or calculating. She had a very giving heart, but he thought it was also a restless one.

Moving over, he crouched in front of her, studied her face. There was a faint line between her brows. She didn't sleep easily, he realized. What dreams chased her? he asked himself. What worries nagged her?

Poor little rich girl, he thought. Still running until you're out of breath and there's nothing to do but go back to the start.

He stroked a thumb over her brow to smooth it, then slid his arms under her. "Come on, baby," he murmured, "time for bed."

"No." She pushed at him, struggled. "Don't."

More nightmares? Concerned, he gathered her close. "It's Seth. It's all right. I've got you."

"Watching me." She turned her face into his shoulder. "Outside. Everywhere. Watching me."

"Shhh… No one's here." He carried her toward the steps, realizing now why every light in the house had been blazing. She'd been afraid to be alone in the dark. Yet she'd stayed. "No one's going to hurt you, Grace. I promise."

"Seth." She surfaced to the sound of his voice, and her heavy eyes opened and focused on his face. "Seth," she said again. She touched a hand to his cheek, then her lips. "You look so tired."

"We can switch. You can carry me."

She slid her arms around him, pressed her cheek, warm to his. "I heard, on the news. The family in Bethesda."

"You didn't have to wait."

"Seth." She eased back, met his eyes.

"I won't talk about it," he said flatly. "Don't ask."

"You won't talk about it because it troubles you to talk about it, or because you won't share those troubles with me?"

He set her down beside the bed, turned away and peeled off his shirt. "I'm tired, Grace. I have to be back in a few hours. I need to sleep."

"All right." She rubbed the heel of her hand over her heart, where it hurt the most. "I've already had some sleep. I'll go downstairs and call a cab."

He hung his shirt over the back of a chair, sat to take off his shoes. "If that's what you want."

"It's not what I want, but it seems it's what you want." She barely lifted a brow when he heaved his shoe across the room. Then he stared at it as if it had leaped there on its own.

"I don't do things like that," he said between his teeth. "I never do things like that."

"Why not? It always makes me feel better." And because he looked so exhausted, and so baffled by himself, she relented. Walking to him, she stepped in close to where he sat and began to knead the stiff muscles of his shoulders. "You know what you need around here, Lieutenant?" She dipped her head to kiss the top of his. "Besides me, of course. You need to get yourself a bubble tub, something you can sink down into that'll beat all these knots out of you. But for now we'll see what I can do about them."

Her hands felt like glory, smoothing out the knotted muscles in his shoulders. "Why?"

"That's one of your favorite questions, isn't it? Come on, lie down, let me work on this rock you call a back."

"I just need to sleep."

"Um-hmm." Taking charge, she nudged him back, climbed onto the bed to kneel beside him. "Roll over, handsome."

"I like this view better." He managed a half smile, toyed with the ends of her hair. "Why don't you come here? I'm too tired to fight you off."

"I'll keep that in mind." She gave him a push. "Roll over, big boy."

With a grunt, he rolled over on his stomach, then let out a second grunt when she straddled him and those wonderful hands began to press and stroke and knead.

"You, being you, would consider a regular massage an indulgence. But that's where you're wrong." She pressed down with the heels of her hands, worked forward to knead with her fingertips. "You give your body relief, it works better for you. I get one every week at the club. Stefan could do wonders for you."

"Stefan." He closed his eyes and tried not to think about another man with his hands all over her. "Figures."

"He's a professional," she said dryly. "And his wife is a pediatric therapist. She's wonderful with the children at the hospital."

He thought of the children, and that was what weakened him. That, and her soothing hands, her quiet voice. Sunlight filtered, a warm red, through his closed lids, but he could still see.

"The kids were in bed."

Her hands froze for a moment. Then, with a long, quiet breath, she moved them again, up and down his spine, over his shoulder blades, up to the tight length of his neck. And she waited.

"The youngest girl had a doll—one of those Raggedy Anns. An old one. She was still holding it. There were Disney posters all over the walls. All those fairy tales and happy endings. The way it's supposed to be when you're a kid. The older girl had one of those teen magazines beside the bed—the kind ten-year-olds read because they can't wait to be sixteen. They never woke up. Never knew neither one of them would get to be sixteen."

She said nothing. There was nothing that could be said. But, leaning down, she touched her lips to the back of his shoulder and felt him let loose a long, ragged breath.

"It twists you when it's kids. I don't know a cop who can deal with it without having it twist his guts. The mother was on the stairs. Looks like she heard the shots, starting running up to her kids. After, he went back to the living room, sat down on the sofa and finished it."

She curled herself into him, hugged herself to his back and just held on. "Try to sleep," she murmured.

"Stay. Please."

"I will." She closed her eyes, listened to his breathing deepen. "I'll stay."

But he woke alone. As sleep was clearing, he wondered if he'd dreamed the meeting at dawn. Yet he could smell her—on the air, on his own skin where she'd curled close. He was still stretched crosswise over the bed, and he tilted his wrist to check the watch he'd neglected to take off.

Whatever else was going on inside him, his internal clock was still in working order.

He gave himself an extra two minutes under the shower to beat back fatigue, and when shaving promised himself to do nothing more than vegetate on his next personal day. He pretended it wasn't going to be another hot, humid, hazy day while he knotted his tie.

Then he swore, scooped fingers though his just-combed hair, remembering he'd neglected to set the timer on his coffeemaker. The minutes it would take to brew it would not only set his teeth on edge, they would eat into his schedule.

But the one thing he categorically refused to do was start the day with the poison that simmered at the cop shop.

His mind was so focused on coffee that when the scent of it wafted like a siren's call as he came down the stairs, he thought it was an illusion.

Not only was the pot full of gloriously rich black liquid, Grace was sitting at his kitchen table, reading the morning paper and nibbling on a bagel. Her hair was scooped back from her face, and she appeared to be wearing nothing more than one of his shirts.

"Good morning." She smiled up at him, then shook her head. "Are you human? How can you look so official and intimidating on less than three hours' sleep?"

"Practice. I thought you'd gone."

"I told you I'd stay. Coffee's hot. I hope you don't mind that I helped myself."

"No." He stood exactly where he was. "I don't mind."

"If it's all right with you, I'll just loiter over coffee awhile before I get dressed. I'll get myself back to Cade's and change. I want to drop by the hospital later this morning, then I'm going home. It's time I did. The cleaning crew should be finished by this afternoon, so I thought…" She trailed off as he just continued to stare at her.

"What is it?" She gave an uncertain smile and rubbed at her nose.

Keeping his eyes on hers, he took the phone from the wall and punched in a number on memory. "This is Buchanan," he said. "I won't be in for a couple hours. I'm taking personal time." He hung up, held out a hand. "Come back to bed. Please."

She rose, and put her hand in his.

When clothes were scattered carelessly on the floor, the sheets turned back, the shades pulled to filter the beat of the sun, he covered her.

He needed to hold, to touch, to indulge himself for one hour with the flow of emotion she caused in him. Only an hour, yet he didn't hurry. Instead, he lingered over slow, deep, drugging kisses that lasted eons, loitered over long, smooth, soft caresses that stretched into forever.

She was there for him. Simply there. Open, giving, offering a seemingly endless supply of warmth.

She sighed, shakily, as he stroked her to helpless response, moving over her tenderly, his patience infinite. Each time their mouths met, with that slow slide of tongue, her heart shuddered in her breast.

There were the soft, slippery sounds of intimacy, the quiet murmurs of lovers, drifting into sighs and moans. Both of them were lost, mired in thick layers of sensation, the air around them like syrup, causing movement to slow and pleasure to last.

Her breath sighed out as he trailed lazily down her

body with hands and mouth, as her own hands stroked over his back, then his shoulders. She opened for him, arching up in welcome, then shuddering as his tongue brought on a long, rolling climax.

And because he needed it as much as she, she let her hands fall limply, let him take her wherever he chose. Her blood beat hot and the heat brought a dew of roused passion to her skin. His hands slicked over her skin like silk.

"Tell me you want me." He trailed slow, openmouthed kisses up her torso.

"Yes." She gripped his hips, urged him. "I want you."

"Tell me you need me." His tongue slid over her nipple.

"Yes." She moaned again when he suckled gently. "I need you."

Tell me you love me. But that he demanded only in his mind as he brought his mouth to hers again, sank into that wet, willing promise.

"Now." He kept his eyes open and on hers.

"Yes." She rose to meet him. "Now."

He glided inside her, filling her so slowly, so achingly, that they both trembled. He saw her eyes swim with tears and found the urge for tenderness stronger than any other. He kissed her again, softly, moved inside her one slow beat at a time.

The sweetness of it had a tear spilling over, trailing down her glowing cheek. Her lips trembled, and he felt her muscles contract and clutch him. "Don't close your eyes." He whispered it, sipped the tear from her cheek. "I want to see your eyes when I take you over."

She couldn't stop it. The tenderness stripped her. Her vision blurred with tears, and the blue of her eyes deepened to midnight. She said his name, then murmured it again against his lips. And her body quivered as the next long, undulating wave swamped her.

"I can't—"

"Let me have you." He was falling, falling, falling, and he buried his face in her hair. "Let me have all of you."

Chapter 10

In the nursery, Grace was rocking an infant. The baby girl was barely big enough to fill the crook of her arm from elbow to wrist, but the tiny infant watched her steadily with the deeply blue eyes of a newborn.

The hole in her heart had been repaired, and her prognosis was good.

"You're going to be fine, Carrie. Your mama and papa are so worried about you, but you're going to be just fine. She stroked the baby's cheek and thought—hoped—Carrie smiled a little.

Grace was tempted to sing her to sleep, but knew the nursing staff rolled their eyes and snickered whenever she tried a lullaby. Still, the babies were rarely critical of her admittedly poor singing voice, so she half sang, half murmured, until Carrie's baby owl's eyes grew heavy.

Even when she slept, Grace continued to rock. It was

self-serving now, she knew. Anyone who had ever rocked a baby understood that it soothed the adult, as well as the child. And here, with an infant dozing in her arms, and her own eyes heavy, she could admit her deepest secret.

She pined for children of her own. She longed to carry them inside her, to feel the weight, the movement within, to push them into life with that last sharp pang of childbirth, to hold them to her breast and feel them drink from her.

She wanted to walk the floor with them when they were fretful, to watch them sleep. To raise them and watch them grow, she thought, closing her eyes as she rocked. To care for them, to comfort them in the night, even to watch them take that first wrenching step away from her.

Motherhood was her greatest wish and her most secret desire.

When she first involved herself with the pediatric wing, she'd worried that she was doing so to assuage that gnawing ache inside her. But she knew it wasn't true. The first time she held a sick child in her arms and gave comfort, she'd understood that her commitment encompassed so much more.

She had so much to give, such an abundance of love that needed to be offered. And here it could be accepted without question, without judgment. Here, at least, she could do something worthwhile, something that mattered.

"Carrie matters," she murmured, kissing the top of the sleeping baby's head before she rose to settle her in her crib. "And one day soon you'll go home, strong and healthy. You won't remember that I once rocked you to sleep when your mama couldn't be here. But I will."

She smiled at the nurse who came in, stepped back. "She seems so much better."

"She's a tough little fighter. You've got a wonderful touch with the babies, Ms. Fontaine." The nurse picked up charts, began to make notes.

"I'll try to give you an hour or so in a couple of days. And you'll be able to reach me at home again, if you need to."

"Oh?" The nurse looked up, peered over the top of wire-framed glasses. The murder at Grace's home, and the ensuing investigation, were hot topics at the hospital. "Are you sure you'll be… comfortable at home?"

"I'm going to make sure I'm comfortable." Grace gave Carrie a final look, then stepped out into the hall.

She just had time, she decided, to stop by the pediatric ward and visit the older children. Then she could call Seth's office and see if he was interested in a little dinner for two at her place.

She turned and nearly walked into DeVane.

"Gregor?" She fixed a smile on her face to mask the sudden odd bumping of her heart. "What a surprise. Is someone ill?"

He stared at her, unblinking. "Ill?"

What was wrong with his eyes? she wondered, that they seemed so pale and unfocused. "We are in the hospital," she said, keeping the smile on her face, and, vaguely concerned, she laid a hand on his arm. "Are you all right?"

He snapped back, appalled. For a moment, his mind seemed to have switched off. He'd only been able to see her, to smell her. "Quite well," he assured her. "Momentarily distracted. I didn't expect to see you, either."

Of course, that was a lie, he'd planned the meeting meticulously. He took her hand, bowed over it, kissed her fingers.

"It is, of course, a pleasure to see you anywhere. I've

come by here as our mutual friends interested me in the care children receive here. Children and their welfare are a particular interest of mine."

"Really?" Her smile warmed immediately. "Mine, too. Would you like a quick tour?"

"With you as my guide, how could I not?" He turned, signaled to two men who stood stiffly several paces back. "Bodyguards," he told Grace, tucking her hand into the crook of his arm and patting it. "Distressingly necessary in today's climate. Tell me, why am I so fortunate as to find you here today?"

As she usually did, she covered the truth and kept her privacy. "The Fontaines donated significantly to this particular wing. I like to stop in from time to time to see what the hospital's doing with it." She flashed a twinkling look. "And you just never know when you might run into a handsome doctor—or ambassador."

She strolled along, explaining various sections and wondering how much she might, with a little time and charm, wheedle out of him for the children. "General pediatrics is on the floor above. Since this section houses maternity, they wouldn't want kids zooming down the corridors while mothers are in labor or resting."

"Yes, children can be quite boisterous." He detested them. "It's one of my deepest regrets that I have none of my own. But having never found the right woman…" He gestured with his free hand. "As I grow older, I'm resigned to having no one to carry on my name."

"Gregor, you're in your prime. A strong, vital man who can have as many children as he likes for years yet."

"Ah." He looked into her eyes again. "But there is still the right woman to be found."

She felt a shiver of discomfort at his pointed statement and intense gaze. "I'm sure you'll find her. We have some preemies here." She stepped closer to the glass. "So tiny," she said softly. "So defenseless."

"It's a pity when they're flawed."

She frowned at his choice of words. "Some of them need more time under controlled conditions and medical care to fully develop. But I wouldn't call them flawed."

Another error, he thought with an inner sense of irritation. He could not seem to keep his mind sharp with her scent invading his senses. "Ah, my English is sometimes awkward. You must forgive me."

She smiled again, wanting to ease his obvious discomfort. "Your English is wonderful."

"Is it clever enough to convince you to share a quiet lunch with me? As friends," he said, lacing his smile with regret. "With similar interests."

She glanced, as he did, at the babies. It was tempting, she admitted. He was a charming man—a wealthy and influential one. She might, with careful campaigning, persuade him to assist her in setting up an international branch of Falling Star, an ambition that had been growing in her lately.

"I would love to, Gregor, but right now I'm simply swamped. I was just on my way home when I ran into you. I have to check on some...repairs." That seemed the simplest way to explain it. "But I'd love to have a rain check. One I'd hope to cash in very soon. There's something concerning our similar interestss that I'd love to have your advice on, and your input."

"I would love to be of any service whatsoever." He kissed her hand again. Tonight, he thought. He would have her tonight, and there would be no more need for this charade.

"That's so kind of you." Because she felt guilty for her disinterest and coolness in the face of his interest, she kissed his cheek. "I really must run. Do call me about that rain check. Next week, perhaps, for lunch." With a final, flashing smile, she dashed off.

As he watched her, his fisted fingers dug crescents into his palms. Fighting for control, he nodded to one of the silent men who waited for him. "Follow her only," he ordered. "And wait for instructions."

Cade didn't think of himself as a whiner—and, considering how well he tolerated his own family, he believed himself one of the most patient, most amiable, of men. But he was certain that if Grace had him shift one more piece of furniture from one end of her enormous living area to the other, he would break down and weep.

"It looks great."

"Hmm…" She stood, one hand on her hip, the fingers of the other tapping against her lip.

The gleam in her eye was enough to strike terror in Cade's heart and had his already aching muscles crying out in protest. "Really, fabulous. A hundred percent. Get the camera. I see a cover of *House and Garden* here."

"You're wheedling, Cade," she said absently. "Maybe the conversation pit did look better facing the other way." His moan was pitiful, and only made her lips twitch. "Of course, that would mean the coffee table and those two accent pieces would have to shift. And the palm tree—isn't it a beauty?—would have to go there."

The beauty weighed fifty pounds if it weighed an

ounce. Cade abandoned pride and whined. "I still have stitches," he reminded her.

"Ah, what's a few stitches to a big, strong man like you?" She fluttered at him, patted his cheek and watched his ego war with his sore back. Giving in, she let loose a long, rolling laugh. "Gotcha. It's fine, darling, absolutely fine. You don't have to carry another cushion."

"You mean it?" His eyes went puppylike with hope. "It's done?"

"Not only is it done, but you're going to sit down, put up your feet, while I go get you an icy beer that I stocked in my fridge just for tall, handsome private investigators."

"You're a goddess."

"So I've been told. Make yourself at home. I'll be right back."

When Grace came back bearing a tray, she saw that Cade had taken her invitation to heart. He sat back on the thick cobalt-blue cushions of her new U-shaped sofa arrangement, his feet propped on the mirror-bright surface of the ebony coffee table, his eyes shut.

"I really did wear you out, didn't I?"

He grunted, opened one eye. Then both popped open in appreciation when she set the loaded tray on the table. "Food," he said, and sprang for it.

She had to laugh as he dived into her offer of glossy green grapes, Brie and crackers, the heap of caviar on ice with toast points. "It's the least I can do for such an attractive moving man." Settling beside him, she picked up the glass of wine she'd poured for herself. "I owe you, Cade."

With his mouth half-full, he scanned the living room, nodded. "Damn straight."

"I don't just mean the manual labor. You gave me a

safe haven when I needed one. And most of all, I owe you for Bailey."

"You don't owe me for Bailey. I love her."

"I know. So do I. I've never seen her happier. She was just waiting for you." Leaning over, Grace kissed his cheek. "I always wanted a brother. Now, with you and Jack, I have two. Instant family. They fit, too, don't they?" she commented. "M.J. and Jack. As if they've always been a team."

"They keep each other on their toes. It's fun to watch."

"It is. And speaking of Jack, I thought he was going to give you a hand with our little redecorating project."

Cade scooped caviar onto a piece of toast. "He had a skip to trace."

"A what?"

"A bail jumper to bring in. He didn't think it was going to take him long." Cade swallowed, sighed. "He doesn't know what he's missing."

"I'll give him the chance to find out." She smiled. "I still have plans for a couple of the rooms upstairs."

It gave Cade his opening. "You know, Grace, I wonder if you're rushing this a little. It's going to take some time to put a house this size back in shape. Bailey and I would like you to stay at our place for a while."

Their place, Grace mused. Already it was their place. "It's more than livable here, Cade. M.J. and I talked about it," she continued. "She and Jack are going to her apartment. It's time we all got back to our routines."

But M.J. wasn't going to be alone, Cade thought, and thoughtfully sipped his beer. "There's still somebody pulling the strings out there. Somebody who wants the Three Stars."

"I don't have them," Grace reminded him. "I can't get them. There's no reason to bother with me at this point."

"I don't know how much reason has to do with it, Grace. I don't like you being here alone."

"Just like a brother." Delighted with him, she gave his arm a squeeze. "Listen, Cade, I've got a new alarm system, and I'm considering buying a big, mean, ugly dog." She started to mention the pistol she had in her nightstand, and the fact that she knew how to use it, but thought that would only worry him more. "I'll be fine."

"What does Buchanan think?"

"I haven't asked him. He's going to come by later—so I won't really be alone."

Satisfied with that, Cade handed her a grape. "You've got him worried."

Her lips curved as she popped the grape into her mouth. "Do I?"

"I don't know him well—I don't think anyone does. He's…I guess *self-contained* would be the word. Doesn't let a lot show on the surface. But when I walked in yesterday, after you'd gone upstairs, he was just standing there, looking up after you." Now Cade grinned. "There was plenty on the surface then. It was pretty illuminating. Seth Buchanan, human being." Then he winced, tipped back his beer. "Sorry, I didn't mean to—"

"It's all right. I know exactly what you mean. He's got an almost terrifying self control, and that impenetrable aura of authority."

"It seems to me that you've managed to dent the armor. In my opinion, that's just what he needed. You're just what he needed."

"I hope he thinks so. It turns out he's just what I needed.

I'm in love with him." With a half laugh, she shook her head and sipped her wine. "I can't believe I told you that. I rarely tell men my secrets."

"Brothers are different."

She smiled at him. "Yes, they are."

"I hope Seth appreciates just how lucky he is."

"I don't think Seth believes in luck."

She suspected Seth didn't believe in the Three Stars of Mithra, either. And she had discovered that she did. In a very short time, she'd simply opened her mind, stretched her imagination and accepted. They had magic, and they had power. She had been touched by both—as had Bailey and M.J. and the men who were linked to them.

Grace had no doubt that whoever wanted that magic, that power, would stop at nothing to gain them. It wouldn't matter when they were in the museum. He would still crave them, still plot to possess them.

But he could no longer reach the stones through her. That part of her connection, she thought with relief, was over. She was safe in her own home, and would learn to live there again. Starting now.

She dressed carefully in a long white dress of thin watered silk that left her shoulders bare and flirted with her ankles. Beneath the flowing silk she wore only skin, creamed and scented.

She left her hair loose, scooped back at the sides with silver combs, her mother's sapphire drops at her ears, gleaming like twin stars. On impulse, she'd clasped a thick silver bracelet high on her forearm—a touch of pagan.

When she looked into the mirror after dressing, she'd

felt an odd jolt—as if she could see herself in the glass, with the faint ghost of someone else merged with her.

But she'd laughed it off, chalked it up to nerves and anticipation, and busied herself completing her preparations.

She filled the rooms she'd redone with candles and flowers, pleased with the welcome they offered. On the table by the window facing her side garden she arranged the china and crystal for her meticulously plotted dinner for two.

The champagne was iced, the music was on low and the lights were romantically dimmed. All she needed was the man.

Seth saw the candles in the windows when he pulled up in the drive. Fatigue layered over frustration and had him, in the dim light of the car, rubbing gritty eyes.

And there were candles in the windows.

He was forced to admit that for the first time in his adult life he didn't have a handle on himself, or on the world around him. He certainly didn't have a handle on the woman who had lit those candles, and who was waiting in that soft, flickering light.

He'd moved on DeVane on pure instinct—and part of that instinct, he knew, was territorial. Nothing could have been more out of character for him. Perhaps that was why he was feeling slightly…out of himself. Out of control. Grace had become a center, a focal point.

Or was it an obsession?

Hadn't he come here because he couldn't keep away? Just as he had dug into DeVane's background because the man roused some primal defense mechanism.

Maybe that was how it started, Seth admitted, but his

cop's instincts were still honed. DeVane was dirty. And with a little more time, a little more digging, he would link the man with the deaths surrounding the diamonds.

Without the diplomatic block, Seth thought, he had enough already to bring the man in for questioning. DeVane liked to collect—and he collected the rare, the precious, and frequently those items that held some whiff of magic.

And Gregor DeVane had financed an expedition the year before to search for the legendary Stars. A rival archaeologist had found them first, and the Washington museum had acquired them.

DeVane had lost more than two million dollars on the hunt and the Stars had slipped through his fingers.

And the rival archaeologist had met with a tragic and fatal accident three months after the find, in the jungles of Costa Rica.

Seth didn't believe in coincidence. The man who had kept DeVane from possessing the diamonds was dead. And so, Seth had discovered, was the head of the expedition DeVane had put together.

No, he didn't believe in coincidence.

DeVane had been a resident of D.C. for nearly two years, on and off, without ever meeting Grace. Now, directly after Grace's connection with the Stars, the man was not only at the same social function, but happened to make a play for her?

Life simply wasn't that tidy.

A little more time, Seth promised himself, rubbing his temples to clear the headache. He'd find the solid connection—link DeVane to the Salvinis, to the bail bondsman, to the men who had died in a crashed van, to Carlo

Monturri. He needed only one link, and then the rest of the chain would fall into place.

But at the moment, he needed to get out of the stuffy car, go inside and face what was happening to his personal life.

With a short laugh, Seth climbed out of the car. A personal life. Wasn't that part of the problem? He'd never had one, hadn't allowed himself one. Now, a matter of days after he'd met Grace, it was threatening to swallow him.

He needed time there, too, he told himself. Time to step back, gain some distance for a more objective look. He'd allowed things to move too fast, to get out of control. That would have to be fixed. A man who fell in love overnight couldn't trust himself. It was time to reassert some logic.

They were dynamically different—in backgrounds, in life-styles and in goals. Physical attraction was bound to fade, or certainly stabilize. He could already foresee her easing back once the initial excitement peaked. She'd grow restless, certainly annoyed with the demands on his work. He would be neither willing nor able to spin her through the social whirl that was such an intricate part of her life.

She was bound to look toward someone else who would. A beautiful woman, vital, sought-after, flattered at every turn, wouldn't be content to light a candle in the window for many nights.

He'd be doing them both a favor by slowing down, stepping back. As he lifted a hand to the gleaming brass knocker, he refused to hear the mocking voice inside his head that called him a liar—and a coward.

She answered the knock quickly, as if she'd only been waiting for it. She stood in the doorway, soft light filtering through the long flow of white silk. The power of her, pure and pagan, stopped his breath.

Though he kept his arms at his sides, she moved into him, and ripped at his heart with a welcoming kiss.

"It's good to see you." Grace skimmed her fingers along his cheekbones, under his shadowed eyes. "You've had a long one, Lieutenant. Come in and relax."

"I haven't got a lot of time. I've got work." He waited, saw the flicker of disappointment in her eyes. It helped justify what he was determined to do. But then she smiled, took his hand.

"Well, let's not waste what time you've got standing in the foyer. You haven't eaten, have you?"

Why didn't she ask him why he couldn't stay? he wondered, irrationally irritated. Why wasn't she complaining? "No."

"Good. Sit down and have a drink. Can you have a drink, or are you officially on duty?" She walked into the living area as she spoke, then drew the chilling champagne from its silver bucket. "I don't suppose one glass would matter, in any case. And I won't tell." She released the cork with an expert's twist and a muffled, celebratory pop. "I've just put the canapés out, so help yourself."

She gestured toward the silver tray on the coffee table before moving off with a quiet, slippery rustle of silk to pour two flutes.

"Tell me what you think. I worked poor Cade to death pushing things around in here, but I wanted to get at least the living space in order again quickly."

It looked as if it had been clipped from a glossy magazine on perfect living. Nothing was out of place, everything was gleaming and lovely. Bold colors mixed with whites and blacks, tasteful knickknacks, and artwork that appeared to have been selected with incredible care over a long period of time.

Yet she'd done it in days—or hours. That, Seth supposed, was the power of wealth and breeding.

Yet the room didn't look calculated or cold. It looked generous and welcoming. Soft surfaces, soft edges, with touches that were so Grace everywhere. Antique bottles in jewel tones, a china cat curled up for a nap, a lush, thriving fern in a copper pot.

And flowers, candlelight.

He looked up, noted the unbroken gleam of wood circling the balcony. "I see you've had it repaired."

Something's wrong, was all she could think as she stepped forward and handed him his glass. "Yes, I wanted that done as soon as possible. That, and the new security system. I think you'll approve."

"I'll take a look at it, if you like."

"I'd like it better if you'd relax while you can. Why don't I bring dinner in?"

"You cooked?"

Now she laughed. "I wouldn't do that to you, but I'm an expert at ordering in—and at presentation. Try to unwind. I'll be right back."

As she glided out, he looked down at the tray. A silver bowl of glossy black caviar, little fancy bites of elegant finger foods. He turned his back on them and, carrying his glass, walked over to study her portrait.

When she came back, wheeling an antique cart, he continued to look at her painted face. "He was in love with you, wasn't he? The artist?"

Grace drew a careful breath at that cool tone. "Yes, he

was. He knew I didn't love him. I often wished I could
have. Charles is one of the kindest, gentlest men I know."

"Did you sleep with him?"

A chill snaked up her spine, but she kept her hands steady
as she set plates on the candle- and flower-decked table.
"No. It wouldn't have been fair, and I care about him too
much."

"You'd rather sleep with men you don't care about."

She hadn't seen it coming, Grace realized. How foolish
of her not to have seen this coming. "No, but I won't sleep
with men who I could hurt like that. I would have hurt
Charles by being his lover, so I stayed his friend."

"And the wives?" He did turn now, eyes narrowed as
he studied the woman instead of the portrait. "Like the
woman who was married to that earl you were mixed up
with? Didn't you worry about hurting her?"

Grace picked up her wine again, quite deliberately
cocked her head. She had never slept with the earl he'd
mentioned, or with any other married man. But she had
never bothered to argue with public perception. Nor would
she bother to deny it now.

"Why would I? I wasn't married to her."

"And the guy who tried to kill himself after you broke
your engagement?"

She touched the glass to her lips, swallowed frothy
wine that burned like shards of glass in her throat. "Overly
dramatic of him, wasn't it? I don't think you're in the
mood for Caesar salad and steak Diane, are you, Lieutenant? Rich food doesn't set well during interrogations."

"No one's interrogating you, Grace."

"Oh, yes, you are. But you neglected to read me my
rights."

Her frigid anger helped justify his own. It wasn't the men—he knew it wasn't the men he'd very deliberately tossed in her face that scraped at him. It was the fact that they didn't matter to him, that somehow nothing seemed to matter but her.

"It's odd you're so sensitive about answering questions about men, Grace. You hadn't troubled to hide your…track record."

"I expected better from you." She said it softly, so he barely heard, then shook her head, smiled coolly. "Foolish of me. No, I've never troubled to hide anything—unless it mattered. The men didn't matter, for the most part. Do you want me to tell you that you're different? Would you believe me if I did?"

He was afraid he would. Terrified he would. "It isn't necessary. We've moved too fast, Grace. I'm not comfortable with it."

"I see." She thought she did now, perfectly. "You'd like to slow things down." She set her glass aside, knowing her hand would start to shake. "It appears you've taken a couple of those giant steps while I've had my back turned. I really should have played that game as a child, so I'd be more alert for sudden moves."

"This isn't a game."

"No, I suppose it isn't." She had her pride, but she also had her heart. And she had to know. "How could you have made love with me like that this morning, Seth, and do this tonight? How could you have touched me the way you have—the way no one ever has—and hurt me like this?"

It was because of what had swamped him that morning, he realized. The helplessness of his need. "I'm not trying to hurt you."

"No, that only makes it worse. You're doing both of us a favor, aren't you? Isn't that how you've worked it out? Break things off before they get too messy? Too late." Her voice broke, but she managed to shore it up again. "It's already messy."

"Damn it." He took a step toward her, then stopped dead when her head whipped up, and those hot blue eyes scorched him.

"Don't even think about touching me now, when those thoughts are still in your head. You go your tidy way, Lieutenant, and I'll go mine. I don't believe in slowing down. You either go forward, or you stop."

Furious with herself, she lifted a hand and flicked a tear off her cheek. "Apparently, we've stopped."

Chapter 11

He stood there wondering what in the hell he was doing. Here was the woman he loved, who—by some wild twist of fate—might actually love him. Here was a chance for that life he'd never allowed himself, the family, the home, the woman. He was pushing them all away, with both hands, and couldn't seem to stop.

"Grace…I want to give us both time to consider what we're doing, where this is going."

"No, you don't." She tossed back her hair with one angry jerk of her head. "Do you think because I've only known you a matter of days that I don't understand how your head works? I've been more intimate with you than I've been with anyone in my life. I *know* you." She managed a deep, ragged breath. "What you want is to get that wheel back under your hands, that control button back under your thumb. This whole thing has run away from you, and you just can't let that happen."

"That may be true." Was true, he realized. Was absolutely, mortifyingly true. "But it doesn't change the point. I'm in the middle of an investigation, and I'm not as objective as I need to be, because I'm involved with you. After it's done—"

"After it's done, what?" she demanded. "We pick up where you left off? I don't think so, Lieutenant. What happens when you're in the middle of the next investigation? And the next? Do I strike you as someone who's going to wait around until you have the time, and the room, to continue an on-again, off-again relationship with me?"

"No." His spine stiffened. "I'm a cop, and my work takes priority."

"I don't believe I've ever asked you to change that. In fact, I found your dedication to your work admirable, attractive. Even heroic." Her smile was thin and brief. "But that's irrelevant, and so is this conversation." She turned away, picked up her wine again. "You know the way out."

No, she'd never asked him to change anything. Never questioned his work. What the hell had he done? "This needs to be discussed."

"That's your style, not mine. Do you actually think you can stand here, in my home…" Her voice began to hitch and jerk. "In my home, and break my heart, dump me and expect a civilized conversation? I want you *out*." She slammed her glass down, snapping the fragile stem of the glass, splattering wine. "Right now."

Where had the panic come from? he wondered. His

beeper went off and was ignored. "We're not leaving it this way."

"Exactly this way," she corrected. "Do you think I'm stupid? Do you think I don't see that you walked in here tonight looking to pick a fight so that it would end exactly this way? Do you think I don't know now that no matter how much I gave you, you'd hold back from me, question, analyze, dissect everything? Well, analyze this. I was willing to give more, whatever you wanted to take. Now you can spend the rest of your life wondering just what you lost here tonight."

As his beeper sounded again, she swept by him, wrenched open the front door. "You'll have to answer that call of duty elsewhere, Lieutenant."

He stepped to her, but, though his arms ached, he resisted the need to reach out. "When I'm done with this, I'm coming back."

"You won't be welcome."

He could feel himself step up to a line he'd never crossed. "That isn't going to matter. I'm coming back."

She said nothing at all, simply shut the door in his face and turned the lock with a hard, audible click.

She leaned back against the door, her breath shallow now, and hot, as pain swept through her. It was worse now that the door was closed, now that she had shut him out. And the candles still flickered, the flowers still bloomed.

She saw that every step she'd taken that day, and the day before, all they way back to the moment she'd walked into her own home and seen him coming down the stairs toward her, had been leading to this moment of blind grief and loss.

She'd been powerless to stop it, she thought, to change what she was, what had come before or what would come after. It was only fools who believed they controlled their own destiny as she'd once believed she controlled hers.

And she'd been a fool to indulge in those pathetic fantasies, dreams where they had belonged together, where they'd made a life together, a home and children together. Where she'd believed she was only waiting for him to finally make all those longings that had always, always, been one handspan out of her reach, come true.

The mythical power of the stones, she thought with a half laugh. Love, knowledge and generosity. Their magic had been cruel to her, giving her that tantalizing glimpse of her every desire, then wrenching it away again and leaving her alone.

The knock on the door had her closing her eyes. How dare he come back, she thought. How dare he, after he'd smashed all her dreams, her hopes, her needs. And how dare she still love him in spite of it.

Well, he wouldn't see her cry, she promised herself, and straightened to scrub her hands over her damp cheeks. He wouldn't see her crawl. He wouldn't see her at all, because she wouldn't let him in.

Resolutely she headed for the phone. He wouldn't be pleased when she called 911 and reported an intruder, she mused. But it would make her point. She picked up the receiver just as the sound of shattering glass had her whirling toward her terrace doors.

She had time to see the man burst through them, time to hear her alarm scream in warning. She even had time to struggle as thick arms grabbed her. Then the cloth was over her face, smelling sickeningly of chloroform.

And she had time only to think of Seth before her world spun and went black.

* * *

Seth was barely three miles away when the next call came through. He jerked up his phone, snarled into it. "Buchanan."

"Lieutenant, Detective Marshall again. I just heard an automatic come through on dispatch. Suspected break-in, 2918 East Lark Lane, Potomac."

"What?" For one stunning moment, his mind went blank. "Grace?"

"I recognized the address from the homicide. Her alarm system's been triggered, she didn't answer the check-in call."

"I'm five minutes from there." He was already swinging around in a fast, tire-squealing turn. "Get the two closest black-and-whites on the scene. Now."

"I'm already on it. Lieutenant—"

But Seth had already tossed the phone aside.

It was a new system, Seth told himself, fighting for calm and logic. New systems often had glitches.

She was upset, not answering her phone, ignoring the confusion. It would be just like her. She was even now defiantly pouring herself another glass of champagne, cursing him.

Maybe she'd even set off the alarm herself, just so he'd come streaking back with his stomach encased in ice and his heart paralyzed. It would be just like her.

And that was one more lie, he thought as he careened around a corner. It was nothing like her at all.

The candles were still burning in her windows. He tried to be relieved by that as he stood on the brakes in her driveway and bolted out of his car. Dinner would still be warm, the music would still be playing, and Grace would be there, standing under her portrait, furious with him.

He beat on the door foolishly, wildly, before he snapped himself back. She wouldn't answer. She was too angry to answer. When the first patrol car pulled up, he turned, flashed his badge.

"Check the east side," he ordered. "I'll take the west."

He turned on his heel, started around the side. He caught the glimmer of the blue water in her pool in the moonlight, and the thought slid in and out of his mind that they'd never used it together, never slipped into that cool water naked.

Then he saw the broken glass. His heart simply stopped. His weapon was in his hand and he was through the shattered door, with no thought to procedure. Someone was shouting her name, racing from room to room in blind panic. It couldn't be him, yet he found himself on the stairs, short of breath, ice cold, dizzy with fear and watching a uniformed cop bend to pick up a scrap of cloth.

"Smells like chloroform, Lieutenant." The officer hesitated, took a step toward the man clinging to the banister. "Lieutenant?"

He couldn't speak. His voice was gone, and every sweaty hour of training with it. Seth's dulled gaze shifted, focused on the face, the portrait. Slowly, and with great effort, he widened his vision again, pulled on the mask of control.

"Search the house. Every inch of it." His eyes locked on the second uniform. "Call in for backup. Now. Then make a sweep of the grounds. Move."

Grace came to slowly, with a roll of nausea and a blinding headache. A nightmare, still black at the edges, circled dully, like a vulture patiently waiting to drop. She squeezed her eyes tighter, rolled her head on the pillow, then cautiously opened them.

Where? The thought was dull, foolish. Not my room, she realized, and struggled to fight off the clinging mists that clouded her brain.

It was satin beneath her cheek. She knew the cool, slippery feel of satin against the skin. White satin, like a bride's dress. Baffled, she skimmed her hand over the thick, luxurious spread of the huge canopied bed.

She could smell jasmine, and roses, and vanilla. All white scents, cool white scents. The walls of the room were ivory and had a sheen like silk. For a moment, she thought she was in a coffin, a huge, elaborate coffin, and her heart beat thick and fast.

She made herself sit up, almost afraid that her head would hit the lid and she would find herself screaming and clawing for freedom as she smothered. But there was nothing, only that fragrant air, and she took a long, unsteady breath of it.

She remembered now—the crash of glass, the big man in black with thick arms. She wanted to panic and forced herself to take another of those jerky breaths. Carefully, hampered by her spinning head, she slid her legs over the edge of the bed until her feet sank into thick, virginal white carpet. She swayed, nearly retched, then forced her feet over that sea of white to the door.

She went slippery with panic when the knob resisted her. Her breath came in ragged gulps as she fought and tugged on the knob of faceted crystal. Then she turned her back, leaned against it and made herself survey what she understood now was her prison.

White on white on white, blinding to the eye. A dainty Queen Anne chair brocaded in white, filmy lace curtains hung like ghosts, heaps of white pillows on a curved white chaise. There were edges of gold that only enhanced the avalanche of white, elegant furniture in pale wood smothered in that snowfall.

She went to the windows first, shuddered when she found them barred, the slices of night beyond them silvered by the moon. She saw nothing familiar—a long roll of lawn, meticulously planted flowers and shrubs, tall, shielding trees.

Wheeling, she saw another door, bolted for it, nearly wept when the knob turned easily. But beyond was a lustrous bath, white-tiled, the frosted-glass windows barred, the angled skylight a soaring ten feet above the floor.

And on the long gleaming counter were jars, bottles, creams, powders. All her own preferences, her scents, her lotions. Her stomach knotted greasily.

Ransom, she told herself. It was a kidnapping, someone who believed her family could be forced to pay for her safe return.

But she knew that was a lie.

The Stars. She leaned weakly against the jamb, pressed her lips together to keep the whimper silent. She'd been taken because of the Three Stars. They would be her ransom.

Her knees trembled as she turned away, ordered herself to calm down, to think clearly. There had to be a way out. There always was.

Her alarm had gone off, she remembered. Seth couldn't have been far away. Would he have gotten the report, come back? It didn't matter. He would have gotten it soon enough. Whatever had happened between them, he would do everything in his power to find her. From duty, if nothing else.

In the meantime, she was on her own. But that didn't mean she was defenseless.

She took two stumbling steps back when the lock on her door clicked, then forced herself to stop, straighten. The door opened, and two men stepped inside. One she recognized quickly enough as her abductor. The other was smaller, wiry, dressed in formal black, with a face as giving as rock.

"Ms. Fontaine," he said in a voice both British and cultured. "If you'd come with me, please."

A butler, she realized, and had to swallow a bubble of hysteria. She knew the type too well, and she assumed an amused and annoyed expression. "Why?"

"He's ready to see you now."

When she made no move to obey, the bigger man stepped in, towering over her, then jerked a thumb toward the doorway.

"Charming," she said dryly. She took a step forward, calculating how quickly she would have to move. The butler inclined his head impassively.

"You're on the third floor," he told her. "Even if you could somehow reach the main level on your own, there are guards. They are under order not to harm you, unless it's unavoidable. If you'll pardon me, I would advise against risking it."

She would risk it, she thought, and a great deal more. But not until she had at least an even chance of success. Without so much as a flick of a glance at the man beside her, she followed the butler out of the room and down a gently lit corridor.

The house was old, she calculated, but beautifully restored. At least three stories, so it was large. A glimpse at her watch told her it had been less than two hours since she was drugged. Time enough to drive some distance, she imagined.

But the view through the bars hadn't been countryside. She'd seen lights—city lights, houses through the trees. A neighborhood, she decided. Exclusive, wealthy, but a neighborhood.

Where there were houses, there were people. And where there were people, there was help.

She was led down a wide, curving staircase of gleaming oak. And saw the guard at the landing, his gun holstered but visible.

Down another hallway. Antiques, paintings, artwork. Her eye was expert enough to recognize the Monet on the wall, the porcelain vase from the Han dynasty on a pedestal, the Nok terra-cotta head from Nigeria.

Her host, she thought, had excellent and eclectic taste. The treasures she saw, small and large, spanned continents and centuries.

A collector, she realized with a chill. Now he had her, and was hoping to trade her for the Three Stars of Mithra.

With what Grace considered absurd formality, under the circumstances, the butler approached tall double doors, opened them, and with seamless expertise bowed slightly from the waist.

"Miss Grace Fontaine."

Seeing no immediate alternative, she stepped through the open doors into an enormous dining room with a frescoed ceiling and a dazzling trio of chandeliers. She scanned the long mahogany table, the Georgian candelabra gaily lit and spaced at precise intervals down its length, and focused on the man who rose and smiled charmingly.

Her worlds overlapped—reality and fear. "Gregor."

"Grace." Elegant in his tux, diamonds winking, he crossed to her, took her numb hand in his. "How delightful to see you." He tucked her arm through his, patted it affectionately. "I don't believe you've dined."

He knew where she was. Seth had no doubt of it, but his first fiery urge to rush to the elegant estate in D.C. and tear it apart single-handedly had to be suppressed.

He could get her killed.

He was certain Ambassador Gregor DeVane had killed before.

The call that interrupted his scene with Grace had been confirmation of yet another woman who had once been linked to the ambassador, a beautiful German scientist who had been found murdered in her home in Berlin, the apparent victim of a bungled burglary.

The dead woman had been an anthropologist who had a keen interest in Mithraism. For six months during the previous year, she had been romantically linked with Gregor DeVane. Then she was dead, and none of her research notes on the Three Stars of Mithra had been recovered.

He knew DeVane was responsible, just as he knew DeVane had Grace. But he couldn't prove it, and he didn't have probable cause to sway any judge to issue a search warrant into the home of a foreign ambassador.

Once more he stood in Grace's living room. Once more he stared up at her portrait and imagined her dead. But this time, he wasn't thinking like a cop.

He turned as Mick Marshall stepped beside him. "We won't find anything here to link him. In twelve hours, the diamonds will be turned over to the museum. He's going to use her to see that doesn't happen. I'm going to stop him."

Mick looked up at the portrait. "What do you need?"

"No. No cops."

"Lieutenant…Seth, if you're right, and he's got her, you're not going to get her out alone. You need to put together a team. You need a hostage negotiator."

"There's no time. We both know that." His eyes weren't flat and cool now, weren't cop's eyes. They were full of storms and passions. "He'll kill her."

His heart was coated with a sheet of ice, but it beat with fiery heat inside the casing. "She's smart. She'll play whatever game she needs to in order to stay alive, but if she makes the wrong move he'll kill her. I don't need a psychiatric profile to see into his head. He's a sociopath with a god complex and an obsession. He wants those diamonds and what he believes they represent. Right now he wants Grace, but if she doesn't serve his purpose, she'll end up like the others. That's not going to happen, Mick."

He reached into his pocket, took out his badge and held it out. This time he wouldn't go by the book, couldn't afford to play by the rules. "You take this for me, hang on to it. I may want it back."

"You're going to need help," Mick insisted. "You're going to need men."

"No cops," Seth repeated, and pushed his badge into Mick's reluctant hand. "Not this time."

"You can't go in solo. It's suicide, professional and literal."

Seth cast one last glance at the portrait. "I won't be alone."

* * *

She wouldn't tremble, Grace promised herself. She wouldn't show him how frightened she was. Instead, she brushed her hair from her shoulder with a careless hand.

"Do you always have your dinner companions abducted from their homes and drugged, Ambassador?"

"You must forgive the clumsiness." Considerately he drew out a chair for her. "It was necessary to be quick. I trust you're suffering no ill effects."

"Other than great annoyance, no." She sat, skimmed her gaze over the dish of marinated mushrooms a silent servant placed before her. They reminded her, painfully, of the noise-filled cookout at Cade's. "And a loss of appetite."

"Oh, you must at least sample the food." He sat at the head of the table, picked up his fork. It was gold and heavy and had once slipped between the lips of an emperor. "I've gone to considerable trouble to have your favorites prepared." His smile remained genial, but his eyes went cold. "Eat, Grace. I detest waste."

"Since you've gone to such lengths." She forced down a bite, ordered her hand not to shake, her stomach not to revolt.

"I hope your room is comfortable. I had to have it prepared for you rather quickly. You'll find appropriate clothing in the armoire and bureau. You've only to ask if there's something else you wish."

"I prefer windows without bars, and doors without locks."

"Temporary precautions, I promise you. Once you're at home here…" His hand covered hers, the grip tightening cruelly when she attempted to pull away. "…and I do very much want you to be at home here, such measures won't be necessary."

She didn't wince as the bones in her hand ground together. When she stopped the resistance, his fingers relaxed, stroked once, then slid away.

"And just how long do you intend to keep me here?"

He smiled, picked up her wineglass, held it out to her. "Eternity. You and I, Grace, are destined to share eternity."

Under the table, her aching hand shook and went clammy. "That's quite some time." She started to set her wine down, untouched, then caught the hard glint in his eye and sipped. "I'm flattered, but confused."

"It's pointless to pretend you don't understand. You held the Star in your hand. You survived death, and you came to me. I've seen your face in my dreams."

"Yes." She could feel her blood drain slowly, as if leeched out of her veins. Looking into his eyes she remembered the nightmares—the shadow in the woods. Watching. "I've seen you in mine."

"You'll bring me the Stars, Grace, and the power. I understand why I failed now. Every step was simply another on the path that brought us here. Together we'll possess the Stars. And I will possess you. Don't worry," he said when she flinched. "You'll come to me a willing bride. But my patience has limits. Beauty is my weakness," he continued, and skimmed a fingertip down her bare arm, toyed idly with the thick silver bracelet she wore. "And perfection my greatest delight. You, my dear, have both. Understand, you'll have no choice should my patience run out. My household staff is…well trained."

Fear was a bright, icy flash, but her voice was steady with disgust. "And would turn a deaf ear and blind eye to rape?"

"I don't enjoy that word during dinner." He gave a sulky little shrug and signaled for the next course. "A woman of your appetites will grow hungry soon enough. And one of your intelligence will undoubtedly see the wisdom of an amiable partnership."

"It's not sex you want, Gregor." She couldn't bear to look down at the tender pink salmon on her plate. "It's subjugation. I'm so poor at subjugation."

"You misunderstand me." He forked up fish and ate with enjoyment. "I intend to make you a goddess, and subject to no one. And I will have everything. No mortal man will come between us." He smiled again. "Certainly not Lieutenant Buchanan. The man is becoming a nuisance. He's probing into my affairs, where he has no business probing. I've seen him…"

DeVane's voice trailed off to a whisper, and there was a hint of fear in it. "In the night. In my dreams. He comes back. He always comes back. No matter how often I kill him." Then his eyes cleared, and he sipped wine the color of melted gold. "Now he's stirring up old business and looking for new."

She could feel the alarming beat of her pulse in her throat, at her wrists, in her temples. "He'll be looking for me, very soon now."

"Possibly. I'll deal with him, when and if the time comes. That could have been tonight, had he not left you so abruptly. Oh, I have considered just what will be done about the lieutenant. But I prefer to wait until I have the Stars. It's possible…" Thoughtfully DeVane picked up his napkin, dabbed at his lips. "I may spare him once I have what belongs to me. If you wish it. I can be magnanimous…under the right circumstances."

Her heart was in her throat now, filling it, blocking it. "If I do what you want, you'll leave him alone?"

"It's possible. We'll discuss it. But I'm afraid I developed an immediate dislike for the man. And I am still annoyed with you, dear Grace, for rejecting my own invitation for such an ordinary man."

She didn't hesitate, couldn't afford to, while her mind whirled with fear for Seth. She made her lips curve silkily. "Gregor, surely you forgive me for that. I was so…crushed when you didn't press your case. A woman, after all, enjoys a more determined pursuit."

"I don't pursue. I take."

"Obviously." She pouted. "It was horrid of you to have manhandled me that way, and frightened me half to death. I may not forgive you for it."

"Be careful how deep you play the game." His voice was low with warning and, she thought, with interest. "I'm not green."

"No." She skimmed a hand over his cheek before she rose. "But maturity has so many advantages."

Her legs were watery, but she roamed the cavernous room, her gaze traveling quickly toward windows, exits. Escape. "You have such a beautiful home. So many treasures." She angled her head, hoped the challenge she issued was worth the risk. "I do love…things. But I warn you, Gregor, I won't be any man's pretty toy."

She walked to him slowly, skimming a fingertip down her throat, between her breasts, while the silk she wore whispered around her. "And when I'm backed into a corner…I scratch."

Seductively she laid a hand on the table, leaned toward him. "You want me?" she breathed it, purred it, watching his eyes darken, sliding her fingers toward the knife beside his plate. "To touch me? To have me?" Her fingers closed over the handle, gripped hard.

"Not in a hundred lifetimes," she said as she struck.

She was fast, and she was desperate. But he'd shifted to draw her to him, and the knife struck his shoulder instead of his heart. As he cried out in shock and rage, she whirled. Grabbing one of the heavy chairs, she smashed the long window and sent glass raining out. But when she leaped forward, strong arms grabbed her from behind.

She fought viciously, her breath panting out. The fragile silk she wore ripped. Then she froze when the knife she had used was pressed against her throat. She didn't bother to struggle against the arms that held her as DeVane leaned his face close to hers. His eyes were mad with fury.

"I could kill you for that. But it would be too little and too quick. I would have made you my equal. I would have shared that with you. Now I'll just take what I choose from you. Until I tire of you."

"You'll never get the Stars," she said steadily. "And you'll never get Seth."

"I'll have exactly what I choose. And you'll help me."

She started to shake her head, flinched as the blade nicked. "I'll do nothing to help you."

"But you will. If you don't do exactly as I tell you, I will pick up the phone. With one single word from me, Bailey James and M. J. O'Leary will die tonight. It will only take a word."

He saw the wild fear come into her eyes, the helpless terror that hadn't been there for her own life. "I have men waiting for that word. If I give it, there will be a terrible and tragic explosion in the night at Cade Parris's home. Another at a small neighborhood pub, just before closing. And as one last twist, a third explosion will destroy the home, and the single occupant, of a certain Lieutenant Buchanan's residence. Their fate is in your hands, Grace. And the choice is yours."

She wanted to call his bluff, but, staring into his eyes, she understood that he wouldn't hesitate to do as he threatened. No, he longed to do it. Their lives meant nothing to him. And everything to her.

"What do you want me to do?"

Bailey was fighting against panic when the phone rang. She stared at it as if it were a snake that had rattled into life. With a silent prayer, she lifted the receiver. "Hello?"

"Bailey."

"Grace." Her fingers went white-knuckled as she whirled. Seth shook his head, held up a hand in caution. "Are you all right?"

"For the moment. Listen very carefully, Bailey, my life depends on it. Do you understand?"

"No. Yes." Stall, she knew she'd been ordered to stall. "Grace, I'm so frightened for you. What happened? Where are you?"

"I can't go into that now. You have to be calm, Bailey. You have to be strong. You were always the calm one. Like when we took that art history exam in college and I was so intimidated by Professor Greenbalm, and you were so cool. You have to be cool now, Bailey, and you have to follow my instructions."

"I will. I'll try." She looked helplessly at Seth as he signaled her to stretch it out. "Just tell me if you're hurt."

"Not yet. But he will hurt me. He'll kill me, Bailey, if you don't do what he wants. Get him what he wants. I know I'm asking a great deal. He wants the stones. You have to go get them. You can't take Cade. You can't call…the police."

String it out, Bailey reminded herself. Keep Grace talking. "You don't want me to call Seth?"

"No. He isn't important. He's just another cop. You know he doesn't matter. You're to wait until 1:30 exactly, then you're to leave the house. Go to Salvini, Bailey. You've got to go to Salvini. Leave M.J. out of it, just like we used to. Understand?"

Bailey nodded, kept her eyes on Seth's. "Yes, I understand."

"Once you get to Salvini, put the stones in a briefcase. Wait there. You'll get a call with the next set of instructions. You'll be all right. You know how you used to like to sneak out of the dorm at night and go out driving alone after curfew? Just think of it that way. Exactly that way, Bailey, and you'll be fine. If you don't, he'll take everything away from me. Do you understand?"

"Yes. Grace—"

"I love you," she managed before the phone went dead.

"Nothing," Cade said tightly as he stared down at the tracing equipment. "He's got it jammed. The signal's all over the board. It wouldn't home in."

"She wants me to go to Salvini," Bailey said quietly.

"You're not going anywhere," Cade said, interrupting her, but Bailey laid a hand on his arm, looked toward M.J.

"No, she meant that part. You understood?"

"Yeah." M.J. pressed her fingers to her eyes, tried to think past the terror. "She was pumping in as much as she could. Bailey and Grace never left me out of anything, so she wanted me along. She wants us out of here, but she was stringing him about the stones. Bailey never jumped curfew."

"She was giving you signals," Jack said. "Trying to punch in what she could manage."

"She knew we'd understand. He must have told her something would happen to us if she didn't cooperate." Bailey reached out for M.J.'s hand. "She wanted us to contact Seth. That's why she said you didn't matter— because we know you do."

Seth dragged a hand through his hair—a rare wasted motion. He had no choice but to trust their instincts. No choice but to trust Grace's sense of survival. "All right. She wants me to know what's happening, and wants you out of the house."

"Yes. She wants us out of the house, thinks we'll be safer at Salvini."

"You'll be safer at the precinct," Seth told her. "And that's where both of you are going."

"No." Bailey's voice remained calm. "She wants us at Salvini. She made a point of it."

Seth studied her, and gauged his options. He could have them taken into protective custody. That was the logical step. Or he could let the game play out. That was a risk. But it was the risk that fit.

"Salvini, then. But Detective Marshall will arrange for guards. You'll stay put until you hear differently."

M.J. bristled. "You expect us to just sit around and wait while Grace is in trouble?"

"That's exactly what you're going to do," Seth said coolly. "She's risking her life to see that you're safe. I'm not going to disappoint her."

"He's right, M.J." Jack lifted a brow as she snarled at him. "Go ahead and fume. But you're outnumbered here. You and Bailey follow instructions."

Seth noted with some surprise that M.J. closed her mouth, gave one brisk nod in assent. "What was the business about the art history exam, Bailey?"

Bailey sucked in air. "Professor Greenbalm's first name was Gregory."

"Gregory." *Gregor.* "Close enough." Seth looked at the two men he needed. "We don't have a lot of time."

Chapter 12

Grace doubted very much that she would live through the night. There were so many things she hadn't done. She had never shown Bailey and M.J. Paris, as they had always planned. She would never see the willow she'd planted on her country hillside grow tall and bend gracefully over her tiny pond. She had never had a child.

The unfairness clawed at her, along with the fear. She was only twenty-six years old, and she was going to die.

She'd seen her sentence in DeVane's eyes. And she knew he intended to kill those she loved, as well. He wouldn't be satisfied with anything less than erasing all the lives that had touched what his obsessed mind considered his.

All she could hang on to now was the hope that Bailey had understood her.

"I'm going to show you what you could have had." His

arm bandaged, a fresh tuxedo covering the damage, DeVane led her through a concealed panel, and down a well-lit set of stone stairs that were polished like ebony. He'd taken a painkiller. His eyes were glassy with it, and vicious.

They were the eyes that had stared out of the woods in her nightmares. And as he walked down the curve of those glossy black stairs, she felt the tug of some deep memory.

By torchlight then, she thought hazily. Down and down, with the torches flickering and the Stars glittering in their home of gold, on a white stone. And death waiting.

The harsh breathing of the man beside her. DeVane's? Someone else's? It was a hot, secret sound that chilled the skin. A room, she thought, struggling to grip the slippery chain of memories. A secret room of white and gold. And she had been locked in it for eternity.

She stopped at the last curve, not so much in fear as in shock. Not here, she thought frantically, but somewhere else. Not her, but part of her. Not him, but someone like him.

DeVane's fingers dug into her arm, but she barely felt the pain. Seth—the man with Seth's eyes, dressed as a warrior, coated with dust and the dents of battle. He'd come for her, and for the Stars.

And died for it.

"No." The stairway spun, and she gripped the cool wall for balance. "Not again. Not this time."

"There's little choice." DeVane jerked her forward, pulled her down the remaining steps. He stopped at a thick door, gestured impatiently for his guard to step back. Holding Grace's arm in a bruising grip, he drew out a heavy key, fit it in an old lock that for reasons Grace couldn't fathom made her think of Alice's rabbit hole.

"I want you to see what could have been yours. What I would have shared with you."

At his rough shove, she stumbled inside and stood blinking in shock.

No, not the rabbit hole, she realized, her dazzled eyes wide and stunned. Ali Baba's cave. Gold gleamed in mountains, jewels winked in rivers. Paintings she recognized as works of the masters crowded together on the walls. Statues and sculpture, some as small as the Fabergé eggs perched on gold stands, others soaring to the ceiling, were jammed inside.

Furs and sweeps of silk, ropes of pearls, carvings and crowns, were jammed into every available space. Mozart played brilliantly on hidden speakers.

It was, she realized, not a fairy-tale cave at all. It was merely a spoiled boy's elaborate and greedy clubhouse. Here he could hide his possessions from the world, keep them all to himself and chortle over them, she imagined.

And how many of these toys had he stolen? she wondered. How many had he killed for?

She wouldn't die here, she promised herself. And neither would Seth. If this was indeed history overlapping, she wouldn't allow it to repeat itself. She would fight with whatever weapons she had.

"You have quite a collection, Gregor, but your presentation could use some work." The first weapon was mild disdain, laced with amusement. "Even the precious loses impact when crammed together in such a disorganized manner."

"It's mine. All of it. A lifetime's work. Here." Like that spoiled boy, he snatched up a goblet of gold, thrust it out to her for admiration. "Queen Guinevere sipped from this before she cuckolded Arthur. He should have cut out her heart for that."

Grace turned the cup in her hand and felt nothing. It was empty not only of wine, she mused, but of magic.

"And here." He grabbed a pair of ornate diamond earrings, thrust them into Grace's face. "Another queen— Marie Antoinette—wore these while her country plotted her death. You might have worn them."

"While you plotted mine." With deliberate scorn, she dismissed the offering and turned away. "No, thank you."

"I have an arrow the goddess Diana hunted with. The girdle worn by Juno."

Her heart thrummed like a harp, but she only chuckled. "Do you really believe that?"

"They're mine." Furious with her reaction, he pushed his way through his collection, laid a hand over the cold marble slab he'd had built. "I'll have the Stars soon. They will be the apex of my collection. I'll set them here, with my own hands. And I'll have everything."

"They won't help you. They won't change you." She didn't know where the words came from, or the knowledge behind them, but she saw his eyes flicker in surprise. "Your fate's already sealed. They'll never be yours. It's not meant, not this time. They're for the light, and for the good. You'll never see them here in the dark."

His stomach jittered. There was power in her words, in her eyes, when she should have been cowed and frightened. It unnerved him. "By sunrise I'll have them here. I'll show them to you." His breath was short and shallow as he approached her. "And I'll have you. I'll keep you as long as I wish. Do with you what I wish."

The hand against her cheek was cold, made her think

wildly of a snake, but she didn't cringe away. "You'll never have the Stars, and you'll never have me. Even if you hold us, you'll never have us. That was true before, but it's only more true now. And that will eat away at you, day after day, until there's nothing left of you but madness."

He struck her, hard enough to knock her back against the wall, to have pain spinning in her head. "Your friends will die tonight." He smiled at her, as if he were discussing a small mutual interest. "You've already sent them to oblivion. I'm going to let you live a long time knowing that."

He took her by the arm and, pulling open the door, dragged her from the room.

"He'll have surveillance cameras," Seth said as they prepared to scale the wall at the rear of DeVane's D.C. estate. "He's bound to have guards patrolling the grounds."

"So we'll be careful." Jack checked the point of his knife, stuck it in his boot, then examined the pistol he'd tucked in his belt. "And we'll be quiet."

"We stick together until we reach the house." Cade went over the plan in his head. "I find security, disarm it."

"Failing that, set the whole damn business off. We could get lucky in the confusion. It'll bring the cops. If things don't go well, you could be dealing with a lot more than a bust for a B-and-E."

Jack issued a pithy one-word opinion on that. "Let's go get her out." He shot Seth one quick grin as he boosted himself up. "Man, I hope he doesn't have dogs. I really hate when they have dogs."

They landed on the soft grass on the other side. It was

possible their presence was detected from that moment. It was a risk they were willing to take. Like shadows, they moved through the starstruck night, slipping through the heavy dark amid the sheltering trees.

Before, on his quest for the Stars and the woman, he'd come alone, and perhaps that arrogance had been his defeat. Baffled by the sudden thought, the quick spurt of what some might have called vision, Seth pushed the feeling aside.

He could see the house through the trees, the glimmer of lights in windows. Which room was she in? How badly was she frightened? Was she hurt? Had he touched her?

Baring his teeth, he bit off the thoughts. He had to focus only on getting inside, finding her. For the first time in years, he felt the weight of his weapon at his side. Knew he intended to use it.

He gave no thought to rules, to his career, to the life he'd built step by deliberate step.

He saw the guard pass by, only a yard beyond the verge of the grove. When Jack tapped his shoulder and signaled, Seth met his eyes, nodded.

Seconds later, Jack sprang at the man from behind, and with a quick twist, rammed his head into the trunk of an oak and then dragged the unconscious body into the shadows.

"One down," he breathed and tucked his newly acquired weapon away.

"They'll have regular check-in," Cade murmured. "We can't know how soon they'll miss his contact."

"Then let's move." Seth signaled Jack to the north, Cade to the south. Staying low, they rushed those gleaming lights.

* * *

The guard who escorted Grace back to her room was silent. At least two hundred and fifty pounds of muscle, she calculated. But she'd seen his eyes flicker down over her bodice, scan the ripped silk that exposed flesh at her side.

She knew how to use her looks as a weapon. Deliberately she tipped her face up to his, let her eyes fill helplessly. "I'm so frightened. So alone." She risked touching a hand to his arm. "You won't hurt me, will you? Please don't hurt me. I'll do anything you want."

He said nothing, but his eyes were keen on her face when she moistened her lips with the tip of her tongue, keeping the movement slow and provocative. "Anything," she repeated, her voice husky, intimate. "You're so strong, so…in charge." Did he even speak English? she wondered. What did it matter? The communication was clear enough.

At the door to her prison, she turned, flashed a smoldering look, sighed deeply. "Don't leave me alone," she murmured. "I'm so afraid of being alone. I need… someone." Taking a chance, she lifted a fingertip, rubbed it over his lips. "He doesn't have to know," she whispered. "No one has to know. It's our secret."

Though it revolted her, she took his hand, placed it on her breast. The flex of his fingers chilled her skin, but she made herself smile invitingly as he lowered his head and crushed her mouth.

Don't think of it, don't think, she warned herself as his hands roamed her. It's not you. He's not touching you.

"Inside." She hoped he interpreted her quick shudder as desire. "Come inside with me. We'll be alone."

He opened the door, his eyes still hungry on her face,

on her body. She would either win here, she thought, or lose everything. She let out a teasing laugh as he grabbed for her the moment the door was locked behind him.

"Oh, there's no hurry now, handsome." She tossed her hair back, glided out of his reach. "No need to rush such a lovely friendship. I want to freshen up for you."

Still he said nothing, but his eyes were narrowing with impatience, suspicion. Still smiling, she reached for the heavy cut-crystal atomizer on the bureau. A woman's weapon, she thought coldly as she gently spritzed her skin, the air. "I prefer using all of my senses." Her fingers tightened convulsively on the bottle as she swayed toward him.

She jerked the bottle up and sprayed perfume directly into his leering eyes. He hissed in shock, grabbed instinctively for his stinging eyes. Putting all her strength behind it, she smashed the crystal into his face, and her knee into his groin.

He staggered, but didn't go down. There was blood on his face, and beneath it, his skin had gone a pasty shade of white. He was fumbling for his gun and, frantic, she kicked out, aiming low again. This time he went to his knees, but his hands were still reaching for the gun snapped to his side.

Sobbing now, she heaved up a footstool, upholstered in white, tasseled in gold. She rammed it into his already bleeding face, then, lifting it high, crashed it onto his head. Desperately she scrabbled to unstrap his gun, her clammy hands slipping off leather and steel. When she held it in two shaking hands, prepared to do whatever was necessary, she saw that he was unconscious.

Her breath tore out of her lungs in a wild laugh. "I guess

I'm just not that kind of girl." Too frightened for caution, she yanked the keys free of his clip, stabbed one after the other at the lock until it gave. And raced like a deer fleeing wolves, down the corridor, through the golden light.

A shadow moved at the head of the stairs, and with a low, keening moan, she lifted the gun.

"That's the second time you've pointed a weapon in my direction."

Her vision grayed at the sound of Seth's voice. Clamping down hard on her lip, she cleared it as he stepped out of the shadows and into the light. "You. You came."

It wasn't armor he wore, she thought dizzily. But black—shirt, slacks, shoes. It wasn't a sword he carried, but a gun.

It wasn't a memory. It was real.

Her dress was torn, bloody. Her face was bruised, her eyes were glassy with shock. He'd killed two men to get this far. And seeing her this way, he thought it hadn't been enough. Not nearly enough.

"It's all right now." He resisted the urge to rush to her, grab her close. She looked as though she might shatter at a touch. "We're going to get you out. No one's going to hurt you."

"He's going to kill them." She forced air in and out of her lungs. "He's going to kill them no matter what I do. He's insane. They're not safe from him. We're none of us safe from him. He killed you before," she ended on a whisper. "He'll try again."

He took her arm to steady her, gently slipped the gun from her hand. "Where is he, Grace?"

"There's a room, through a panel in the library, down

the stairs. Just like before...lifetimes ago. Do you remember?" Spinning between images, she pressed a hand to her head. "He's there with his toys, all the glittering toys. I stabbed him with a dinner knife."

"Good girl." How much of the blood was hers? He could detect no wound other than the bruises on her face and arms. "Come on now, come with me."

He led her down the stairs. There was the guard she'd seen before. But he wasn't standing now. Averting her eyes, she stepped around him, gestured. She was steadier now. The past didn't always run in a loop, she knew. Sometimes it changed. People made it change.

"It's back there, the third door down on the left." She cringed when she caught a movement. But it was Jack, melting out of a doorway.

"It's clear," he said to Seth.

"Take her out." His eyes said everything as he nudged her into Jack's arms. *Take care of her. I'm trusting you.*

Jack hitched her against his side to keep his weapon hand free. "You're okay, honey."

"No." She shook her head. "He's going to kill them. He has explosives, something, at the house, at the pub. You have to stop him. The panel. I'll show you."

She wrenched away from Jack, staggered like a drunk toward the library. "Here." She turned a rosette in the carving of the chair rail. "I watched him." The panel slid smoothly open.

"Jack, get her out. Call in a 911. I'll deal with him."

She was floating, just under the surface of thick, warm water. "He'll have to kill him," she said faintly as Seth disappeared into the opening. "This time he can't fail."

"He knows what he has to do."

"Yes, he always does." And the room spun once, wildly. "Jack, I'm sorry," she managed before she spun with it.

He hadn't locked the door, Seth noted. Arrogant bastard, so sure no one would trespass on his sacred ground. With his weapon lifted, Seth eased the heavy door open, blinked once at the bright gleam of gold.

He stepped inside, focused on the man sitting in a thronelike chair in the center of all the glory. "It's done, DeVane."

DeVane wasn't surprised. He'd known the man would come. "You risk a great deal." His smile was cold as a snake's, his eyes mad as a hatter's. "You did before. You remember, don't you? Dreamed of it, didn't you? You came to steal from me before, to take the Stars and the woman. You had a sword then, heavy and unjeweled."

Something vague and quick passed through Seth's mind. A stone castle, a stormy sky, a room of great wealth. A woman beloved. On an altar, a triangle wrenched from the hands of the god, adorned with diamonds as blue as stars.

"I killed you." DeVane laughed softly. "Left your body for the crows."

"That was then." Seth stepped forward. "This is now."

DeVane's smile spread. "I am beyond you." He lifted his hand, and the gun he held in it.

Two shots were fired, so close together they sounded as one. The room shook, echoed, settled, and went back to gleaming. Slowly Seth stepped closer, looked down at the man who lay facedown on a hill of gold.

"Now you are," Seth murmured. "You're beyond me now."

She heard the shots. For one unspeakable moment everything inside her stopped. Heart, mind, breath, blood. Then it started again, a tidal wave of feeling that had her springing off the bench where Jack had put her, the air heaving in and out of her lungs.

And she knew, because she felt, because her heart could beat, that it hadn't been Seth who'd met the bullet. If he had died, she would have known. Some piece of her heart would have broken off from the whole and shattered.

Still, she waited, her eyes on the house, because she had to see.

The stars wheeled overhead, the moon shot light through the trees. Somewhere in the distance, a night bird began to call out, with hope and joy.

Then he walked out of the house. Whole. Tears clogged her throat and were swallowed. They stung her eyes and were willed away. She had to see him clearly, the man she had accepted that she loved, and couldn't have.

He walked to her, his eyes dark and cool, his gait steady.

He'd already regained control, she realized. Already tucked whatever he'd had to do away in some compartment where it wouldn't interfere with what had to be done next.

She wrapped her arms around herself, hands clamped tight on her forearms. She'd never know that one gesture, that turning into herself and not him, was what stopped him from reaching for her.

So he stood, with an armspan of distance between them and looked at the woman he accepted that he loved, and had pushed away.

She was pale, and even now he could see the quick trembles that ripped through her. But he wouldn't have said she was fragile. Even now, with death shimmering between them, she wasn't fragile.

Her voice was strong and steady. "It's over?"

"Yeah, it's over."

"He was going to kill them."

"That's over, too." His need to touch her, to hold on, was overwhelming. He felt that his knees were about to give way. But she turned, shifted her body away, and looked out into the dark.

"I need to see them. Bailey and M.J."

"I know."

"You need my statement."

God. His control wavered enough for him to press his fingers against burning eyes. "It can wait."

"Why? I want it over. I need to put it behind me." She steadied herself again, then turned slowly. And when she faced him, his hands were at his sides and his eyes clear. "I need to put it all behind me."

Her meaning was clear enough, Seth thought. He was part of that all.

"Grace, you're hurt and you're in shock. An ambulance is on the way."

"I don't need an ambulance."

"Don't tell me what the hell you need." Fury swarmed through him, buzzed in his head like a nest of mad hornets. "I said the damn statement can wait. You're shaking. For God's sake, sit down."

When he reached out to take her arm, she jerked back, her chin snapping up, her shoulders hunching. "Don't touch me. Just...don't." If he touched her, she might break. If she broke she would weep. And weeping, she would beg.

The words were a knife in the gut, the deep and desperate blue of her eyes a blow to the face. Because he felt his fingers tremble, he stuffed them into his pockets, took a step back. "All right. Sit down. Please."

Had he thought she wasn't fragile? She looked as if she would shatter into pieces with one hard thought. She was sheet pale, her eyes enormous. Blood and bruises marked her face.

And there was nothing he could do. Nothing she would let him do.

He heard the distant wail of sirens, and footsteps from behind him. Cade, his face grim, walked to Grace, tucked a blanket he'd brought from the house over her shoulders.

Seth watched as she turned into him, how her body seemed to go fluid and flow into the arms Cade offered her. He heard the fractured sob even as she muffled it against Cade's shoulder.

"Get her out of here." His fingers burned to reach out, stroke her hair, to take something away with him. "Get her the hell out of here."

He walked back into the house to do what needed to be done.

The birds sang their morning song as Grace stepped out into her garden. The woods were quiet and green. And safe. She'd needed to come here, to her country escape. To come alone. To be alone.

Bailey and M.J. had understood. In a few days, she thought, she would go into town, call, see if they'd like to come up, bring Jack and Cade. She would need to see them soon. But she couldn't bear to go back yet. Not yet.

She could still hear the shots, the quick jolt of them

shuddering through her as Jack had taken her outside. She'd known it was DeVane and not Seth who had met the bullet. She'd simply known.

She hadn't seen Seth again that night. It had been easy to avoid him in the confusion that followed. She'd answered all the questions the local police had asked, made statements to the government officials. She'd stood up to it, then quietly demanded that Cade or Jack take her to Salvini, take her to Bailey and M.J.

And the Three Stars.

Stepping down onto her blooming terraces, she brought it back into her head, and her heart. The three of them standing in the near dark of a near-empty room, she with her torn and bloody dress.

Each of them had taken a point of the triangle, had felt the sing of power, seen the flicker of impossible light. And had known it was done.

"It's as if we've done this before," Bailey had murmured. "But it wasn't enough then. It was lost, and so were we."

"It's enough now." M.J. had looked up, met each of their eyes in turn. "Like a cycle, complete. A chain, with the links forged. It's weird, but it's right."

"A museum instead of a temple this time." Regret and relief had mixed within Grace as they set the Stars down again. "A promise kept, and, I suppose, destinies fulfilled."

She'd turned to both of them, embraced them. Another triangle. "I've always loved you both, needed you both. Can we go somewhere? The three of us." The tears had come then, flooding. "I need to talk."

She'd told them everything, poured out heart and soul, hurt and terror, until she was empty. And she supposed, because it was them, she'd healed a little.

Now she would heal on her own.

She could do it here, Grace knew, and, closing her eyes, she just breathed. Then, because it always soothed, she set down her gardening basket, and began to tend her blooms.

She heard the car coming, the rumble of wheels on gravel, and her brow creased in mild irritation. Her neighbors were few and far between and rarely intruded. She wanted no company but her plants, and she stood, her flowers flowing at her feet, determined to politely and firmly send the visitor away again.

Her heart kicked once, hard, when she saw that the car was Seth's. She watched in silence as it stopped in the middle of her lane and he got out and started toward her.

She looked like something out of a misty legend herself, he thought. Her hair blowing in the breeze, the long, loose skirt of her dress fluttering, and flowers in a sea around her. His nerves jangled.

And his stomach clutched when he saw the bruise marring her cheek.

"You're a long way from home, Seth." She spoke without expression as he stopped two steps beneath her.

"You're a hard woman to find, Grace."

"That's the way I prefer it. I don't care for company here."

"Obviously." Both to give himself time to settle and because he was curious, he scanned the land, the house perched on the hill, the deep secrets of the woods. "It's a beautiful spot."

"Yes."

"Remote." His gaze shifted back to hers so quickly, so intensely, he nearly made her jolt. "Peaceful. You've earned some peace."

"That's why I'm here." She lifted a brow. "And why are you here?"

"I needed to talk to you. Grace—"

"I intended to see you when I came back," she said quickly. "We didn't talk much that night. I suppose I was more shaken up than I realized. I never even thanked you."

It was worse, he realized, that cool, polite voice was worse than a shouted curse. "You don't have anything to thank me for."

"You saved my life and, I believe, the lives of the people I love. I know you broke rules, even the law, to find me, to get me away from him. I'm grateful."

The palms of his hands went clammy. She was making him see it again, feel it again. All that rage and terror. "I'd have done anything to get you away from him."

"Yes, I think I know that." She had to look away. It hurt too much to look into his eyes. She'd promised herself, sworn to herself she wouldn't be hurt again. "And I wonder if any of us had a choice in what happened over that short, intense period of time. Or," she added with a ghost of a smile, "if you choose to believe what happened, over centuries. I hope you haven't—that your career won't suffer because of what you did for me."

His eyes went dark, flat. "The job's secure, Grace."

"I'm glad." He had to leave, she thought. He had to leave now, before she crumbled. "I still intend to write a letter to your superiors. And you might know I have an uncle in the Senate. I wouldn't be surprised, when the smoke clears, if you got a promotion out of it."

His throat was raw. He couldn't clear it. "Look at me, damn it." When her gaze shot back to his face, he curled his hands into fists to keep from touching her. "Do you think that matters?"

"Yes, I do. It matters, Seth, certainly to me. But for now, I'm taking a few days, so if you'll excuse me, I want to get to my gardening before the heat of the day."

"Do you think this ends it?"

She leaned over, took up her clippers and snipped off wilted blooms. They faded all too quickly, she thought. And that left an ache in the heart. "I think you already ended it."

"Don't turn away from me." He took her arm, hauled her toward him, as panic and fury spiraled through him. "You can't just turn away. I can't—" He broke off, his hand lifting to lie on the bruise on her cheek. "Oh, God, Grace. He hurt you."

"It's nothing." She stepped back quickly, nearly flinching, and his hand fell heavily to his side. "Bruises fade. And he's gone. You saw to that. He's gone, and it's over. The Three Stars are where they belong, and everything's back in its place. Everything's as it was meant to be."

"Is it?" He didn't step to her, couldn't bear to see her shrink back from him again. "I hurt you, and you won't forgive me for it."

"Not entirely," she agreed, fighting to keep it light. "But saving my life goes a long way to—"

"Stop it," he said in a voice both ragged and quiet. "Just stop it." Undone, he whirled away, pacing, nearly trampling her bedding plants. He hadn't known he could suffer like this—the ice in the belly, the heat in the brain.

He spoke, looking out into her woods, into shadows and cool green shade. "Do you know what it did to me, knowing he had you? Knowing it. Hearing your voice on the phone, the fear in it?"

"I don't want to think about it. I don't want to think about any of that."

"I can't do anything but think of it. And see you— every time I close my eyes, I see you the way you stood there in that hallway, blood on your dress, marks on your skin. Not knowing—not knowing what he'd done to you. And remembering—half remembering some other time when I couldn't stop him."

"It's over," she said again, because her legs were turning to water. "Leave it alone."

"You might have gotten away without me," he continued. "You took out a guard twice your size. You might have pulled it off without any help from me. You might not have needed me at all. And I realized that was part of my problem all along. Believing, being certain, I needed you so much more than you could possibly need me. Being afraid of that. Stupid to be afraid of that," he said as he came up the steps again. "Once you understand real fear, the fear of knowing you could lose the most important thing in your life in one single heartbeat, nothing else can touch you."

He gathered her to him, too desperate to heed her resistance. And, with a shuddering gulp of air, buried his face in her hair. "Don't push me away, don't send me away."

"This isn't any good." It hurt to be held by him, yet she wished she could go on being held just like this, with the sun warm on her skin and his face pressed into her hair.

"I need you. I need you," he repeated, and turned his urgent mouth to hers.

The hammer blow of emotion struck and she buckled. It swirled from one of them to the other in an unbridled storm, left her heart shaken and weak. She closed her eyes, slid her arms around him. Need would be enough, she promised herself. She would make it enough for both of them. There was too much inside her that she ached to give for her to turn him away.

"I won't send you away." Her hands stroked over his back, soothed the tension. "I'm glad you're here. I want you here." She drew back, brought his hand to her cheek. "Come inside, Seth. Come to bed."

His fingers tightened on hers. Then gently lifted her head up. It made him ache to realize she believed there was only that he wanted from her. That he'd let her think it.

"Grace, I didn't come here to take you to bed. I didn't come here to start where we left off."

Why had he been so resistant to seeing what was in her eyes? he wondered. Why had he refused to believe what was so blatantly real, so generously offered to him.

"I came here to beg. The third Star is generosity," he said, almost to himself. "You didn't make me beg. I didn't come here for sex, Grace. Or for gratitude."

Confused, she shook her head. "What do you want, Seth? Why did you come?"

He wasn't sure he'd fully realized why until just now. "To hear you tell me what you want. What you need."

"Peace." She gestured. "I have that here. Friendship. I have that, too."

"And that's it? That's enough?"

"It's been enough all my life."

He caught her face in his hands before she could step away. "If you could have more? What do you want, Grace?"

"Wanting what you can't have only makes you unhappy."

"Tell me." He kept his eyes focussed on hers. "Straight out, for once. Just say what you want."

"Family. Children. I want children and a man who loves me—who wants to make that family with me." Her lips curved slowly, but the smile didn't reach her eyes. "Surprised I'd want to spoil my figure? Spend a few years of my life changing diapers?"

"No." He slid his hands down to her shoulders, firming his grip. She was poised to move, he noted. To run. "No, I'm not surprised."

"Really? Well." She moved her shoulders as if to shrug off the weight of his touch. "If you're going to stay, let's go inside. I'm thirsty."

"Grace, I love you." He watched her smile slide away from her face, felt her body go absolutely still.

"What? What did you say to me?"

"I love you." Saying it, he realized, was power. True power. "I fell in love with you before I'd seen you. Fell in love with an image, a memory, a wish. I can't be sure which it is, or if it was all of them. I don't know if it was fate, or choice, or luck. But it was so fast, so hard, so deep, I wouldn't let myself believe, and I wouldn't let myself trust. And I turned you away because you let yourself do both. I came here to tell you that." His hands slid down her arms and clasped hers.

"Grace, I'm asking you to believe in us again, to trust in us again. And to marry me."

"You—" She had to take a step back, had to press a hand to her heart. "You want to marry me."

"I'm asking you to come back with me today. I know it's old-fashioned, but I want you to meet my family."

The pressure in her chest all but burst her heart. "You want me to meet your family."

"I want them to meet the woman I love, the woman I

want to have a life with. The life I've been waiting to start—waiting for her to start." He brought her hand to his cheek, held it there while his eyes looked deep into hers. "The woman I want to make children with."

"Oh." The weight on her chest released in a flood, poured out of her…until her heart was in her swimming eyes.

"Don't cry." It seemed he would beg after all. "Grace, please, don't. Don't tell me I left it too late." Awkwardly he brushed at her tears with his thumbs. "Don't tell me I ruined it."

"I love you so much." She closed her fingers around his wrists, watched the emotion leap into his eyes. "I've been so unhappy waiting for you. I was so sure I'd missed you. Again. Somehow."

"Not this time." He kept his hands on her face, kissed her gently. "Not ever again."

"No, not ever again," she murmured against his lips.

"Say yes," he asked her. "I want to hear you say yes."

"Yes. To everything."

She held him close in the flower-scented morning where the stars slept behind the sky. And felt the last link of an endless chain fall into place.

"Seth."

He kept his eyes shut, his cheek on her hair. And his smile bloomed slow and easy. "Grace."

"We're where we're supposed to be. Can you feel it?" She drew a deep breath. "All of us are where we belong now."

She lifted her face, found his mouth waiting. "And now," he said quietly, "it begins."

* * * * *

Treasures Lost,
Treasures Found

To Dixie Browning,
the true lady of the island.

Chapter 1

He had believed in it. Edwin J. Hardesty hadn't been the kind of man who had fantasies or followed dreams, but sometime during his quiet, literary life he had looked for a pot of gold. From the information in the reams of notes, the careful charts and the dog-eared research books, he thought he'd found it.

In the panelled study, a single light shot a beam across a durable oak desk. The light fell over a hand—narrow, slender, without the affectation of rings or polish. Yet even bare, it remained an essentially feminine hand, the kind that could be pictured holding a porcelain cup or waving a feather fan. It was a surprisingly elegant hand for a woman who didn't consider herself elegant, delicate or particularly feminine. Kathleen Hardesty was, as her father had been, and as he'd directed her to be, a dedicated educator.

Minds were her concern—the expanding and the fulfilling of them. This included her own as well as every one
of her students'. For as long as she could remember, her
father had impressed upon her the importance of education. He'd stressed the priority of it over every other aspect
of life. Education was the cohesiveness that held civilization together. She grew up surrounded by the dusty smell
of books and the quiet, placid tone of patient instruction.

She'd been expected to excel in school, and she had.
She'd been expected to follow her father's path into education. At twenty-eight, Kate was just finishing her first
year at Yale as an assistant professor of English literature.

In the dim light of the quiet study, she looked the part.
Her light brown hair was tidily secured at the nape of her
neck with all the pins neatly tucked in. Her practical tor-
toiseshell reading glasses seemed dark against her milk-
pale complexion. Her high cheekbones gave her face an
almost haughty look that was often dispelled by her warm,
doe-brown eyes.

Though her jacket was draped over the back of her
chair, the white blouse she wore was still crisp. Her cuffs
were turned back to reveal delicate wrists and a slim
Swiss watch on her left arm. Her earrings were tasteful
gold studs given to Kate by her father on her twenty-first
birthday, the only truly personal gift she could ever
remember receiving from him.

Seven long years later, one short week after her father's
funeral, Kate sat at his desk. The room still carried the
scent of his cologne and a hint of the pipe tobacco he'd
only smoked in that room.

She'd finally found the courage to go through his
papers.

She hadn't known he was ill. In his early sixties, Hardesty had looked robust and strong. He hadn't told his daughter about his visits to the doctor, his check-ups, ECG results or the little pills he carried with him everywhere. She'd found his pills in his inside pocket after his fatal heart attack. Kate hadn't known his heart was weak because Hardesty never shared his shortcomings with anyone. She hadn't known about the charts and research papers in his desk; he'd never shared his dreams either.

Now that she was aware of both, Kate wasn't certain she ever really knew the man who'd raised her. The memory of her mother was dim; that was to be expected after more than twenty years. Her father had been alive just a week before.

Leaning back for a moment, she pushed her glasses up and rubbed the bridge of her nose between her thumb and forefinger. She tried, with only the desk lamp between herself and the dark, to think of her father in precise terms.

Physically, he'd been a tall, big man with a full head of steel-gray hair and a patient face. He had favored dark suits and white shirts. The only vanity she could remember had been his weekly manicures. But it wasn't a physical picture Kate struggled with now. As a father…

He was never unkind. In all her memories, Kate couldn't remember her father ever raising his voice to her, ever striking her. He never had to, she thought with a sigh. All he had to do was express disappointment, disapproval, and that was enough.

He had been brilliant, tireless, dedicated. But all of that had been directed toward his vocation. As a father, Kate reflected… He'd never been unkind. That was all that would come to her, and because of it she felt a fresh wave of guilt and grief.

She hadn't disappointed him, that much she could cling to. He had told her so himself, in just those words, when she was accepted by the English Department at Yale. Nor had he expected her ever to disappoint him. Kate knew, though it had never been discussed, that her father wanted her to become head of the English Department within ten years. That had been the extent of his dream for her.

Had he ever realized just how much she'd loved him? She wondered as she shut her eyes, tired now from the hours of reading her father's handwriting. Had he ever known just how desperately she'd wanted to please him? If he'd just once said he was proud...

In the end, she hadn't had those few intense last moments with her father one reads about in books or sees in the movies. When she'd arrived at the hospital, he was already gone. There'd been no time for words. No time for tears.

Now she was on her own in the tidy Cape Cod house she'd shared with him for so long. The housekeeper would still come on Wednesday mornings, and the gardener would come on Saturdays to cut the grass. She alone would have to deal with the paperwork, the sorting, the shifting, the clearing out.

That could be done. Kate leaned back farther in her father's worn leather chair. It could be done because all of those things were practical matters. She dealt easily with the practical. But what about these papers she'd found? What would she do about the carefully drawn charts, the notebooks filled with information, directions, history, theory? In part, because she was raised to be logical, she considered filing them neatly away.

But there was another part, the part that enabled one to

lose oneself in fantasies, in dreams, in the "perhapses" of life. This was the part that allowed Kate to lose herself totally in the possibilities of the written word, in the wonders of a book. The papers on her father's desk beckoned her.

He'd believed in it. She bent over the papers again. He'd believed in it or he never would have wasted his time documenting, searching, theorizing. She would never be able to discuss it with him. Yet, in a way, wasn't he telling her about it through his words?

Treasure. Sunken treasure. The stuff of fiction and Hollywood movies. Judging by the stack of papers and notebooks on his desk, Hardesty must have spent months, perhaps years, compiling information on the location of an English merchant ship lost off the coast of North Carolina two centuries before.

It brought Kate an immediate picture of Edward Teach—Blackbeard, the bloodthirsty pirate with the crazed superstitions and reign of terror. The stuff of romances, she thought. Of romance...

Ocracoke Island. The memory was sharp, sweet and painful. Kate had blocked out everything that had happened that summer four years before. Everything and everyone. Now, if she was to make a rational decision about what was to be done, she had to think of those long, lazy months on the remote Outer Banks of North Carolina.

She'd begun work on her doctorate. It had been a surprise when her father had announced that he planned to spend the summer on Ocracoke and invited her to accompany him. Of course, she'd gone, taking her portable typewriter, boxes of books, reams of paper. She hadn't expected to be seduced by white sand beaches and the call of gulls.

She hadn't expected to fall desperately and insensibly in love.

Insensibly, Kate repeated to herself, as if in defense. She'd have to remember that was the most apt adjective. There'd been nothing sensible about her feelings for Ky Silver.

Even the name, she mused, was unique, unconventional, flashy. They'd been as suitable for each other as a peacock and a wren. Yet that hadn't stopped her from losing her head, her heart and her innocence during that balmy, magic summer.

She could still see him at the helm of the boat her father had rented, steering into the wind, laughing, dark hair flowing wildly. She could still remember that heady, weightless feeling when they'd gone scuba diving in the warm coastal waters. Kate had been too caught up in what was happening to herself to think about her father's sudden interest in boating and diving.

She'd been too swept away by her own feelings of astonishment that a man like Ky Silver should be attracted to someone like her to notice her father's preoccupation with currents and tides. There'd been too much excitement for her to realize that her father never bothered with fishing rods like the other vacationers.

But now her youthful fancies were behind her, Kate told herself. Now, she could clearly remember how many hours her father had closeted himself in his hotel room, reading book after book that he brought with him from the mainland library. He'd been researching even then. She was sure he'd continued that research in the following summers when she had refused to go back. Refused to go back, Kate remembered, because of Ky Silver.

Ky had asked her to believe in fairy tales. He asked her to give him the impossible. When she refused, frightened, he shrugged and walked away without a second look. She had never gone back to the white sand and gulls since then.

Kate looked down again at her father's papers. She had to go back now—go back and finish what her father had started. Perhaps, more than the house, the trust fund, the antique jewelry that had been her mother's, this was her father's legacy to her. If she filed those papers neatly away, they'd haunt her for the rest of her life.

She had to go back, Kate reaffirmed as she took off her glasses and folded them neatly on the blotter. And it was Ky Silver she'd have to go to. Her father's aspirations had drawn her away from Ky once; now, four years later, they were drawing her back.

But Dr. Kathleen Hardesty knew the difference between fairy tales and reality. Reaching in her father's desk drawer, she drew out a sheet of thick creamy stationery and began to write.

Ky let the wind buffet him as he opened the throttle. He liked speed in much the same way he liked a lazy afternoon in the hammock. They were two of the things that made life worthwhile. He was used to the smell of salt spray, but he still inhaled deeply. He was well accustomed to the vibration of the deck under his feet, but he still felt it. He wasn't a man to let anything go unnoticed or unappreciated.

He grew up in this quiet, remote little coastal town, and though he'd traveled and intended to travel more, he didn't plan to live anywhere else. It suited him—the freedom of the sea, and the coziness of a small community.

He didn't resent the tourists because he knew they helped keep the village alive, but he preferred the island in winter. Then the storms blew wild and cold, and only the hearty would brave the ferry across Hatteras Inlet.

He fished, but unlike the majority of his neighbors, he rarely sold what he caught. What he pulled out of the sea, he ate. He dove, occasionally collecting shells, but again, this was for his own pleasure. Often he took tourists out on his boat to fish or to scuba dive, because there were times he enjoyed the company. But there were afternoons, like this sparkling one, when he simply wanted the sea to himself.

He had always been restless. His mother had said that he came into the world two weeks early because he grew impatient waiting. Ky turned thirty-two that spring, but was far from settled. He knew what he wanted—to live as he chose. The trouble was that he wasn't certain just what he wanted to choose.

At the moment, he chose the open sky and the endless sea. There were other moments when he knew that that wouldn't be enough.

But the sun was hot, the breeze cool and the shoreline was drawing near. The boat's motor was purring smoothly and in the small cooler was a tidy catch of fish he'd cook up for his supper that night. On a crystal, sparkling afternoon, perhaps it was enough.

From the shore he looked like a pirate might if there were pirates in the twentieth century. His hair was long enough to curl over his ears and well over the collar of a shirt had he worn one. It was black, a rich, true black that might have come from his Arapaho or Sicilian blood. His eyes were the deep, dark green of the sea on a cloudy day.

His skin was bronzed from years in the sun, taut from the years of swimming and pulling in nets. His bone structure was also part of his heritage, sculpted, hard, defined.

When he smiled as he did now, racing the wind to shore, his face took on that reckless freedom women found irresistible. When he didn't smile, his eyes could turn as cold as a lion's before a leap. He discovered long ago that women found that equally irresistible.

Ky drew back on the throttle so that the boat slowed, rocked, then glided into its slip in Silver Lake Harbor. With the quick, efficient movements of one born to the sea, he leaped onto the dock to secure the lines.

"Catch anything?"

Ky straightened and turned. He smiled, but absently, as one does at a brother seen almost every day of one's life. "Enough. Things slow at the Roost?"

Marsh smiled, and there was a brief flicker of family resemblance, but his eyes were a calm light brown and his hair was carefully styled. "Worried about your investment?"

Ky gave a half-shrug. "With you running things?"

Marsh didn't comment. They knew each other as intimately as men ever know each other. One was restless, the other calm. The opposition never seemed to matter. "Linda wants you to come up for dinner. She worries about you."

She would, Ky thought, amused. His sister-in-law loved to mother and fuss, even though she was five years younger than Ky. That was one of the reasons the restaurant she ran with Marsh was such a success—that, plus Marsh's business sense and the hefty investment and shrewd renovations Ky had made. Ky left the managing up to his brother and his sister-in-law. He didn't mind owning a restaurant, even keeping half an eye on the profit and loss, but he certainly had no interest in running one.

After the lines were secure, he wiped his palms down the hips of his cut-offs. "What's the special tonight?"

Marsh dipped his hands into his front pockets and rocked back on his heels. "Bluefish."

Grinning, Ky tossed back the lid of his cooler revealing his catch. "Tell Linda not to worry. I'll eat."

"That's not going to satisfy her." Marsh glanced at his brother as Ky looked out to sea. "She thinks you're alone too much."

"You're only alone too much if you don't like being alone." Ky glanced back over his shoulder. He didn't want to debate now, when the exhilaration of the speed and the sea were still upon him. But he'd never been a man to placate. "Maybe you two should think about having another baby, then Linda would be too busy to worry about big brothers."

"Give me a break. Hope's only eighteen months old."

"You've got to add nine to that," Ky reminded him carelessly. He was fond of his niece, despite—no, because she was a demon. "Anyway, it looks like the family lineage is in your hands."

"Yeah." Marsh shifted his feet, cleared his throat and fell silent. It was a habit he'd carried since childhood, one that could annoy or amuse Ky depending on his mood. At the moment, it was only mildly distracting.

Something was in the air. He could smell it, but he couldn't quite identify it. A storm brewing, he wondered? One of those hot, patient storms that seemed capable of brewing for weeks. He was certain he could smell it.

"Why don't you tell me what else is on your mind?"

Ky suggested. "I want to get back to the house and clean these."

"You had a letter. It was put in our box by mistake."

It was a common enough occurrence, but by his brother's expression Ky knew there was more. His sense of an impending storm grew sharper. Saying nothing, he held out his hand.

"Ky…" Marsh began. There was nothing he could say, just as there'd been nothing to say four years before. Reaching in his back pocket, he drew out the letter.

The envelope was made from heavy cream-colored paper. Ky didn't have to look at the return address. The handwriting and the memories it brought leaped out at him. For a moment, he felt his breath catch in his lungs as it might if someone had caught him with a blow to the solar plexus. Deliberately, he expelled it. "Thanks," he said, as if it meant nothing. He stuck the letter in his pocket before he picked up his cooler and gear.

"Ky—" Again Marsh broke off. His brother had turned his head, and the cool, half-impatient stare said very clearly—back off. "If you change your mind about dinner," Marsh said.

"I'll let you know." Ky went down the length of the dock without looking back.

He was grateful he hadn't bothered to bring his car down to the harbor. He needed to walk. He needed the fresh air and the exercise to keep his mind clear while he remembered what he didn't want to remember. What he never really forgot.

Kate. Four years ago she'd walked out of his life with the same sort of cool precision with which she'd walked into it. She had reminded him of a Victorian doll—a little prim, a little aloof. He'd never had much patience with neatly folded hands or haughty manners, yet almost from the first instant he'd wanted her.

At first, he thought it was the fact that she was so different. A challenge—something for Ky Silver to conquer. He enjoyed teaching her to dive, and watching the precise step-by-step way she learned. It hadn't been any hardship to look at her in a snug scuba suit, although she didn't have voluptuous curves. She had a trim, neat, almost boylike figure and what seemed like yards of thick, soft hair.

He could still remember the first time she took it down from its pristine knot. It left him breathless, hurting, fascinated. Ky would have touched it—touched her then and there if her father hadn't been standing beside her. But if a man was clever, if a man was determined, he could find a way to be alone with a woman.

Ky had found ways. Kate had taken to diving as though she'd been born to it. While her father had buried himself in his books, Ky had taken Kate out on the water—under the water, to the silent, dreamlike world that had attracted her just as it had always attracted him.

He could remember the first time he kissed her. They had been wet and cool from a dive, standing on the deck of his boat. He was able to see the lighthouse behind her and the vague line of the coast. Her hair had flowed down her back, sleek from the water, dripping with it. He'd reached out and gathered it in his hand.

"What are you doing?"

Four years later, he could hear that low, cultured, eastern voice, the curiosity in it. It took no effort for him to see the curiosity that had been in her eyes.

"I'm going to kiss you."

The curiosity had remained in her eyes, fascinating him. "Why?"

"Because I want to."

It was as simple as that for him. He wanted to. Her body had stiffened as he'd drawn her against him. When her lips parted in protest, he closed his over them. In the time it takes a heart to beat, the rigidity had melted from her body. She'd kissed him with all the young, stored-up passion that had been in her—passion mixed with innocence. He was experienced enough to recognize her innocence, and that too had fascinated him. Ky had, foolishly, youthfully and completely, fallen in love.

Kate had remained an enigma to him, though they shared impassioned hours of laughter and long, lazy talks. He admired her thirst for learning and she had a predilection for putting knowledge into neat slots that baffled him. She was enthusiastic about diving, but it hadn't been enough for her simply to be able to swim freely underwater, taking her air from tanks. She had to know how the tanks worked, why they were fashioned a certain way. Ky watched her absorb what he told her, and knew she'd retain it.

They had taken walks along the shoreline at night and she had recited poetry from memory. Beautiful words, Byron, Shelley, Keats. And he, who'd never been overly impressed by such things, had eaten it up because her voice had made the words somehow personal. Then she'd begin to talk about syntax, iambic pentameters, and Ky would find new ways to divert her.

For three months, he did little but think of her. For the first time, Ky had considered changing his lifestyle. His little cottage near the beach needed work. It needed furniture. Kate would need more than milk crates and the hammock that had been his style. Because he'd been young and had never been in love before, Ky had taken his own plans for granted.

She'd walked out on him. She'd had her own plans, and he hadn't been part of them.

Her father came back to the island the following summer, and every summer thereafter. Kate never came back. Ky knew she had completed her doctorate and was teaching in a prestigious ivy league school where her father was all but a cornerstone. She had what she wanted. So, he told himself as he swung open the screen door of his cottage, did he. He went where he wanted, when he wanted. He called his own shots. His responsibilities extended only as far as he chose to extend them. To his way of thinking, that itself was a mark of success.

Setting the cooler on the kitchen floor, Ky opened the refrigerator. He twisted the top off a beer and drank half of it in one icy cold swallow. It washed some of the bitterness out of his mouth.

Calm now, and curious, he pulled the letter out of his pocket. Ripping it open, he drew out the single neatly written sheet.

Dear Ky,
You may or may not be aware that my father suffered a fatal heart attack two weeks ago. It was very sudden, and I'm currently trying to tie up the many details this involves.

In going through my father's papers, I find that he had again made arrangements to come to the island this summer, and engage your services. I now find it necessary to take his place. For reasons which I'd rather explain in person, I need your help. You have my father's deposit. When I arrive in Ocracoke on the fifteenth, we can discuss terms.

If possible, contact me at the hotel, or leave a message. I hope we'll be able to come to a mutually agreeable arrangement. Please give my best to Marsh. Perhaps I'll see him during my stay.

Best,
Kathleen Hardesty

So the old man was dead. Ky set down the letter and lifted his beer again. He couldn't say he'd had any liking for Edwin Hardesty. Kate's father had been a stringent, humorless man. Still, he hadn't disliked him. Ky had, in an odd way, gotten used to his company over the last few summers. But this summer, it would be Kate.

Ky glanced at the letter again, then jogged his memory until he remembered the date. Two days, he mused. She'd be there in two days…to discuss terms. A smile played around the corners of his mouth but it didn't have anything to do with humor. They'd discuss terms, he agreed silently as he scanned Kate's letter again.

She wanted to take her father's place. Ky wondered if she'd realized, when she wrote that, just how ironic it was. Kathleen Hardesty had been obediently dogging her father's footsteps all her life. Why should that change after his death?

Had she changed? Ky wondered briefly. Would that fascinating aura of innocence and aloofness still cling to her? Or perhaps that had faded with the years. Would that rather sweet primness have developed into a rigidity? He'd see for himself in a couple of days, he realized, but tossed the letter onto the counter rather than into the trash.

So, she wanted to engage his services, he mused. Leaning both hands on either side of the sink, he looked out the window in the direction of the water he could smell, but not quite see. She wanted a business arrangement—the rental of his boat, his gear and his time. He felt the bitterness well up and swallowed it as cleanly as he had the beer. She'd have her business arrangement. And she'd pay. He'd see to that.

Ky left the kitchen with his catch still in the cooler. The appetite he'd worked up with salt spray and speed had vanished.

Kate pulled her car onto the ferry to Ocracoke and set the brake. The morning was cool and very clear. Even so, she was tempted to simply lean her head back and close her eyes. She wasn't certain what impulse had pushed her to drive from Connecticut rather than fly, but now that she'd all but reached her destination, she was too weary to analyze.

In the bucket seat beside her was her briefcase, and inside, all the papers she'd collected from her father's desk. Perhaps once she was in the hotel on the island, she could go through them again, understand them better. Perhaps the feeling that she was doing the right thing would come back. Over the last few days she'd lost that sense.

The closer she came to the island, the more she began to think she was making a mistake. Not to the island, Kate corrected ruthlessly—the closer she came to Ky. It was a fact, and Kate knew it was imperative to face facts so that they could be dealt with logically.

She had a little time left, a little time to calm the feelings that had somehow gotten stirred up during the drive south. It was foolish, and somehow it helped Kate to remind herself of that. She wasn't a woman returning to a lover, but a woman hoping to engage a diver in a very specific venture. Past personal feelings wouldn't enter into it because they were just that. Past.

The Kate Hardesty who'd arrived on Ocracoke four years ago had little to do with the Dr. Kathleen Hardesty who was going there now. She wasn't young, inexperienced or impressionable. Those reckless, wild traits of Ky's wouldn't appeal to her now. They wouldn't frighten her. They would be, if Ky agreed to her terms, business partners.

Kate felt the ferry move beneath her as she stared through the windshield. Yes, she thought, unless Ky had changed a great deal, the prospect of diving for treasure would appeal to his sense of adventure.

She knew enough about diving in the technical sense to be sure she'd find no one better equipped for the job. It was always advisable to have the best. More relaxed and less weary, Kate stepped out of her car to stand at the rail. From there she could watch the gulls swoop and the tiny uninhabited islands pass by. She felt a sense of homecoming, but pushed it away. Connecticut was home. Once Kate did what she came for, she'd go back.

The water swirled behind the boat. She couldn't hear it over the motor, but looking down she could watch the wake. One island was nearly imperceptible under a flock of big, brown pelicans. It made her smile, pleased to see the odd, awkward-looking birds again. They passed the long spit of land, where fishermen parked trucks and tried their luck, near the point where bay met sea. She could watch the waves crash and foam where there was no shore, just a turbulent marriage of waters. That was something she hadn't forgotten, though she hadn't seen it since she left the island. Nor had she forgotten just how treacherous the current was along that verge.

Excitement. She breathed deeply before she turned back to her car. The treacherous was always exciting.

When the ferry docked, she had only a short wait before she could drive her car onto the narrow blacktop. The trip to town wouldn't take long, and it wasn't possible to lose your way if you stayed on the one long road. The sea battered on one side, the sound flowed smoothly on the other—both were deep blue in the late morning light.

Her nerves were gone, at least that's what she told herself. It had just been a case of last minute jitters—very normal. She was prepared to see Ky again, speak to him, work with him if they could agree on the terms.

With the windows down, the soft moist air blew around her. It was soothing. She'd almost forgotten just how soothing air could be, or the sound of water lapping constantly against sand. It was right to come. When she saw the first faded buildings of the village, she felt a wave of relief. She was here. There was no turning back now.

The hotel where she had stayed that summer with her father was on the sound side of the island. It was small and quiet. If the service was a bit slow by northern standards, the view made up for it.

Kate pulled up in front and turned off the ignition. Self-satisfaction made her sigh. She'd taken the first step and was completely prepared for the next.

Then as she stepped out of the car, she saw him. For an

instant, the confident professor of English literature vanished. She was only a woman, vulnerable to her own emotions.

Oh God, he hasn't changed. Not at all. As Ky came closer, she could remember every kiss, every murmur, every crazed storm of their loving. The breeze blew his hair back from his face so that every familiar angle and plane was clear to her. With the sun warm on her skin, bright in her eyes, she felt the years spin back, then forward again. He hadn't changed.

He hadn't expected to see her yet. Somehow he thought she'd arrive that afternoon. Yet he found it necessary to go by the Roost that morning knowing the restaurant was directly across from the hotel where she'd be staying.

She was here, looking neat and a bit too thin in her tailored slacks and blouse. Her hair was pinned up so that the soft femininity of her neck and throat were revealed. Her eyes seemed too dark against her pale skin—skin Ky knew would turn golden slowly under the summer sun.

She looked the same. Soft, prim, calm. Lovely. He ignored the thud in the pit of his stomach as he stepped in front of her. He looked her up and down with the arrogance that was so much a part of him. Then he grinned because he had an overwhelming urge to strangle her.

"Kate. Looks like my timing's good."

She was almost certain she couldn't speak and was therefore determined to speak calmly. "Ky, it's nice to see you again."

"Is it?"

Ignoring the sarcasm, Kate walked around to her trunk and released it. "I'd like to get together with you as soon as possible. There are some things I want to show you, and some business I'd like to discuss."

"Sure, always open for business."

He watched her pull two cases from her trunk, but didn't offer to help. He saw there was no ring on her hand—but it wouldn't have mattered.

"Perhaps we can meet this afternoon then, after I've settled in." The sooner the better, she told herself. They would establish the purpose, the ground rules and the payment. "We could have lunch in the hotel."

"No, thanks," he said easily, leaning against the side of her car while she set her cases down. "You want me, you know where to find me. It's a small island."

With his hands in the pockets of his jeans, he walked away from her. Though she didn't want to, Kate remembered that the last time he'd walked away, they'd stood in almost the same spot.

Picking up her cases, she headed for the hotel, perhaps a bit too quickly.

Chapter 2

She knew where to find him. If the island had been double in size, she'd still have known where to find him. Kate acknowledged that Ky hadn't changed. That meant if he wasn't out on his boat, he would be at home, in the small, slightly dilapidated cottage he owned near the beach. Because she felt it would be a strategic error to go after him too soon, she dawdled over her unpacking.

But there were memories even here, where she'd spent one giddy, whirlwind night of love with Ky. It had been the only time they were able to sleep together through the night, embracing each other in the crisp hotel sheets until the first light of dawn crept around the edges of the window shades. She remembered how reckless she'd felt during those few stolen hours, and how dull the morning had seemed because it brought them to an end.

Now she could look out the same window she had

stood by then, staring out in the same direction she'd stared out then when she watched Ky walk away. She remembered the sky had been streaked with a rose color before it had brightened to a pure, pale blue.

Then, with her skin still warm from her lover's touch and her mind glazed with lack of sleep and passion, Kate had believed such things could go on forever. But of course they couldn't. She had seen that only weeks later. Passion and reckless nights of loving had to give way to responsibilities, obligations.

Staring out the same window, in the same direction, Kate could feel the sense of loss she'd felt that long ago dawn without the underlying hope that they'd be together again. And again.

They wouldn't be together again, and there'd been no one else since that one heady summer. She had her career, her vocation, her books. She had had her taste of passion.

Turning away, she busied herself by rearranging everything she'd just arranged in her drawers and closet. When she decided she'd stalled in her hotel room long enough, Kate started out. She didn't take her car. She walked, just as she always walked to Ky's home.

She told herself she was over the shock of seeing him again. It was only natural that there be some strain, some discomfort. She was honest enough to admit that it would have been easier if there'd been only strain and discomfort, and not that one sharp quiver of pleasure. Kate acknowledged it, now that it had passed.

No, Ky Silver hadn't changed, she reminded herself. He was still arrogant, self-absorbed and cocky. Those traits might have appealed to her once, but she'd been very young. If she were wise, she could use those same traits to persuade Ky to help her. Yes, those traits, she thought, and the tempting offer of a treasure hunt. Even at her most pessimistic, she couldn't believe Ky would refuse. It was his nature to take chances.

This time she'd be in charge. Kate drew in a deep breath of warm air that tasted of sea. Somehow she felt it would steady her. Ky was going to find she was no longer naive, or susceptible to a few careless words of affection.

With her briefcase in hand, Kate walked through the village. This too was the same, she thought. She was glad of it. The simplicity and solitude still appealed to her. She enjoyed the dozens of little shops, the restaurants and small inns tucked here and there, all somehow using the harbor as a central point, the lighthouse as a landmark. The villagers still made the most of their notorious one-time resident and permanent ghost, Blackbeard. His name or face was lavishly displayed on store signs.

She passed the harbor, unconsciously scanning for Ky's boat. It was there, in the same slip he'd always used—clean lines, scrubbed deck, shining hardware. The flying bridge gleamed in the afternoon light and looked the same as she remembered. Reckless, challenging. The paint was fresh and there was no film of salt spray on the bridge windows. However careless Ky had been about his own appearance or his home, he'd always pampered his boat.

The *Vortex*. Kate studied the flamboyant lettering on the stern. He could pamper, she thought again, but he also expected a lot in return. She knew the speed he could urge out of the second-hand cabin cruiser he'd lovingly reconstructed himself. Nothing could block the image of the days she'd stood beside him at the helm. The wind had whipped her hair as he'd laughed and pushed for speed, and more speed. Her heart thudded, her pulse raced until she was certain nothing and no one could catch them. She'd been afraid, of him, of the rush of wind—but she'd stayed with both. In the end, she'd left both.

He enjoyed the demanding, the thrilling, the frightening. Kate gripped the handle of her briefcase tighter. Isn't that why she came to him? There were dozens of other experienced divers, many, many other experts on the coastal waters of the Outer Banks. There was only one Ky Silver.

"Kate? Kate Hardesty?"

At the sound of her name, Kate turned and felt the years tumble back again. "Linda!" This time there was no restraint. With an openness she showed to very few, Kate embraced the woman who dashed up to her, "It's wonderful to see you." With a laugh, she drew Linda away to study her. The same chestnut hair cut short and pert, the same frank, brown eyes. It seemed very little had changed on the island. "You look wonderful."

"When I looked out the window and saw you, I could hardly believe it. Kate, you've barely changed at all." With her usual candor and lack of pretension, Linda took a quick, thorough survey. It was quick only because she did things quickly, but it wasn't subtle. "You're too thin," she decided. "But that might be jealousy."

"You still look like a college freshman," Kate returned. "That is jealousy."

As swiftly as the laugh had come, Linda sobered. "I'm sorry about your father, Kate. These past weeks must've been difficult for you."

Kate heard the sincerity, but she'd already tied up her grief and stored it away. "Ky told you?"

"Ky never tells me anything," Linda said with a sniff.

In an unconscious move, she glanced in the direction of his boat. It was in its slip and Kate had been walking north—in the direction of Ky's cottage. There could be only one place she could have been going. "Marsh did. How long are you going to stay?"

"I'm not sure yet." She felt the weight of her briefcase. Dreams held the same weight as responsibilities. "There are some things I have to do."

"One of the things you have to do is have dinner at the Roost tonight. It's the restaurant right across from your hotel."

Kate looked back at the rough wooden sign. "Yes, I noticed it. Is it new?"

Linda glanced over her shoulder with a self-satisfied nod. "By Ocracoke standards. We run it."

"We?"

"Marsh and I." With a beaming smile, Linda held out her left hand. "We've been married for three years." Then she rolled her eyes in a habit Kate remembered. "It only took me fifteen years to convince him he couldn't live without me."

"I'm happy for you." She was, and if she felt a pang, she ignored it. "Married and running a restaurant. My father never filled me in on island gossip."

"We have a daughter too. Hope. She's a year and a half old and a terror. For some reason, she takes after Ky." Linda sobered again, laying a hand lightly on Kate's arm. "You're going to see him now." It wasn't a question; she didn't bother to disguise it as one.

"Yes." Keep it casual, Kate ordered herself. Don't let the questions and concern in Linda's eyes weaken you. There were ties between Linda and Ky, not only newly formed family ones, but the older tie of the island. "My father was working on something. I need Ky's help with it."

Linda studied Kate's calm face. "You know what you're doing?"

"Yes." She didn't show a flicker of unease. Her stomach slowly wrapped itself in knots. "I know what I'm doing."

"Okay." Accepting Kate's answer, but not satisfied, Linda dropped her hand. "Please come by—the restaurant or the house. We live just down the road from Ky. Marsh'll want to see you, and I'd like to show off Hope—and our menu," she added with a grin. "Both are outstanding."

"Of course I'll come by." On impulse, she took both of Linda's hands. "It's really good to see you again. I know I didn't keep in touch, but—"

"I understand." Linda gave her hands a quick squeeze. "That was yesterday. I've got to get back, the lunch crowd's pretty heavy during the season." She let out a little sigh, wondering if Kate was as calm as she seemed. And if Ky were as big a fool as ever. "Good luck," she murmured, then dashed across the street again.

"Thanks," Kate said under her breath. She was going to need it.

The walk was as beautiful as she remembered. She passed the little shops with their display windows showing handmade crafts or antiques. She passed the blue and white clapboard houses and the neat little streets on the outskirts of town with their bleached green lawns and leafy trees.

A dog raced back and forth on the length of his chain as she wandered by, barking at her as if he knew he was supposed to but didn't have much interest in it. She could see the tower of the white lighthouse. There'd been a keeper there once, but those days were over. Then she was on the narrow path that led to Ky's cottage.

Her palms were damp. She cursed herself. If she had to remember, she'd remember later, when she was alone. When she was safe.

The path was as it had been, just wide enough for a car, sparsely graveled, lined with bushes that always grew out a bit too far. The bushes and trees had always had a wild, overgrown look that suited the spot. That suited him.

Ky had told her he didn't care much for visitors. If he wanted company, all he had to do was go into town where he knew everyone. That was typical of Ky Silver, Kate mused. If I want you, I'll let you know. Otherwise, back off.

He'd wanted her once…. Nervous, Kate shifted the briefcase to her other hand. Whatever he wanted now, he'd have to hear her out. She needed him for what he was best at—diving and taking chances.

When the house came into view, she stopped, staring. It was still small, still primitive. But it no longer looked as though it would keel over on its side in a brisk wind.

The roof had been redone. Obviously Ky wouldn't need to set out pots and pans during a rain any longer. The porch he'd once talked vaguely about building now ran the length of the front, sturdy and wide. The screen door that had once been patched in a half a dozen places had been replaced by a new one. Yet nothing looked new, she observed. It just looked right. The cedar had weathered to silver, the windows were untrimmed but gleaming. There was, much to her surprise, a spill of impatiens in a long wooden planter.

She'd been wrong, Kate decided as she walked closer. Ky Silver had changed. Precisely how, and precisely how much, she had yet to find out.

She was nearly to the first step when she heard sounds coming from the rear of the house. There was a shed back there, she remembered, full of boards and tools and salvage. Grateful that she didn't have to meet him in the house, Kate walked around the side to the tiny backyard. She could hear the sea and knew it was less than a two-minute walk through high grass and sand dunes.

Did he still go down there in the evenings? she wondered. Just to look, he'd said. Just to smell. Sometimes he'd pick up driftwood or shells or whatever small treasures the sea gave up to the sand. Once he'd given her a small smooth shell that fit into the palm of her hand—very white with a delicate pink center. A woman with her first gift of diamonds could not have been more thrilled.

Shaking the memories away, she went into the shed. It was as tall as the cottage and half as wide. The last time she'd been there, it'd been crowded with planks and boards and boxes of hardware. Now she saw the hull of a boat. At a worktable with his back to her, Ky sanded the mast.

"You've built it." The words came out before she could stop them, full of astonished pleasure. How many times had he told her about the boat he'd build one day? It had seemed to Kate it had been his only concrete ambition. Mahogany on oak, he'd said. A seventeen-foot sloop that would cut through the water like a dream. He'd have bronze fastenings and teak on the deck. One day he'd sail the inner coastal waters from Ocracoke to New England. He'd described the boat so minutely that she'd seen it then just as clearly as she saw it now.

"I told you I would." Ky turned away from the mast and faced her. She, in the doorway, had the sun at her back. He was half in shadow.

"Yes." Feeling foolish, Kate tightened her grip on the briefcase. "You did."

"But you didn't believe me." Ky tossed aside the sandpaper. Did she have to look so neat and cool, and impossibly lovely? A trickle of sweat ran down his back. "You always had a problem seeing beyond the moment."

Reckless, impatient, compelling. Would he always bring those words to her mind? "You always had a problem dealing with the moment," she said.

His brow lifted, whether in surprise or derision she couldn't be sure. "Then it might be said *we* always had a problem." He walked to her, so that the sun slanting through the small windows fell over him, then behind him. "But it didn't always seem to matter." To satisfy himself that he still could, Ky reached out and touched her face. She didn't move, and her skin was as soft and cool as he remembered. "You look tired Kate."

The muscles in her stomach quivered, but not her voice. "It was a long trip."

His thumb brushed along her cheekbone. "You need some sun."

This time she backed away. "I intend to get some."

"So I gathered from your letter." Pleased that she'd retreated first, Ky leaned against the open door. "You wrote that you wanted to talk to me in person. You're here. Why don't you tell me what you want?"

The cocky grin might have made her melt once. Now it stiffened her spine. "My father was researching a project. I intend to finish it."

"So?"

"I need your help."

Ky laughed and stepped past her into the sunlight. He needed the air, the distance. He needed to touch her again. "From your tone, there's nothing you hate more than asking me for it."

"No." She stood firm, feeling suddenly strong and bitter. "Nothing."

There was no humor in his eyes as he faced her again. The expression in them was cold and flat. She'd seen it before. "Then let's understand each other before we start. You left the island and me, and took what I wanted."

He couldn't make her cringe now as he once had with only that look. "What happened four years ago has nothing to do with today."

"The hell it doesn't." He came toward her again so that she took an involuntary step backward. "Still afraid of me?" he asked softly.

As it had a moment ago, the question turned the fear to anger. "No," she told him, and meant it. "I'm not afraid of you, Ky. I've no intention of discussing the past, but I will agree that I left the island and you. I'm here now on business. I'd like you to hear me out. If you're interested, we'll discuss terms, nothing else."

"I'm not one of your students, professor." The drawl crept into his voice, as it did when he let it. "Don't instruct."

She curled her fingers tighter around the handle of her briefcase. "In business, there are always ground rules."

"Nobody agreed to let you make them."

"I made a mistake," Kate said quietly as she fought for control. "I'll find someone else."

She'd taken only two steps away when Ky grabbed her arm. "No, you won't." The stormy look in his eyes made her throat dry. She knew what he meant. She'd never find anyone else that could make her feel as he made her feel, or want as he made her want. Deliberately, Kate removed his hand from her arm.

"I came here on business. I've no intention of fighting with you over something that doesn't exist any longer."

"We'll see about that." How long could he hold on? Ky wondered. It hurt just to look at her and to feel her withdrawing with every second that went by. "But for now, why don't you tell me what you have in that businesslike briefcase, professor."

Kate took a deep breath. She should have known it wouldn't be easy. Nothing was ever easy with Ky. "Charts," she said precisely. "Notebooks full of research, maps, carefully documented facts and precise theories. In my opinion, my father was very close to pinpointing the exact location of the *Liberty*, an English merchant vessel that sank, stores intact, off the North Carolina coast two hundred and fifty years ago."

He listened without a comment or a change of expression from beginning to end. When she finished, Ky studied her face for one long moment. "Come inside," he said and turned toward the house. "Show me what you've got."

His arrogance made her want to turn away and go back to town exactly as she'd come. There were other divers, others who knew the coast and the waters as well as Ky did. Kate forced herself to calm down, forced herself to think. There were others, but if it was a choice between the devil she knew and the unknown, she had no choice. Kate followed him into the house.

This, too, had changed. The kitchen she remembered had had a paint splattered floor, with the only usable counter space being a tottering picnic table. The floor had been stripped and varnished, the cabinets redone, and scrubbed butcher block counters lined the sink. He had put in a skylight so that the sun spilled down over the picnic table, now re-worked and re-painted, with benches along either side.

"Did you do all of this yourself?"

"Yeah. Surprised?"

So he didn't want to make polite conversation. Kate set her briefcase on the table. "Yes. You always seemed content that the walls were about to cave in on you."

"I was content with a lot of things, once. Want a beer?"

"No." Kate sat down and drew the first of her father's notebooks out of her briefcase. "You'll want to read these. It would be unnecessary and time-consuming for you to read every page, but if you'd look over the ones I've marked, I think you'll have enough to go by."

"All right." Ky turned from the refrigerator, beer in hand. He sat, watching her over the rim as he took the first swallow, then he opened the notebook.

Edwin Hardesty's handwriting was very clear and precise. He wrote down his facts in didactic, unromantic terms. What could have been exciting was as dry as a thesis, but it was accurate. Ky had no doubt of that.

The *Liberty* had been lost, with its stores of sugar, tea, silks, wine and other imports for the colonies. Hardesty had listed the manifest down to the last piece of hardtack. When it had left England, the ship had also been carrying gold. Twenty-five thousand in coins of the realm. Ky glanced up from the notebook to see Kate watching him.

"Interesting," he said simply, and turned to the next page she marked.

There'd been only three survivors who'd washed up on the island. One of the crew had described the storm that had sunk the *Liberty*, giving details on the height of the waves, the splintering wood, the water gushing into the hole. It was a grim, grisly story which Hardesty had recounted in his pragmatic style, complete with footnotes. The crewman had also given the last known location of the ship before it had gone down. Ky didn't require Hardesty's calculations to figure the ship had sunk two-and-a-half miles off the coast of Ocracoke.

Going from one notebook to another, Ky read through Hardesty's well-drafted theories, his clear to-the-point documentations, corroborated and recorroborated. He scanned the charts, then studied them with more care. He remembered the man's avid interest in diving, which had always seemed inconsistent with his precise lifestyle.

So he'd been looking for gold, Ky mused. All these years the man had been digging in books and looking for gold. If it had been anyone else, Ky might have dismissed it as another fable. Little towns along the coast were full of stories about buried treasure. Edward Teach had used the shallow waters of the inlets to frustrate and outwit the crown until his last battle off the shores of Ocracoke. That alone kept the dreams of finding sunken treasures alive.

But it was Dr. Edwin J. Hardesty, Yale professor, an unimaginative, humorless man who didn't believe there was time to be wasted on the frivolous, who'd written these notebooks.

Ky might still have dismissed it, but Kate was sitting

across from him. He had enough adventurous blood in him to believe in destinies.

Setting the last notebook aside, he picked up his beer again. "So, you want to treasure hunt."

She ignored the humor in his voice. With her hands folded on the table, she leaned forward. "I intend to follow through with what my father was working on."

"Do you believe it?"

Did she? Kate opened her mouth and closed it again. She had no idea. "I don't believe that all of my father's time and research should go for nothing. I want to try. As it happens, I need you to help me do it. You'll be compensated."

"Will I?" He studied the liquid left in the beer bottle with a half smile. "Will I indeed?"

"I need you, your boat and your equipment for a month, maybe two. I can't dive alone because I just don't know the waters well enough to risk it, and I don't have the time to waste. I have to be back in Connecticut by the end of August."

"To get more chalk dust under your fingernails."

She sat back slowly. "You have no right to criticize my profession."

"I'm sure the chalk's very exclusive at Yale," Ky commented. "So you're giving yourself six weeks or so to find a pot of gold."

"If my father's calculations are viable, it won't take that long."

"If," Ky repeated. Setting down his bottle, he leaned forward. "I've got no timetable. You want six weeks of my time, you can have it. For a price."

"Which is?"

"A hundred dollars a day and fifty percent of whatever we find."

Kate gave him a cool look as she slipped the notebooks back into her briefcase. "Whatever I was four years ago, Ky, I'm not a fool now. A hundred dollars a day is outrageous when we're dealing with monthly rates. And fifty percent is out of the question." It gave her a certain satisfaction to bargain with him. This made it business, pure and simple. "I'll give you fifty dollars a day and ten percent."

With the maddening half grin on his face he swirled the beer in the bottle. "I don't turn my boat on for fifty a day."

She tilted her head a bit to study him. Something tore inside him. She'd often done that whenever he said something she wanted to think over. "You're more mercenary than you once were."

"We've all got to make a living, professor." Didn't she feel anything? he thought furiously. Wasn't she suffering just a little, being in the house where they'd made love their first and last time? "You want a service," he said quietly, "you pay for it. Nothing's free. Seventy-five a day and twenty-five percent. We'll say it's for old-times' sake."

"No, we'll say it's for business' sake." She made herself extend her hand, but when his closed over it, she regretted the gesture. It was callused, hard, strong. Kate knew how his hand felt skimming over her skin, driving her to desperation, soothing, teasing, seducing.

"We have a deal." Ky thought he could see a flash of remembrance in her eyes. He kept her hand in his knowing she didn't welcome his touch. Because she didn't. "There's no guarantee you'll find your treasure."

"That's understood."

"Fine. I'll deduct your father's deposit from the total."

"All right." With her free hand, she clutched at her briefcase. "When do we start?"

"Meet me at the harbor at eight tomorrow." Deliberately, he placed his other free hand over hers on the leather case. "Leave this with me. I want to look over the papers some more."

"There's no need for you to have them," Kate began, but his hands tightened on hers.

"If you don't trust me with them, you take them along." His voice was very smooth and very quiet. At its most dangerous. "And find yourself another diver."

Their gazes locked. Her hands were trapped and so was she. Kate knew there would be sacrifices she'd have to make. "I'll meet you at eight."

"Fine." He released her hands and sat back. "Nice doing business with you, Kate."

Dismissed, she rose. Just how much had she sacrificed already? she wondered. "Goodbye."

He lifted and drained his half-finished beer when the screen shut behind her. Then he made himself sit there until he was certain that when he rose and walked to the window she'd be out of sight. He made himself sit there until the air flowing through the screens had carried her scent away.

Sunken ships and deep-sea treasure. It would have excited him, captured his imagination, enthusiasm and interest if he hadn't had an overwhelming urge to just get in his boat and head toward the horizon. He hadn't believed she could still affect him that way, that much, that completely. He'd forgotten that just being within touching distance of her tied his stomach in knots.

He'd never gotten over her. No matter what he filled his life with over the past four years, he'd never gotten over the slim, intellectual woman with the haughty face and doe's eyes.

Ky sat, staring at the briefcase with her initials stamped discreetly near the handle. He'd never expected her to come back, but he'd just discovered he'd never accepted the fact that she'd left him. Somehow, he'd managed to deceive himself through the years. Now, seeing her again, he knew it had just been a matter of pure survival and nothing to do with truth. He'd had to go on, to pretend that that part of his life was behind him, or he would have gone mad.

She was back now, but she hadn't come back to him. A business arrangement. Ky ran his hand over the smooth leather of the case. She simply wanted the best diver she knew and was willing to pay for him. Fee for services, nothing more, nothing less. The past meant little or nothing to her.

Fury grew until his knuckles whitened around the bottle. He'd give her what she paid for, he promised himself. And maybe a bit extra.

This time when she went away, he wouldn't be left feeling like an inadequate fool. She'd be the one who would have to go on pretending for the rest of her life. This time when she went away, he'd be done with her. God, he'd have to be.

Rising quickly, he went out to the shed. If he stayed inside, he'd give in to the need to get very, very drunk.

Chapter 3

Kate had the water in the tub so hot that the mirror over the white pedestal sink was fogged. Oil floated on the surface, subtly fragrant and soothing. She'd lost track of how long she lay there—soaking, recharging. The next irrevocable step had been taken. She'd survived. Somehow during her discussion with Ky in his kitchen she had fought back the memories of laughter and passion. She couldn't count how many meals they'd shared there, cooking their catch, sipping wine.

Somehow during the walk back to her hotel, she'd overcome the need to weep. Tomorrow would be just a little easier. Tomorrow, and every day that followed. She had to believe it.

His animosity would help. His derision toward her kept Kate from romanticizing what she had to tell herself had never been more than a youthful summer fling. Perspective. She'd always been able to stand back and align everything in its proper perspective.

Perhaps her feelings for Ky weren't as dead as she had hoped or pretended they were. But her emotions were tinged with bitterness. Only a fool asked for more sorrow. Only a romantic believed that bitterness could ever be sweet. It had been a long time since Kate had been a romantic fool. Even so, they would work together because both had an interest in what might be lying on the sea floor.

Think of it. Two hundred and fifty years. Kate closed her eyes and let her mind drift. The silks and sugar would be gone, but would they find brass fittings deep in corrosion after two-and-a-half centuries? The hull would be covered with fungus and barnacles, but how much of the oak would still be intact? Might the log have been secured in a waterproof hold and still be legible? It could be donated to a museum in her father's name. It would be something—the last something she could do for him. Perhaps then she'd be able to lay all her ambiguous feelings to rest.

The gold, Kate thought as she rose from the tub, the gold would survive. She wasn't immune to the lure of it. Yet she knew it would be the hunt that would be exciting, and somehow fulfilling. If she found it…

What would she do? Kate wondered. She dropped the hotel towel over the rod before she wrapped herself in her robe. Behind her, the mirror was still fogged with steam from the water that drained slowly from the tub. Would she put her share tidily in some conservative investments? Would she take a leisurely trip to the Greek islands to see what Byron had seen and fallen in love with there? With a laugh, Kate walked through to the other room to pick up her brush. Strange, she hadn't thought beyond the search yet. Perhaps that was for the best, it wasn't wise to plan too far ahead.

You always had a problem seeing beyond the moment.

Damn him! With a sudden fury, Kate slammed the brush onto the dresser. She'd seen beyond the moment. She'd seen that he'd offered her no more than a tentative affair in a run-down beach shack. No guarantees, no commitment, no future. She only thanked God she'd had enough of her senses left to understand it and to walk away from what was essentially nothing at all. She'd never let Ky know just how horribly it had hurt to walk away from nothing at all.

Her father had been right to quietly point out the weaknesses in Ky, and her obligation to herself and her chosen profession. Ky's lack of ambition, his careless attitude toward the future weren't qualities, but flaws. She'd had a responsibility, and by accepting it had given herself independence and satisfaction.

Calmer, she picked up her brush again. She was dwelling on the past too much. It was time to stop. With the deft movements of habit, she secured her hair into a sleek twist. From this time on, she'd think only of what was to come, not what had, or might have been.

She needed to get out.

With panic just under the surface, Kate pulled a dress out of her closet. It no longer mattered that she was tired, that all she really wanted to do was to crawl into bed and let her mind and body rest. Nerves wouldn't permit it. She'd go across the street, have a drink with Linda and Marsh. She'd see their baby, have a long, extravagant dinner. When she came back to the hotel, alone, she'd make certain she'd be too tired for dreams.

Tomorrow, she had work to do.

Because she dressed quickly, Kate arrived at the Roost just past six. What she saw, she immediately approved of. It wasn't elegant, but it was comfortable. It didn't have the dimly lit, cathedral feel of so many of the restaurants she'd dined in with her father, with colleagues, back in Connecticut. It was relaxed, welcoming, cozy.

There were paintings of ships and boats along the stuccoed walls, of armadas and cutters. Throughout the dining room was other sailing paraphernalia—a ship's compass with its brass gleaming, a colorful spinnaker draped behind the bar with the stools in front of it shaped like wooden kegs. There was a crow's nest spearing toward the ceiling with ferns spilling out and down the mast.

The room was already half full of couples and families, the bulk of whom Kate identified as tourists. She could hear the comforting sound of cutlery scraping lightly over plates. There was the smell of good food and the hum of mixed conversations.

Comfortable, she thought again, but definitely well organized. Waiters and waitresses in sailor's denims moved smoothly, making every second count without looking rushed. The window opened out to a full evening view of Silver Lake Harbor. Kate turned her back on it because she knew her gaze would fall on the *Vortex* or its empty slip.

Tomorrow was soon enough for that. She wanted one night without memories.

"Kate."

She felt the hands on her shoulders and recognized the voice. There was a smile on her face when she turned around. "Marsh, I'm so glad to see you."

In his quiet way, he studied her, measured her and saw both the strain and the relief. In the same way, he'd had a crush on her that had faded into admiration and respect before the end of that one summer. "Beautiful as ever. Linda said you were, but it's nice to see for myself."

She laughed, because he'd always been able to make her feel as though life could be honed down to the most simple of terms. She'd never questioned why that trait had made her relax with Marsh and tingle with Ky.

"Several congratulations are in order, I hear. On your marriage, your daughter and your business."

"I'll take them all. How about the best table in the house?"

"No less than I expected." She linked her arm through his. "Your life agrees with you," she decided as he led her to a table by the window. "You look happy."

"Look and am." He lifted a hand to brush hers. "We were sorry to hear about your father, Kate."

"I know. Thank you."

Marsh sat across from her and fixed her with eyes so much calmer, so much softer than his brother's. She'd always wondered why the man with the dreamer's eyes had been so practical while Ky had been the real dreamer. "It's tragic, but I can't say I'm sorry it brought you back to the island. We've missed you." He paused, just long enough for effect. "All of us."

Kate picked up the square carmine-colored napkin and ran it through her hands. "Things change," she said deliberately. "You and Linda are certainly proof of that. When I left, you thought she was a bit of a nuisance."

"That hasn't changed," he claimed and grinned. He glanced up at the young, pony-tailed waitress. "This is

Cindy, she'll take good care of you, Miss Hardesty—" He looked back at Kate with a grin. "I guess I should say Dr. Hardesty."

"Miss'll do," Kate told him. "I've taken the summer off."

"Miss Hardesty's a guest, a special one," he added, giving the waitress a smile. "How about a drink before you order? Or a bottle of wine?"

"Piesporter," the reply came from a deep, masculine voice.

Kate's fingers tightened on the linen, but she forced herself to look up calmly to meet Ky's amused eyes.

"The professor has a fondness for it."

"Yes, Mr. Silver."

Before Kate could agree or disagree, the waitress had dashed off.

"Well, Ky," Marsh commented easily. "You have a way of making the help come to attention."

With a shrug, Ky leaned against his brother's chair. If the three of them felt the air was suddenly tighter, each concealed it in their own way. "I had an urge for scampi."

"I can recommend it," Marsh told Kate. "Linda and the chef debated the recipe, then babied it until they reached perfection."

Kate smiled at Marsh as though there were no dark, brooding man looking down at her. "I'll try it. Are you going to join me?"

"I wish I could. Linda had to run home and deal with some crisis—Hope has a way of creating them and brow-beating the babysitter—but I'll try to get back for coffee. Enjoy your dinner." Rising, he sent his brother a cool, knowing look, then walked away.

"Marsh never completely got over that first case of adulation," Ky commented, then took his brother's seat without invitation.

"Marsh has always been a good friend." Kate draped the napkin over her lap with great care. "Though I realize this is your brother's restaurant, Ky, I'm sure you don't want my company for dinner any more than I want yours."

"That's where you're wrong." He sent a quick, dashing smile at the waitress as she brought the wine. He didn't bother to correct Kate's assumption on the Roost's ownership. Kate sat stone-faced, her manners too good to allow her to argue, while Cindy opened the bottle and poured the first sip for Ky to taste.

"It's fine," he told her. "I'll pour." Taking the bottle, he filled Kate's glass to within half an inch of the rim. "Since we've both chosen the Roost tonight, why don't we have a little test?"

Kate lifted her glass and sipped. The wine was cool and dry. She remembered the first bottle they'd shared—sitting on the floor of his cottage the night she gave him her innocence. Deliberately, she took another swallow. "What kind of test?"

"We can see if the two of us can share a civilized meal in public. That was something we never got around to before."

Kate frowned as he lifted his glass. She'd never seen Ky drink from a wineglass. The few times they had indulged in wine, it had been drunk out of one of the half a dozen water glasses he'd owned. The stemware seemed too delicate for his hand, the wine too mellow for the look in his eye.

No, they'd never eaten dinner in public before. Her

father would have exuded disapproval for socializing with someone he'd considered an employee. Kate had known it, and hadn't risked it.

Things were different now, she told herself as she lifted her own glass. In a sense, Ky was now her employee. She could make her own judgments. Recklessly, she toasted him. "To a profitable arrangement then."

"I couldn't have said it better myself." He touched the rim of his glass to hers, but his gaze was direct and uncomfortable. "Blue suits you," he said, referring to her dress, but not taking his eyes off hers. "The deep midnight blue that makes your skin look like something that should be tasted very, very carefully."

She stared at him, stunned at how easily his voice could take on that low, intimate tone that had always made the blood rush out of her brain. He'd always been able to make words seem something dark and secret. That had been one of his greatest skills, one she had never been prepared for. She was no more prepared for it now.

"Would you care to order now?" The waitress stopped beside the table, cheerful, eager to please.

Ky smiled when Kate remained silent. "We're having scampi. The house dressing on the salads will be fine." He leaned back, glass in hand, still smiling. But the smile on his lips didn't connect with his eyes. "You're not drinking your wine. Maybe I should've asked if your taste has changed over the years."

"It's fine." Deliberately she sipped, then kept the glass in her hand as though it would anchor her. "Marsh looks well," she commented. "I was happy to hear about him and Linda. I always pictured them together."

"Did you?" Ky lifted his glass toward the lowering

evening light slanting through the window. He watched the colors spear through the wine and glass and onto Kate's hand. "He didn't. But then…" Shifting his gaze, he met her eyes again. "Marsh always took more time to make up his mind than me."

"Recklessness," she continued as she struggled just to breathe evenly, "was always more your style than your brother's."

"But you didn't come to my brother with your charts and notes, did you?"

"No." With an effort she kept her voice and her eyes level. "I didn't. Perhaps I decided a certain amount of recklessness had its uses."

"Find me useful, do you, Kate?"

The waitress served the salads but didn't speak this time. She saw the look in Ky's eyes.

So had Kate. "When I'm having a job done, I've found that it saves a considerable amount of time and trouble to find the most suitable person." With forced calm, she set down her wine and picked up her fork. "I wouldn't have come back to Ocracoke for any other reason." She tilted her head, surprised by the quick surge of challenge that rushed through her. "Things will be simpler for both of us if that's clear up front."

Anger moved through him, but he controlled it. If they were playing word games, he had to keep his wits. She'd always been clever, but now it appeared the cleverness was glossed over with sophistication. He remembered the innocent, curious Kate with a pang. "As I recall, you were always one for complicating rather than simplifying. I had to explain the purpose, history and mechanics of every piece of equipment before you'd take the first dive."

"That's called caution, not complication."

"You'd know more about caution than I would. Some people spend half their lives testing the wind." He drank deeply of the wine. "I'd rather ride with it."

"Yes." This time it was she who smiled with her lips only. "I remember very well. No plans, no ties, tomorrow the wind might change."

"If you're anchored in one spot too long, you can become like those trees out there." He gestured out the window where a line of sparse junipers bent away from the sea. "Stunted."

"Yet you're still here, where you were born, where you grew up."

Slowly Ky poured her more wine. "The island's too isolated, the life a bit too basic for some. I prefer it to those structured little communities with their parties and country clubs."

Kate looked like she belonged in such a place, Ky thought as he fought against the frustrated desire that ebbed and flowed inside him. She belonged in an elegant silk suit, holding a Dresden cup and discussing an obscure eighteenth-century English poet. Was that why she could still make him feel rough and awkward and too full of longings?

If they could be swept back in time, he'd have stolen her, taken her out to open sea and kept her there. They would have traveled from port to exotic port. If having her meant he could never go home again, then he'd have sailed until his time was up. But he would have had her. Ky's fingers tightened around his glass. By God, he would have had her.

The main course was slipped in front of him discreetly.

Ky brought himself back to the moment. It wasn't the eighteenth century, but today. Still, she had brought him the past with the papers and maps. Perhaps they'd both find more than they'd bargained for.

"I looked over the things you left with me."

"Oh?" She felt a quick tingle of excitement but speared the first delicate shrimp as though it were all that concerned her.

"Your father's research is very thorough."

"Of course."

Ky let out a quick laugh. "Of course," he repeated, toasting her. "In any case, I think he might have been on the right track. You do realize that the section he narrowed it down to goes into a dangerous area."

Her brows drew together, but she continued to eat. "Sharks?"

"Sharks are a little difficult to confine to an area," he said easily. "A lot of people forget that the war came this close in the forties. There are still mines all along the coast of the Outer Banks. If we're going down to the bottom, it'd be smart to keep that in mind."

"I've no intention of being careless."

"No, but sometimes people look so far ahead they don't see what's under their feet."

Though he'd eaten barely half of his meal, Ky picked up his wine again. How could he eat when his whole system was aware of her? He couldn't stop himself from wondering what it would be like to pull those confining pins out of her hair as he'd done so often in the past. He couldn't prevent the memory from springing up about what it had been like to bundle her into his arms and just hold her there with her body fitting so neatly against his.

He could picture those long, serious looks she'd give him just before passion would start to take over, then the freedom he could feel racing through her in those last heady moments of love-making.

How could it have been so right once and so wrong now? Wouldn't her body still fit against his? Wouldn't her hair flow through his hands as it fell—that quiet brown that took on such fascinating lights in the sun. She'd always murmur his name after passion was spent, as if the sound alone sustained her. He wanted to hear her say it, just once more, soft and breathless while they were tangled together, bodies still warm and pulsing. He wasn't sure he could resist it.

Absently Ky signaled for coffee. Perhaps he didn't want to resist it. He needed her. He'd forgotten just how sharp and sure a need could be. Perhaps he'd take her. He didn't believe she was indifferent to him—certain things never fade completely. In his own time, in his own way, he'd take what he once had from her. And pray it would be enough this time.

When he looked back at her, Kate felt the warning signals shiver through her. Ky was a difficult man to understand. She knew only that he'd come to some decision and that it involved her. Grateful for the warming effects of the coffee, she drank. She was in charge this time, she reminded herself, every step of the way and she'd make him aware of it. There was no time like the present to begin.

"I'll be at the harbor at eight," she said briskly. "I'll require tanks of course, but I brought my own wet suit. I'd appreciate it if you'd have my briefcase and its contents on board. I believe we'd be wise to spend between six and eight hours out a day."

"Have you kept up with your diving?"

"I know what to do."

"I'd be the last to argue that you had the best teacher." He tilted his cup back in a quick, impatient gesture Kate found typical of him. "But if you're rusty, we'll take it slow for a day or two."

"I'm a perfectly competent diver."

"I want more than competence in a partner."

He saw the flare in her eyes and his need sharpened. It was a rare and arousing thing to watch her controlled and reasonable temperament heat up. "We're not partners. You're working for me."

"A matter of viewpoint," Ky said easily. He rose, deliberately blocking her in. "We'll be putting in a full day tomorrow, so you'd better go catch up on all the sleep you've been missing lately."

"I don't need you to worry about my health, Ky."

"I worry about my own," he said curtly. "You don't go under with me unless you're rested and alert. You come to the harbor in the morning with shadows under your eyes, you won't make the first dive." Furiously she squashed the urge to argue with the reasonable. "If you're sluggish, you make mistakes," Ky said briefly. "A mistake you make can cost me. That logical enough for you, professor?"

"It's perfectly clear." Bracing herself for the brush of bodies, Kate rose. But bracing herself didn't stop the jolt, not for either of them.

"I'll walk you back."

"It's not necessary."

His hand curled over her wrist, strong and stubborn. "It's civilized," he said lazily. "You were always big on being civilized."

Until you'd touch me, she thought. No, she wouldn't remember that, not if she wanted to sleep tonight. Kate merely inclined her head in cool agreement. "I want to thank Marsh."

"You can thank him tomorrow." Ky dropped the waitress's tip on the table. "He's busy."

She started to protest, then saw Marsh disappear into what must have been the kitchen. "All right." Kate moved by him and out into the balmy evening air.

The sun was low, though it wouldn't set for nearly an hour. The clouds to the west were just touched with mauve and rose. When she stepped outside, Kate decided there were more people in the restaurant than there were on the streets.

A charter fishing boat glided into the harbor. Some of the tourists would be staying on the island, others would be riding back across Hatteras Inlet on one of the last ferries of the day.

She'd like to go out on the water now, while the light was softening and the breeze was quiet. Now, she thought, while others were coming in and the sea would stretch for mile after endless empty mile.

Shaking off the mood, she headed for the hotel. What she needed wasn't a sunset sail but a good solid night's sleep. Daydreaming was foolish, and tomorrow too important.

The same hotel. Ky glanced up at her window. He already knew she had the same room. He'd walked her there before, but then she'd have had her arm through his in that sweet way she had of joining them together. She'd have looked up and laughed at him over something that had happened that day. And she'd have kissed him, warm,

long and lingeringly before the door would close behind her.

Because her thoughts had run the same gamut, Kate
turned to him while they were still outside the hotel.
"Thank you, Ky." She made a business out of shifting her
purse strap on her arm. "There's no need for you to go any
further out of your way."

"No, there isn't." He'd have something to take home
with him that night, he thought with sudden, fierce impatience. And he'd leave her something to take up to the
room where they'd had one long, glorious night. "But
then we've always looked at needs from different angles."
He cupped his hand around the back of her neck, holding
firm as he felt her stiffen.

"Don't." She didn't back away. Kate told herself she
didn't back away because to do so would make her seem
vulnerable. And she was, feeling those long hard fingers
play against her skin again.

"I think this is something you owe me," he told her in
a voice so quiet it shivered on the air. "Maybe something
I owe myself."

He wasn't gentle. That was deliberate. Somewhere
inside him was a need to punish for what hadn't been—
or perhaps what had. The mouth he crushed on hers
hungered, the arms he wrapped around her demanded. If
she'd forgotten, he thought grimly, this would remind her.
And remind her.

With her arms trapped between them, he could feel her
hands ball into tight fists. Let her hate him, loathe him.
He'd rather that than cool politeness.

But God she was sweet. Sweet and as delicate as one
of the frothy waves that lapped and spread along the shore-

line. Dimly, distantly, he knew he could drown in her without a murmur or complaint.

She wanted it to be different. Oh, how she wanted it to be different so that she'd feel nothing. But she felt everything.

The hard, impatient mouth that had always thrilled and bemused her—it was the same. The lean restless body that fit so unerringly against her—no different. The scent that clung to him, sea and salt—hadn't changed. Always when he kissed her, there'd been the sounds of water or wind or gulls. That, too, remained constant. Behind them boats rocked gently in their slips, water against wood. A gull resting on pilings let out a long, lonely call. The light dimmed as the sun dropped closer to the sea. The flood of past feelings rose up to merge and mingle with the moment.

She didn't resist him. Kate had told herself she wouldn't give him the satisfaction of a struggle. But the command to her brain not to respond was lost in the thin clouds of dusk. She gave because she had to. She took because she had no choice.

His tongue played over hers and her fists uncurled until Kate's palms rested against his chest. So warm, so hard, so familiar. He kissed as he always had, with complete concentration, no inhibitions and little patience.

Time tumbled back and she was young and in love and foolish. Why, she wondered while her head swam, should that make her want to weep?

He had to let her go or he'd beg. Ky could feel it rising in him. He wasn't fool enough to plead for what was already gone. He wasn't strong enough to accept that he had to let go again. The tug-of-war going on inside him was fierce enough to make him moan. On the sound he pulled away from her, frustrated, infuriated, bewitched.

Taking a moment, he stared down at her. Her look was the same, he realized—that half surprised, half speculative look she'd given him after their first kiss. It disoriented him. Whatever he'd sought to prove, Ky knew now he'd only proven that he was still as much enchanted with her as he'd ever been. He bit back an oath, instead, giving her a half-salute as he walked away.

"Get eight hours of sleep," he ordered without turning around.

Chapter 4

Some mornings the sun seemed to rise more slowly than others, as if nature wanted to show off her particular majesty just a bit longer. When she'd gone to bed, Kate had left her shades up knowing that the morning light would awaken her before the travel alarm beside her bed rang.

She took the dawn as a gift to herself, something individual and personal. Standing at the window, she watched it bloom. The first quiet breeze of morning drifted through the screen to run over her hair and face, through the thin material of her nightshirt, cool and promising. While she stood, Kate absorbed the colors, the light and the silent thunder of day breaking over water.

The lazy contemplation was far different from her structured routine of the past months and years. Mornings had been a time to dress, a time to run over her schedule and notes for the day's classes over two cups of coffee and a quick breakfast. She never had time to give herself the dawn, so she took it now.

She slept better than she'd expected, lulled by the quiet, exhausted by the days of traveling and the strain on her emotions. There'd been no dreams to haunt her from the time she'd turned back the sheets until the first light had fallen over her face. Then she rose quickly. There'd be no dreams now.

Kate let the morning wash over her with all its new promises, its beginnings. Today was the start. Everything, from the moment she'd taken out her father's papers until she'd seen Ky again, had been a prelude. Even the brief, torrid embrace of the night before had been no more than a ghost of the past. Today was the real beginning.

She dressed and went out into the morning.

Breakfast was impossible. The excitement she'd so meticulously held off was beginning to strain for freedom. The feeling that what she was doing was right was back with her. Whatever it took, whatever it cost her, she'd look for the gold her father had dreamed of. She'd follow his directions. If she found nothing, she'd have looked anyway.

In looking, Kate had come to believe she'd lay all her personal ghosts to rest.

Ky's kiss. It had been aching, disturbing as it had always been. She'd been absorbed, just as she'd always been. Though she knew she had to face both Ky and the past, she hadn't known it would be so frighteningly easy to go back— back to that dark, dreamy world where only he had taken her.

Now that she knew, now that she'd faced even that, Kate had to prepare to fight the wind.

He'd never forgiven her, she realized, for saying no. For bruising his pride. She'd gone back to her world when he'd asked her to stay in his. Asked her to stay, Kate remembered, without offering anything, not even a promise. If he'd given her that, no matter how casual or airy the promise might have been, she wouldn't have gone. She wondered if he knew that.

Perhaps he thought if he could make her lose herself to him again, the scales would be even. She wouldn't lose. Kate stuck her hands into the pockets of her brief pleated shorts. No, she didn't intend to lose. If he had pressed her last night, if he'd known just how weakened she'd been by that one kiss…

But he wouldn't know, she told herself. She wouldn't weaken again. For the summer, she'd make the treasure her goal and her one ambition. She wouldn't leave the island empty-handed this time.

He was already on board the *Vortex*. Kate could see him stowing gear, his hair tousled by the breeze that flowed in from the sea. With only cut-offs and a sleeveless T-shirt between him and the sun she could see the muscles coil and relax, the skin gleam.

Magnificent. She felt the dull ache deep in her stomach and tried to rationalize it away. After all, a well-honed masculine build should make a woman respond. It was natural. One could even call it impersonal, Kate decided. As she started down the dock she wished she could believe it.

He didn't see her. A fishing boat already well out on the water had caught his attention. For a moment, she stopped, just watching him. Why was it she could always sense the restlessness in him? There was movement in him even when he was still, sound even when he was silent. What was it he saw when he looked out over the sea? Challenge? Romance?

He was a man who always seemed poised for action, for doing. Yet he could sit quietly and watch the waves as if there were nothing more important than that endless battle between earth and water.

Just now he stood on the deck of his boat, hands on hips, watching the tubby fishing vessel putt toward the horizon. It was something he'd seen countless times, yet he stopped to take it in again. Kate looked where Ky looked and wished she could see what he was seeing.

Quietly she went forward, her deck shoes making no sound, but he turned, eyes still intense. "You're early," he said, and with no more greeting reached out a hand to help her on board.

"I thought you might be as anxious to start as I am."

Palm met palm, rough against smooth. Both of them broke contact as soon as possible.

"It should be an easy ride." He looked back to sea, toward the boat, but this time he didn't focus on it. "The wind's coming in from the north, no more than ten knots."

"Good." Though it wouldn't have mattered to her nor, she thought, to him, if the wind had been twice as fast. This was the morning to begin.

She could sense the impatience in him, the desire to be gone and doing. Wanting to make things as simple as possible Kate helped Ky cast off, then walked to the stern. That would keep the maximum distance between them. They didn't speak. The engine roared to life, shattering the calm. Smoothly, Ky maneuvered the small cruiser out of the harbor, setting up a small wake that caused the water to lap against pilings. He kept the same steady even speed while they sailed through the shallows of Ocracoke Inlet. Looking back, Kate watched the distance between the boat and the village grow.

The dreamy quality remained. The last thing she saw was a child walking down a pier with a rod cocked rakishly over his shoulder. Then she turned her face to the sea.

Warm wind, glaring sun. Excitement. Kate hadn't been sure the feelings would be the same. But when she closed her eyes, letting the dull red light glow behind her lids, the salty mist touch her face, she knew this was a love that had remained constant, one that had waited for her.

Sitting perfectly still, she could feel Ky increase the speed until the boat was eating its way through the water as sleekly as a cat moves through the jungle. With her eyes closed, she enjoyed the movement, the speed, the sun. This was a thrill that had never faded. Tasting it again, she understood that it never would.

She'd been right, Kate realized, the hunt would be much more exciting than the final goal. The hunt, and no matter how cautious she was, the man at the helm.

He'd told himself he wouldn't look back at her. But he had to—just once. Eyes closed, a smile playing around her mouth, hair dancing around her face where the wind nudged it from the pins. It brought back a flash of memory—to the first time he'd seen her like that and realized he had to have her. She looked calm, totally at peace. He felt there was a war raging inside him that he had no control over.

Even when he turned back to sea again Ky could see her, leaning back against the stern, absorbing what wind and water offered. In defense, he tried to picture her in a classroom, patiently explaining the intricacies of *Don Juan* or *Henry IV*. It didn't help. He could only imagine her sitting behind him, soaking up sun and wind as if she'd been starved for it.

Perhaps she had been. Though she didn't know what direction Ky's thoughts had taken, Kate realized she'd never been further away from the classroom or the demands she placed on herself there than she was at this moment. She was part teacher, there was no question of that, but she was also, no matter how she'd tried to banish it, part dreamer.

With the sun and the wind on her skin, she was too exhilarated to be frightened by the knowledge, too content to worry. It was a wild, free sensation to experience again something known, loved, then lost.

Perhaps... Perhaps it was too much like the one frenzied kiss she'd shared with Ky the night before, but she needed it. It might be a foolish need, even a dangerous one. Just once, only this once, she told herself, she wouldn't question it.

Steady, strong, she opened her eyes again. Now she could watch the sun toss its diamonds on the surface of the water. They rippled, enticing, enchanting. The fishing boat Ky had watched move away from the island before them was anchored, casting its nets. A purse seiner, she remembered. Ky had explained the wide, weighted net to her once and how it was often used to haul in menhaden.

She wondered why he'd never chosen that life, where he could work and live on the water day after day. But not alone, she recalled with a ghost of a smile. Fishermen were their own community, on the sea and off it. It wasn't often

Ky chose to share himself or his time with anyone. There were times, like this one, when she understood that perfectly.

Whether it was the freedom or the strength that was in her, Kate approached him without nerves. "It's as beautiful as I remember."

He dreaded having her stand beside him again. Now, however, he discovered the tension at the base of his neck had eased. "It doesn't change much." Together they watched the gulls swoop around the fishing boat, hoping for easy pickings. "Fishing's been good this year."

"Have you been doing much?"

"Off and on."

"Clamming?"

He had to smile when he remembered how she'd looked, jeans rolled up to her knees, bare feet full of sand as he'd taught her how to dig. "Yeah."

She, too, remembered, but her only memories were of warm days, warm nights. "I've often wondered what it's like on the island in winter."

"Quiet."

She took the single careless answer with a nod. "I've often wondered why you preferred that."

He turned to her, measuring. "Have you?"

Perhaps that had been a mistake. Since it had already been made, Kate shrugged. "It would be foolish of me to say I hadn't thought of the island or you at all during the last four years. You've always made me curious."

He laughed. It was so typical of her to put things that way. "Because all your tidy questions weren't answered. You think too much like a teacher, Kate."

"Isn't life a multiple choice?" she countered. "Maybe

two or three answers would fit, but only one's ultimately right."

"No, only one's ultimately wrong." He saw her eyes take on that thoughtful, considering expression. She was, he knew, weighing the pros and cons of his statement. Whether she agreed or not, she'd consider all the angles. "You haven't changed either," he murmured.

"I thought the same of you. We're both wrong. Neither of us have stayed the same. That's as it should be." Kate looked away from him, further east, then gave a quick cry of pleasure. "Oh, look!" Without thinking, she put her hand on his arm, slender fingers gripping taut muscle. "Dolphins."

She watched them, a dozen, perhaps more, leap and dive in their musical pattern. Pleasure was touched with envy. To move like that, she thought, from water to air and back to water again. It was a freedom that might drive a man mad with the glory of it. But what a madness...

"Fantastic, isn't it?" she murmured. "To be part of the air and the sea. I'd nearly forgotten."

"How much?" Ky studied her profile until he could have etched the shape of it on the wind. "How much have you nearly forgotten?"

Kate turned her head, only then realizing just how close they stood. Unconsciously, she'd moved nearer to him when she'd seen the dolphins. Now she could see nothing but his face, inches from hers, feel nothing but the warm skin beneath her hand. His question, the depth of it, seemed to echo off the surface of the water to haunt her.

She stepped back. The drop before her was very deep and torn with rip tides. "All that was necessary," she said simply. "I'd like to look over my father's charts. Did you bring them on board?"

"Your briefcase is in the cabin." His hands gripped the wheel tightly, as though he were fighting against a storm. Perhaps he was. "You should be able to find your way below."

Without answering, Kate walked around him to the short steep steps that led belowdecks.

There were two narrow bunks with the spreads taut enough to bounce a coin if one was dropped. The galley just beyond would have all the essentials, she knew, in small, efficient scale. Everything would be in its place, as tidy as a monk's cell.

Kate could remember lying with Ky on one of the pristine bunks, flushed with passion while the boat swayed gently in the current and the music from his radio played jazz.

She gripped the leather of her case as if the pain in her fingers would help fight off the memories. To fight everything off entirely was too much to expect, but the intensity eased. Carefully she unfolded one of her father's charts and spread it on the bunk.

Like everything her father had done, the chart was precise and without frills. Though it had certainly not been his field, Hardesty had drawn a chart any sailor would have trusted.

It showed the coast of North Carolina, Pamlico Sound and the Outer Banks, from Manteo to Cape Lookout. As well as the lines of latitude and longitude, the chart also had the thin crisscrossing lines that marked depth.

Seventy-six degrees north by thirty-five degrees east. From the markings, that was the area her father had decided the *Liberty* had gone down. That was southeast of Ocracoke by no more than a few miles. And the depth... Yes, she decided as she frowned over the chart, the depth would still be considered shallow diving. She and Ky would have the relative freedom of wet suits and tanks rather than the leaded boots and helmets required for deep-sea explorations.

X marks the spot she thought, a bit giddy, but made herself fold the chart with the same care she'd used to open it. She felt the boat slow then heard the resounding silence when the engines shut off. A fresh tremor of anticipation went through her as she climbed the steps into the sunlight again.

Ky was already checking the tanks though she knew he would have gone over all the equipment thoroughly before setting out. "We'll go down here," he said as he rose from his crouched position. "We're about half a mile from the last place your father went in last summer."

In one easy motion he pulled off his shirt. Kate knew he was self-aware, but he'd never been self-conscious. Ky had already stripped down to brief bikini trunks before she turned away for her own gear.

If her heart was pounding, it was possible to tell herself it was in anticipation of the dive. If her throat was dry, she could almost believe it was nerves at the thought of giving herself to the sea again. His body was hard and brown and lean, but she was only concerned with his skill and his knowledge. And he, she told herself, was only concerned with his fee and his twenty-five percent of the find.

She wore a snug tank suit under her shorts that clung to subtle curves and revealed long, slender legs that Ky knew were soft as water, strong as a runner's. He began to pull on the thin rubber wet suit. They were here to look for gold, to find a treasure that had been lost. Some treasures, he knew, could never be recovered.

As he thought of it, Ky glanced up to see Kate draw the pins from her hair. It fell, soft and slow, over, then past her shoulders. If she'd shot a dart into his chest, she couldn't have pierced his heart more accurately. Swearing under his breath, Ky lifted the first set of tanks.

"We'll go down for an hour today."

"But—"

"An hour's more than enough," he interrupted without sparing her a glance. "You haven't worn tanks in four years."

Kate slipped into the set he offered her, securing the straps until they were snug, but not tight. "I didn't tell you that."

"No, but you'd sure as hell have told me if you had." The corner of his mouth lifted when she remained silent. After attaching his own tanks, Ky climbed over the side onto the ladder. She could either argue, he figured, or she could follow.

To clear his mask, he spat into it, rubbed, then reached down to rinse it in salt water. Pulling it over his eyes and nose, Ky dropped into the sea. It took less than ten seconds before Kate plunged into the water beside him. He paused a moment, to make certain she didn't flounder or forget to breathe, then he headed for greater depth.

No, she wouldn't forget to breathe, but the first breath was almost a sigh as her body submerged. It was as thrilling to her as it had been the first time, this incredible ability to stay beneath the ocean's surface and breathe air.

Kate looked up to see the sun spearing through the water, and held out a hand to watch the watery light play on her skin. She could have stayed there, she realized, just reveling in it. But with a curl of her body and a kick, she followed Ky into depth and dimness.

Ky saw a school of menhaden and wondered if they'd end up in the net of the fishing boat he'd watched that morning. When the fish swerved in a mass and rushed past him, he turned to Kate again. She'd been right when she'd told him she knew what to do. She swam as cleanly and as competently as ever.

He expected her to ask him how he intended to look for the *Liberty*, what plan he'd outlined. When she hadn't, Ky had figured it was for one of two reasons. Either she didn't want to have any in-depth conversation with him at the moment, or she'd already reasoned it out for herself. It seemed more likely to be the latter, as her mind was also as clean and competent as ever.

The most logical method of searching seemed to be a semi-circular route around Hardesty's previous dives. Slowly and methodically, they would widen the circle. If Hardesty had been right, they'd find the *Liberty* eventually. If he'd been wrong…they'd have spent the summer treasure hunting.

Though the tanks on her back reminded Kate not to take the weightless freedom for granted, she thought she could stay down forever. She wanted to touch—the water, the sea grass, the soft, sandy bottom. Reaching out toward a school of bluefish she watched them scatter defensively then regroup. She knew there were times when, as a diver moved through the dim, liquid world, he could forget the need for the sun. Perhaps Ky had been right in limiting the dive. She had to be careful not to take what she found again for granted.

The flattened disklike shape caught Ky's attention. Automatically, he reached for Kate's arm to stop her forward progress. The stingray that scuttled along the bottom looking for tasty crustaceans might be amusing to watch, but it was deadly. He gauged this one to be as long as he was tall with a tail as sharp and cruel as a razor. They'd give it a wide berth.

Seeing the ray reminded Kate that the sea wasn't all beauty and dreams. It was also pain and death. Even as she watched, the stingray struck out with its whiplike tail and caught a small, hapless bluefish. Once, then twice. It was nature, it was life. But she turned away. Through the protective masks, her eyes met Ky's.

She expected to see derision for an obvious weakness, or worse, amusement. She saw neither. His eyes were gentle, as they were very rarely. Lifting a hand, he ran his knuckles down her cheek, as he'd done years before when he'd chosen to offer comfort or affection. She felt the warmth, it reflected in her eyes. Then, as quickly as the moment had come, it was over. Turning, Ky swam away, gesturing for her to follow.

He couldn't afford to be distracted by those glimpses of vulnerability, those flashes of sweetness. They had already done him in once. Top priority was the job they'd set out to do. Whatever other plans he had, Ky intended to be in full control. When the time was right, he'd have his fill of Kate. That he promised himself. He'd take exactly what he felt she owed him. But she wouldn't touch his emotions again. When he took her to bed, it would be with cold calculation.

That was something else he promised himself.

Though they found no sign of the *Liberty*, Ky saw wreckage from other ships—pieces of metal, rusted, covered with barnacles. They might have been from a sub or a battleship from World War II. The sea absorbed what remained in her.

He was tempted to swim farther out, but knew it would take twenty minutes to return to the boat. Circling around, he headed back, overlapping, double-checking the area they'd just covered.

Not quite a needle in a haystack, Ky mused, but close. Two centuries of storms and currents and sea quakes. Even if they had the exact location where the *Liberty* had sunk, rather than the last known location, it took calculation and guesswork, then luck to narrow the field down to a radius of twenty miles.

Ky believed in luck much the same way he imagined Hardesty had believed in calculation. Perhaps with a mixture of the two, he and Kate would find what was left of the *Liberty*.

Glancing over, he watched Kate gliding beside him. She was looking everywhere at once, but Ky didn't think her mind was on treasure or sunken ships. She was, as she'd been that summer before, completely enchanted with the sea and the life it held. He wondered if she still remembered all the information she'd demanded of him before the first dive. What about the physiological adjustments to the body? How was the CO_2 absorbed? What about the change in external pressure?

Ky felt a flash of humor as they started to ascend. He was dead sure Kate remembered every answer he'd given her, right down to the decimal point in pounds of pressure per square inch.

The sun caught her as she rose toward the surface, slowly. It shone around and through her hair, giving her an ethereal appearance as she swam straight up, legs kicking gently, face tilted toward sun and surface. If there were mermaids, Ky knew they'd look as she did—slim, long, with pale loose hair free in the water. A man could only hold on to a mermaid if he accepted the world she lived in as his own. Reaching out, he caught the tip of her hair in his fingers just before they broke the surface together.

Kate came up laughing, letting her mouthpiece fall and pushing her mask up. "Oh, it's wonderful! Just as I remembered." Treading water, she laughed again and Ky realized it was a sound he hadn't heard in four years. But he remembered it exactly.

"You looked like you wanted to play more than you wanted to look for sunken ships." He grinned at her, enjoying her pleasure and the ease of a smile he'd never expected to see again.

"I did." Almost reluctant, she reached out for the ladder to climb on board. "I never expected to find anything the first time down, and it was so wonderful just to dive again." She stripped off her tanks then checked the valves herself before she set them down. "Whenever I go down I begin to believe I don't need the sun anymore. Then when I come up it's warmer and brighter than I remember."

With the adrenaline still flowing, she peeled off her flippers, then her mask, to stand, face lifted toward the sun. "There's nothing else exactly like it."

"Skin diving." Ky tugged down the zipper of his wet suit. "I tried some in Tahiti last year. It's incredible being in that clear water with no equipment but a mask and flippers, and your own lungs."

"Tahiti?" Surprised and interested, Kate looked back as Ky stripped off the wet suit. "You went there?"

"Couple of weeks late last year." He dropped the wet

suit in the big plastic can he used for storing equipment before rinsing.

"Because of your affection for islands?"

"And grass skirts."

The laughter bubbled out again. "I'm sure you'd look great in one."

He'd forgotten just how quick she could be when she relaxed. Because the gesture appealed, Ky reached over and gave her hair a quick tug. "I wish I'd taken snapshots." Turning, he jogged down the steps into the cabin.

"Too busy ogling the natives to put them on film for posterity?" Kate called out as she dropped down on the narrow bench on the starboard side.

"Something like that. And of course trying to pretend I didn't notice the natives ogling me."

She grinned. "People in grass skirts," she began then let out a muffled shout as he tossed a peach in her direction. Catching it cleanly, Kate smiled at him before she bit into the fruit.

"Still have good reflexes," Ky commented as he came up the last step.

"Especially when I'm hungry." She touched her tongue to her palm where juice dribbled. "I couldn't eat this morning, I was too keyed up."

He held out one of two bottles of cold soda he'd taken from the refrigerator. "About the dive?"

"That and…" Kate broke off, surprised that she was talking to him as if it had been four years before.

"And?" Ky prompted. Though his tone was casual, his gaze had sharpened.

Aware of it, Kate rose, turning away to look back over the stern. She saw nothing there but sky and water. "It was the morning," she murmured. "The way the sun came up over the water. All that color." She shook her head and water dripped from the ends of her hair onto the deck. "I haven't watched a sunrise in a very long time."

Making himself relax again, Ky leaned back, biting into his own peach as he watched her. "Why?"

"No time. No need."

"Do they both mean the same thing to you?"

Restless, she moved her shoulders. "When your life revolves around schedules and classes, I suppose one equals the other."

"That's what you want? A daily timetable?"

Kate looked back over her shoulder, meeting his eyes levelly. How could they ever understand each other? she wondered. Her world was as foreign to him as his to her. "It's what I've chosen."

"One of your multiple choices of life?" Ky countered, giving a short laugh before he tilted his bottle back again.

"Maybe, or maybe some parts of life only have one choice." She turned completely around, determined not to lose the euphoria that had come to her with the dive. "Tell me about Tahiti, Ky. What's it like?"

"Soft air, soft water. Blue, green, white. Those are the colors that come to mind, then outrageous splashes of red and orange and yellow."

"Like a Gauguin painting."

The length of the deck separated them. Perhaps that made it easier for him to smile. "I suppose, but I don't think he'd have appreciated all the hotels and resorts. It isn't an island that's been left to itself."

"Things rarely are."

"Whether they should be or not."

Something in the way he said it, in the way he looked
at her, made Kate think he wasn't speaking of an island
now, but of something more personal. She drank, cooling
her throat, moistening her lips. "Did you scuba?"

"Some. Shells and coral so thick I could've filled a
boat with them if I'd wanted. Fish that looked like they
should've been in an aquarium. And sharks." He remembered one that had nearly caught him half a mile out. Remembering made him grin. "The waters off Tahiti are
anything but boring."

Kate recognized the look, the recklessness that would
always surface just under his skill. Perhaps he didn't look
for trouble, but she thought he'd rarely sidestep it. No, she
doubted they'd ever fully understand each other, if they
had a lifetime.

"Did you bring back a shark's tooth necklace?"

"I gave it to Hope." He grinned again. "Linda won't let
her have it yet."

"I should think not. Does it feel odd, being an uncle?"

"No. She looks like me."

"Ah, the male ego."

Ky shrugged, aware that he had a healthy share and was
comfortable with it. "I get a kick out of watching her run
Marsh and Linda in circles. There's not much entertain-
ment on the island."

She tried to imagine Ky being entertained by something
as tame as a baby girl. She failed. "It's strange," Kate said
after a moment. "Coming back to find Marsh and Linda
married and parents. When I left Marsh treated Linda like
his little sister."

"Didn't your father keep you up on progress on the
island?"

The smile left her eyes. "No."

Ky lifted a brow. "Did you ask?"

"No."

He tossed his empty bottle into a small barrel. "He hadn't told you anything about the ship either, about why he kept coming back to the island year after year."

She tossed her drying hair back from her face. It hadn't been put in the tone of a question. Still, she answered because it was simpler that way. "No, he never mentioned the *Liberty* to me."

"That doesn't bother you?"

The ache came, but she pushed it aside. "Why should it?" she countered. "He was entitled to his own life, his privacy."

"But you weren't."

She felt the chill come and go. Crossing the deck, Kate dropped her bottle beside Ky's before reaching for her shirt. "I don't know what you mean."

"You know exactly what I mean." He closed his hand over hers before she could pull the shirt on. Because it would've been cowardly to do otherwise, she lifted her head and faced him. "You know," he said again, quietly. "You just aren't ready to say it out loud yet."

"Leave it alone, Ky." Her voice trembled, and though it infuriated her, she couldn't prevent it. "Just leave it."

He wanted to shake her, to make her admit, so that he could hear, that she'd left him because her father had preferred it. He wanted her to say, perhaps sob, that she hadn't had the strength to stand up to the man who had shaped and molded her life to suit his values and wants.

With an effort, he relaxed his fingers. As he had before, Ky turned away with something like a shrug. "For now," he said easily as he went back to the helm. "Summer's just beginning." He started the engine before turning around for one last look. "We both know what can happen during a summer."

Chapter 5

"The first thing you have to understand about Hope," Linda began, steadying a vase the toddler had jostled, "is that she has a mind of her own."

Kate watched the chubby black-haired Hope climb onto a wing-backed chair to examine herself in an ornamental mirror. In the fifteen minutes Kate had been in Linda's home, Hope hadn't been still a moment. She was quick, surprisingly agile, with a look in her eyes that made Kate believe she knew exactly what she wanted and intended to get it, one way or the other. Ky had been right. His niece looked like him, in more ways than one.

"I can see that. Where do you find the energy to run a restaurant, keep a home and manage a fireball?"

"Vitamins," Linda sighed. "Lots and lots of vitamins. Hope, don't put your fingers on the glass."

"Hope!" the toddler cried out, making faces at herself in the mirror. "Pretty, pretty, pretty."

"The Silver ego," Linda commented. "It never tarnishes."

With a chuckle, Kate watched Hope crawl backwards out of the chair, land on her diaper-padded bottom and begin to systematically destroy the tower of blocks she'd built a short time before. "Well, she is pretty. It only shows she's smart enough to know it."

"It's hard for me to argue that point, except when she's spread toothpaste all over the bathroom floor." With a contented sigh, Linda sat back on the couch. She enjoyed having Monday afternoons off to play with Hope and catch up on the dozens of things that went by the wayside when the restaurant demanded her time. "You've been here over a week now, and this is the first time we've been able to talk."

Kate bent over to ruffle Hope's hair. "You're a busy woman."

"So are you."

Kate heard the question, not so subtly submerged in the statement, and smiled. "You know I didn't come back to the island to fish and wade, Linda."

"All right, all right, the heck with being tactful." With a mother's skill, she kept her antenna honed on her active toddler and leaned toward Kate. "What *are* you and Ky doing out on his boat every day?"

With Linda, evasions were neither necessary nor advisable. "Looking for treasure," Kate said simply.

"Oh." Expressing only mild surprise, Linda saved a budding African violet from her daughter's curious fingers. "Blackbeard's treasure." She handed Hope a rubber duck in lieu of the plant. "My grandfather still tells stories about it. Pieces of eight, a king's ransom and bottles of rum. I always figured that it was buried on land."

Amused at the way Linda could handle the toddler without breaking rhythm, Kate shook her head. "No, not Blackbeard's."

There were dozens of theories and myths about where the infamous pirate had hidden his booty, and fantastic speculation on just how rich the trove was. Kate had never considered them any more than stories. Yet she supposed, in her own way, she was following a similar fantasy.

"My father'd been researching the whereabouts of an English merchant ship that sank off the coast here in the eighteenth century."

"Your father?" Instantly Linda's attention sharpened. She couldn't conceive of the Edwin Hardesty she remembered from summers past as a treasure searcher. "That's why he kept coming to the island every summer? I could never figure out why…" She broke off, grimaced, then plunged ahead. "I'm sorry, Kate, but he never seemed the type to take up scuba diving as a hobby, and I never once saw him with a fish. He certainly managed to keep what he was doing a secret."

"Yes, even from me."

"You didn't know?" Linda glanced over idly as Hope began to beat on a plastic bucket with a wooden puzzle piece.

"Not until I went through his papers a few weeks ago. I decided to follow through on what he'd started."

"And you came to Ky."

"I came to Ky." Kate smoothed the material of her thin summer skirt over her knees. "I needed a boat, a diver, preferably an islander. He's the best."

Linda's attention shifted from her daughter to Kate.
There was simple understanding there, but it didn't completely mask impatience. "Is that the only reason you came
to Ky?"

Needs rose up to taunt her. Memories washed up in one
warm wave. "Yes, that's the only reason."

Linda wondered why Kate should want her to believe
what Kate didn't believe herself. "What if I told you he's
never forgotten you?"

Kate shook her head quickly, almost frantically.
"Don't."

"I love him." Linda rose to distract Hope who'd discovered tossing blocks was more interesting than stacking
them. "Even though he's a frustrating, difficult man. He's
Marsh's brother." She set Hope in front of a small army
of stuffed animals before she turned and smiled. "He's my
brother. And you were the first mainlander I was ever
really close to. It's hard for me to be objective."

It was tempting to pour out her heart, her doubts. Too
tempting. "I appreciate that, Linda. Believe me, what was
between Ky and me was over a long time ago. Lives
change."

Making a neutral sound, Linda sat again. There were
some people you didn't press. Ky and Kate were both the
same in that area, however diverse they were otherwise.
"All right. You know what I've been doing the past four
years." She sent a long-suffering look in Hope's direction.
"Tell me what your life's been like."

"Quieter."

Linda laughed. "A small border war would be quieter
than life in this house."

"Earning my doctorate as early as I did took a lot of

concentrated effort." She'd needed that one goal to keep herself level, to keep herself…calm. "When you're teaching as well it doesn't leave much time for anything else." Shrugging, she rose. It sounded so staid, she realized. So dull. She'd wanted to learn, she'd wanted to teach, but in and of itself, it sounded hollow.

There were toys spread all over the living room, tiny pieces of childhood. A tie was tossed carelessly over the back of a chair next to a table where Linda had dropped her purse. Small pieces of a marriage. Family. She wondered, with a panic that came and went quickly, how she would ever survive the empty house back in Connecticut.

"This past year at Yale has been fascinating and difficult." Was she defending or explaining? Kate wondered impatiently. "Strange, even though my father taught, I didn't realize that being a teacher is just as hard and demanding as being a student."

"Harder," Linda declared after a moment. "You have to have the answers."

"Yes." Kate crouched down to look at Hope's collection of stuffed animals. "I suppose that's part of the appeal, though. The challenge of either knowing the answer or reasoning it out, then watching it sink in."

"Hoping it sinks in?" Linda ventured.

Kate laughed again. "Yes, I suppose that's it. When it does, that's the most rewarding aspect. Being a mother can't be that much different. You're teaching every day."

"Or trying to," Linda said dryly.

"The same thing."

"You're happy?"

Hope squeezed a bright pink dragon then held it out for

Kate. Was she happy? Kate wondered as she obliged by cuddling the dragon in turn. She'd been aiming for achievement, she supposed, not happiness. Her father had never asked that very simple, very basic question. She'd never taken the time to ask herself. "I want to teach," she answered at length. "I'd be unhappy if I couldn't."

"That's a roundabout way of answering without answering at all."

"Sometimes there isn't any yes or no."

"Ky!" Hope shouted so that Kate jolted, whipping her head around to the front door.

"No." Linda noted the reaction, but said nothing. "She means the dragon. He gave it to her, so it's Ky."

"Oh." She wanted to swear but managed to smile as she handed the baby back her treasured dragon. It wasn't reasonable that just his name should make her hands unsteady, her pulse unsteady, her thoughts unsteady. "He wouldn't pick the usual, would he?" she asked carelessly as she rose.

"No." She gave Kate a very direct, very level look. "His tastes have always run to the unique."

Amusement helped to relax her. Kate's brow rose as she met the look. "You don't give up, do you?"

"Not on something I believe in." A trace of stubbornness came through. The stubbornness, Kate mused, that had kept her determinedly waiting for Marsh to fall in love with her. "I believe in you and Ky," Linda continued. "You two can make a mess of it for as long as you want, but I'll still believe in you."

"You haven't changed," Kate said on a sigh. "I came back to find you a wife, a mother, and the owner of a restaurant, but you haven't changed at all."

"Being a wife and mother only makes me more certain that what I believe is right." She had her share of arrogance, too, and used it. "We don't own the restaurant," she added as an afterthought.

"No?" Surprised, Kate looked up again. "But I thought you said the Roost was yours and Marsh's."

"We run it," Linda corrected. "And we do have a twenty percent interest." Sitting back, she gave Kate a pleased smile. There was nothing she liked better than to drop small bombs in calm water and watch the ripples. "Ky owns the Roost."

"Ky?" Kate couldn't have disguised the astonishment if she'd tried. The Ky Silver she thought she knew hadn't owned anything but a boat and a shaky beach cottage. He hadn't wanted to. Buying a restaurant, even a small one on a remote island took more than capital. It took ambition.

"Apparently he didn't bother to mention it."

"No." He'd had several opportunities, Kate recalled, the night they'd had dinner. "No, he didn't. It doesn't seem characteristic," she murmured. "I can picture him buying another boat, a bigger boat or a faster boat, but I can't imagine him buying a restaurant."

"I guess it surprised everyone except Marsh—but then Marsh knows Ky better than anyone. A couple of weeks before we were married, Ky told us he'd bought the place and intended to remodel. Marsh was ferrying over to Hatteras every day to work, I was helping out in my aunt's craft shop during the season. When Ky asked if we wanted to buy in for twenty percent and take over as managers, we jumped at it." She smiled, pleased, and perhaps relieved. "It wasn't a mistake for any of us."

Kate remembered the homey atmosphere, the excellent

seafood, the fast service. No, it hadn't been a mistake, but Ky… "I just can't picture Ky in business, not on land anyway."

"Ky knows the island," Linda said simply. "And he knows what he wants. To my way of thinking, he just doesn't always know how to get it."

Kate was going to avoid that area of speculation. "I'm going to take a walk down to the beach," she decided. "Would you like to come?"

"I'd love to, but—" With a gesture of her hand Linda indicated why Hope had been quiet for the last few minutes. With her arm hooked around her dragon, she was sprawled over the rest of the animals, sound asleep.

"It's either stop or go with her, isn't it?" Kate observed with a laugh.

"The nice thing is that when she stops, so can I." Expertly Linda gathered up Hope, cradling her daughter on her shoulder. "Have a nice walk, and stop into the Roost tonight if you have the chance."

"I will." Kate touched Hope's head, the thick, dark, disordered hair that was so much like her uncle's. "She's beautiful, Linda. You're very lucky."

"I know. It's something I don't ever forget."

Kate let herself out of the house and walked along the quiet street. Clouds were low, making the light gloomy, but the rain held off. She could taste it in the breeze, the clean freshness of it, mixed with the faintest hint of the sea. It was in that direction she walked.

On an island, she'd discovered, you were much more drawn to the water than to the land. It was the one thing she'd understood completely about Ky, the one thing she'd never questioned.

It had been easier to avoid going to the beach in Connecticut, though she'd always loved the rocky, windy New England coast. She'd been able to resist it, knowing what memories it would bring back. Pain. Kate had learned there were ways of avoiding pain. But here, knowing you could reach the edge of land by walking in any direction, she couldn't resist. It might have been wiser to walk to the sound, or the inlet. She walked to the sea.

It was warm enough that she needed no more than the sheer skirt and blouse, breezy enough so that the material fluttered around her. She saw two men, caps low over foreheads, their rods secured in the sand, talking together while they sat on buckets and waited for a strike. Their voices didn't carry above the roar and thunder of surf, but she knew their conversation would deal with bait and lures and yesterday's catch. She wouldn't disturb them, nor they her. It was the way of the islander to be friendly enough, but not intrusive.

The water was as gray as the sky, but she didn't mind. Kate had learned not just to accept its moods but to appreciate the contrasts of each one. When the sea was like this, brooding, with threats of violence on the surface, that meant a storm. She found it appealed to a restlessness in herself she rarely acknowledged.

Whitecaps tossed with systematic fever. The spray rose high and wide. The cry of gulls didn't seem lonely or plaintive now, but challenging. No, a gray gloomy sky meeting a gray sea was anything but dull. It teamed with energy. It boiled with life.

The wind tugged at her hair, loosening pins. She didn't notice. Standing just away from the edge of the surf, Kate faced wind and sea with her eyes wide. She had to think about what she'd just discovered about Ky. Perhaps what she had been determined not to discover about herself.

Thinking there, alone in the gray threatening light before a storm, was what Kate felt she needed. The constant wind blowing in from the east would keep her head clear. Maybe the smells and sounds of the sea would remind her of what she'd had and rejected, and what she'd chosen to have.

Once she'd had a powerful force that had held her swirling, breathless. That force was Ky, a man who could pull on your emotions, your senses, by simply being. The recklessness had attracted her once, the tough arrogance combined with unexpected gentleness. What she saw as his irresponsibility had disturbed her. Kate sensed that he was a man who would drift through life when she'd been taught from birth to seek out a goal and work for it to the exclusion of all else. It was that very different outlook on life that set them poles apart.

Perhaps he had decided to take on some responsibility in his life with the restaurant, Kate decided. If he had she was glad of it. But it couldn't make any difference. They were still poles apart.

She chose the calm, the ordered. Success was satisfaction in itself when success came from something loved. Teaching was vital to her, not just a job, not even a profession. The giving of knowledge fed her. Perhaps for a moment in Linda's cozy, cluttered home it hadn't seemed like enough. Not quite enough. Still, Kate knew if you wished for too much, you often received nothing at all.

With the wind whipping at her face she watched the rain begin far out to sea in a dark curtain. If the past had been a treasure she'd lost, no chart could take her back. In her life, she'd been taught only one direction.

* * *

Ky never questioned his impulses to walk on the beach. He was a man who was comfortable with his own mood swings, so comfortable, he rarely noticed them. He hadn't deliberately decided to stop work on his boat at a certain time. He simply felt the temptation of sea and storm and surrendered to it.

Ky watched the seas as he made his way up and over the hill of sand. He could have found his way without faltering in the dark, with no moon. He'd stood on shore and watched the rain at sea before, but repetition didn't lessen the pleasure. The wind would bring it to the island, but there was still time to seek shelter if shelter were desired. More often than not, Ky would let the rain flow over him while the waves rose and fell wildly.

He'd seen his share of tropical storms and hurricanes. While he might find them exhilarating, he appreciated the relative peace of a summer rain. Today he was grateful for it. It had given him a day away from Kate.

They had somehow reached a shaky, tense coexistence that made it possible for them to be together day after day in a relatively small space. The tension was making him nervy; nervy enough to make a mistake when no diver could afford to make one.

Seeing her, being with her, knowing she'd withdrawn from him as a person was infinitely more difficult than being apart from her. To Kate, he was only a means to an end, a tool she used in the same way he imagined she used a textbook. If that was a bitter pill, he felt he had only himself to blame. He'd accepted her terms. Now all he had to do was live with them.

He hadn't heard her laugh again since the first dive. He missed that, Ky discovered, every bit as much as he missed the taste of her lips, the feel of her in his arms. She wouldn't give him any of it willingly, and he'd nearly convinced himself he didn't want her any other way.

But at night, alone, with the sound of the surf in his head, he wasn't sure he'd survive another hour. Yet he had to. It was the fierce drive for survival that had gotten him through the last years. Her rejection had eaten away at him, then it had pushed him to prove something to himself. Kate had been the reason for his risking every penny he'd had to buy the Roost. He'd needed something tangible. The Roost had given him that, in much the same way the charter boat he'd recently bought gave him a sense of worth he once thought was unnecessary.

So he owned a restaurant that made a profit, and a boat that was beginning to justify his investment. It had given his innate love of risk an outlet. It wasn't money that mattered, but the dealing, the speculation, the possibilities. A search for sunken treasure wasn't much different.

What was she looking for really? Ky wondered. Was the gold her objective? Was she simply looking for an unusual way to spend her holiday? Was she still trying to give her father the blind devotion he'd expected all her life? Was it the hunt? Watching the wall of rain move slowly closer, Ky found of all the possibilities he wanted it to be the last.

With perhaps a hundred yards between them, both Kate and Ky looked out to the sea and the rain without being aware of each other. He thought of her and she of him, but the rain crept closer and time slipped by. The wind grew bolder. Both of them could admit to the restlessness that churned inside them, but neither could acknowledge simple loneliness.

Then they turned to walk back up the dunes and saw each other.

Kate wondered how long he'd been there, and how, when she could feel the waves of tension and need, she hadn't known the moment he'd stepped onto the beach. Her mind, her body—always so calm and cooperative—sprang to fevered life when she saw him. Kate knew she couldn't fight that, only the outcome. Still she wanted him. She told herself that just wanting was asking for disaster, but that didn't stop the need. If she ran from him now she'd admit defeat. Instead Kate took the first step across the sand toward him.

The thin white cotton of her skirt flapped around her, billowing, then clinging to the slender body he already knew. Her skin seemed very pale, her eyes very dark. Again Ky thought of mermaids, of illusions and of foolish dreams.

"You always liked the beach before a storm," Kate said when she reached him. She couldn't smile though she told herself she would. She wanted, though she told herself she wouldn't.

"It won't be much longer." He hooked his thumbs into the front pockets of his jeans. "If you didn't bring your car, you're going to get wet."

"I was visiting Linda." Kate turned her head to look back at the rain. No, it wouldn't be much longer. "It doesn't matter," she murmured. "Storms like this are over just as quickly as they begin." Storms like this, she thought, and like others. "I met Hope. You were right."

"About what?"

"She looks like you." This time she did manage to smile, though the tension was balled at the base of her neck. "Did you know she named a doll after you?"

"A dragon's not a doll," Ky corrected. His lips curved. He could resist a great deal, be apathetic about a great deal more, but he found it virtually impossible to do either when it came to his niece. "She's a great kid. Hell of a sailor."

"You take her out on your boat?"

He heard the astonishment and shrugged it away. "Why not? She likes the water."

"I just can't picture you…" Breaking off, Kate turned back to the sea again. No, she couldn't picture him entertaining a child with toy dragons and boat rides, just as she couldn't picture him in the business world with ledgers and accountants. "You surprise me," she said a bit more casually. "About a lot of things."

He wanted to reach out and touch her hair, wrap those loose blowing ends around his finger. He kept his hands in his pockets. "Such as?"

"Linda told me you own the Roost."

He didn't have to see her face to know it would hold that thoughtful, considering expression. "That's right, or most of it anyway."

"You didn't mention it when we were having dinner there."

"Why should I?" She didn't have to see him to know he shrugged. "Most people don't care who owns a place as long as the food's good and the service is quick."

"I guess I'm not most people." She said it quietly, so quietly the words barely carried over the sound of the waves. Even so, Ky tensed.

"Why would it matter to you?"

Before she could think, she turned back, her eyes full of emotion. "Because it all matters. The whys, the hows.

Because so much has changed and so much is the same. Because I want…" Breaking off, she took a step back. The look in her eyes turned to panic just before she started to dash away.

"What?" Ky demanded, grabbing her arm. "What do you want?"

"I don't know!" she shouted, unaware that it was the first time she'd done so in years. "I don't know what I want. I don't understand why I don't."

"Forget about understanding." He pulled her closer, holding her tighter when she resisted—or tried to. "Forget everything that's not here and now." The nights of restlessness and frustration already had his mercurial temperament on edge. Seeing her when he hadn't expected to made his emotions teeter. "You walked away from me once, but I won't crawl for you again. And you," he added with his eyes suddenly dark, his face suddenly close, "you damn well won't walk away as easily this time, Kate. Not this time."

With his arms wrapped around her he held her against him. His lips hovered above hers, threatening, promising. She couldn't tell. She didn't care. It was their taste she wanted, their pressure, no matter how harsh, how demanding. No matter what the consequence. Intellect and emotion might battle, and the battle might be eternal. Yet as she stood there crushed against him, feeling the wind whip at both of them, she already knew what the inevitable outcome would be.

"Tell me what you want, Kate." His voice was low, but as demanding as a shout. "Tell me what you want—now."

Now, she thought. If there could only be just now. She started to shake her head, but his breath feathered over her

skin. That alone made future and past fade into insignifi-
cance.

"You," she heard herself murmur. "Just you." Reaching
up she drew his face down to hers.

A wild passionate wind, a thunderous surf, the threat of
rain just moments away. She felt his body—hard and confident against hers. She tasted his lips—soft, urgent. Over
the thunder in her head and the thunder to the east, she
heard her own moan. She wanted, as long as the moment
lasted.

His tongue tempted; she surrendered to it. He dove
deep and took all, then more. It might never be enough.
With no hesitation, Kate met demand with demand, heat
with heat. While mouth sought mouth, her hands roamed
his face, teaching what she hadn't forgotten, reacquaint-
ing her with the familiar.

His skin was rough with a day's beard, the angle of
cheek and jaw, hard and defined. As her fingers inched up
she felt the soft brush of his hair blown by the wind. The
contrast made her tremble before she dove her fingers
deeper.

She could make him blind and deaf with needs. Knowing
it, Ky couldn't stop it. The way she touched him, so sure, so
sweet while her mouth was molten fire. Desire boiled in him,
rising so quickly he was weak with it before his mind
accepted what his body couldn't deny. He held her closer,
hard against soft, rough against smooth, flame against flame.

Through the thin barrier of her blouse he felt her flesh
warm to his touch. He knew the skin here would be
delicate, as fragile as the underside of a rose. The scent
would be as sweet, the taste as honeyed. Memories, the
moment, the dream of more, all these combined to make

him half mad. He knew what it would be like to have her, and knowing alone aroused. He felt her now, and feeling made him irrational.

He wanted to take her right there, next to the sea, while the sky opened up and poured over them.

"I want you." With his face buried against her neck he searched for all the places he remembered. "You know how much. You always knew."

"Yes." Her head was spinning. Every touch, every taste added speed to the whirl. Whatever doubts she'd had, Kate had never doubted the want. She hadn't always understood it, the intensity of it, but she'd never doubted it. It was pulling at her now—his, hers—the mutual, mindless passion they'd always been able to ignite in one another. She knew where it would lead—to dark, secret places full of sound and velocity. Not the eye of the hurricane, never the calm with him, but full fury from beginning to end. She knew where it would lead, and knew there'd be glory and freedom. But Ky had spoken no less than the truth when he'd said she wouldn't walk away so easily this time. It was that truth that made her reach for reason, when it would have been so simple to reach for madness.

"We can't." Breathless, she tried to turn in his arms. "Ky, *I* can't." This time when she took his face in her hands it was to draw it away from hers. "This isn't right for me."

Fury mixed with passion. It showed in his eyes, in the press of his fingers on her arms. "It's right for you. It's never been anything but right for you."

"No." She had to deny it, she had to mean it, because he was so persuasive. "No, it's not. I've always been attracted to you. It'd be ridiculous for me to try to pretend otherwise, but this isn't what I want for myself."

His fingers tightened. If they brought her pain neither of them acknowledged it. "I told you to tell me what you wanted. You did."

As he spoke the sky opened, just as he'd imagined. Rain swept in from the sea, tasting of salt, the damp wind and mystery. Instantly drenched, they stood just as they were, close, distant, with his hands firm on her arms and hers light on his face. She felt the water wash over her body, watched it run over his. It stirred her. She couldn't say why, she wouldn't give in to it.

"At that moment I did want you, I can't deny it."

"And now?" he demanded.

"I'm going back to the village."

"Damn it, Kate, what else do you want?"

She stared at him through the rain. His eyes were dark, stormy as the sea that raged behind him. Somehow he was more difficult to resist when he was like this, volatile, on edge, not quite controlled. She felt desire knot in her stomach, and swim in her head. That was all, Kate told herself. That was all it had ever been. Desire without understanding. Passion without future. Emotion without reason.

"Nothing you can give me," she whispered, knowing she'd have to dig for the strength to walk away, dig for it even to take the first step. "Nothing we can give to each other." Dropping her hands she stepped back. "I'm going back."

"You'll come back to me," Ky said as she took the first steps from him. "And if you don't," he added in a tone that made her hesitate, "it won't make any difference. We'll finish what's been started again."

She shivered, but continued to walk. Finish what's been started again. That was what she most feared.

Chapter 6

The storm passed. In the morning the sea was calm and blue, sprinkled with diamonds of sunlight from a sky where all clouds had been whisked away. It was true that rain freshened things—the air, grass, even the wood and stone of buildings.

The day was perfect, the wind calm. Kate's nerves rolled and jumped.

She'd committed herself to the project. It was her agreement with Ky that forced her to go to the harbor as she'd been doing every other morning. It made her climb on deck when she wanted nothing more than to pack and leave the island the way she'd come. If Ky could complete the agreement after what had passed between them on the beach, so could she.

Perhaps he sensed the fatigue she was feeling, but he made no comment on it. They spoke only when necessary as he headed out to open sea. Ky stood at the helm, Kate at the stern. Still, even the roar of the engine didn't disguise the strained silence. Ky checked the boat's compass, then cut the engines. Silence continued, thunderously.

With the deck separating them, each began to don their equipment—wet suits, the weight belts that would give them neutral buoyancy in the water, headlamps to light the sea's dimness, masks for sight. Ky checked his depth gauge and compass on his right wrist, then the luminous dial of the watch on his left while Kate attached the scabbard for her diver's knife onto her leg just below the knee.

Without speaking, they checked the valves and gaskets on the tanks, then strapped them on, securing buckles. As was his habit, Ky went into the water first, waiting until Kate joined him. Together they jackknifed below the surface.

The familiar euphoria reached out for her. Each time she dived, Kate expected the underwater world to become more commonplace. Each time it was still magic. She acknowledged what made it possible for her to join creatures of the sea—the regulator with its mouthpiece and hose that brought her air from the tanks on her back, the mask that gave her visibility. She knew the importance of every gauge. She acknowledged the technology, then put it in the practical side of her brain while she simply enjoyed.

They swam deeper, keeping in constant visual contact. Kate knew Ky often dived alone, and that doing so was always a risk. She also knew that no matter how much anger and resentment he felt toward her, she could trust him with her life.

She relied on Ky's instincts as much as his ability. It was his expertise that guided her now, perhaps more than her father's careful research and calculations. They were combing the very edge of the territory her father had mapped out, but Kate felt no discouragement. If she hadn't trusted Ky's skill and instincts, she would never have come back to Ocracoke.

They were going deeper now than they had on their other dives. Kate equalized by letting a tiny bit of air into her suit. Feeling the "squeeze" on her eardrums at the change in pressure, she relieved it carefully. A damaged eardrum could mean weeks without being able to dive.

When Ky signaled for her to switch on her headlamp she obeyed without question. Excitement began to rise.

The sunlight was fathoms above them. The world here never saw it. Sea grass swayed in the current. Now and then a fish, curious and brave enough, would swim along beside them only to vanish in the blink of an eye at a sudden movement.

Ky swam smoothly through the water, using his feet to propel him at a steady pace. Their lamps cut through the murk, surprising more fish, illuminating rock formations that had existed under the sea for centuries. Kate discovered shapes and faces in them.

No, she could never dive alone, Kate decided as Ky slowed his pace to keep rhythm with her more meandering one. It was so easy for her to lose her sense of time and direction. Air came into her lungs with a simple drawing of breath as long as the tanks held oxygen, but the gauges on her wrist only worked if she remembered to look at them.

Even mortality could be forgotten in enchantment. And

enchantment could too easily lead to a mistake. It was a lesson she knew, but one that could slip away from her. The timelessness, the freedom was seductive. The feeling was somehow as sensual as the timeless freedom felt in a lover's arms. Kate knew this pleasure could be as dangerous as a lover, but found it as difficult to resist.

There was so much to see, to touch. Crustaceans of different shapes, sizes and hues. They were alive here in their own milieu, so different from when they washed up helplessly on the beach for children to collect in buckets. Fish swam in and out of waving grass that would be limp and lifeless on land. Unlike dolphins or man, some creatures would never know the thrill of both air and water.

Her beam passed over another formation, crusted with barnacles and sea life. She nearly passed it, but curiosity made her turn back so that the light skimmed over it a second time. Odd, she thought, how structured some of the shapes could be. It almost looked like…

Hesitating, using her arms to reverse her progress, Kate turned in the water to play her light over the shape from end to end. Excitement rose so quickly she grabbed Ky's arm in a grip strong enough to make him stop to search for a defect in her equipment. With a shake of her head Kate warded him off, then pointed.

When their twin lights illuminated the form on the ocean floor, Kate nearly shouted with the discovery. It wasn't a shelf of rock. The closer they swam toward it the more apparent that became. Though it was heavily corroded and covered with crustaceans, the shape of the cannon remained recognizable.

Ky swam around the barrel. When he removed his knife and struck the cannon with the hilt the metallic sound rang out strangely. Kate was certain she'd never heard anything more musical. Her laughter came out in a string of bubbles that made Ky look in her direction and grin.

They'd found a corroded cannon, he thought, and she was as thrilled as if they'd found a chest full of doubloons. And he understood it. They'd found something perhaps no one had seen for two centuries. That in itself was a treasure.

With a movement of his hand he indicated for her to follow, then they began to swim slowly east. If they'd found a cannon, it was likely they'd find more.

Reluctant to leave her initial discovery, Kate swam with him, looking back as often as she looked ahead. She hadn't realized the excitement would be this intense. How could she explain what it felt like to discover something that had lain untouched on the sea floor for more than two centuries? Who would understand more clearly, she wondered, her colleagues at Yale or Ky? Somehow she felt her colleagues would understand intellectually, but they would never understand the exhilaration. Intellectual pleasure didn't make you giddy enough to want to turn somersaults.

How would her father have felt if he'd found it? She wished she knew. She wished she could have given him that one instant of exultation, perhaps shared it with him as they'd so rarely shared anything. He'd only known the planning, the theorizing, the bookwork. With one long look at that ancient weapon, she'd known so much more.

When Ky stopped and touched her shoulders, her emotions were as mixed as her thoughts. If she could have spoken she'd have told him to hold her, though she wouldn't have known why. She was thrilled, yet running through the joy was a thin shaft of sorrow—for what was lost, she thought. For what she'd never be able to find again.

Perhaps he knew something of what moved her. They couldn't communicate with words, but he touched her cheek—just a brush of his finger over her skin. It was more comforting to her than a dozen soft speeches.

She understood then that she'd never stopped loving him. No matter how many years, how many miles had separated them, what life she had she'd left with him. The time in between had been little more than existence. It was possible to live with emptiness, even to be content with it until you had that heady taste of life again.

She might have panicked. She might have run if she hadn't been trapped there, fathoms deep in the midst of a discovery. Instead she accepted the knowledge, hoping that time would tell her what to do.

He wanted to ask her what was going through her mind. Her eyes were full of so many emotions. Words would have to wait. Their time in the sea was almost up. He touched her face again and waited for the smile. When she gave it to him, Ky pointed at something behind her that he had just noticed moments before.

An oaken plank, old, splintered and bumpy with parasites. For the second time Ky removed his knife and began to pry the board from its bed. Silt floated up thinly, cutting visibility before it settled again. Replacing his knife, Ky gave the thumbs-up signal that meant they'd surface. Kate shook her head indicating that they should continue to search, but Ky merely pointed to his watch, then again to the surface.

Frustrated with the technology that allowed her to dive, but also forced her to seek air again, Kate nodded.

They swam west, back toward the boat. When she passed the cannon again, Kate felt a quick thrill of pride. She'd found it. And the discoveries were only beginning.

The moment her head was above water, she started to laugh. "We found it!" She grabbed the ladder with one hand as Ky began to climb up, placing his find and his tanks on the deck first. "I can't believe it, after hardly more than a week. It's incredible, that cannon lying down there all these years." Water ran down her face but she didn't notice. "We have to find the hull, Ky." Impatient, she released her tanks and handed them up to him before she climbed aboard.

"The chances are good—eventually."

"Eventually?" Kate tossed her wet hair out of her eyes. "We found this in just over a week." She indicated the board on the deck. She crouched over it, just wanting to touch. "We found the *Liberty*."

"We found a wreck," he corrected. "It doesn't have to be the *Liberty*."

"It is," she said with a determination that caused his brow to lift. "We found the cannon and this just on the edge of the area my father had charted. It all fits too well."

"Regardless of what wreck it is, it's undocumented. You'll get your name in the books, professor."

Annoyed she rose. They stood facing each other on either side of the plank they'd lifted out of the sea. "I don't care about having my name in the books."

"Your father's name then." He unzipped his wet suit to let his skin dry.

She remembered her feelings after spotting the cannon, how Ky had seemed to understand them. Could they only be kind to each other, only be close to each other, fathoms under the surface? "Is there something wrong with that?"

"Only if it's an obsession. You always had a problem with your father."

"Because he didn't approve of you?" she shot back.

His eyes took on that eerily calm, almost flat expression that meant his anger was lethal. "Because it mattered too much to you what he approved of."

That stung. The truth often did. "I came here to finish my father's project," she said evenly. "I made that clear from the beginning. You're still getting your fee."

"You're still following directions. His directions." Before she could retort, he turned toward the cabin. "We'll eat and rest before we go back under."

With an effort, she held on to her temper. She wanted to dive again, badly. She wanted to find more. Not for her father's approval, Kate thought fiercely. Certainly not for Ky's. She wanted this for herself. Pulling down the zipper of her wet suit, she went down the cabin steps.

She'd eat because strength and energy were vital to a diver. She'd rest for the same reason. Then, she determined, she'd go back to the wreck and find proof that it was the *Liberty*.

Calmer, she watched Ky go through a small cupboard. "Peanut butter?" she asked when she saw the jar he pulled out.

"Protein."

Her laugh helped her to relax again. "Do you still eat it with bananas?"

"It's still good for you."

Though she wrinkled her nose at the combination, she reminded herself that beggars couldn't be choosers. "When we find the treasure," she said recklessly, "I'll buy you a bottle of champagne."

Their fingers brushed as he handed her the first sandwich. "I'll hold you to it." He picked up his own sandwich and a quart of milk. "Let's eat on deck."

He wasn't certain if he wanted the sun or the space, but it wasn't any easier to be with her in that tiny cabin than it had been the first time, or the last. Taking her assent for granted, Ky went up the stairs again, without looking back. Kate followed.

"It might be good for you," Kate commented as she took the first bite, "but it still tastes like something you give five-year-olds when they scrape their knees."

"Five-year-olds require a lot of protein."

Giving up, Kate sat cross-legged on the deck. The sun was bright, the movement of the boat gentle. She wouldn't let his digs get to her, nor would she dig back. They were in this together, she reminded herself. Tension and sniping wouldn't help them find what they sought.

"It's the *Liberty*, Ky," she murmured, looking at the plank again. "I know it is."

"It's possible." He stretched out with his back against the port side. "But there are a lot of wrecks, unidentified and otherwise, all through these waters. Diamond Shoals is a graveyard."

"Diamond Shoals is fifty miles north."

"And the entire coastline along these barrier islands is full of littoral currents, rip currents and shifting sand ridges. Two hundred years ago they didn't have modern navigational devices. Hell, they didn't even have the lighthouses until the nineteenth century. I couldn't even give you an educated guess as to how many ships went down from the time Columbus set out until World War II."

Kate took another bite. "We're only concerned with one ship."

"Finding one's no big problem," he returned. "Finding a specific one's something else. Last year, after a couple of hurricanes breezed through, they found wrecks uncovered on the beach on Hatteras. There are plenty of houses on the island that were built from pieces of wreckage like that." He pointed to the plank with the remains of his sandwich.

Kate frowned at the board again. "It could be the *Liberty* just as easily as it couldn't."

"All right." Appreciating her stubbornness, Ky grinned. "But whatever it is, there might be treasure. Anything lost for more than two hundred years is pretty much finders keepers."

She didn't want to say that it wasn't any treasure she wanted. Just the *Liberty*'s. From what he said before, Kate was aware he already understood that. It was simply different for him. She took a long drink of cold milk. "What do you plan to do with your share?"

With his eyes half closed, he shrugged. He could do as he pleased now, a cache of gold wouldn't change that. "Buy another boat, I imagine."

"With what two-hundred-year-old gold would be worth today, you'd be able to buy a hell of a boat."

He grinned, but kept his eyes shaded. "I intend to. What about you?"

"I'm not sure." She wished she had some tangible goal for the money, something exciting, even fanciful. It just didn't seem possible to think beyond the hunt yet. "I thought I might travel a bit."

"Where?"

"Greece maybe. The islands."

"Alone?"

The food and the motion of the boat lulled her. She made a neutral sound as she shut her eyes.

"Isn't there some dedicated teacher you'd take with you? Someone you could discuss the Trojan War with?"

"Mmm, I don't want to go to Greece with a dedicated teacher."

"Someone else?"

"There's no one."

Sitting on the deck with her face lifted, her hair blowing, she looked like a finely crafted piece of porcelain. Something a man might look at, admire, but not touch. When her eyes were open, hot, her skin flushed with passion, he burned for her. When she was like this, calm, distant, he ached. He let the needs run through him because he knew there was no stopping them.

"Why?"

"Hmm?"

"Why isn't there anyone?"

Lazily she opened her eyes. "Anyone?"

"Why don't you have a lover?"

The sleepy haze cleared from her eyes instantly. He saw her fingers tense on the dark blue material that stretched snugly over her knees. "It's none of your business whether I do or not."

"You've just told me you don't."

"I told you there's no one I'd travel with," she corrected, but when she started to rise, he put a hand on her shoulder.

"It's the same thing."

"No, it's not, but it's still none of your business, Ky, any more than your personal life is mine."

"I've had women," he said easily. "But I haven't had a lover since you left the island."

She felt the pain and the pleasure sweep up through her.

It was dangerous to dwell on the sensation. As dangerous as it was to lose yourself deep under the ocean. "Don't." She lifted her hand to remove his from her shoulder. "This isn't good for either of us."

"Why?" His fingers linked with hers. "We want each other. We both know the rules this time around."

Rules. No commitment, no promises. Yes, she understood them this time, but like mortality during a dive, they could easily be forgotten. Even now, with his eyes on hers, her fingers caught in his, the structure of those rules became dimmer and dimmer. He would hurt her again. There was never any question of that. Somehow, in the last twenty-four hours, it had become a matter of *how* she would deal with the pain, not *if.*

"Ky, I'm not ready." Her voice was low, not pleading, but plainly vulnerable. Though she wasn't aware of it, there was no defense she could put to better use.

He drew her up so that they were both standing, touching only hand to hand. Though she was tall, her slimness made her appear utterly fragile. It was that and the way she looked at him, with her head tilted back so their eyes could meet, that prevented him from taking what he was determined to have, without questions, without her willingness. Ruthlessly, that was how he told himself he wanted to take her, even though he knew he couldn't.

"I'm not a patient man."

"No."

He nodded, then released her hand while he still could. "Remember it," he warned before he turned to go to the helm. "We'll take the boat east, over the wreck and dive again."

An hour later they found a piece of rigging, broken and corroded, less than three yards from the cannon. By hand signals, Ky indicated that they'd start a stockpile of the salvage. Later they'd come back with the means of bringing it up. There were more planks, some too big for a man to carry up, some small enough for Kate to hold in one hand.

When she found a pottery bowl, miraculously unbroken, she realized just what an archaeologist must feel after hours of digging when he unearths a fragment of another era. Here it was, cupped in her hand, a simple bowl, covered with silt, covered with age. Someone had eaten from it once, a seaman, relaxing briefly below deck, perhaps on his first voyage across the Atlantic to the New World. His last journey in any event, Kate mused as she turned the bowl over in her hand.

The rigging, the cannon, the planks equaled ship. The bowl equaled man.

Though she put the bowl with the other pieces of their find, she intended to take it up with her on this dive. Whatever other artifacts they found could go to a museum, but the first, she'd keep.

They found pieces of glass that might have come from bottles that held whiskey, chunks of crockery that hadn't survived intact like the bowl. Bits of cups, bowls, plates littered the sea floor.

The galley, she decided. They must have found the galley. Over the years, the water pressure would have simply disintegrated the ship until it was all pieces spread on and under the floor of the ocean. It would, in essence, have become part of the sea, a home for the creatures and plant life that dwelt there.

But they'd found the galley. If they could find something, just one thing with the ship's name inscribed on it, they'd be certain.

Diligently, using her knife as a digging tool, Kate worked at the floor of the sea. It wasn't a practical way to search, but she saw no harm in trying her luck. They'd found crockery, glass, the unbroken bowl. Even as she glanced up she saw Ky examining what might have been half a dinner plate.

When she unearthed a long wooden ladle, Kate found that her excitement increased. They *had* found the galley, and in time, she'd prove to Ky that they'd found the *Liberty*.

Engrossed in her find, she turned to signal to Ky and moved directly into the path of a stingray.

He saw it. Ky was no more than a yard from Kate when the movement of the ray unearthing itself from its layer of sand and silt had caught his eye. His movement was pure reflex, done without thought or plan. He was quick. But even as he grabbed Kate's hand to swing her back behind him, out of range, the wicked, saw-toothed tail lashed out.

Her scream was muffled by the water, but the sound went through Ky just as surely as the stingray's poison went through Kate. Her body went stiff against his, rigid in pain and shock. The ladle she'd found floated down, out of her grip, until it landed silently on the bottom.

He knew what to do. No rational diver goes down unless he has a knowledge of how to handle an emergency. Still Ky felt a moment of panic. This wasn't just another diver, it was Kate. Before his mind could clear, her stiffened body went limp against him. Then he acted.

Cool, almost mechanically, he tilted her head back with the chin carry to keep her air passage open. He held her securely, pressing his chest into her tanks, keeping his hand against her ribcage. It ran through his mind that it was best she'd fainted. Unconscious she wouldn't struggle as she might had she been awake and in pain. It was best she'd fainted because he couldn't bear to think of her in pain. He kicked off for the surface.

On the rise he squeezed her, hard, forcing expanding air out of her lungs. There was always the risk of embolism. They were going up faster than safety allowed. Even while he ventilated his own lungs, Ky kept a lookout. She would bleed, and blood brought sharks.

The minute they surfaced, Ky released her weight belt. Supporting her with his arm wrapped around her, his hand grasping the ladder, Ky unhooked his tanks, slipped them over the side of the boat, then removed Kate's. Her face was waxy, but as he pulled the mask from her face she moaned. With that slight sound of life some of the blood came back to his own body. With her draped limply over his shoulder, he climbed the ladder onto the *Vortex*.

He laid her down on the deck, and with hands that didn't hesitate, began to pull the wet suit from her. She moaned again when he drew the snug material over the wound just above her ankle, but she didn't reach the surface of consciousness. Grimly, Ky examined the laceration the ray had caused. Even through the protection of her suit, the tail had penetrated deep into her skin. If Ky had only been quicker...

Cursing himself, Ky hurried to the cabin for the first aid kit.

As consciousness began to return, Kate felt the ache

swimming up from her ankle to her head. Spears of pain shot through her, sharp enough to make her gasp and struggle, as if she could move away from it and find ease again.

"Try to lie still."

The voice was gentle and calm. Kate balled her hands into fists and obeyed it. Opening her eyes, she stared up at the pure blue sky. Her mind whirled with confusion, but she stared at the sky as though it were the only tangible thing in her life. If she concentrated, she could rise above the hurt. The ladle. Opening her hand she found it empty, she'd lost the ladle. For some reason it seemed vital that she have it.

"We found the galley." Her voice was hoarse with anguish, but her one hand remained open and limp. "I found a ladle. They'd have used it for spooning soup into that bowl. The bowl—it wasn't even broken. Ky…" Her voice weakened with a new flood of sensation as memory began to return. "It was a stingray. I wasn't watching for it, it just seemed to be there. Am I going to die?"

"No!" His answer was sharp, almost angry. Bending over her, he placed both hands on her shoulders so that she'd look directly into his face. He had to be sure she understood everything he said. "It was a stingray," he confirmed, not adding that it had been a good ten feet long. "Part of the spine's broken off, lodged just above your ankle."

He watched her eyes cloud further, part pain, part fear. His hands tightened on her shoulders. "It's not in deep. I can get it out, but it'll hurt like hell."

She knew what he was saying. She could stay as she was until he got her back to the doctor on the island, or she could trust him to treat her now. Though her lips trembled, she kept her eyes on his and spoke clearly.

"Do it now."

"Okay." He continued to stare at her, into the eyes that were glazed with shock. "Hang on. Don't try to be brave. Scream as much as you want but try not to move. I'll be quick." Bending farther, he kissed her hard. "I promise."

Kate nodded, then concentrating on the feeling of his lips against hers, shut her eyes. He was quick. Within seconds she felt the hurt rip through her, over the threshold she thought she could bear and beyond…. She pulled in air to scream, but went back under the surface into liquid dimness.

Ky let the blood flow freely onto the deck for a moment, knowing it would wash away some of the poison. His hands had been rock steady when he'd pulled the spine from her flesh. His mind had been cold. Now with her blood on his hands, they began to shake. Ignoring them, and the icy fear of seeing Kate's smooth skin ripped and raw, Ky washed the wound, cleansed it, bound it. Within the hour, he'd have her to a doctor.

With unsteady fingers, he checked the pulse at the base of her neck. It wasn't strong, but it was steady. Lifting an eyelid with his thumb, he checked her pupils. He didn't believe she was in shock, she'd simply escaped from the pain. He thanked God for that.

On a long breath he let his forehead rest against hers, only for a moment. He prayed that she'd remain unconscious until she was safely under a doctor's care.

He didn't take the time to wash her blood from his hands before he took the helm. Ky whipped the boat around in a quick circle and headed full throttle back to Ocracoke.

Chapter 7

As she started to float toward consciousness, Kate focused, drifted, then focused again. She saw the whirl of a white ceiling rather than the pure blue arc of sky. Even when the mist returned she remembered the hurt and thrashed out against it. She couldn't face it a second time. Yet she found as she rose closer to the surface that she didn't have the will to fight against it. That brought fear. If she'd had the strength, she might have wept.

Then she felt a cool hand on her cheek. Ky's voice pierced the last layers of fog, low and gentle. "Take it easy, Kate. You're all right now. It's all over."

Though her breath hitched as she inhaled, Kate opened her eyes. The pain didn't come. All she felt was his hand on her cheek, all she saw was his face. "Ky." When she said his name, Kate reached for his hand, the one solid thing she was sure of. Her own voice frightened her. It was hardly more than a wisp of air.

"You're going to be fine. The doctor took care of you." As he spoke, Ky rubbed his thumb over her knuckles, establishing a point of concentration, and kept his other hand lightly on her cheek, knowing that contact was important. He'd nearly gone mad waiting for her to open her eyes again. "Dr. Bailey, you remember. You met him before."

It seemed vital that she should remember so she forced her mind to search back. She had a vague picture of a tough, weathered old man who looked more suited to the sea than the examining room. "Yes. He likes…likes ale and flounder."

He might have laughed at her memory if her voice had been stronger. "You're going to be fine, but he wants you to rest for a few more days."

"I feel…strange." She lifted a hand to her own head as if to assure herself it was still there.

"You're on medication, that's why you're groggy. Understand?"

"Yes." Slowly she turned her head and focused on her surroundings. The walls were a warm ivory, not the sterile white of a hospital. The dark oak trim gleamed dully. On the hardwood floor lay a single rug, its muted Indian design fading with age. It was the only thing Kate recognized. The last time she'd been in Ky's bedroom only half the drywall had been in place and one of the windows had had a long thin crack in the bottom pane. "Not the hospital," she managed.

"No." He stroked her head, needing to touch as much as to check for her fever that had finally broken near dawn. "It was easier to bring you here after Bailey took care of you. You didn't need a hospital, but neither of us liked the idea of your being in a hotel right now."

"Your house," she murmured, struggling to concentrate her strength. "This is your bedroom, I remember the rug."

They'd made love on it once. That's what Ky remembered. With an effort, he kept his hands light. "Are you hungry?"

"I don't know." Basically, she felt nothing. When she tried to sit up, the drug spun in her head, making both the room and reality reel away. That would have to stop, Kate decided while she waited for the dizziness to pass. She'd rather have some pain than that helpless, weighted sensation.

Without fuss, Ky moved the pillows and shifted her to a sitting position. "The doctor said you should eat when you woke up. Just some soup." Rising he looked down on her, in much the same way, Kate thought, as he'd looked at a cracked mast he was considering mending. "I'll fix it. Don't get up," he added as he walked to the door. "You're not strong enough yet."

As he went into the hall he began to swear in a low steady stream.

Of course she wasn't strong enough, he thought with a last vicious curse. She was pale enough to fade into the sheets she lay on. No resistance, that's what Bailey had said. Not enough food, not enough sleep, too much strain. If he could do nothing else, Ky determined as he pulled open a kitchen cupboard, he could do something about that. She was going to eat, and lie flat on her back until the doctor said otherwise.

He'd known she was weak, that was the worst of it. Ky

dumped the contents of a can into a pot then hurled the empty container into the trash. He'd seen the strain on her face, the shadows under her eyes, he'd heard the traces of fatigue come and go in her voice, but he'd been too wrapped up in his own needs to do anything about it.

With a flick of the wrist, he turned on the burner under the soup, then the burner under the coffee. God, he needed coffee. For a moment he simply stood with his fingers pressed against his eyes waiting for his system to settle.

He couldn't remember ever spending a more frantic twenty-four hours. Even after the doctor had checked and treated her, even when Ky had brought her home and she'd been fathoms deep under the drug, his nerves hadn't eased. He'd been terrified to leave the room for more than five minutes at a time. The fever had raged through her, though she'd been unaware. Most of the night he'd sat beside her, bathing away the sweat and talking to her, though she couldn't hear.

Through the night he'd existed on coffee and nerves. With a half-laugh he reached for a cup. It looked like that wasn't going to change for a while yet.

He knew he still wanted her, knew he still felt something for her, under the bitterness and anger. But until he'd seen her lying unconscious on the deck of his boat, with her blood on his hands, he hadn't realized that he still loved her.

He'd known what to do about the want, even the bitterness, but now, faced with love, Ky hadn't a clue. It didn't seem possible for him to love someone so frail, so calm, so…different than he. Yet the emotion he'd once felt for her had grown and ripened into something so solid he couldn't see any way around it. For now, he'd concentrate on getting her on her feet again. He poured the soup into a bowl and carried it upstairs.

It would have been an easy matter to close her eyes and slide under again. Too easy. Willing herself to stay awake, Kate concentrated on Ky's room. There were a number of changes here as well, she mused. He'd trimmed the windows in oak, giving them a wide sill where he'd scattered the best of his shells. A piece of satiny driftwood stood, beautiful as a piece of sculpture. There was a paneled closet door with a faceted glass knob where there'd once been a rod, a round-backed rattan chair where there'd been packing crates.

Only the bed was the same, she mused. The wide four-poster had been his mother's. She knew he'd given the rest of his family's furniture to Marsh. Ky had told her once he'd felt no need or desire for it, but he kept the bed. He was born there, unexpectedly, during a night in which the island had been racked by a storm.

And they'd made love there, Kate remembered as she ran her fingers over the sheets. The first time, and the last.

Stopping the movement of her fingers, she looked over as Ky came back into the room. Memories had to be pushed aside. "You've done a lot of work in here."

"A bit." He set the tray over her lap as he sat on the edge of the bed.

As the scent of the soup reached her, Kate shut her eyes. Just the aroma seemed to be enough. "It smells wonderful."

"The smell won't put any meat on you."

She smiled, and opened her eyes again. Then before she'd realized it, Ky had spoon-fed her the first bite. "It tastes wonderful too." Though she reached for the spoon, he dipped it into the bowl himself then held it to her lips. "I can do it," she began, then was forced to swallow more broth.

"Just eat." Fighting off waves of emotion he spoke briskly. "You look like hell."

"I'm sure I do," she said easily. "Most people don't look their best a couple of hours after being stung by a stingray."

"Twenty-four," Ky corrected as he fed her another spoon of soup.

"Twenty-four what?"

"Hours." Ky slipped in another spoonful when her eyes widened.

"I've been unconscious for twenty-four hours?" She looked to the window and the sunlight as if she could find some means of disproving it.

"You slipped in and out quite a bit before Bailey gave you the shot. He said you probably wouldn't remember." Thank God, Ky added silently. Whenever she'd fought her way back to consciousness, she'd been in agony. He could still hear her moans, feel the way she'd clutched him. He never knew a person could suffer physically for another's pain the way he'd suffered for hers. Even now it made his muscles clench.

"That must've been some shot he gave me."

"He gave you what you needed." His eyes met hers. For the first time Kate saw the fatigue in them, and the anger.

"You've been up all night," she murmured. "Haven't you had any rest at all?"

"You needed to be watched," he said briefly. "Bailey wanted you to stay under, so you'd sleep through the worst of the pain, and so you'd just sleep period." His voice changed as he lost control over the anger. He couldn't prevent the edge of accusation from showing, partly for her, partly for himself. "The wound wasn't that bad, do you understand? But you weren't in any shape to handle it. Bailey said you've been well on the way to working yourself into exhaustion."

"That's ridiculous. I don't—"

Ky swore at her, filling her mouth with more soup. "Don't tell me it's ridiculous. I had to listen to him. I had to look at you. You don't eat, you don't sleep, you're going to fall down on your face."

There was too much of the drug in her system to allow her temper to bite. Instead of annoyance, her words came out like a sigh. "I didn't fall on my face."

"Only a matter of time." Fury was coming too quickly. Though his fingers tightened on the spoon, Ky held it back. "I don't care how much you want to find the treasure, you can't enjoy it if you're flat on your back."

The soup was warming her. As much as her pride urged her to refuse, her system craved the food. "I won't be," she told him, not even aware that her words were beginning to slur. "We'll dive again tomorrow, and I'll prove it's the *Liberty*."

He started to swear at her, but one look at the heavy eyes and the pale cheeks had him swallowing the words. "Sure." He spooned in more soup knowing she'd be asleep again within moments.

"I'll give the ladle and the rigging and the rest to a museum." Her eyes closed. "For my father."

Ky set the tray on the floor. "Yes, I know."

"It was important to him. I need...I just need to give him something." Her eyes fluttered open briefly. "I didn't know he was ill. He never told me about his heart, about the pills. If I'd known..."

"You couldn't have done any more than you did." His voice was gentle again as he shifted the pillows down.

"I loved him."

"I know you did."

"I could never seem to make the people I love understand what I need. I don't know why."

"Rest now. When you're well, we'll find the treasure."

She felt herself sinking into warmth, softness, the dark. "Ky." Kate reached out and felt his fingers wrap around hers. With her eyes closed, it was all the reality she needed.

"I'll stay," he murmured, brushing the hair from her cheek. "Just rest."

"All those years…" He could feel her fingers relaxing in his as she slipped deeper. "I never forgot you. I never stopped wanting you. Not ever…"

He stared down at her as she slept. Her face was utterly peaceful, pale as marble, soft as silk. Unable to resist, he lifted her fingers to his own cheek, just to feel her flesh against his. He wouldn't think about what she'd said now. He couldn't. The strain of the last day had taken a toll on him as well. If he didn't get some rest, he wouldn't be able to care for her when she woke again.

Rising, Ky pulled down the shades, and took off his shirt. Then he lay down next to Kate in the big four-poster bed and slept for the first time in thirty-six hours.

The pain was a dull, consistent throb, not the silvery sharp flash she remembered, but a gnawing ache that wouldn't pass. When it woke her, Kate lay still, trying to orient herself. Her mind was clearer now. She was grateful for that, even though with the drug out of her system she was well aware of the wound. It was dark, but the moonlight slipped around the edges of the shades Ky had drawn. She was grateful for that too. It seemed she'd been a prisoner of the dark for too long.

It was night. She prayed it was only hours after she'd last awoken, not another full day later. She didn't want that quick panic at the thought of losing time again. Because she needed to be certain she was in control this time, she went over everything she remembered.

The pottery bowl, the ladle, then the stingray. She closed her eyes a moment, knowing it would be a very long time before she forgot what it had felt like to be struck with that whiplike tail. She remembered waking up on the deck of the *Vortex*, the pure blue sky overhead, and the strong, calm way Ky had spoken to her before he'd pulled out the spine. That pain, the horror of that one instant was very clear. Then, there was nothing else.

She remembered nothing of the journey back to the island, or of Dr. Bailey's ministrations or of being transported to Ky's home. Her next clear image was of waking in his bedroom, of dark oak trim on the windows, wide sills with shells set on them.

He'd fed her soup—yes, that was clear, but then things started to become hazy again. She knew he'd been angry, though she couldn't remember why. At the moment, it was more important to her that she could put events in some sort of sequence.

As she lay in the dark, fully awake and finally aware, she heard the sound of quiet, steady breathing beside her. Turning her head, Kate saw Ky beside her, hardly more than a silhouette with the moonlight just touching the skin of his chest so that she could see it rise and fall.

He'd said he would stay, she remembered. And he'd

been tired. Abruptly Kate remembered there'd been fatigue in his eyes as well as temper. He'd been caring for her.

A mellow warmth moved through her, one she hadn't felt in a very long time. He had taken care of her, and though it had made him angry, he'd done it. And he'd stayed. Reaching out, she touched his cheek.

Though the gesture was whisper light, Ky awoke immediately. His sleep had been little more than a half doze so that he could recharge his system yet be aware of any sign that Kate needed attention. Sitting up, he shook his head to clear it.

He looked like a boy caught napping. For some reason the gesture moved Kate unbearably. "I didn't mean to wake you," she murmured.

He reached for the lamp beside the bed and turned it on low. Though his body revolted against the interruption, his mind was fully awake. "Pain?"

"No."

He studied her face carefully. The glazed look from the drug had left her eyes, but the color hadn't returned. "Kate."

"All right. Some."

"Bailey left some pills."

As he started to rise, Kate reached for him again. "No, I don't want anything. It makes me groggy."

"It takes away the pain."

"Not now, Ky, please. I promise I'll tell you if it gets bad."

Because her voice was close to desperate he made himself content with that. At the moment, she looked too fragile to argue with. "Are you hungry?"

She smiled, shaking her head. "No. It must be the middle of the night. I was only trying to orient myself." She touched him again, in gratitude, in comfort. "You should sleep."

"I've had enough. Anyway, you're the patient."

Automatically, he put his hand to her forehead to check for fever. Touched, Kate laid hers over it. She felt the quick reflexive tensing of his fingers.

"Thank you." When he would have removed his hand, she linked her fingers with his. "You've been taking good care of me."

"You needed it," he said simply and much too swiftly. He couldn't allow her to stir him now, not when they were in that big, soft bed surrounded by memories.

"You haven't left me since it happened."

"I had no place to go."

His answer made her smile. Kate reached up her free hand to touch his cheek. There had been changes, she thought, many changes. But so many things had stayed the same. "You were angry with me."

"You haven't been taking care of yourself." He told himself he should move away from the bed, from Kate, from everything that weakened him there.

He stayed, leaning over her, one hand caught in hers. Her eyes were dark, soft in the dim light, full of the sweetness and innocence he remembered. He wanted to hold her until there was no more pain for either of them, but he knew, if he pressed his body against hers now, he wouldn't stop. Again he started to move, pulling away the hand that held hers. Again Kate stopped him.

"I would've died if you hadn't gotten me up."

"That's why it's smarter to dive with a partner."

"I might still have died if you hadn't done everything you did."

He shrugged this off, too aware that the fingers on his face were stroking lightly, something she had done in the past. Sometimes before they'd made love, and often afterward, when they'd talked in quiet voices, she'd stroke his face, tracing the shape of it as though she'd needed to memorize it. Perhaps she, too, sometimes awoke in the middle of the night and remembered too much.

Unable to bear it, Ky put his hand around her wrist and drew it away. "The wound wasn't that bad," he said simply.

"I've never seen a stingray that large." She shivered and his hand tightened on her wrist.

"Don't think about it now. It's over."

Was it? she wondered as she lifted her head and looked into his eyes. Was anything ever really over? For four years she'd told herself there were joys and pains that could be forgotten, absorbed into the routine that was life as it had to be lived. Now, she was no longer sure. She needed to be. More than anything else, she needed to be sure.

"Hold me," she murmured.

Was she trying to make him crazy? Ky wondered. Did she want him to cross the border, that edge he was trying so desperately to avoid? It took most of the strength he had left just to keep his voice even. "Kate, you need to sleep now. In the morning—"

"I don't want to think about the morning," she murmured. "Only now. And now I need you to hold me." Before he could refuse, she slipped her arms around his waist and rested her head on his shoulder.

She felt his hesitation, but not his one vivid flash of longing before his arms came around her. On a long breath Kate closed her eyes. Too much time had passed since she'd had this, the gentleness, the sweetness she'd experienced only with Ky. No one else had ever held her with such kindness, such simple compassion. Somehow, she never found it odd that a man could be so reckless and arrogant, yet kind and compassionate at the same time.

Perhaps she'd been attracted to the recklessness, but it had been the kindness she had fallen in love with. Until now, in the quiet of the deep night, she hadn't understood. Until now, in the security of his arms, she hadn't accepted what she wanted.

Life as it had to be lived, she thought again. Was taking what she so desperately needed part of that?

She was so slender, so soft beneath the thin nightshirt. Her hair lay over his skin, loose and free, its color muted in the dim light. He could feel her palms against his back, those elegant hands that had always made him think more of an artist than a teacher. Her breathing was quiet, serene, as he knew it was when she slept. The light scent of woman clung to the material of the nightshirt.

Holding her didn't bring the pain he'd expected but a contentment he'd been aching for without realizing it. The tension in his muscles eased, the knot in his stomach vanished. With his eyes closed, he rested his cheek on her hair. It seemed like a lifetime since he'd known the pleasure of quiet satisfaction. She'd asked him to hold her, but had she known he needed to be held just as badly?

Kate felt him relax degree by degree and wondered if it had been she who'd caused the tension in him, and she who'd ultimately released it. Had she hurt him more than she'd realized? Had he cared more than she'd dared to believe? Or was it simply that the physical need never completely faded? It didn't matter, not tonight.

Ky was right. She knew the rules this time around. She wouldn't expect more than he offered. Whatever he offered was much, much more than she'd had in the long, dry years without him. In turn, she could give what she ached to give. Her love.

"It's the same for me as it always was," she murmured. Then, tilting her head back, she looked at him. Her hair streamed down her back, her eyes were wide and honest. He felt the need slam into him like a fist.

"Kate—"

"I never expected to feel the same way when I came back," she interrupted. "I don't think I'd have come. I wouldn't have had the courage."

"Kate, you're not well." He said it very slowly, as if he had to explain to them both. "You've lost blood, had a fever. It's taken a lot out of you. It'd be best, I think, if you tried to sleep now."

She felt no fever now. She felt cool and light and full of needs. "That day on the beach during the storm, you said I'd come to you." Kate brought her hands up his back until they reached his shoulders. "Even then I knew you were right. I'm coming to you now. Make love with me, Ky, here, in the bed where you loved me that first time."

And the last, he remembered, fighting back a torrent of desire. "You're not well," he managed a second time.

"Well enough to know what I want." She brushed her lips over his chin where his beard grew rough with neglect. So long…that was all that would come clearly to her. It had been so long. Too long. "Well enough to know what

I need. It's always been you." Her fingers tightened on his shoulders, her lips inches from his. "It's only been you."

Perhaps moving away from her was the answer. But some answers were impossible. "Tomorrow you may be sorry."

She smiled in her calm, quiet way that always moved him. "Then we'll have tonight."

He couldn't resist her. The warmth. He didn't want to hurt her. The softness. The need building inside him threatened to send them both raging even though he knew she was still weak, still fragile. He remembered how it had been the first time, when she'd been innocent. He'd been so careful, though he had never felt the need to care before, and hadn't since. Remembering that, he laid her back.

"We'll have tonight," he repeated and touched his lips to hers.

Sweet, fresh, clean. Those words went through his head, those sensations went through his system as her lips parted for his. So he lingered over her kiss, enjoying with tenderness what he'd once promised himself to take ruthlessly. His mouth caressed, without haste, without pressure. Tasting, just tasting, while the hunger grew.

Her hands reached for his face, fingers stroking, the rough, the smooth. She could hear her own heart beat in her head, feel the slow, easy pleasure that came in liquid waves. He murmured to her, lovely, quiet words that made her thrill when she felt them formed against her mouth. With his tongue he teased hers in long, lazy sweeps until she felt her mind cloud as it had under the drug. Then when she felt the first twinge of desperation, he kissed her with an absorbed patience that left her weak.

He felt it—that initial change from equality to submission that had always excited him. The aggression would come later, knocking the breath from him, taking him to the edge. He knew that too. But for the moment, she was soft, yielding.

He slid his hands over the nightshirt, stroking, lingering. The material between his flesh and hers teased them both. She moved to his rhythm, glorying in the steady loss of control. He took her deeper with a touch, still deeper with a taste. She dove, knowing the full pleasure of ultimate trust. Wherever he took her, she wanted to go.

With a whispering movement he took his hand over the slender curve of her breast. She was soft, the material smooth, making her hardening nipple a sensuous contrast. He loitered there while her breathing grew unsteady, reveling in the changes of her body. Lingering over each separate button of her nightshirt, Ky unfastened them, then slowly parted the material, as if he were unveiling a priceless treasure.

He'd never forgotten how lovely she was, how exciting delicacy could be. Now that he had her again, he allowed himself the time to look, to touch carefully, all the while watching the contact of his lean tanned hand against her pale skin. With tenderness he felt seldom and demonstrated rarely, he lowered his mouth, letting his lips follow the progress his fingers had already begun.

She was coming to life under him. Kate felt her blood begin to boil as though it had lain dormant in her veins for years. She felt her heart begin to thump as though it had been frozen in ice until that moment. She heard her name as only he said it. As only he could.

Sensations? Could there be so many of them? Could she have known them all once, experienced them all once, then lived without them? A whisper, a sigh, the brush of a fingertip along her skin. The scent of a man touched by the sea, the taste of her lover lingering yet on her lips. The glow of soft lights against closed lids. Time faded. No yesterday. No tomorrow.

She could feel the slick material of the nightshirt slide away, then the warm, smooth sheets beneath her back. The skim of his tongue along her ribcage incited a thrill that began in her core and exploded inside her head.

She remembered the dawn breaking slowly over the sea. Now she knew the same magnificence inside her own body. Light and warmth spread through her, gradually, patiently, until she was glowing with a new beginning.

He hadn't known he could hold such raging desire in check and still feel such complete pleasure, such whirling excitement. He was aware of every heightening degree of passion that worked through her. He understood the changing, rippling thrill she felt if he used more pressure here, a longer taste there. It brought him a wild sense of power, made only more acute by the knowledge that he must harness it. She was fluid. She was silk. And then with a suddenness that sent him reeling, she was fire.

Her body arched on the first tumultuous crest. It ripped through her like a madness. Greedy, ravenous for more, she began to demand what he'd only hinted at. Her hands ran over him, nearly destroying his control in a matter of seconds. Her mouth was hot, hungry, and sought his with an urgency he couldn't resist. Then she rained kisses over his face, down his throat until he gripped the sheets with his hands for fear of crushing her too tightly and bruising her skin.

She touched him with those slender, elegant fingers so

that the blood rushed fast and furious into his head. "You make me crazy," he murmured.

"Yes." She could do no more than whisper, but her eyes opened. "Yes."

"I want to watch you go up," he said softly as he slid into her. "I want to see what making love with me does to you."

She arched again, the moan inching out of her as she experienced a second wild peak. He saw her eyes darken, cloud as he took her slowly, steadily toward the verge between passion and madness. He watched the color come into her cheeks, saw her lips tremble as she spoke his name. Her hands gripped his shoulders, but neither of them knew her short tapered nails dug into his skin.

They moved together, neither able to lead, both able to follow. As pleasure built, he never took his eyes from her face.

All sensation focused into one. They were only one. With a freedom that reaches perfection only rarely, they gave perfection to each other.

Chapter 8

She was sleeping soundly when Ky woke. Ky observed a hint of color in her cheeks and was determined to see that it stayed there. The touch of his hand to her hair was gentle but proprietary. Her skin was cool and dry, her breathing quiet but steady.

What she'd given him the night before had been offered with complete freedom, without shadows of the past, with none of the bitter taste of regret. It was something else he intended to keep constant.

No, he wasn't going to allow her to withdraw from him again. Not an inch. He'd lost her four years ago, or perhaps he'd never really had her—not in the way he'd believed, not in the way he'd taken for granted. But this time, Ky determined, it would be different.

In his own way, he needed to take care of her. Her fragility drew that from him. In another way, he needed a partner on equal terms. Her strength offered him that. For reasons he never completely understood, Kate was exactly what he'd always wanted.

Clumsiness, arrogance, inexperience, or perhaps a combination of all three made him lose her once. Now that he had a second chance, he was going to make sure it worked. With a little more time, he might figure out how.

Rising, he dressed in the shaded light of the bedroom, then left her to sleep.

When she woke slowly, Kate was reluctant to surface from the simple pleasure of a dream. The room was dim, her mind was hazy with sleep and fantasy. The throb in her leg came as a surprise. How could there be pain when everything was so perfect? With a sigh, she reached for Ky and found the bed empty.

The haze vanished immediately, as did all traces of sleep and the pretty edge of fantasy. Kate sat up, and though the movement jolted the pain in her leg, she stared at the empty space beside her.

Had that been a dream as well? she wondered. Tentatively, she reached out and found the sheets cool. All a fantasy brought on by medication and confusion? Unsure, unsteady, she pushed the hair away from her face. Was it possible that she'd imagined it all—the gentleness, the sweetness, the passion?

She'd needed Ky. That hadn't been a dream. Even now she could feel the dull ache in her stomach that came from need. Had the need caused her to fantasize all that strange, stirring beauty during the night? The bed beside her was empty, the sheets cool. She was alone.

The pleasure she awoke with drained, leaving her empty, leaving her grateful for the pain that was her only grip on reality. She wanted to weep, but found she hadn't the energy for tears.

"So you're up."

Ky's voice made her whip her head around. Her nerves were strung tight. He walked into the bedroom carrying a tray, wearing an easy smile.

"That saves me from having to wake you up to get some food into you." Before he approached the bed, he went to both windows and drew up the shades. Light poured into the room and the warm breeze that had been trapped behind the shades rushed in to ruffle the sheets. Feeling it, she had to control a shudder. "How'd you sleep?"

"Fine." The awkwardness was unexpected. Kate folded her hands and sat perfectly still. "I want to thank you for everything you've done."

"You've already thanked me once. It wasn't necessary then or now." Because her tone had put him on guard, Ky stopped next to the bed to take a good long look at her. "You're hurting."

"It's not bad."

"This time you take a pill." After setting the tray on her lap, he walked to the dresser and picked up a small bottle. "No arguments," he said, anticipating her refusal.

"Ky, it's really not bad." When had he offered her a pill before? The struggle to remember brought only more frustration. "There's barely any pain."

"Any pain's too much." He sat on the bed, and putting the pill into her palm curled her hand over it with his own. "When it's you."

With her fingers curled warmly under his, she knew. Elation came so quietly she was afraid to move and chase it away. "I didn't dream it, did I?" she whispered.

"Dream what?" He kissed the back of her hand before he handed her the glass of juice.

"Last night. When I woke up, I was afraid it had all been a dream."

He smiled and, bending, touched his lips to hers. "If it was, I had the same dream." He kissed her again, with humor in his eyes. "It was wonderful."

"Then it doesn't matter whether it was a dream or not."

"Oh no, I prefer reality."

With a laugh, she started to drop the pill on the tray, but he stopped her. "Ky—"

"You're hurting," he said again. "I can see it in your eyes. Your medication wore off hours ago, Kate."

"And kept me unconscious for an entire day."

"This is mild, just to take the edge off. Listen—" His hand tightened on hers. "I had to watch you in agony."

"Ky, don't."

"No, you'll do it for me if not for yourself. I had to watch you bleed and faint and drift in and out of consciousness." He ran his hand down her hair, then cupped her face so she'd look directly into his eyes. "I can't tell you what it did to me because I don't know how to describe it. I know I can't watch you in pain anymore."

In silence, she took the pill and drained the glass of juice. For him, as he said, not for herself. When she swallowed the medication, Ky tugged at her hair. "It hardly has more punch than an aspirin, Kate. Bailey said he'd give you something stronger if you needed it, but he'd rather you go with this."

"It'll be fine. It's really more uncomfortable than painful." It wasn't quite the truth, nor did he believe her, but they both let it lie for the moment. Each of them moved cautiously, afraid to spoil what might have begun to bloom again. Kate glanced down at the empty juice glass. The cold, fresh flavor still lingered on her tongue. "Did Dr. Bailey say when I could dive again?"

"Dive?" Ky's brows rose as he uncovered the plate of bacon, eggs and toast. "Kate, you're not even getting up out of bed for the rest of the week."

"Out of bed?" she repeated. "A week?" She ignored the overloaded plate of food as she gaped at him. "Ky, I was stung by a stingray, not attacked by a shark."

"You were stung by a stingray," he agreed. "And your system was so depleted Bailey almost sent you to a hospital. I realize things might've been rough on you since your father died, but you haven't helped anything by not taking care of yourself."

It was the first time he'd mentioned her father's death, and Kate noted he still expressed no sympathy. "Doctors tend to fuss," she began.

"Bailey doesn't," he interrupted. The anger came back and ran along the edge of his words. "He's a tough, cynical old goat, but he knows his business. He told me that you'd apparently worked yourself right to the edge of exhaustion, that your resistance was nil, and that you were a good ten pounds underweight." He held out the fork. "We're going to do something about that, professor. Starting now."

Kate looked down at what had to be four large eggs, scrambled, six slices of bacon and four pieces of toast. "I can see you intend to," she murmured.

"I'm not having you sick." He took her hand again and his grip was firm. "I'm going to take care of you, Kate, whether you like it or not."

She looked back at him in her calm, considering way. "I don't know if I do like it," she decided. "But I suppose we'll both find out."

Ky dipped the fork into the eggs. "Eat."

A smile played at the corners of her mouth. She'd never been pampered in her life and thought it might be entirely too easy to get used to it. "All right, but this time I'll feed myself."

She already knew she'd never finish the entire meal, but for his sake, and the sake of peace, she was determined to deal with half of it. That had been precisely his strategy. If he'd have brought her a smaller portion, she'd have eaten half of that, and have eaten less. He knew her better than either one of them fully realized.

"You're still a wonderful cook," she commented, breaking a piece of bacon in half. "Much better than I."

"If you're good, I might broil up some flounder tonight."

She remembered just how exquisitely he prepared fish. "How good?"

"As good as it takes." He accepted the slice of toast she offered him but dumped on a generous slab of jam. "Maybe I'll beg some of the hot fudge cake from the Roost."

"Looks like I'll have to be on my best behavior."

"That's the idea."

"Ky…" She was already beginning to poke at her eggs. Had eating always been quite such an effort? "About last night, what happened—"

"Should never have stopped," he finished.

Her lashes swept up, and her eyes were quiet and candid. "I'm not sure."

"I am," he countered. Taking her face in his hands, he kissed her, softly, with only a hint of passion. But the hint was a promise of much more. "Let it be enough for now, Kate. If it has to get complicated, let's wait until other things are a little more settled."

Complicated. Were commitments complicated, the future, promises? She looked down at her plate knowing she simply didn't have the strength to ask or to answer. Not now. "In a way I feel as though I'm slipping back—to that summer four years ago. And yet…"

"It's like a step forward."

Kate looked at him again, but this time reached out. He'd always understood. Though he said little, though his way was sometimes rough, he'd always understood. "Yes. Either way it's a little unnerving."

"I've never liked smooth water. You get a better ride with a few waves."

"Perhaps." She shook her head. Slipping back, stepping forward, it hardly mattered. Either way, she was moving toward him. "Ky, I can't eat any more."

"I figured." Easily, he picked up an extra fork from the tray and began eating the cooling eggs himself. "It's still probably more than you eat for breakfast in a week."

"Probably," she agreed in a murmur, realizing just how well he'd maneuvered her. Kate lay back against the propped-up pillows, annoyed that she was growing sleepy again. No more medication, she decided silently as Ky polished off their joint breakfast. If she could just avoid that, and go out for a little while, she'd be fine. The trick would be to convince Ky.

Kate looked toward the window, and the sunshine. "I don't want to lose a week's time going over the wreck."

He didn't have to follow the direction of her gaze to follow the direction of her thoughts. "I'll be going down," he said easily. "Tomorrow, the next day anyway." Sooner, he thought to himself, depending on how Kate mended.

"Alone?"

He caught the tone as he bit into the last piece of bacon. "I've gone down alone before."

She would have protested, stating how dangerous it was, if she'd believed it would have done any good. Ky did a great deal alone because that was how he preferred it. Instead, Kate chose another route.

"We're looking for the *Liberty* together, Ky. It isn't a one-man operation."

He sent her a long, quiet look before he picked up the coffee she hadn't touched. "Afraid I'll take off with the treasure?"

"Of course not." She wouldn't allow her emotions to get in the way. "If I hadn't trusted your integrity," she said evenly, "I wouldn't have shown you the chart in the first place."

"Fair enough," he allowed with a nod. "So if I continue to dive while you're recuperating, we won't lose time."

"I don't want to lose you either." It was out before she could stop it. Swearing lightly, Kate looked toward the window again. The sky was the pale blue sometimes seen on summer mornings.

Ky merely sat for a moment while the pleasure of her words rippled through him. "You'd worry about me?"

Angry, Kate turned back. He looked so smug, so infuriatingly content. "No, I wouldn't worry. God usually makes a point of looking after fools."

Grinning, he set the tray on the floor beside the bed. "Maybe I'd like you to worry, a little."

"Sorry I can't oblige you."

"Your voice gets very prim when you're annoyed," he commented. "I like it."

"I'm not prim."

He ran a hand down her loosened hair. No, she looked anything but prim at the moment. Soft and feminine, but not prim. "Your voice is. Like one of those pretty, lacy ladies who used to sit in parlors eating finger sandwiches."

She pushed his hand aside. He wouldn't get around her with charm. "Perhaps I should shout instead."

"Like that too, but more…" He kissed one cheek, then the other. "I like to see you smile at me. The way you smile at nobody else."

Her skin was already beginning to warm. No, he might not get around her with charm, but…he'd distract her from her point if she wasn't careful. "I'd be bored, that's all. If I have to sit here, hour after hour with nothing to do."

"I've got lots of books." He slipped her nightshirt down her shoulder then kissed her bare skin with the lightest of touches. "Probably lay my hands on some crossword puzzles, too."

"Thanks a lot."

"There's a copy of Byron downstairs."

Despite her determination not to, Kate looked toward him again. "Byron?"

"I bought it after you left. The words are wonderful." He had the three buttons undone with such quick expertise, she never noticed. "But I could always hear the way you'd say them. I remember one night on the beach, when the moon was full on the water. I don't remember the name of the poem, but I remember how it started, and how it sounded when you said it. 'It is the hour'," he began, then smiled at her.

"'It is the hour'," Kate continued, "'when from the boughs the nightingale is heard/It is the hour when lovers' vows seem sweet in every whisper'd word/And gentle winds, and waters near make music to the lonely ear'…" She trailed off, remembering even the scent of that night. "You were never very interested in Byron's technique."

"No matter how hard you tried to explain it to me."

Yes, he was distracting her. Kate was already finding it difficult to remember what point she'd been trying to make. "He was one of the leading poets of his day."

"Hmm." Ky caught the lobe of her ear between his teeth.

"He had a fascination for war and conflict, and yet he had more love affairs in his poems than Shelley or Keats."

"How about out of his poems?"

"There too." She closed her eyes as his tongue began to do outrageous things to her nervous system. "He used humor, satire as well as a pure lyrical style. If he'd ever completed *Don Juan*…" She trailed off with a sigh that edged toward a moan.

"Did I interrupt you?" Ky brushed his fingers down her thigh. "I really love to hear you lecture."

"Yes."

"Good." He traced her lips with his tongue. "I just thought maybe I could give you something to do for a while." He skimmed his hand over her hip then up to the side of her breast. "So you won't be bored by staying in bed. Want to tell me more about Byron?"

With a long quiet breath, she wound her arms around his neck. The point she'd been trying to make didn't seem important any longer. "No, but I might like staying in bed after all, even without the crossword puzzles."

"You'll relax." He said it softly, but the command was unmistakable. She might have argued, but the kiss was long and lingering, leaving her slow and helplessly yielding.

"I don't have a choice," she murmured. "Between the medication and you."

"That's the idea." He'd love her, Ky thought, but so gently she'd have nothing to do but feel. Then she'd sleep. "There are things I want from you." He lifted his head until their eyes met. "Things I need from you."

"You never tell me what they are."

"Maybe not." He laid his forehead on hers. Maybe he just didn't know how to tell her. Or how to ask. "For now, what I want is to see you well." Again he lifted his head, and his eyes focused on hers. "I'm not an unselfish man, Kate. I want that just as much for myself as I want it for you. I fully intended to have you back in my bed, but I didn't want it for you. I fully intended to have you back in my bed, but I didn't care to have you unconscious here first."

"Whatever you intended, I make my own choices." Her hands slid up his shoulders to touch his face. "I chose to make love with you then. I choose to make love with you now."

He laughed and pressed her palm to his lips. "Professor, you think I'd have given you a choice? Maybe we don't know each other as well as we should at this point, but you should know that much."

Thoughtfully, she ran her thumb down his cheekbone. It was hard, elegantly defined. Somehow it suited him in the same way the unshaven face suited him. But did she? Kate wondered. Were they, despite all their differences, right for each other?

It seemed when they were like this, there was no question of suitability, no question of what was right or wrong. Each completed the other. Yet there had to be more. No matter how much each of them denied it on the surface, there had to be more. And ultimately, there had to be a choice.

"When you take what isn't offered freely, you have nothing." She felt the rough scrape of his unshaven face on her palm and the thrill went through her system. "If I give, you have whatever you need without asking."

"Do I?" he murmured before he touched his lips to hers again. "And you? What do you have?"

She closed her eyes as her body drifted on a calm, quiet plane of pleasure. "What I need."

For how long? The question ran through his mind, prodding against his contentment. But he didn't ask. There'd be a time, he knew, for more questions, for the hundreds of demands he wanted to make. For ultimatums. Now she was sleepy, relaxed in the way he wanted her to be.

With no more words he let her body drift, stroking gently, letting her system steep in the pleasure he could give. With no one else could he remember asking so little for himself and receiving so much. She was the hinge that could open or close the door on the better part of him.

He listened to her sigh as he touched her. The second was a kind of pure contentment that mirrored his own feelings. It seemed neither of them required any more.

Kate knew it shouldn't be so simple. It had never been

simple with anyone else, so that in the end she'd never given herself to anyone else. Only with Ky had she ever known that full excitement that left her free. Only with Ky had she ever known the pure ease that felt so right.

They'd been apart four years, yet if it had been forty, she would have recognized his touch in an instant. That touch was all she needed to make her want him.

She remembered the demands and fire that had always been threaded through their lovemaking before. It had been the excitement she'd craved even while it had baffled her. Now there was patience touched with a consideration she didn't know he was capable of.

Perhaps if she hadn't loved him already, she would have fallen in love at that moment when the sun filtered through the windows and his hands were on her skin. She wanted to give him the fire, but his hands kept it banked. She wanted to meet any demands, but he made none. Instead, she floated on the clouds he brought to her.

Though the heat smoldered inside him, she kept him sane. Just by her pliancy. Though passion began to take over, she kept him calm. Just by her serenity. He'd never looked for serenity in his life. It had simply come to him, as Kate had. He'd never understood what it meant to be calm, but he had known the emptiness and the chaos of living without it.

Without urgency or force, he slipped inside her. Slowly, with a sweetness that made her weak, he gave her the ultimate gift. Passion, fulfillment, with the softer emotions covering a need that seemed insatiable.

Then she slept, and he left her to her dreams.

When she awoke again, Kate wasn't groggy, but weak. Even as sleep cleared, a sense of helpless annoyance went though her. It was midafternoon. She didn't need a clock, the angle of the sunlight that slanted through the window across from the bed told her what time it was. More hours had been lost without her knowledge. And where was Ky?

Kate groped for her nightshirt and slipped into it. If he followed his pattern, he'd be popping through the door with a loaded lunch tray and a pill. Not this time, Kate determined as she eased herself out of bed. Nothing else was going into her system that made her lose time.

But as she stood, the dregs of the medication swam in her head. Reflexively, she nearly sat again before she stopped herself. Infuriated, she gripped the bedpost, breathed deeply then put her weight on her injured foot. It took the pain to clear her head.

Pain had its uses, she thought grimly. After she'd given the hurt a moment to subside, it eased into a throb. That could be tolerated, she told herself and walked to the mirror over Ky's dresser.

She didn't like what she saw. Her hair was listless, her face washed-out and her eyes dull. Swearing, she put her hands to her cheeks and rubbed as though she could force color into them. What she needed, Kate decided, was a hot shower, a shampoo and some fresh air. Regardless of what Ky thought, she was going to have them.

Taking a deep breath, she headed for the door. Even as she reached for the knob, it opened.

"What're you doing up?"

Though they were precisely the words she'd expected, Kate had expected them from Ky, not Linda. "I was just—"

"Do you want Ky to skin me alive?" Linda demanded, backing Kate toward the bed with a tray of steaming soup in her hand. "Listen, you're supposed to rest and eat, then eat and rest. Orders."

Realizing abruptly that she was retreating, Kate held her ground. "Whose?"

"Ky's. And," she continued before Kate could retort, "Dr. Bailey's."

"I don't have to take orders from either of them."

"Maybe you don't," Linda agreed dryly. "But I don't argue with a man who's protecting his woman, or with the man who poked a needle into my bottom when I was three. Both of them can be nasty. Now lie down."

"Linda…" Though she knew the sigh sounded long suffering, Kate couldn't prevent it. "I've a cut on my leg. I've been in bed for something like forty-eight hours straight. If I don't have a shower and a breath of air soon, I'm going to go crazy."

A smile tugged at Linda's mouth that she partially concealed by nibbling on her lower lip. "A bit grumpy, are we?"

"I can be more than a bit." This time the sigh was simply bad tempered. "Look at me!" Kate demanded, tugging on her hair. "I feel as though I've just crawled out from under a rock."

"Okay. I know how I felt after I'd delivered Hope. After I'd had my cuddle with her I wanted a shower and shampoo so bad I was close to tears." She set the tray on the table beside the bed. "You can have ten minutes in the shower, then you can eat while I change your bandage. But Ky made me swear I'd make you eat every bite." She put her hands on her hips. "So that's the deal."

"He's overreacting," Kate began. "It's absurd. I don't need to be babied this way."

"Tell me that when you don't look like I could blow you over. Now come on, I'll give you a hand in the shower."

"No, damn it, I'm perfectly capable of taking a shower by myself." Ignoring the pain in her leg, she stormed out of the room, slamming the door at her back. Linda swallowed a laugh and sat down on the bed to wait.

Fifteen minutes later, refreshed and thoroughly ashamed of herself, Kate came back in. Wrapped in Ky's robe, she rubbed a towel over her hair. "Linda—"

"Don't apologize. If I'd been stuck in bed for two days, I'd snap at the first person who gave me trouble. Besides—" Linda knew how to play her cards "—if you're really sorry you'll eat all your soup, so Ky won't yell at me."

"All right." Resigned, Kate sat back in the bed and took the tray on her lap. She swallowed the first bite of soup and stifled her objection as Linda began to fiddle with her bandage. "It's wonderful."

"The seafood chowder's one of our specialties. Oh, honey." Linda's eyes darkened with concern after she removed the gauze. "This must've hurt like hell. No wonder Ky's been frantic."

Drumming up her courage, Kate leaned over enough to look at the wound. There was no inflammation as she'd feared, no puffiness. Though the slice was six inches in length, it was clean. Her stomach muscles unknotted. "It's not so bad," she murmured. "There's no infection."

"Look, I've been caught by a stingray, a small one. I probably had a cut half an inch across and I cried like a baby. Don't tell me it's not so bad."

"Well, I slept through most of it." She winced, then deliberately relaxed her muscles.

Linda narrowed her eyes as she studied Kate's face.

"Ky said you should have a pill if there was any pain when you woke."

"If you want to do me a favor, you can dump them out." Calmly, Kate ate another spoonful of soup. "I really hate to argue with him, or with you, but I'm not taking any more pills and losing any more time. I appreciate the fact that he wants to pamper me. It's unexpectedly sweet, but I can only take it so far."

"He's worried about you. He feels responsible."

"For my carelessness?" With a shake of her head, Kate concentrated on finishing the soup. "It was an accident, and if there's blame, it's mine. I was so wrapped up in looking for salvage I didn't take basic precautions. I practically bumped into the ray." With an effort, she controlled a shudder. "Ky acted much more quickly than I. He'd already started to pull me out of range. If he hadn't, things would have been much more serious."

"He loves you."

Kate's fingers tightened on the spoon. With exaggerated care, she set it back on the tray. "Linda, there's a vast difference between concern, attraction, even affection and love."

Linda simply nodded in agreement. "Yes. I said Ky loves you."

She managed to smile and pick up the tea that had been cooling beside the soup. "*You* said," Kate returned simply. "*Ky* hasn't."

"Well neither did Marsh until I was ready to strangle him, but that didn't stop me."

"I'm not you." Kate lay back against the pillows, grateful that most of the weakness and the weariness had passed. "And Ky isn't Marsh."

Impatient, Linda rose and swirled around the room. "People who complicate simple things make me so mad!"

Smiling, Kate sipped her tea. "Others simplify the complicated."

With a sniff, Linda turned back. "I've known Ky Silver all my life. I watched him bounce around from one cute girl to the next, then one attractive woman to another until I lost count. Then you came along." Stopping, she leaned against the bedpost. "It was as if someone had hit him over the head with a blunt instrument. You dazed him, Kate, almost from the first minute. You fascinated him."

"Dazing, fascinating." Kate shrugged while she tried to ignore the ache in her heart. "Flattering, I suppose, but neither of those things equals love."

The stubborn line came and went between Linda's brows. "I don't believe love comes in an instant, it grows. If you could have seen the way Ky was after you left four years ago, you'd know—"

"Don't tell me about four years ago," Kate interrupted. "What happened four years ago is over. Ky and I are two different people today, with different expectations. This time…" She took a deep breath. "This time when it ends, I won't be hurt because I know the limits."

"You've just gotten back together and you're already talking about endings and limitations!" Dragging a hand through her hair, Linda came forward to sit on the edge of the bed. "What's wrong with you? Don't you know how to wish anymore? How to dream?"

"I was never very good at either. Linda…" She hesitated, wanting to choose her phrasing carefully. "I don't want to expect any more from Ky than what he can easily give. After August, I know we'll each go back to our separate worlds—there's no bridge between them. Maybe I was meant to come back so we could make up for whatever pain we caused each other before. This time I want to leave still being friends. He's..." She hesitated again because this phrasing was even more important. "He's always been a very important part of my life."

Linda waited a moment, then narrowed her eyes. "That's about the dumbest thing I've ever heard."

Despite herself, Kate laughed. "Linda—"

Holding up her hands, she shook her head and cut Kate off. "No, I can't talk about it anymore, I get too mad and I'm supposed to be taking care of you." She let out her breath on a huff as she removed Kate's tray. "I just can't understand how anyone so smart could be so stupid, but the more I think about it the more I can see that you and Ky deserve each other."

"That sounds more like an insult than a compliment."

"It was."

Kate pushed her tongue against her teeth to hold back a smile. "I see."

"Don't look so smug just because you've made me so angry I don't want to talk about it anymore." She drew her shoulders back. "I might just give Ky a piece of my mind when he gets home."

"That's his problem," Kate said cheerfully. "Where'd he go?"

"Diving."

Amusement faded. "Alone?"

"There's no use worrying about it." Linda spoke briskly

as she cursed herself for not thinking of a simple lie. "He dives alone ninety percent of the time."

"I know." But Kate folded her hands, preparing to worry until he returned.

Chapter 9

"I'm going with you."

The sunlight was strong, the scent of the ocean pure. Through the screen the sound of gulls from a quarter of a mile away could be heard clearly. Ky turned from the stove where he poured the last cup of coffee and eyed Kate as she stood in the doorway.

She'd pinned her hair up and had dressed in thin cotton pants and a shirt, both of which were baggy and cool. It occured to him that she looked more like a student than a college professor.

He knew enough of women and their illusions to see that she'd added color to her cheeks. She hadn't needed blusher the evening before when he'd returned from the wreck. Then she had been angry, and passionate. He nearly smiled as he lifted his cup.

"You wasted your time getting dressed," he said easily. "You're going back to bed."

Kate disliked stubborn people, people who demanded their own way flatly and unreasonably. At that moment, she decided they were *both* stubborn. "No." On the surface she remained as calm as he was while she walked into the kitchen. "I'm going with you."

Unlike Kate, Ky never minded a good argument. Preparing for one, he leaned back against the stove. "I don't take down a diver against doctor's orders."

She'd expected that. With a shrug, she opened the refrigerator and took out a bottle of juice. She knew she was being bad tempered, and though it was completely out of character, she was enjoying the experience. The simple truth was that she had to do something or go mad.

As far as she could remember, she'd never spent two more listless days. She had to move, think, feel the sun. It might have been satisfying to stomp her feet and demand, but, she thought, fruitless. If she had to compromise to get her way, then compromise she would.

"I can rent a boat and equipment and go down on my own." With the glass in hand, she turned, challenging. "You can't stop me."

"Try me."

It was said simply, quietly, but she'd seen the flare of anger in his eyes. Better, she thought. Much better. "I've a right to do precisely as I choose. We both know it." Perhaps her leg was uncomfortable, but as to the rest of her body, it was charged up and ready to move. Nor was there anything wrong with her mind. Kate had plotted her strategy very well. After all, she thought grimly, there'd certainly been enough time to think it through.

"We both know you're not in any shape to dive." His first urge was to carry her back to bed, his second to shake her until she rattled. Ky did neither, only drank his coffee and watched her over the rim. A power struggle wasn't something he'd expected, but he wouldn't back away from it. "You're not stupid, Kate. You know you can't go down yet, and you know I won't let you."

"I've rested for two days. I feel fine." As she walked toward him she was pleased to see him frown. He understood she had a mind of her own, and that he had to deal with it. The truth was, she was stronger than either of them had expected her to be. "As far as diving goes, I'm willing to leave that to you for the next couple of days, but…" She paused, wanting to be certain he knew she was negotiating, not conceding. "I'm going out on the *Vortex* with you. And I'm going out this morning."

He lifted a brow. She'd never intended to dive, but she'd used it as a pressure point to get what she wanted. He couldn't blame her. Ky remembered recovering from a broken leg when he was fourteen. The pain was vague in his mind now, but the boredom was still perfectly clear. "You'll lie down in the cabin when you're told."

She smiled and shook her head. "I'll lie down in the cabin if I need to."

He took her chin in his hand and squeezed. "Damn right you will. Okay, let's go. I want an early start."

Once he was resigned, Ky moved quickly. She could either keep up, or be left behind. Within minutes he parked his car near his slip at Silver Lake Harbor and was boarding the *Vortex*. Content, Kate took a seat beside him at the helm and prepared to enjoy the sun and the wind. Already she felt the energy begin to churn.

"I've done a chart of the wreck as of yesterday's dive," he told her as he maneuvered out of the harbor.

"A chart?" Automatically she pushed at her hair as she turned toward him. "You didn't show me."

"Because you were asleep when I finished it."

"I've been asleep ninety percent of the time," she mumbled.

As he headed out to sea, Ky laid a hand on her shoulder. "You look better, Kate, no shadows. No strain. That's more important."

For a moment, just a moment, she pressed her cheek against his hand. Few women could resist such soft concern, and yet...she didn't want his concern to cloud their reason for being together. Concern could turn to pity. She needed him to see her as a partner, as equal. As long as she was his lover, it was vital that they meet on the same ground. Then when she left... When she left there'd be no regrets.

"I don't need to be pampered anymore, Ky."

His shoulders moved as he glanced at the compass. "I enjoyed it."

She was resisting being cared for. He understood it, appreciated it and regretted it. There had been something appealing about seeing to her needs, about having her depend on him. He didn't know how to tell her he wanted her to be well and strong just as much as he wanted her to turn to him in times of need.

Somehow, he felt their time together had been too short for him to speak. He didn't deal well with caution. As a diver, he knew its importance, but as a man... As a man he fretted to go with his instincts, with his impulses.

His fingers brushed her neck briefly before he turned

to the wheel. He'd already decided he'd have to approach his relationship with Kate as he'd approach a very deep, very dangerous dive—with an eye on currents, pressure and the unexpected.

"That chart's in the cabin," he told her as he cut the engine. "You might want to look it over while I'm down."

She agreed with a nod, but the restlessness was already on her as Ky began to don his equipment. She didn't want to make an issue of his diving alone. He wouldn't listen to her in any case; if anything came of it, it would only be an argument. In silence she watched him check his tanks. He'd be down for an hour. Kate was already marking time.

"There are cold drinks in the galley." He adjusted the strap of his mask before climbing over the side. "Don't sit in the sun too long."

"Be careful," she blurted out before she could stop herself.

Ky grinned, then was gone with a quiet splash.

Though she ran over to the side, Kate was too late to watch him dive. For a long time after, she simply leaned over the boat, staring at the water's surface. She imagined Ky going deeper, deeper, adjusting his pressure, moving out with power until he'd reached the bottom and the wreck.

He'd brought back the bowl and ladle the evening before. They sat on the dresser in his bedroom while the broken rigging and pieces of crockery were stored downstairs. Thus far he'd done no more than gather what they'd already found together, but today, Kate thought with a twinge of impatience, he'd extend the search. Whatever he found, he'd find alone.

She turned away from the water, frustrated that she

was excluded. It occurred to her that all her life she'd been an onlooker, someone who analyzed and explained the action rather than causing it. This search had been her first opportunity to change that, and now she was back to square one.

Stuffing her hands in her pockets, Kate looked up at the sky. There were clouds to the west, but they were thin and white. Harmless. She felt too much like that herself at the moment—something unsubstantial. Sighing, she went below deck. There was nothing to do now but wait.

Ky found two more cannons and sent up buoys to mark their position. It would be possible, if he didn't find something more concrete, to salvage the cannons and have them dated by an expert. Though he swam from end to end, searching carefully, he knew it was unlikely he'd find a date stamp through the layers of corrosion. But in time… Satisfied, he swam north.

If he accomplished nothing else on this dive, he wanted to establish the size of the site. With luck it would be fairly small, perhaps no bigger than a football field. However, there was always the chance that the wreckage could be scattered over several square miles. Before they brought in a salvage ship, he wanted to take a great deal of care with the preliminary work.

They would need tools. A metal detector would be invaluable. Thus far, they'd done no more than find a wreck, no matter how certain Kate was that it was the *Liberty*. For the moment he had no way to determine the origin of the ship, he had to find cargo. Once he'd found that, perhaps treasure would follow.

Once he'd found the treasure… Would she leave?

Would she take her share of the gold and the artifacts and drive home?

Not if he could help it, Ky determined as he shone his headlamp over the sea floor. When the search was over and they'd salvaged what could be salvaged from the sea, it would be time to salvage what they'd once had—what had perhaps never truly been lost. If they could find what had been buried for centuries, they could find what had been buried for four years.

He couldn't find much without tools. Most of the ship—or what remained of it—was buried under silt. On another dive, he'd use the prop-wash, the excavation device he'd constructed in his shop. With that he could blow away inches of sediment at a time—a slow but safe way to uncover artifacts. But someone would have to stay on board to run it.

He thought of Kate and rejected the idea immediately. Though he had no doubt she could handle the technical aspect—it would only have to be explained to her once—she'd never go for it. Ky began to think it was time they enlisted Marsh.

He knew his air time was almost up and he'd have to surface for fresh tanks. Still, he lingered near the bottom, searching, prodding. He wanted to take something up for Kate, something tangible that would put the enthusiasm back in her eyes.

It took him more than half of his allotted time to find it, but when Ky held the unbroken bottle in his hand, he knew Kate's reaction would be worth the effort. It was a common bottle, not priceless crystal, but he could see no mold marks, which meant it had been hand blown. Crust was weathered over it in layers, but Ky took the time to carefully chip some away, from the bottom only. If the date wasn't on the bottom, he'd need the crust to have the bottle dated. Already he was thinking of the Corning Glass Museum and their rate of success.

Then he saw the date, and with a satisfied grin placed the find in the goodie bag on his belt. With his air supply running short, he started toward the surface.

His hour was up. Or so nearly up, Kate thought, that he should have surfaced already if he'd allowed himself any safety factor. She paced from port to starboard and back again. Would he always risk his own welfare to the limit?

She'd long since given up sitting quietly in the cabin, going over the makeshift chart Ky had begun. She'd found a book on shipwrecks that Ky had obviously purchased recently, and though it had also been among her father's research books, she'd skimmed through it again.

It gave a detailed guide to identifying and excavating a wreck, listed common mistakes and hazards. She found it difficult to read about hazards while Ky was alone beneath the surface. Still, even the simple language of the book couldn't disguise the adventure. For perhaps half the time Ky had been gone, she'd lost herself in it. Spanish galleons, Dutch merchant ships, English frigates.

She'd found the list of wrecks off North Carolina alone extensive. But these, she'd thought, had already been located, documented. The adventure there was over. One day, because of the chain her father had started and she'd continued, the *Liberty* would be among them.

Fretfully, Kate waited for Ky to surface. She thought of her father. He'd pored over this same book as well— planning, calculating. Yet his calculations hadn't taken him beyond the initial stage. If he'd shared his goal with her, would he have taken her on his summer quests? She'd never know, because she'd never been given the choice.

She was making her own choices now, Kate mused. Her first had been to return to Ocracoke, accepting the consequences. Her next had been to give herself to Ky without conditions. Her last, she thought as she stared down at the quiet water, would be to leave him again. Yet, in reality, perhaps she'd still been given no choice. It was all a matter of currents. She could only swim against them for so long.

Relief washed over her when she spotted the flow of bubbles. Ky grabbed the bottom rung of the ladder as he pushed up his mask. "Waiting for me?"

Relief mixed with annoyance for the time she'd spent worrying about him. "You cut it close."

"Yeah, a little." He passed up his tanks. "I had to stop and get you a present."

"It's not a joke, Ky." Kate watched him come over the side, agile, lean and energetic. "You'd be furious with me if I'd cut my time that close."

"Leave it up to Linda to fuss," he advised as he pulled down the zipper of his wet suit. "She was born that way." Then he grabbed her, crushing her against him so that she felt the excitement he'd brought up with him. His mouth closed over hers, tasting of salt from the sea. Because he was wet, her clothes clung to him, binding them together for the brief instant he held her. But when he would have released her, she held fast, drawing the kiss out into something that warmed his cool skin.

"I worry about you, Ky." For one last moment, she held on fiercely. "Damn it, is that what you want to hear?"

"No." He took her face in his hands and shook his head. "No."

Kate broke away, afraid she'd say too much, afraid she'd say things neither of them were ready to hear. She knew the rules this time. She groped for something calm, something simple. "I suppose I got a bit frantic waiting up here. It's different when you're down."

"Yeah." What did she want from him? he wondered. Why was it that every time she started to show her concern for him, she clammed up? "I've got some more things to add to the chart."

"I saw the buoys you sent up." Kate moistened her lips and relaxed, muscle by muscle.

"Two more cannons. From the size of them, I'd say she was a fairly small ship. It's unlikely she was constructed for battle."

"She was a merchant ship."

"Maybe. I'm going to take the metal detector down and see what I come up with. From the stuff we've found, I don't think she's buried too deep."

Kate nodded. Delve into business, keep the personal aspect light. "I'd like to send off a piece of the planking and some of the glass to be analyzed. I think we'll have more luck with the glass, but it doesn't hurt to cover all the angles."

"No, it doesn't. Don't you want your present?"

At ease again, she smiled. "I thought you were joking. Did you bring me a shell?"

"I thought you'd like this better." Reaching into his bag, Ky brought out the bottle. "It's too bad it's not still corked. We could've had wine with peanut butter."

"Oh, Ky, it's not damaged!" Thrilled, she reached out for it, but he pulled it back out of reach and grinned.

"Bottoms up," he told her and turned the bottle upside down.

Kate stared at the smeared bottom of the bottle. "Oh, God," she whispered. "It's dated. 1749." Gingerly, she took the bottle in both hands. "The year before the *Liberty* sank."

"It's another ship, maybe," Ky reminded her. "But it does narrow down the time element."

"Over two hundred years," she murmured. "Glass, it's so breakable, so vulnerable, and yet it survived two centuries." Her eyes lit with enthusiasm as she looked back at him. "Ky, we should be able to find out where the bottle was made."

"Probably, but most glass bottles found on wrecks from the seventeenth and eighteenth century were manufactured in England anyway. It wouldn't prove the ship was English."

She let out a huff of breath, but her energy hadn't dimmed. "You've been doing your research."

"I don't go into any project until I know the angles." Ky knelt down to check the fresh tanks.

"You're going back down now?"

"I want to get as much mapped out as I can before we start dealing with too much equipment."

She'd done enough homework herself to know that the most common mistake of the modern day salvor was in failing to map out a site. Yet she couldn't stem her impatience. It seemed so time-consuming when they could be concentrating on getting under the layers of silt.

It seemed to her that she and Ky had changed positions somehow. She'd always been the cautious one, proceeding step by logical step, while he'd taken the risks. Struggling with the impotence of having to wait and watch, she stood back while he strapped on the fresh tanks. As she watched, Ky picked up a brass rod.

"What's that for?"

"It's the base for this." He held out a device that resembled a compass. "It's called an azimuth circle. It's a cheap, effective way to map out the site. I drive this into the approximate center of the wreck so that it becomes the datum point, align the circle with the magnetic north, then I use a length of chain to measure the distance to the cannons, or whatever I need to map. After I get it set, I'll be back up for the metal detector."

Frustration built again. He was doing all the work while she simply stood still. "Ky, I feel fine. I could help if—"

"No." He didn't bother to argue or list reasons. He simply went over the side and under.

It was midafternoon when they started back. Ky spent the last hour at sea adding to the chart, putting in the information he'd gathered that day. He'd brought more up in his goodie bag—a tankard, spoons and forks that might have been made of iron. It seemed they had indeed found the galley. Kate decided she'd begin a detailed list of their finds that evening. If it was all she could do at the moment, she'd do it with pleasure.

Her mood had lifted a bit since she'd caught three good-sized bluefish while Ky had been down at the wreck the second time. No matter how much Ky argued, she fully intended to cook them herself and eat them sitting at the table, not lying in bed.

"Pretty pleased with yourself, aren't you?"

She gave him a cool smile. They were cruising back toward Silver Lake Harbor and though she felt a weariness, it was a pleasant feeling, not the dragging fatigue of the past days. "Three bluefish in that amount of time's a very respectable haul."

"No argument there. Especially since I intend to eat half of them."

"I'm going to grill them."

"Are you?"

She met his lifted brow with a neutral look. "I caught, I cook."

Ky kept the boat at an even speed as he studied her. She looked a bit tired, but he thought he could convince her to take a nap if he claimed he wanted one himself. She was healing quickly. And she was right. He couldn't pamper her. "I could probably bring myself to start the charcoal for you."

"Fair enough. I'll even let you clean them."

He laughed at the bland tone and ruffled her hair until the pins fell out.

"Ky!" Automatically, Kate reached up to repair the damage.

"Wear it up in the school room," he advised, tossing some of the pins overboard. "I find it difficult to resist you when your hair's down and just a bit mussed."

"Is that so?" She debated being annoyed, then decided there were more productive ways to pass the time. Kate let the wind toss her hair as she moved closer to him so that their bodies touched. She smiled at the quick look of surprise in his eyes as she slipped both hands under his T-shirt. "Why don't you turn off the engine and show me what happens when you stop resisting?"

For all her generosity and freedom in lovemaking, she'd never been the initiator. Ky found himself both baffled and aroused as she smiled up at him, her hands stroking slowly over his chest. "You know what happens when I stop resisting," he murmured.

She gave a low, quiet laugh. "Refresh my memory." Without waiting for an answer, she drew back on the throttle herself until the boat was simply idling. "You didn't make love with me last night." Her hands slid around and up his back.

"You were sleeping." She was seducing him in the middle of the afternoon, in the middle of the ocean. He found he wanted to savor the new experience as much as he wanted to bring it to fruition.

"I'm not sleeping now." Rising on her toes, she brushed her lips over his, lightly, temptingly. She felt his heartbeat race against her body and reveled in a sense of power she'd never explored. "Or perhaps you're in a hurry to get back, and uh, clean fish."

She was taunting him. Why had he never seen the witch in her before? Ky felt his stomach knot with need, but when he drew her closer, she resisted. Just slightly. Just enough to torment. "If I make love with you now, I won't be gentle."

She kept her lips inches from his. "Is that a warning?" she whispered. "Or a promise?"

He felt the first tremor move through him and was astonished. Not even for her had he ever trembled. Not even for her. The need grew, stretching restlessly, recklessly. "I'm not sure you know what you're doing, Kate."

Nor did she, but she smiled because it no longer mattered. Only the outcome mattered. "Come down to the cabin with me and we'll both find out." She slipped away from him and without a word disappeared below deck.

His hand wasn't steady when he reached for the key to turn off the engines. He needed a moment, perhaps a bit more, to regain the control he'd held so carefully since they'd become lovers again. Ever since he'd had her blood on his hands, he had a tremendous fear of hurting her. Since he'd had a taste of her again, he had an equal fear of driving her away. Caution was a strain, but he'd kept it in focus with sheer will. As Ky started down the steps, he told himself he'd continue to be cautious.

She'd unbuttoned her blouse but hadn't removed it. When he came into the narrow cabin with her, Kate smiled. She was afraid, though she hardly knew why. But over the fear was a heady sense of power and strength that fought for full release. She wanted to take him to the edge, to push him to the limits of passion. At that moment, she was certain she could.

When he came no closer to her, Kate stepped forward and pulled his shirt over his head. "Your skin's gold," she murmured. "It's always excited me." Taking her pleasure slowly, she ran her hands up his sides, feeling the quiver she caused. "You've always excited me."

Her hands were steady, her pulse throbbed as she unsnapped his cut-offs. With her eyes on his, she slowly, slowly, undressed him. "No one's ever made me want the way you make me want."

He had to stop her and take control again. She couldn't know the effect of those long, fragile fingers when they brushed easily over his skin, or how her calm eyes made him rage inside.

"Kate…" He took her hands in his and bent to kiss her. But she turned her head, meeting his neck with warm lips that sent a spear of fire up his spine.

Then her body was pressed against his, flesh meeting flesh where her blouse parted. Her mouth trailed over his chest, her hands down his back to his hips. He felt the fury of desire whip through him as though it had sharp, hungry teeth.

So he forgot control, gentleness, vulnerability. She drove him to forget. She intended to.

They were tangled on the narrow bunk, her blouse halfway down her back and parted so that her breasts pushed into his chest, driving him mad with their firm, subtle curves. She nipped at his lips, demanding, pushing for more, still more. Waves of passion overtook them.

His need was incendiary. She was like a flame, impossible to hold, searing here, singeing there until his body was burning with needs and fierce fantasies.

Her hands were swift, sending sharp gasping pleasure everywhere at once until he wasn't sure he could take it anymore. Yet he no longer thought of stopping her. Less of stopping himself.

His hands gripped her with an urgency that made her moan from the sheer strength in them. She wanted his strength now—mindless strength that would carry them both to a place they'd never gone before. And she was leading. The knowledge made her laugh aloud as she tasted his skin, his lips, his tongue.

She slid down his body, feeling each jolt of pleasure as it shot through him. There could be no slow, lingering loving now. They'd pushed each other beyond reason. The air here was dark and thin and whirling with sound. Kate drank it in.

When he found her moist, hot and ready she let him take her over peak after shuddering peak, knowing as he drove her, she drove him. Her body was filled with sensations that came and went like comets, slipped away and burst on her again, and again. Through the thunder in her head she heard herself say his name, clear and quick.

On the sound, she took him into her and welcomed the madness.

Chapter 10

She was wrong.

Kate had thought she'd be ready, even anxious to dive again. There hadn't been a day during her recuperation that she hadn't thought of going down. Every time Ky had brought back an artifact, she was thrilled with the discovery and frustrated with her own lack of participation. Like a schoolgirl approaching summer, she'd begun to count the days.

Now, a week after the accident, Kate stood on the deck of the *Vortex* with her mouth dry and her hands trembling as she pulled on her wet suit. She could only be grateful that Ky was already over the side, hooking up his home-rigged prop-wash to the boat's propeller. Drafted to the crew, Marsh stood at the stern watching his brother. With Linda's eager support, he'd agreed to give Ky a few hours a day of his precious free time while he was needed.

Kate took the moment she had alone to gather her thoughts and her nerve.

It was only natural to be anxious about diving after the experience she'd had. Kate told herself that was logical. But it didn't stop her hands from trembling as she zipped up her suit. She could equate it with falling off a horse and having to mount again. It was psychological. But it didn't ease the painful tension in her stomach.

Trembling hands and nerves. With or without them she told herself as she hooked on her weight belt, she was going down. Nothing, not even her own fears, was going to stop her from finishing what she'd begun.

"He's got it," Marsh called out when Ky signaled him.

"I'll be ready." Kate picked up the cloth bag she'd use to bring up small artifacts. With luck, and if the prop-wash did its job, she knew they'd soon need more sophisticated methods to bring up the salvage.

"Kate."

She didn't look up, but continued to hook on the goodie bag. "Yes?"

"You know it's only natural that you'd be nervous going down." Marsh touched a hand to her shoulder, but she busied herself by strapping on her diving knife. "If you want a little more time, I'll work with Ky and you can run the wash."

"No." She said it too quickly, then cursed herself. "It's all right, Marsh." With forced calm she hung the under-water camera she'd purchased only the day before around her neck. "I have to take the first dive sometime."

"It doesn't have to be now."

She smiled at him again thinking how calm, how steady he appeared when compared to Ky. This was the sort of man it would have made sense for her to be attracted to. Confused emotions made no sense. "Yes, it does. Please." She put her hand on his arm before he could speak again. "Don't say anything to Ky."

Did she think he'd have to? Marsh wondered as he inclined his head in agreement. Unless he was way off the mark, Marsh was certain Ky knew every expression, every gesture, every intonation of her voice.

"Let's run it a couple of minutes at full throttle." Ky climbed over the side, dripping and eager. "With the depth and the size of the prop, we're going to have to test the effect. There might not be enough power to do us any good."

In agreement, Marsh went to the helm. "Are you thinking about using an air lift?"

Ky's only answer was a noncommittal grunt. He had thought of it. The metal tube with its stream of compressed air was a quick, efficient way to excavate on silty bottoms. They might get away with the use of a small air lift, if it became necessary. But perhaps the prop-wash would do the job well enough. Either way, he was thinking more seriously about a bigger ship, with more sophisticated equipment and more power. As he saw it, it all depended on what they found today.

He picked up one last piece of equipment—a small powerful spear gun. He'd take no more chances with Kate.

"Okay, slow it down to the minimum," he ordered. "And keep it there. Once Kate and I are down, we don't want the prop-wash shooting cannonballs around."

Kate stopped the deep breathing she was using to ease tension. Her voice was cool and steady. "Would it have that kind of power?"

"Not at this speed." Ky adjusted his mask then took her hand. "Ready?"

"Yes."

Then he kissed her, hard. "You've got guts, professor," he murmured. His eyes were dark, intense as they passed over her face. "It's one of the sexiest things about you." With this he was over the side.

He knew. Kate gave a quiet unsteady sigh as she started down the ladder. He knew she was afraid, and that had been his way of giving her support. She looked up once and saw Marsh. He lifted his hand in salute. Throat dry, nerves jumping, Kate let the sea take her.

She felt a moment's panic, a complete disorientation the moment she was submerged. It ran through her head that down here, she was helpless. The deeper she went, the more vulnerable she became. Choking for air, she kicked back toward the surface and the light.

Then Ky had her hands, holding her to him, holding her under. His grip was firm, stilling the first panic. Feeling the wild race of her pulse, he held on during her first resistance.

Then he touched her cheek, waiting until she'd calmed enough to look at him. In his eyes she saw strength and challenge. Pride alone forced her to fight her way beyond the fear and meet him, equal to equal.

When she'd regulated her breathing, accepting that her air came through the tanks on her back, he kissed the back of her hand. Kate felt the tension give. She wouldn't be helpless, she reminded herself. She'd be careful.

With a nod, she pointed down, indicating she was ready to dive. Keeping hands linked, they started toward the bottom.

The whirlpool action created by the wash of the prop had already blasted away some of the sediment. At first glance Ky could see that if the wreck was buried under more than a few feet, they'd need something stronger than his home-made apparatus and single prop engine. But for now, it would do. Patience, which came to him only with deliberate effort, was more important at this stage than speed. With the wreck, he thought, and—he glanced over at the woman beside him—with a great deal more. He had to take care not to hurry.

It was still working, blowing away some of the overburden at a rate Ky figured would equal an inch per minute. He and Kate alone couldn't deal with any more speed. He watched the swirl of water and sediment while she swam a few feet away to catalog one of the cannons on film. When she came closer, he grinned as she placed the camera in front of her face again. She was relaxed, her initial fear forgotten. He could see it simply in the way she moved. Then she let the camera fall so they could begin the search again.

Kate saw something solid wash away from the hole being created by the whirl of water. Grabbing it up, she found herself holding a candlestick. In her excitement, she turned it over and over in her hand.

Silver? she wondered with a rush of adrenaline. Had they found their first real treasure? It was black with oxidation, so it was impossible to be certain what it was made of. Still, it thrilled her. After days and days of only waiting, she was again pursuing the dream.

When she looked up, Ky was already gathering the uncovered items and laying them in the mesh basket. There were more candleholders, more tableware, but not the plain unglazed pottery they'd found before. Kate's pulse began to drum with excitement while she meticulously snapped pictures. They'd be able to find a hallmark, she was certain of it. Then they'd know if they had indeed found a British ship. Ordinary seamen didn't use silver, or even pewter table service. They'd uncovered more than the galley now. And they were just beginning.

When Ky found the first piece of porcelain he signaled to her. True, the vase—if that's what it once had been—had suffered under the water pressure and the years. It was broken so that only half of the shell remained, but so did the manufacturer's mark.

When Kate read it, she gripped Ky's arm. *Whieldon.* English. The master potter who'd trained the likes of Wedgwood. Kate cupped the broken fragment in her hands as though it were alive. When she lifted her eyes to Ky's they were filled with triumph.

Fretting against her inability to speak, Kate pointed to the mark again. Ky merely nodded and indicated the basket. Though she was loath to part with it, Kate found herself even more eager to discover more. She settled the porcelain in the mesh. When she swam back, Ky's hands were filled with other pieces. Some were hardly more than shards, others were identifiable as pieces left from bowls or lids.

No, it didn't prove it was a merchant ship, Kate told herself as she gathered what she could herself. So far, it only proved that the officers and perhaps some passengers had eaten elegantly on their way to the New World. English officers, she reminded herself. In her mind they'd taken the identification that far.

The force of the wash sent an object shooting up. Ky

reached out for it and found a crusted, filthy pot he guessed would have been used for tea or coffee. Perhaps it was cracked under the layers, but it held together in his hands. He tapped on his tank to get Kate's attention.

She knew it was priceless the moment she saw it. Stemming impatience, she signaled for Ky to hold it out as she lifted the camera again. Obliging, he crossed his legs like a genie and posed.

It made her giggle. They'd perhaps just found something worth thousands of dollars, but he could still act silly. Nothing was too serious for Ky. As she brought him into frame, Kate felt the same foolish pleasure. She'd known the hunt would be exciting, perhaps rewarding, but she'd never known it would be fun. She swam forward and reached for the pot herself.

Running her fingers over it, she could detect some kind of design under the crust. Not ordinary pottery, she was sure. Not utility-ware. She held something elegant, something well crafted.

He understood its worth as well as she. Taking it from her, Ky indicated they would bring it and the rest of the morning's salvage to the surface. Pointing to his watch he showed her that their tanks were running low.

She didn't argue. They'd come back. The *Liberty* would wait for them. Each took a handle of the mesh basket and swam leisurely toward the surface.

"Do you know how I feel?" Kate demanded the moment she could speak.

"Yes." Ky gripped the ladder with one hand and waited for her to unstrap her tanks and slip them over onto the deck. "I know just how you feel."

"The teapot." Breathing fast, she hauled herself up the

ladder. "Ky, it's priceless. It's like finding a perfectly formed rose inside a mass of briars." Before he could answer, she was laughing and calling out to Marsh. "It's fabulous! Absolutely fabulous."

Marsh cut the engine then walked over to help them. "You two work fast." Bending he touched a tentative finger to the pot. "God, it's all in one piece."

"We'll be able to date it as soon as it's cleaned. But look." Kate drew out the broken vase. "This is the mark of an English potter. English," she repeated, turning to Ky. "He trained Wedgwood, and Wedgwood didn't begin manufacturing until the 1760s, so—"

"So this piece more than likely came from the era we're looking for," Ky finished. "*Liberty* or not," he continued, crouching down beside her. "It looks like you've found yourself an eighteenth-century wreck that's probably of English origin and certainly hasn't been recorded before." He took one of her hands between both of his. "Your father would've been proud of you."

Stunned, she stared at him. Emotions raced through her with such velocity she had no way of controlling or channeling them. The hand holding the broken vase began to tremble. Quickly, she set it down in the basket again and rose.

"I'm going below," she managed and fled.

Proud of her. Kate put a hand over her mouth as she stumbled into the cabin. His pride, his love. Wasn't it all she'd really ever wanted from her father? Was it possible she could only gain it after his death?

She drank in deep gulps of air and struggled to level her emotions. No, she wanted to find the *Liberty*, she wanted to bring her father's dream to reality, have his name on a plaque in a museum with the artifacts they'd found. She owed him that. But she'd promised herself she'd find the *Liberty* for herself as well. For herself.

It was her choice, her first real decision to come in from the sidelines and act on her own. For herself, Kate thought again as she brought the first surge of emotion under control.

"Kate?"

She turned, and though she thought she was perfectly calm, Ky could see the turmoil in her eyes. Unsure how to handle it, he spoke practically.

"You'd better get out of that suit."

"But we're going back down."

"Not today." To prove his point he began to strip out of his own suit just as Marsh started the engines.

Automatically, she balanced herself as the boat turned. "Ky, we've got two more sets of tanks. There's no reason for us to go back when we're just getting started."

"Your first dive took most of the strength you've built up. If you want to dive tomorrow, you've got to take it slow today."

Her anger erupted so quickly, it left them both astonished. "The hell with that!" she exploded. "I'm sick to death of being treated as if I don't know my own limitations or my own mind and body."

Ky walked into the galley and picked up a can of beer. With a flick of his wrist, air hissed out. "I don't know what you're talking about."

"I lay in bed for the better part of a week because of pressure from you and Linda and anyone else who came around me. I'm not tolerating this any longer."

With one hand, he pushed dripping hair from his

forehead as he lifted the can. "You're tolerating exactly what's necessary until I say differently."

"You say?" she tossed back. Cheeks flaming, she strode over to him. "I don't have to do what you say, or what anyone says. Not anymore. It's about time you remember just who's in charge of this salvage operation."

His eyes narrowed. "In charge?"

"I hired you. Seventy-five a day and twenty-five percent. Those were the terms. There was nothing in there about you running my life."

He abruptly went still. For a moment, all that could be heard over the engines was her angry breathing. Dollars and percents, he thought with a deadly sort of calm. Just dollars and percents. "So that's what it comes down to?"

Too overwrought to see beyond her own anger, she continued to lash out. "We made an agreement. I fully intend to see that you get everything we arranged, but I won't have you telling me when I can go down. I won't have you judging when I'm well and when I'm not. I'm sick to death of being dictated to. And I won't be—not by you, not by anyone. Not any longer."

The metal of the can gave under his fingers. "Fine. You do exactly what you want, professor. But while you're about it, get yourself another diver. I'll send you a bill." Ky went up the cabin steps the way he came down. Quickly and without a sound.

With her hands gripped together, Kate sat down on the bunk and waited until she heard the engines stop again. She refused to think. Thinking hurt. She refused to feel. There was too much to feel. When she was certain she was in control, she stood and went up on deck.

Everything was exactly as she'd left it—the wire basket filled with bits of porcelain and tableware, her nearly depleted tanks. Ky was gone. Marsh walked over from the stern where he'd been waiting for her.

"You're going to need a hand with these."

Kate nodded and pulled a thigh length T-shirt over her tank suit. "Yes. I want to take everything back to my room at the hotel. I have to arrange for shipping."

"Okay." But instead of reaching down for the basket, he took her arm. "Kate, I don't like to give advice."

"Good." Then she swore at her own rudeness. "I'm sorry, Marsh. I'm feeling a little rough at the moment."

"I can see that, and I know things aren't always smooth for you and Ky. Look, he has a habit of closing himself up, of not saying everything that's on his mind. Or worse," Marsh added. "Of saying the first thing that comes to mind."

"He's perfectly free to do so. I came here for the specific purpose of finding and excavating the *Liberty*. If Ky and I can't deal together on a business level, I have to do without his help."

"Listen, he has a few blind spots."

"Marsh, you're his brother. Your allegiance is with him as it should be."

"I care about both of you."

She took a deep breath, refusing to let the emotion surface and carry her with it. "I appreciate that. The best thing you can do for me now, perhaps for both of us, is to tell me where I can rent a boat and some equipment. I'm going back out this afternoon."

"Kate."

"I'm going back out this afternoon," she repeated. "With or without your help."

Resigned, Marsh picked up the mesh basket. "All right, you can use mine."

It took the rest of the morning for Kate to arrange everything, including the resolution of a lengthy argument with Marsh. She refused to let him come with her, ending by saying she'd simply rent a boat and do without his assistance altogether. In the end, she stood at the helm of his boat alone and headed out to sea.

She craved the solitude. Almost in defiance, she pushed the throttle forward. If it was defiance, she didn't care, any more than she cared whom she was defying. It was vital to do this one act for herself.

She refused to think about Ky, about why she'd exploded at him. If her words had been harsh, they'd also been necessary. She comforted herself with that. For too long, for a lifetime, she'd been influenced by someone else's opinion, someone else's expectations.

Mechanically, she stopped the engines and put on her equipment, checking and rechecking as she went. She'd never gone down alone before. Even that seemed suddenly a vital thing to do.

With a last look at her compass, she took the mesh basket over the side.

As she went deep, a thrill went through her. She was alone. In acres and acres of sea, she was alone. The water parted for her like silk. She was in control, and her destiny was her own.

She didn't rush. Kate found she wanted that euphoric feeling of being isolated under the sea where only curious fish bothered to give her a passing glance. Ultimately, her only responsibility here was to herself. Briefly, she closed her eyes and floated. At last, only to herself.

When she reached the site, she felt a new surge of pride. This was something she'd done without her father. She wouldn't think of the whys or the hows now, but simply the triumph. For two centuries, it had waited. And now, *she'd* found it. She circled the hole the prop-wash had created and began to fan using her hand.

Her first find was a dinner plate with a flamboyant floral pattern around the rim. She found one, then half a dozen, two of which were intact. On the back was the mark of an English potter. There were cups as well, dainty, exquisite English china that might have graced the table of a wealthy colonist, might have become a beloved heirloom, if nature hadn't interfered. Now they looked like something out of a horror show—crusted, misshapen with sea life. They couldn't have been more beautiful to her.

As she continued to fan, Kate nearly missed what appeared to be a dark sea shell. On closer examination she saw it was a silver coin. She couldn't make out the currency, but knew it didn't matter. It could just as easily be Spanish, as she'd read that Spanish currency had been used by all European nations with settlements in the New World.

The point was, it was a coin. The first coin. Though it was silver, not gold, and unidentifiable at the moment, she'd found it by herself.

Kate started to slip it into her goodie bag when her arm was jerked back.

The thrill of fear went wildly from her toes to her throat. The spear gun was on board the *Vortex*. She had no weapon. Before she could do more than turn in defense, she was caught by the shoulders with Ky's furious hands.

Terror died, but the anger in his eyes only incited her own. Damn him for frightening her, for interfering. Shaking him away, Kate signaled for him to leave. With one arm, he encircled her waist and started for the surface.

Only once did she even come close to breaking away from him. Ky simply banded his arm around her again, more tightly, until she had a choice between submitting or cutting off her own air.

When they broke the surface, Kate drew in breath to shout, but even in this, she was out-maneuvered.

"Idiot!" he shouted at her, dragging her to the ladder. "One day off your back and you jump into forty feet of water by yourself. I don't know why in hell I ever thought you had any brains."

Breathless, she heaved her tanks over the side. When she was on solid ground again, she intended to have her say. For now, she'd let him have his.

"I take my eyes off you for a couple hours and you go off half-cocked. If I'd murdered Marsh, it would have been on your head."

To her further fury, Kate saw that she'd boarded the *Vortex*. Marsh's boat was nowhere in sight.

"Where's the *Gull*?" she demanded.

"Marsh had the sense to tell me what you were doing." The words came out like bullets as he stripped off his gear. "I didn't kill him because I needed him to come out with me and take the *Gull* back." He stood in front of her, dripping, and as furious as she'd ever seen him. "Don't you have any more sense than to dive out here alone?"

She tossed her head back. "Don't you?"

Infuriated, he grabbed her and started to peel the wet suit from her himself. "We're not talking about me, damn it. I've been diving since I was six. I know the currents."

"*I* know the currents."

"And I haven't been flat on my back for a week."

"I was flat on my back for a week because you were overreacting." She struggled away from him, and because the wet suit was already down to her waist, peeled it off. "You've no right to tell me when and where I can dive, Ky. Superior strength gives you no right to drag me up when I'm in the middle of salvaging."

"The hell with what I have a right to do." Grabbing her again, he shook her with more violence than he'd ever shown her. A dozen things might have happened to her in the thirty minutes she'd been down. A dozen things he knew too well. "I make my own rights. You're not going down alone if I have to chain you up to stop it."

"You told me to get another diver," she said between her teeth. "Until I do, I dive alone."

"You threw that damn business arrangement in my face. Percentages. Lousy percentages and a daily rate. Do you know how that made me feel?"

"No!" she shouted, pushing him away. "No, I don't know how that made you feel. I don't know how anything makes you feel. You don't tell me." Dragging both hands through her dripping hair she walked away. "We agreed to the terms. That's all I know."

"That was before."

"Before what?" she demanded. Tears brimmed for no reason she could name, but she blinked them back again. "Before I slept with you?"

"Damn it, Kate." He was across the deck, backing her into the rail before she could take a breath. "Are you trying to get at me for something I did or didn't do four years ago? I don't even know what it is. I don't know what you want from me or what you don't want and I'm sick of trying to outguess you."

"I don't want to be pushed into a corner," she told him fiercely. "That's what I don't want. I don't want to be expected to fall in passively with someone else's plans for me. That's what I don't want. I don't want it assumed that I simply don't have any personal goals or wishes of my own. Or any basic competence of my own. *That's* what I don't want!"

"Fine." They were both losing control, but he no longer gave a damn. Ky ripped off his wet suit and tossed it aside. "You just remember something, lady. I don't expect anything of you and I don't assume. Once maybe, but not anymore. There was only one person who ever pushed you into a corner and it wasn't me." He hurled his mask across the deck where it bounced and smacked into the side. "I'm the one who let you go."

She stiffened. Even with the distance between them he could see her eyes frost over. "I won't discuss my father with you."

"You caught on real quick though, didn't you?"

"You resented him. You—"

"I?" Ky interrupted. "Maybe you better look at yourself, Kate."

"I loved him," she said passionately. "All my life I tried to show him. You don't understand."

"How do you know that I don't understand?" he exploded. "Don't you know I can see what you're feeling every time we find something down there? Do you think I'm so blind I don't see that you're hurting because *you* found it, not him? Don't you think it tears me apart to see that you punish yourself for not being what you think he wanted you to be? And I'm tired," he continued as her breath started to hitch. "Damn tired of being compared to and measured by a man you loved without ever being close to him."

"I don't." She covered her face, hating the weakness but powerless against it. "I don't do that. I only want..."

"What?" he demanded. "What do you want?"

"I didn't cry when he died," she said into her hands. "I didn't cry, not even at the funeral. I owed him tears, Ky. I owed him something."

"You don't owe him anything you didn't already give him over and over again." Frustrated, he dragged a hand through his hair before he went to her. "Kate." Because words seemed useless, he simply gathered her close.

"I didn't cry."

"Cry now," he murmured. He pressed his lips to the top of her head. "Cry now."

So she did, desperately, for what she'd never been able to quite touch, for what she'd never been able to quite hold. She'd ached for love, for the simple companionship of understanding. She wept because it was too late for that now from her father. She wept because she wasn't certain she could ask for love again from anyone else.

Ky held her, lowering her onto the bench as he cradled her in his lap. He couldn't offer her words of comfort. They were the most difficult words for him to come by. He could only offer her a place to weep, and silence.

As the tears began to pass, she kept her face against his

shoulder. There was such simplicity there, though it came from a man of complications. Such gentleness, though it sprang from a restless nature. "I couldn't mourn for him before," she murmured. "I'm not sure why."

"You don't have to cry to mourn."

"Maybe not," she said wearily. "I don't know. But it's true, what you said. I've wanted to do all this for him because he'll never have the chance to finish what he started. I don't know if you can understand, but I feel if I do this I'll have done everything I could. For him, and for myself."

"Kate." Ky tipped back her head so he could see her face. Her eyes were puffy, rimmed with red. "I don't have to understand. I just have to love you."

He felt her stiffen in his arms and immediately cursed himself. Why was it he never said things to her the way they should be said? Sweetly, calmly, softly. She was a woman who needed soft words, and he was a man who always struggled with them.

She didn't move, and for a long, long moment, they stayed precisely as they were.

"Do you?" she managed after a moment.

"Do I what?"

Would he make her drag it from him? "Love me?"

"Kate." Frustrated, he drew away from her. "I don't know how else to show you. You want bouquets of flowers, bottles of French champagne, poems? Damn it, I'm not made that way."

"I want a straight answer."

He let out a short breath. Sometimes her very calmness drove him to distraction. "I've always loved you. I've never stopped."

That went through her, sharp, hot, with a mixture of pain and pleasure she wasn't quite sure how to deal with. Slowly, she rose out of his arms, and walking across the deck, looked out to sea. The buoys that marked the site bobbed gently. Why were there no buoys in life to show you the way?

"You never told me."

"Look, I can't even count the number of women I've said it to." When she turned back with her brow raised, he rose, uncomfortable. "It was easy to say it to them because it didn't mean anything. It's a hell of a lot harder to get the words out when you mean them, and when you're afraid someone's going to back away from you the minute you do."

"I wouldn't have done that."

"You backed away, you went away for four years, when I asked you to stay."

"You asked me to stay," she reminded him. "You asked me not to go back to Connecticut, but to move in with you. Just like that. No promises, no commitment, no sign that you had any intention of building a life with me. I had responsibilities."

"To do what your father wanted you to do."

She swallowed that. It was true in its way. "All right, yes. But you never said you loved me."

He came closer. "I'm telling you now."

She nodded, but her heart was in her throat. "And I'm not backing away. I'm just not sure I can take the next step. I'm not sure you can either."

"You want a promise."

She shook her head, not certain what she'd do if indeed

he gave her one. "I want time, for both of us. It seems we both have a lot of thinking to do."

"Kate." Impatient, he came to her, taking her hands. They trembled. "Some things you don't have to think about. Some things you can think about too much."

"You've lived your life a certain way a long time, and I mine," she said quickly. "Ky, I've just begun to change— to feel the change. I don't want to make a mistake, not with you. It's too important. With time—"

"We've lost four years," he interrupted. He needed to resolve something, he discovered, and quickly. "I can't wait any longer to hear it if it's inside you."

Kate let out the breath she'd been holding. If he could ask, she could give. It would be enough. "I love you, Ky. I never stopped either. I never told you when I should have."

He felt the weight drain from his body as he cupped her face. "You're telling me now."

It was enough.

Chapter 11

Love. Kate had read hundreds of poems about that one phenomenon. She'd read, analyzed and taught from countless novels where love was the catalyst to all action, all emotion. With her students, she'd dissected innumerable lines from books, plays and verse that all led back to that one word.

Now, for perhaps the first time in her life, it was offered to her. She found it had more power than could possibly be taught. She found she didn't understand it.

Ky hadn't Byron's way with words, or Keat's romantic phrasing. What he'd said, he'd said simply. It meant everything. She still didn't understand it.

She could, in her own way, understand her feelings. She'd loved Ky for years, since that first revelation one summer when she'd come to know what it meant to want to fully share oneself with another.

But what, she wondered, did Ky find in her to love? It wasn't modesty that caused her to ask herself this question, but the basic practicality she'd grown up with. Where there was an effect, there was a cause. Where there was reaction, there was action. The world ran on this principle. She'd won Ky's love—but how?

Kate had no insecurity about her own intelligence. Perhaps, if anything, she overrated her mind, and it was this that caused her to underrate her other attributes.

He was a man of action, of restless and mercurial nature. She, on the other hand, considered herself almost blandly level. While she thrived on routine, Ky thrived on the unexpected. Why should he love her? Yet he did.

If she accepted that, it was vital to come to a resolution. Love led to commitment. It was there that she found the wall solid, without footholds.

He lived on a remote island because he was basically a loner, because he preferred moving at his own pace, in his own time. She was a teacher who lived by a day-to-day schedule. Without the satisfaction of giving knowledge, she'd stagnate. In the structured routine of a college town, Ky would go mad.

Because she could find no compromise, Kate opted to do what she'd decided to do in the beginning. She'd ride with the current until the summer was over. Perhaps by then, an answer would come.

They spoke no more of percentages. Kate quietly dropped the notion of keeping her hotel room. These, she told herself, were small matters when so much more hung in the balance during her second summer with Ky.

The days went quickly with her and Ky working together with the prop-wash or by hand. Slowly, painstakingly, they uncovered more salvage. The candlesticks had turned out to be pewter, but the coin had been Spanish silver. Its date had been 1748.

In the next two-week period, they uncovered much more—a heavy intricately carved silver platter, more china and porcelain, and in another area dozens of nails and tools.

Kate documented each find on film, for practical and personal reasons. She needed the neat, orderly way of keeping track of the salvage. She wanted to be able to look back on those pictures and remember how she felt when Ky held up a crusted teacup or an oxidized tankard. She'd be able to look and remember how he'd played an outstaring game with a large lazy bluefish. And lost.

More than once Ky had suggested the use of a larger ship equipped for salvage. They discussed it, and its advantages, but they never acted on it. Somehow, they both felt they wanted to move slowly, working basically with their own hands until there came a time when they had to make a decision.

The cannons and the heavier pieces of ship's planking couldn't be brought up without help, so these they left to the sea for the time being. They continued to use tanks, rather than changing to a surface-supplied source of air, so they had to surface and change gear every hour or so. A diving rig would have saved time—but that wasn't their goal.

Their methods weren't efficient by professional salvor standards, but they had an unspoken agreement. Stretch time. Make it last.

The nights they spent together in the big four-poster, talking of the day's finds, or of tomorrow's, making love, marking time. They didn't speak of the future that loomed after the summer's end. They never talked of what they'd do the day after the treasure was found.

The treasure became their focus, something that kept them from reaching out when the other wasn't ready.

The day was fiercely hot as they prepared to dive. The sun was baking. It was mid-July. She'd been in Ocracoke for a month. For all her practicality, Kate told herself it was an omen. Today was the turning point of summer.

Even as she pulled the wet suit up to her waist, sweat beaded on her back. She could almost taste the cool freshness of the water. The sun glared on her tanks as she lifted them, bouncing off to spear her eyes.

"Here." Taking them from her, Ky strapped them onto her back, checking the gauges himself. "The water's going to feel like heaven."

"Yeah." Marsh tipped up a quart bottle of juice. "Think of me baking up here while you're having all the fun."

"Keep the throttle low, brother," Ky said with a grin as he climbed over the side. "We'll bring you a reward."

"Make it something round and shiny with a date stamped on it," Marsh called back, then winked at Kate as she started down the ladder. "Good luck."

She felt the excitement as the water lapped over her ankles. "Today, I don't think I need it."

The noise of the prop-wash disturbed the silence of the water, but not the mystery. Even with technology and equipment, the water remained an enigma, part beauty, part danger. They went deeper and deeper until they reached the site with the scoops in the silt caused by their earlier explorations.

They'd already found what they thought had been the officers' and passengers' quarters, identifying it by the discovery of a snuff box, a silver bedside candleholder and Ky's personal favorite—a decorated sword. The few pieces of jewelry they'd found indicated a personal cache rather than cargo.

Though they fully intended to excavate in the area of the cache, it was the cargo they sought. Using the passengers' quarters and the galley as points of reference, they concentrated on what should have been the stern of the ship.

There were ballast rocks to deal with. This entailed a slow, menial process that required moving them by hand to an area they'd already excavated. It was time consuming, unrewarding and necessary. Still, Kate found something peaceful in the mindless work, and something fascinating about the ability to do it under fathoms of water with basically little effort. She could move a ballast pile as easily as Ky, whereas on land, she would have tired quickly.

Reaching down to clear another area, Ky's fingers brushed something small and hard. Curious, he fanned aside a thin layer of silt and picked up what at first looked like a tab on a can of beer. As he brought it closer, he saw it was much more refined, and though there were layers of crust on the knob of the circle, he felt his heart give a quick jerk.

He'd heard of diamonds in the rough, but he'd never thought to find one by simply reaching for it. He was no expert, but as he painstakingly cleaned what he could from the stone, he judged it to be at least two carats. With a tap on Kate's shoulder, he got her attention.

It gave him a great deal of pleasure to see her eyes widen and to hear the muffled sound of her surprise. Together, they turned it over and over again. It was dull and dirty, but the gem was there.

They were finding bits and pieces of civilization. Perhaps a woman had worn the ring while dining with the captain on her way to America. Perhaps some British officer had carried it in his vest pocket, waiting to give it to the woman he'd hoped to marry. It might have belonged to an elderly widow, or a young bride. The mystery of it, and its tangibility, were more precious than the stone itself. It was…lasting.

Ky held it out to her, offering. Their routine had fallen into a finders-keepers arrangement, in that whoever found a particular piece carried it in their own bag to the surface where everything was carefully cataloged on film and paper. Kate looked at the small, water-dulled piece of the past in Ky's fingers.

Was he offering her the ring because it was a woman's fancy, or was he offering her something else? Unsure, she shook her head, pointing to the bag on his belt. If he were asking her something, she needed it to be done with words.

Ky dropped the ring into his bag, secured it, then went back to work.

He thought he understood her, in some ways. In other ways, Ky found she was as much a mystery as the sea. What did she want from him? If it was love, he'd given her that. If it was time, they were both running out of it. He wanted to demand, was accustomed to demanding, yet she blocked his ability with a look.

She said she'd changed—that she was just beginning to feel in control of her life. He thought he understood that, as well as her fierce need for independence. And yet... He'd never known anything but independence. He, too, had changed. He needed her to give him the boundaries and the borders that came with dependence. His for her, and hers for him. Was the timing wrong again? Would it ever be right?

Damn it, he wanted her, he thought as he heaved another rock out of his way. Not just for today, but for tomorrow. Not tied against him, but bound to him. Why couldn't she understand that?

She loved him. It was something she murmured in the night when she was sleepy and caught close against him. She wasn't a woman to use words unless they had meaning. Yet with the love he offered and the love she returned, she'd begun to hold something back from him, as though he could have only a portion of her, but not all. Edged with frustration, he cleared more ballast. He needed, and would have, all.

Marriage? Was he thinking of marriage? Kate found herself flustered and uneasy. She'd never expected Ky to look for that kind of commitment, that kind of permanency. Perhaps she'd misread him. After all, it was difficult to be certain of someone's intention, yet she knew just how clearly Ky and she had been able to communicate underwater.

There was so much to consider, so many things to weigh. He wouldn't understand that, Kate mused. Ky was a man who made decisions in an instant and took the consequences. He wouldn't think about all the variables, all the what-ifs, all the maybes. She had to think about them all. She simply knew no other way.

Kate watched the silt and sand blowing away, causing

a cuplike indentation to form on the ocean floor. Outside influences, she mused. They could eat away at the layers and uncover the core, but sometimes what was beneath couldn't stand up to the pressure.

Is that what would happen between her and Ky? How would their relationship hold up under the pressure of variant lifestyles—the demands of her profession and the free-wheeling tone of his? Would it stay intact, or would it begin to sift away, layer by layer? How much of herself would he ask her to give? And in loving, how much of herself would she lose?

It was a possibility she couldn't ignore, a threat she needed to build a solid defense against. Time. Perhaps time was the answer. But summer was waning.

The force of the wash made a small object spin up, out of the layer of silt and into the water. Kate grabbed at it and the sharp edge scraped her palm. Curious, she turned it over for examination. A buckle? she wondered. The shape seemed to indicate it, and she could just make out a fastening. Even as she started to hold it out for Ky another, then another was pushed off the ocean bed.

Shoe buckles, Kate realized, astonished. Dozens of them. No, she realized as more and more began to twist up in the water's spin and reel away. Hundreds. With a quick frenzy, she began to gather what she could. More than hundreds, she discovered as her heart thudded. There were thousands of them, literally thousands.

She held a buckle in her hand and looked at Ky in triumph. They'd found the cargo. There'd been shoe buckles on the manifest of the *Liberty*. Five thousand of them. Nothing but a merchantman carried something like that in bulk.

Proof. She waved the buckle, her arm sweeping out in slow motion to take in the swarm of them swirling away from the wash and dropping again. Proof, her mind shouted out. The cargo-hold was beneath them. And the treasure. They had only to reach it.

Ky took her hands and nodded, knowing what was in her mind. Beneath his fingers he could feel the race of her pulse. He wanted that for her, the excitement, the thrill that came from discovering something only half believed in. She brought the back of his hand to her cheek, her eyes laughing, buckles spinning around them. Kate wanted to laugh until she was too weak to stand. Five thousand shoe buckles would guide them to a chest of gold.

Kate saw the humor in his eyes and knew Ky's thoughts ran along the same path as hers. He pointed to himself, then thumbs up. With a minimum of signaling, he told Kate that he would surface to tell Marsh to shut off the engines. It was time to work by hand.

Excited, she nodded. She wanted only to begin. Resting near the bottom, Kate watched Ky go up and out of sight. Oddly, she found she needed time alone. She'd shared the heady instant of discovery with Ky, and now she needed to absorb it.

The *Liberty* was beneath her, the ship her father had searched for. The dream he'd kept close, carefully researching, meticulously calculating, but never finding.

Joy and sorrow mixed as she gathered a handful of the buckles and placed them carefully in her bag. For him. In that moment she felt she'd given him everything she'd always needed to.

Carefully, and this time for personal reasons rather than the catalog, she began to shoot pictures. Years from now, she thought. Years and years from now, she'd look at a snapshot of swirling silt and drifting pieces of metal, and she'd remember. Nothing could ever take that moment of quiet satisfaction from her.

She glanced up at the sudden silence. The wash had stilled. Ky had reached the surface. Silt and the pieces of crusted, decorated metal began to settle again without the agitation of the wash. The sea was a world without sound, without movement.

Kate looked down at the scoop in the ocean floor. They were nearly there. For a moment she was tempted to begin to fan and search by herself, but she'd wait for Ky. They began together, and they'd finish together. Content, she watched for his return.

When Kate saw the movement above her, she started to signal. Her hand froze in place, then her arm, her shoulder and the rest of her body, degree by degree. It came smoothly through the water, sleek and silent. Deadly.

The noise of the prop-wash had kept the sea life away. Now the abrupt quiet brought out the curious. Among the schools of harmless fish glided the long bulletlike shape of a shark.

Kate was still, hardly daring to breathe as she feared even the trail of bubbles might attract him. He moved without haste, apparently not interested in her. Perhaps he'd already hunted successfully that day. But even with a full belly, a shark would attack what annoyed his uncertain temper.

She gauged him to be ten feet in length. Part of her mind registered that he was fairly small for what she recognized as a tiger shark. They could easily double that length. But she knew the jaws, those large sickle-shaped teeth, would be strong, merciless and fatal.

If she remained still, the chances were good that he would simply go in search of more interesting waters. Isn't that what she'd read sitting cozily under lamplight at her own desk? Isn't that what Ky had told her once when they'd shared a quiet lunch on his boat? All that seemed so remote, so unreal now, as she looked above and saw the predator between herself and the surface.

It was movement that attracted them, she reminded herself as she forced her mind to function. The movement a swimmer made with kicking feet and sweeping arms.

Don't panic. She forced herself to breathe slowly. No sudden moves. She forced her nervous hands to form tight, still fists.

He was no more than ten feet away. Kate could see the small black eyes and the gentle movement of his gills. Breathing shallowly, she never took her eyes from his. She had only to be perfectly still and wait for him to swim on.

But Ky. Kate's mouth went dry as she looked toward the direction where Ky had disappeared moments before. He'd be coming back, any minute, unaware of what was lurking near the bottom. Waiting. Cruising.

The shark would sense the disturbance in the water with the uncanny ability the hunter had. The kick of Ky's feet, the swing of his arms would attract the shark long before Kate would have a chance to warn him of any danger.

He'd be unaware, helpless, and then… Her blood seemed to freeze. She'd heard of the sensation but now she experienced it. Cold seemed to envelop her. Terror made her head light. Kate bit down on her lip until pain cleared her thoughts. She wouldn't stand by idly while Ky came blindly into a death trap.

Glancing down, she saw the spear gun. It was over five feet away and unloaded for safety. Safety, she thought hysterically. She'd never loaded one, much less shot one. And first, she'd have to get to it. There'd only be one chance. Knowing she'd have no time to settle her nerves, Kate made her move.

She kept her eyes on the shark as she inched slowly toward the gun. At the moment, he seemed to be merely cruising, not particularly interested in anything. He never even glanced her way. Perhaps he would move on before Ky came back, but she needed the weapon. Fingers shaking, she gripped the butt of the gun. Time seemed to crawl. Her movements were so slow, so measured, she hardly seemed to move at all. But her mind whirled.

Even as she gripped the spear she saw the shape that glided down from the surface. The shark turned lazily to the left. To Ky.

No! her mind screamed as she rammed the spear into position. Her only thought that of protecting what she loved. Kate swam forward without hesitation, taking a path between Ky and the shark. She had to get close.

Her mind was cold now, with fear, with purpose. For the second time, she saw those small, deadly eyes. This time, they focused on her. If she'd never seen true evil before, Kate knew she faced it now. This was cruelty, and a death that wouldn't come easily.

The shark moved toward her with a speed that made her heart stop. His jaws opened. There was a black, black cave behind them.

Ky dove quickly, wanting to get back to Kate, wanting

to search for what had brought them back together. If it was the treasure she needed to settle her mind, he'd find it. With it, they could open whatever doors they needed to open, lock whatever needed to be locked. Excitement drummed through him as he dove deeper.

When he spotted the shark, he pulled up short. He'd felt that deep primitive fear before, but never so sharply. Though it was less than useless against such a predator, he reached for his diver's knife. He'd left Kate alone. Cold-bloodedly, he set for the attack.

Like a rocket, Kate shot up between himself and the shark. Terror such as he'd never known washed over him. Was she mad? Was she simply unaware? Giving no time to thought, Ky barreled through the water toward her.

He was too far away. He knew it even as the panic hammered into him. The shark would be on her before he was close enough to sink the knife in.

When he saw what she held in her hand, and realized her purpose he somehow doubled his speed. Everything was in slow motion, and yet it seemed to happen in the blink of an eye. He saw the gaping hole in the shark's mouth as it closed in on Kate. For the first time in his life, prayers ran through him like water.

The spear shot out, sinking deep through the shark's flesh. Instinctively, Kate let herself drop as the shark came forward full of anger and pain. He would follow her now, she knew. If the spear didn't work, he would be on her in moments.

Ky saw blood gush from the wound. It wouldn't be enough. The shark jerked as if to reject the spear, and slowed his pace. Just enough. Teeth bared, Ky fell on its back, hacking with the knife as quickly as the water would allow. The shark turned, furious. Using all his strength, Ky turned with it, forcing the knife into the underbelly and ripping down. It ran through his mind that he was holding death, and it was as cold as the poets said.

From a few feet away, Kate watched the battle. She was numb, body and mind. Blood spurted out to dissipate in the water. Letting the empty gun fall, she too reached for her knife and swam forward.

But it was over. One instant the fish and Ky were as one form, locked together. Then they were separate as the body of the shark sank lifelessly toward the bottom. She saw the eyes one last time.

Her arm was gripped painfully. Limp, Kate allowed herself to be dragged to the surface. Safe. It was the only clear thought her mind could form. He was safe.

Too breathless to speak, Ky pulled her toward the ladder, tanks and all. He saw her slip near the top and roll onto the deck. Even as he swung over himself, he saw two fins slice through the water and disappear below where the blood drew them.

"What the hell—" Jumping up from his seat, Marsh ran across the deck to where Kate still lay, gasping for air.

"Sharks." Ky cut off the word as he knelt beside her. "I had to bring her up fast. Kate." Ky reached a hand beneath her neck, lifting her up as he began to take off her tanks. "Are you dizzy? Do you have any pain—your knees, elbows?"

Though she was still gasping for air, she shook her head. "No, no, I'm all right." She knew he worried about decompression sickness and tried to steady herself to reassure him. "Ky, we weren't that deep after—when we came up."

He nodded, grimly acknowledging that she was winded, not incoherent. Standing, he pulled off his mask and heaved it across the deck. Temper helped alleviate the helpless shaking. Kate merely drew her knees up and rested her forehead on them.

"Somebody want to fill me in?" Marsh asked, glancing from one to the other. "I left off when Ky came up raving about shoe buckles."

"Cargo-hold," Kate murmured. "We found it."

"So Ky said." Marsh glanced at his brother whose knuckles were whitening against the rail as he looked out to sea. "Run into some company down there?"

"There was a shark. A tiger."

"She nearly got herself killed," Ky explained. Fury was a direct result of fear, and just as deadly. "She swam right in front of him." Before Marsh could make any comment, Ky turned on Kate. "Did you forget everything I taught you?" he demanded. "You manage to get a doctorate but you can't remember that you're supposed to minimize your movements when a shark's cruising? You know that arm and leg swings attract them, but you swim in front of him, flailing around as though you wanted to shake hands—holding a damn spear gun that's just as likely to annoy him as do any real damage. If I hadn't been coming down just then, he'd have torn you to pieces."

Kate lifted her head slowly. Whatever emotion she'd felt up to that moment was replaced by an anger so deep it overshadowed everything. Meticulously she removed her flippers, her mask and her weight belt before she rose. "If you hadn't been coming down just then," she said precisely, "there'd have been no reason for me to swim in front of him." Turning, she walked to the steps and down into the cabin.

For a full minute there was utter silence on deck. Above, a gull screeched, then swerved west. Knowing there'd be no more dives that day, Marsh went to the helm. As he glanced over he saw the deep stain of blood on the water's surface.

"It's customary," he began with his back to his brother, "to thank someone when they save your life." Without waiting for a comment, he switched on the engine.

Shaken, Ky ran a hand through his hair. Some of the shark's blood had stained his fingers. Standing still, he stared at it.

Not through carelessness, he thought with a jolt. It had been deliberate. Kate had deliberately put herself in the path of the shark. For him. She'd risked her life to save him. He ran both hands over his face before he started below deck.

He saw her sitting on a bunk with a glass in her hand. A bottle of brandy sat at her feet. When she lifted the glass to her lips her hand shook lightly. Beneath the tan the sun had given her, her face was drawn and pale. No one had ever put him first so completely, so unselfishly. It left him without any idea of what to say.

"Kate…"

"I'm not in the mood to be shouted at right now," she told him before she drank again. "If you need to vent your temper, you'll have to save it."

"I'm not going to shout." Because he felt every bit as unsteady as she did, he sat beside her and lifted the bottle, drinking straight from it. The brandy ran hot and strong through him. "You scared the hell out of me."

"I'm not going to apologize for what I did."

"I should thank you." He drank again and felt the nerves

in his stomach ease. "The point is, you had no business doing what you did. Nothing but blind luck kept you from being torn up down there."

Turning her head, she stared at him. "I should've stayed safe and sound on the bottom while you dealt with the shark—with your diver's knife."

He met the look levelly. "Yes."

"And you'd have done that, if it'd been me?"

"That's different."

"Oh." Glass in hand, she rose. She took a moment to study him, that raw-boned, dark face, the dripping hair that needed a trim, the eyes that reflected the sea. "Would you care to explain that little piece of logic to me?"

"I don't have to explain it, it just is." He tipped the bottle back again. It helped to cloud his imagination which kept bringing images of what might have happened to her.

"No, it just isn't, and that's one of your major problems."

"Kate, have you any idea what could have happened if you hadn't lucked out and hit a vital spot with that spear?"

"Yes." She drained her glass and felt some of the edge dull. The fear might come back again unexpectedly, but she felt she was strong enough to deal with it. And the anger. No matter how it slashed at her, she would put herself between him and danger again. "I understand perfectly. Now, I'm going up with Marsh."

"Wait a minute." He stood to block her way. "Can't you see that I couldn't stand it if anything happened to you? I want to take care of you. I need to keep you safe."

"While you take all the risks?" she countered. "Is that supposed to be the balance of our relationship, Ky? You man, me woman? I bake bread, you hunt the meat?"

"Damn it, Kate, it's not as basic as that."

"It's just as basic as that," she tossed back. The color had come back to her face. Her legs were steady again. And she would be heard. "You want me to be quiet and content—and amenable to the way you choose to live. You want me to do as you say, bend to your will, and yet I know how you felt about my father."

It didn't seem she had the energy to be angry any longer. She was just weary, bone weary from slamming herself up against a wall that didn't seem ready to budge.

"I spent all my life doing what it pleased him to have me do," she continued in calmer tones. "No waves, no problems, no rebellion. He gave me a nod of approval, but no true respect and certainly no true affection. Now, you're asking me to do the same thing again with you." She felt no tears, only that weariness of spirit. "Why do you suppose the only two men I've ever loved should want me to be so utterly pliant to their will? Why do you suppose I lost both of them because I tried so hard to do just that?"

"No." He put his hands on her shoulders. "No, that's not true. It's not what I want from you or for you. I just want to take care of you."

She shook her head. "What's the difference, Ky?" she whispered. "What the hell's the difference?" Pushing past him, Kate went out on deck.

Chapter 12

Because in her quiet, immovable way Kate had demanded it, Ky left her alone. Perhaps it was for the best as it gave him time to think and to reassess what he wanted.

He realized that because of his fear for her, because of his need to care for her, he'd hurt her and damaged their already tenuous relationship.

On a certain level, she'd hit the mark in her accusations. He did want her to be safe and cared for while he sweated and took the risks. It was his nature to protect what he loved—in Kate's case, perhaps too much. It was also his nature to want other wills bent to his. He wanted Kate, and was honest enough to admit that he'd already outlined the terms in his own mind.

Her father's quiet manipulating had infuriated Ky and yet, he found himself doing the same thing. Not so quietly, he admitted, not nearly as subtly, but he was doing the same thing. Still, it wasn't for the same reasons. He wanted Kate to be with him, to align herself to him. It was as simple as that. He was certain, if she'd just let him, that he could make her happy.

But he never fully considered that she'd have demands or terms of her own. Until now, Ky hadn't thought how he'd adjust to them.

The light of dawn was quiet as Ky added the finishing touches to the lettering on his sailboat. For most of the night, he'd worked in the shed, giving Kate her time alone, and himself the time to think. Now that the night was over, only one thing remained clear. He loved her. But it had come home to him that it might not be enough. Though impatience continued to push at him, he reined it in. Perhaps he had to leave it to her to show him what would be.

For the next few days, they would concentrate on excavating the cargo that had sunk two centuries before. The longer they searched, the more the treasure became a symbol for him. If he could give it to her, it would be the end of the quest for both of them. Once it was over, they'd both have what they wanted. She, the fulfillment of her father's dream, and he, the satisfaction of seeing her freed from it.

Ky closed the shed doors behind him and headed back for the house. In a few days, he thought with a glance over his shoulder, he'd have something else to give her. Something else to ask her.

He was still some feet away from the house when he smelled the morning scents of bacon and coffee drifting through the kitchen windows. When he entered, Kate was standing at the stove, a long T-shirt over her tank suit, her feet bare, her hair loose. He could see the light dusting of freckles over the bridge of her nose, and the pale soft curve of her lips.

His need to gather her close rammed into him with such power, he had to stop and catch his breath. "Kate—"

"I thought since we'd be putting in a long day we should have a full breakfast." She'd heard him come in, sensed it. Because it made her knees weak, she spoke briskly. "I'd like to get an early start."

He watched her drop eggs into the skillet where the white began to sizzle and solidify around the edges. "Kate, I'd like to talk to you."

"I've been thinking we might consider renting a salvage ship after all," she interrupted, "and perhaps hiring another couple of divers. Excavating the cargo's going to be very slow work with just the two of us. It's certainly time we looked into lifting bags and lines."

Long days in the sun had lightened her hair. There were shades upon shades of variation so that as it flowed it reminded him of the smooth soft pelt of a deer. "I don't want to talk business now."

"It's not something we can put off too much longer." Efficiently, she scooped up the eggs and slid them onto plates. "I'm beginning to think we should expedite the excavation rather than dragging it out for what may very well be several more weeks. Then, of course, if we're talking about excavating the entire site, it would be months."

"Not now." Ky turned off the burner under the skillet. Taking both plates from Kate, he set them on the table.

"Look, I have to do something, and I'm not sure I'll do it very well."

Turning, Kate took silverware from the drawer and went to the table. "What?"

"Apologize." When she looked back at him in her cool, quiet way, he swore. "No, I won't do it well."

"It isn't necessary."

"Yes, it's necessary. Sit down." He let out a long breath as she remained standing. "Please," he added, then took a chair himself. Without a word, Kate sat across from him. "You saved my life yesterday." Even saying it aloud, he felt uneasy about it. "It was no less than that. I never could have taken that shark with my diver's knife. The only reason I did was because you'd weakened and distracted him."

Kate lifted her coffee and drank as though they were discussing the weather. It was the only way she had of blocking out images of what might have been. "Yes."

With a frustrated laugh, Ky stabbed at his eggs. "Not going to make it easy on me, are you?"

"No, I don't think I am."

"I've never been that scared," he said quietly. "Not for myself, certainly not for anyone else. I thought he had you." He looked up and met her calm, patient eyes. "I was still too far away to do anything about it. If…"

"Sometimes it's best not to think about the ifs."

"All right." He nodded and reached for her hand. "Kate, realizing you put yourself in danger to protect me only made it worse somehow. The possibility of anything happening to you was bad enough, but the idea of it happening because of me was unbearable."

"You would've protected me."

"Yes, but—"

"There shouldn't be any buts, Ky."

"Maybe there shouldn't be," he agreed, "but I can't promise there won't be."

"I've changed." The fact filled her with an odd sense of power and unease. "For too many years I've channeled my own desires because I thought somehow that approval could be equated with love. I know better now."

"I'm not your father, Kate."

"No, but you also have a way of imposing your will on me. My fault to a point." Her voice was calm, level, as it was when she lectured her students. She hadn't slept while Ky had spent his hours in the shed. Like him, she'd spent her time in thought, in search for the right answers. "Four years ago, I had to give to one of you and deny the other. It broke my heart. Today, I know I have to answer to myself first." With her breakfast hardly touched, she took her plate to the sink. "I love you, Ky," she murmured. "But I have to answer to myself first."

Rising, he went to her and laid his hands on her shoulders. Somehow the strength that suddenly seemed so powerful in her both attracted him yet left him uneasy. "Okay." When she turned into his arms, he felt the world settle a bit. "Just let me know what the answer is."

"When I can." She closed her eyes and held tight. "When I can."

For three long days they dove, working away the silt to find new discoveries. With a small air lift and their own hands, they found the practical, the beautiful and the ordinary. They came upon more than eight thousand of the ten thousand decorated pipes on the *Liberty*'s manifest. At least half of them, to Kate's delight, had their bowls intact. They were clay, long-stemmed pipes with the bowls decorated with oak leaves or bunches of grapes and flowers. In a heady moment of pleasure, she snapped Ky's picture as he held one up to his lips.

She knew that at auction, they would more than pay for the investment she'd made. And, with them, the donation she'd make to a museum in her father's name was steadily growing. But more than this, the discovery of so many pipes on a wreck added force to their claim that the ship was English.

There were also snuff boxes, again thousands, leaving literally no doubt in her mind that they'd found the merchantman *Liberty*. They found tableware, some of it elegant, some basic utility-ware, but again in quantity. Their list of salvage grew beyond anything Kate had imagined, but they found no chest of gold.

They took turns hauling their finds to the surface, using an inverted plastic trash can filled with air to help them lift. Even with this, they stored the bulk of it on the sea floor. They were working alone again, without a need for Marsh to man the prop-wash. As it had been in the beginning, the project became a personal chore for only the two of them. What they found became a personal triumph. What they didn't find, a personal disappointment.

Kate delegated herself to deal with the snuff boxes, transporting them to the mesh baskets. Already, she was planning to clean several of them herself as part of the discovery. Beneath the layers of time there might be something elegant, ornate or ugly. She didn't believe it mattered what she found, as long as she found it.

Tea, sugar and other perishables the merchant ship had

carried were long since gone without a trace. What she and Ky found now were the solid pieces of civilization that had survived centuries in the sea. A pipe meant for an eighteenth-century man had never reached the New World. It should have made her sad but, because it had survived, because she could hold it in her hand more than two hundred years later, Kate felt a quiet triumph. Some things last, whatever the odds.

Reaching down, she disturbed something that lay among the jumbled snuff boxes. Automatically, she jerked her hand back. Memories of the stingray and other dangers were still very fresh. When the small round object clinked against the side of a box and lay still, her heart began to pound. Almost afraid to touch, Kate reached for it. Between her fingers, she held a gold coin from another era.

Though she had read it was likely, she hadn't expected it to be as bright and shiny as the day it was minted. The pieces of silver they'd found had blackened, and other metal pieces had corroded, some of them crystalized almost beyond recognition. Yet, the gold, the small coin she'd plucked from the sea floor, winked back at her.

Its origin was English. The long-dead king stared out at her. The date was 1750.

Ky! Foolishly, she said his name. Though the sound was muffled and indistinguishable, he turned. Unable to wait, Kate swam toward him, clutching the coin. When she reached him, she took his hand and pressed the gold into his palm.

He knew at the moment of contact. He had only to look into her eyes. Taking her hand, he brought it to his lips. She'd found what she wanted. For no reason he could name, he felt empty. He pressed the coin back into her hand, closing her fingers over it tightly. The gold was hers.

Swimming beside her, Ky moved to the spot where Kate had found the coin. Together, they fanned, using all the patience each of them had stored. In the twenty minutes of bottom time they had left, they uncovered only five more coins. As if they were as fragile as glass, Kate placed them in her bag. Each took a mesh basket filled with salvage and surfaced.

"It's there, Ky." Kate let her mouthpiece drop as Ky hauled the first basket over the rail. "It's the *Liberty*, we've proven it."

"It's the *Liberty*," he agreed, taking the second basket from her. "You've finished what your father started."

"Yes." She unhooked her tanks, but it was more than their weight she felt lifted from her shoulders. "I've finished." Digging into her bag, she pulled out the six bright coins. "These were loose. We still haven't found the chest. If it still exists."

He'd already thought of that, but not how he'd tell her his own theory. "They might have taken the chest to another part of the boat when the storm hit." It was a possibility; it had given them hope that the chest was still there.

Kate looked down. The glittery metal seemed to mock her. "It's possible they put the gold in one of the lifeboats when they manned them. The survivor's story wasn't clear after the ship began to break up."

"A lot of things are possible." He touched her cheek briefly before he started to strip off his gear. "With a little luck and a little more time, we might find it all."

She smiled as she dropped the coins back into her bag. "Then you could buy your boat."

"And you could go to Greece." Stripped down to his bathing trunks, Ky went to the helm. "We need to give ourselves the full twelve hours before we dive again, Kate. We've been calling it close as it is."

"That's fine." She made a business of removing her own suit. She needed the twelve hours, she discovered, for more than the practical reason of residual nitrogen.

They spoke little on the trip back. They should've been ecstatic. Kate knew it, and though she tried, she couldn't recapture that quick boost she'd felt when she picked up the first coin.

She discovered that if she'd had a choice she would have gone back weeks, to the time when the gold was a distant goal and the search was everything.

It took the rest of the day to transport the salvage from the *Vortex* to Ky's house, to separate and catalog it. She'd already decided to contact the Park Service. Their advice in placing many of the artifacts would be invaluable. After taxes, she'd give her father his memorial. And, she mused, she'd give Ky whatever he wanted out of the salvage.

Their original agreement no longer mattered to her. If he wanted half, she'd give it. All she wanted, Kate realized, was the first bowl she'd found, the blackened silver coin and the gold one that had led her to the five other coins.

"We might think about investing in a small electrolytic reduction bath," Ky murmured as he turned what he guessed was a silver snuff box in his palm. "We could treat a lot of this salvage ourselves." Coming to a decision, he set the box down. "We're going to have to think about a bigger ship and equipment. It might be best to stop diving for the next couple of days while we arrange for it. It's been six weeks, and we've barely scratched the surface of what's down there."

She nodded, not entirely sure why she wanted to weep. He was right. It was time to move on, to expand. How could she explain to him, when she couldn't explain to herself, that she wanted nothing else from the sea? While the sun set, she watched him meticulously list the salvage.

"Ky…" She broke off because she couldn't find the words to tell him what moved through her. Sadness, emptiness, needs.

"What's wrong?"

"Nothing." But she took his hands as she rose. "Come upstairs now," she said quietly. "Make love with me before the sun goes down."

Questions ran through him, but he told himself they could wait. The need he felt from her touched off his own. He wanted to give her, and to take from her, what couldn't be found anywhere else.

When they entered the bedroom it was washed with the warm, lingering light of the sun. The sky was slowly turning red as he lay beside her. Her arms reached out to gather him close. Her lips parted. Refusing to rush, they undressed each other. No boundaries. Flesh against flesh they lay. Mouth against mouth they touched.

Kisses—long and deep—took them both beyond the ordinary world of place and time. Here, there were dozens of sensations to be felt, and no questions to be asked. Here, there was no past, no tomorrow, only the moment. Her body went limp under his, but her mouth hungered and sought.

No one else… No one else had ever taken her beyond herself so effortlessly. Never before had anyone made her so completely aware of her own body. A feathery touch along her skin drove pleasure through her with inescapable force.

The scent of sea still clung to both of them. As pleasure became liquid, they might have been fathoms under the ocean, moving freely without the strict rules of gravity. There were no rules here.

As his hands brought their emotions rising to the surface, so did hers for him. She explored the rippling muscles of his back, near the shoulders. Lingering there, she enjoyed just the feel of one of the subtle differences between them. His skin was smooth, but muscles bunched under it. His hands were gentle, but the palms were hard. He was lean, but there was no softness there.

Again and again she touched and tasted, needing to absorb him. Above all else, she needed to experience everything they'd ever had together this one time. They made love here, she remembered, that first time. The first time…and the last. Whenever she thought of him, she'd remember the quieting light of dusk and the distant sound of surf.

He didn't understand why he felt such restrained urgency from her, but he knew she needed everything he could give her. He loved her, perhaps not as gently as he could, but more thoroughly than ever before.

He touched. "Here," Ky murmured, using his fingertips to drive her up. As she gasped and arched, he watched her. "You're soft and hot."

He tasted. "And here…" With his tongue, he pushed her to the edge. As her hands gripped his, he groaned. Pleasure heaped upon pleasure. "You taste like temptation—sweet and forbidden. Tell me you want more."

"Yes." The word came out on a moan. "I want more."

So he gave her more.

Again and again, he took her up, watching the astonished pleasure on her face, feeling it in the arch of her body, hearing it in her quick breaths. She was helpless, mindless, his. He drove his tongue into her and felt her explode, wave after wave.

As she shuddered, he moved up her body, hands fast, mouth hot and open. Suddenly, on a surge of strength, she rolled on top of him. Within seconds, she'd devastated his claim to leadership. All fire, all speed, all woman, she took control.

Heedless, greedy, they moved over the bed. Murmurs were incoherent, care was forgotten. They took with only one goal in mind. Pleasure—sweet, forbidden pleasure.

Shaking, locked tight, they reached the goal together.

Dawn was breaking, clear and calm as Kate lay still, watching Ky sleep. She knew what she had to do for both of them, to both of them. Fate had brought them together a second time. It wouldn't bring them together again.

She'd bargained with Ky, offering him a share of gold for his skill. In the beginning, she'd believed that she wanted the treasure, needed it to give her all the options she'd never had before. That choice. Now, she knew she didn't want it at all. A hundred times more gold wouldn't change what was between her and Ky—what drew them to each other, and what kept them apart.

She loved him. She understood that, in his way, he loved her. Did that change the differences between them?

Did that make her able and willing to give up her own life to suit his, or able and willing to demand that he do the same?

Their worlds were no closer together now than they'd been four years ago. Their desires no more in tune. With the gold she'd leave for him, he'd be able to do what he wanted with his life. She needed no treasure for that.

If she stayed... Unable to stop herself, Kate reached out to touch his cheek. If she stayed she'd bury herself for him. Eventually, she'd despise herself for it, and he'd resent her. Better that they take what they'd had for a few weeks than cover it with years of disappoinments.

The treasure was important to him. He'd taken risks for it, worked for it. She'd give her father his memorial. Ky would have the rest.

Quietly, still watching him sleep, she dressed.

It didn't take Kate long to gather what she'd come with. Taking her suitcase downstairs, she carefully packed what she'd take with her from the *Liberty*. In a box, she placed the pottery bowl wrapped in layers of newspaper. The coins, the blackened silver and the shiny gold, she zipped into a small pouch. With equal care, she packed the film she'd taken during their days under the ocean.

What she'd designated for the museum she'd already marked. Leaving the list on the table, she left the house.

She told herself it would be cleaner if she left no note, yet she found herself hesitating. How could she make him understand? After putting her suitcase in her car, she went back into the house. Quietly, she took the five gold coins upstairs and placed them on Ky's dresser. With a last look at him as he slept, she went back out again.

She'd have a final moment with the sea. In the quiet air of morning, Kate walked over the dunes.

She'd remember it this way—empty, endless and full of sound. Surf foamed against the sand, white on white. What was beneath the surface would always call her—the memories of peace, of excitement, of sharing both with Ky. Only a summer, she thought. Life was made of four seasons, not one.

Day was strengthening, and her time was up. Turning, she scanned the island until she saw the tip of the light-house. Some things lasted, she thought with a smile. She'd learned a great deal in a few short weeks. She was her own woman at last. She could make her own way. As a teacher, she told herself that knowledge was precious. But it made her ache with loneliness. She left the empty sea behind her.

Though she wanted to, Kate deliberately kept herself from looking at the house as she walked back to her car. She didn't need to see it again to remember it. If things had been different... Kate reached for the door handle of her car. Her fingers were still inches from it when she was spun around.

"What the hell're you doing?"

Facing Ky, she felt her resolve crumble, then rebuild. He was barely awake, and barely dressed. His eyes were heavy with sleep, his hair disheveled from it. All he wore was a pair of ragged cut-offs. She folded her hands in front of her and hoped her voice would be strong and clear.

"I had hoped to be gone before you woke."

"Gone?" His eyes locked on hers. "Where?"

"I'm going back to Connecticut."

"Oh?" He swore he wouldn't lose his temper. Not this time. This time, it might be fatal for both of them. "Why?"

Her nerves skipped. The question had been quiet enough, but she knew that cold, flat expression in his eyes. The wrong move, and he'd leap. "You said it yourself yesterday, Ky, when we came up from the last dive. I've done what I came for."

He opened his hand. Five coins shone in the morning sun. "What about this?"

"I left them for you." She swallowed, no longer certain how long she could speak without showing she was breaking in two. "The treasure isn't important to me. It's yours."

"Damn generous of you." Turning over his hand, he dropped the coins into the sand. "That's how much the gold means to me, professor."

She stared at the gold on the ground in front of her. "I don't understand you."

"*You* wanted the treasure," he tossed at her. "It never mattered to me."

"But you said," she began, then shook her head. "When I first came to you, you took the job because of the treasure."

"I took the job because of you. You wanted the gold, Kate."

"It wasn't the money." Dragging a hand through her hair, she turned away. "It was never the money."

"Maybe not. It was your father."

She nodded because it was true, but it no longer hurt. "I finished what he started, and I gave myself something. I don't want any more coins, Ky."

"Why are you running away from me again?"

Slowly, she turned back. "We're four years older than we were before, but we're the same people."

"So?"

"Ky, when I went away before, it was partially because of my father, because I felt I owed him my loyalty. But if I'd thought you'd wanted me. *Me*," she repeated, placing her palm over her heart, "not what you wanted me to be. If I'd thought that, and if I'd thought you and I could make a future together, I wouldn't have gone. I wouldn't be leaving now."

"What the hell gives you the right to decide what I want, what I feel?" He whirled away from her, too furious to remain close. "Maybe I made mistakes, maybe I just assumed too much four years ago. Damn it, I paid for it, Kate, every day from the time you left until you came back. I've done everything I could to be careful this time around, not to push, not to assume. Then I wake up and find you leaving without a word."

"There aren't any words, Ky. I've always given you too many of them, and you've never given me enough."

"You're better with words than I am."

"All right, then I'll use them. I love you." She waited until he turned back to her. The restlessness was on him again. He was holding it off with sheer will. "I've always loved you, but I think I know my own limitations. Maybe I know yours too."

"No, you think too much about limitations, Kate, and not enough about possibilities. I let you walk away from me before. It's not going to be so easy this time."

"I have to be my own person, Ky. I won't live the rest of my life as I've lived it up to now."

"Who the hell wants you to?" he exploded. "Who the hell wants you to be anything but what you are? It's about time you stopped equating love with responsibility and started looking at the other side of it. It's sharing, giving and taking and laughing. If I ask you to give part of yourself to me, I'm going to give part of myself right back."

Unable to stop himself he took her arms in his hands, just holding, as if through the contact he could make his words sink in.

"I don't want your constant devotion. I don't want you to be obliged to me. I don't want to go through life thinking that whatever you do, you do because you want to please me. Damn it, I don't want that kind of responsibility."

Without words, she stared at him. He'd never said anything to her so simply, so free of half meanings. Hope rose in her. Yet still, he was telling her only what he didn't want. Once he gave her the flip side of that coin hope could vanish.

"Tell me what you do want."

He had only one answer. "Come with me a minute." Taking her hand, he drew her toward the shed. "When I started this, it was because I'd always promised myself I would. Before long, the reasons changed." Turning the latch, he pulled the shed doors open.

For a moment, she saw nothing. Gradually, her eyes adjusted to the dimness and she stepped inside. The boat was nearly finished. The hull was sanded and sealed and painted, waiting for Ky to take it outside and attach the mast. It was lovely, clean and simple. Just looking at it, Kate could imagine the way it would flow with the wind. Free, light and clever.

"It's beautiful, Ky. I always wondered…" She broke off as she read the name printed boldly on the stern.

Second Chance.

"That's all I want from you," Ky told her, pointing to the two words. "The boat's yours. When I started it, I thought I was building it for me. But I built it for you, because I knew it was one dream you'd share with me. I only want what's printed on it, Kate. For both of us." Speechless, she watched him lean over the starboard side and open a small compartment. He drew out a tiny box.

"I had this cleaned. You wouldn't take it from me before." Opening the lid, he revealed the diamond he'd found, sparkling now in a simple gold setting. "It didn't cost me anything and it wasn't made especially for you. It's just something I found among a bunch of rocks."

When she started to speak, he held up a hand. "Hold on. You wanted words, I haven't finished with them yet. I know you have to teach, I'm not asking you to give it up. I am asking that you give me one year here on the island. There's a school here, not Yale, but people still have to be taught. A year, Kate. If it isn't what you want after that, I'll go back with you."

Her brows drew together. "Back? To Connecticut? You'd live in Connecticut?"

"If that's what it takes."

A compromise…she thought, baffled. Was he offering to adjust his life for hers? "And if that isn't right for you?"

"Then we'll try someplace else, damn it. We'll find someplace in between. Maybe we'll move half a dozen times in the next few years. What does it matter?"

What did it matter? she wondered as she studied him. He was offering her what she'd waited for all of her life. Love without chains.

"I want you to marry me." He wondered if that simple

statement shook her as much as it did him. "Tomorrow isn't soon enough, but if you'll give me the year, I can wait."

She nearly smiled. He'd never wait. Once he had her promise of the year, he'd subtly and not so subtly work on her until she found herself at the altar. It was nearly tempting to make him go through the effort.

Limitations? Had she spoken of limitations? Love had none.

"No," she decided aloud. "You only get the year if I get the ring. And what goes with it."

"Deal." He took her hand quickly as though she might change her mind. "Once it's on, you're stuck, professor." Pulling the ring from the box he slipped it onto her finger. Swearing lightly, he shook his head. "It's too big."

"It's all right. I'll keep my hand closed for the next fifty years or so." With a laugh, she went into his arms. All doubts vanished. They'd make it, she told herself. South, north or anywhere in between.

"We'll have it sized," he murmured, nuzzling into her neck.

"Only if they can do it while it's on my finger." Kate closed her eyes. She'd just found everything. Did he know it? "Ky, about the *Liberty*, the rest of the treasure."

He tilted her face up to kiss her. "We've already found it."

* * * * *

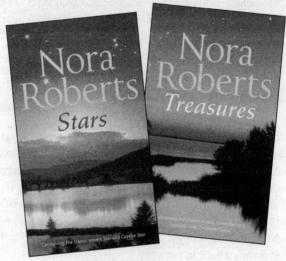

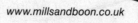

A meeting under the mistletoe

SHERRYL WOODS HOLLY JACOBS
DARLENE GARDNER

*A meeting under
the mistletoe*

*Christmas
Eve Kisses*

Amy's gift-wrapped cop...
Merry's holiday surprise...
The true **Joy** of the season...

For these three special women,
Christmas will bring unexpected gifts!

Available 5th December 2008

www.millsandboon.co.uk

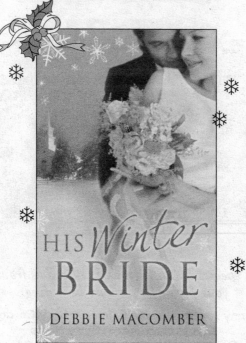